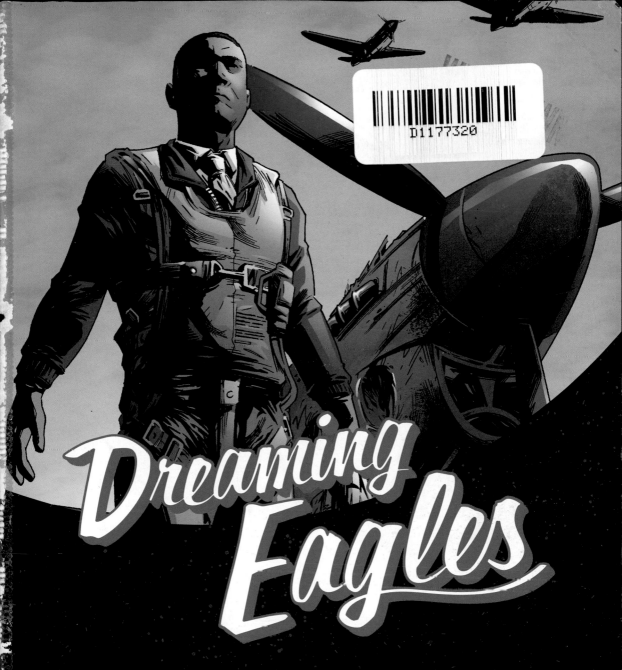

Dreaming Eagles

GARTH ENNIS

SIMON COLEBY

JOHN KALISZ

ROB STEEN

FRANCESCO FRANCAVILLA

AFTERSHOCK

DREAMING EAGLES

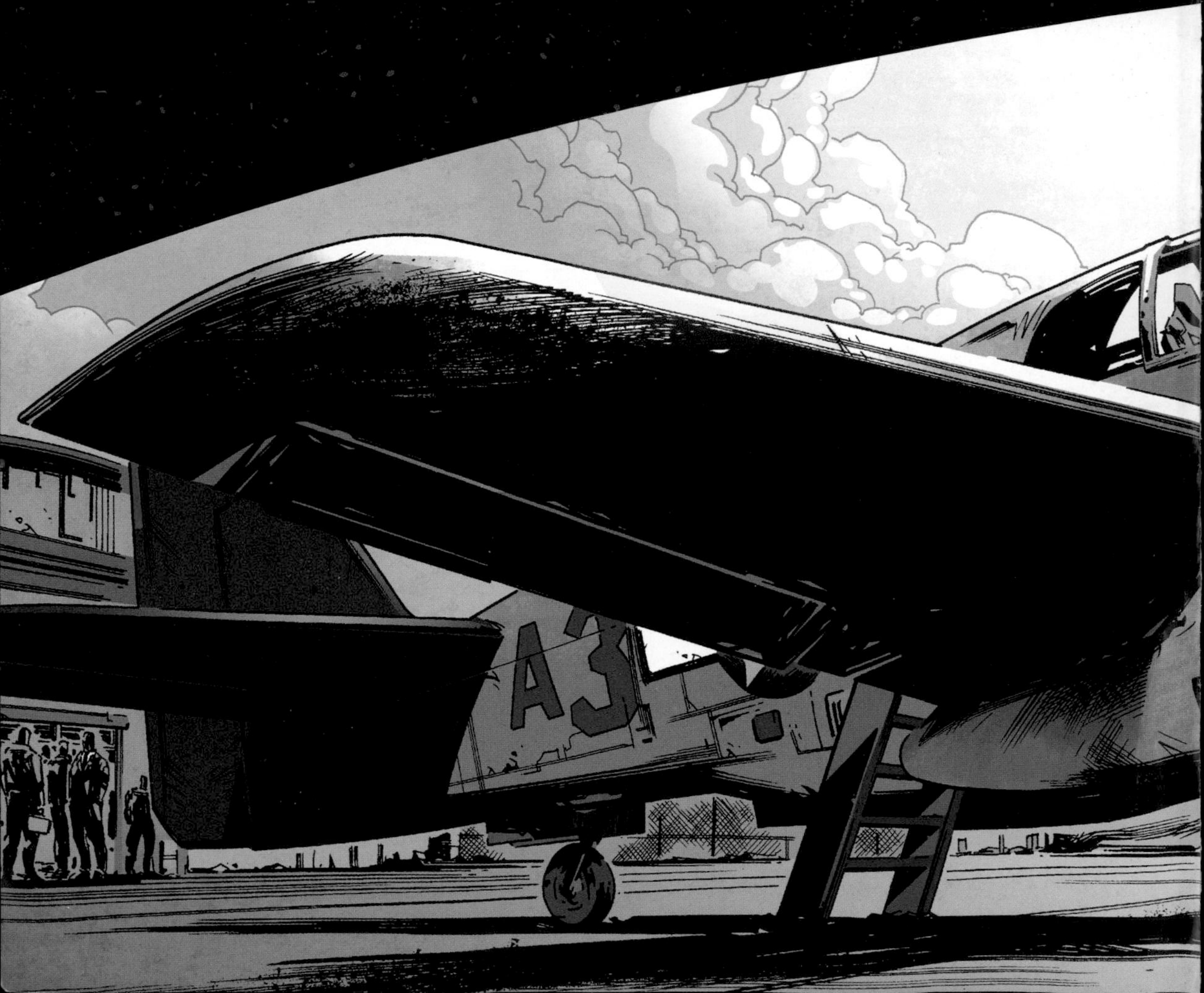
A3

GARTH ENNIS creator & writer **SIMON COLEBY** artist

JOHN KALISZ colorist **ROB STEEN** letterer

FRANCISCO FRANCAVILLA front & original series covers

PHIL HESTER, DECLAN SHALVEY & **BRIAN STELFREEZE** variant covers

JARED K. FLETCHER logo designer **JOHN J. HILL** & **COREY BREEN** book designers

MIKE MARTS editor

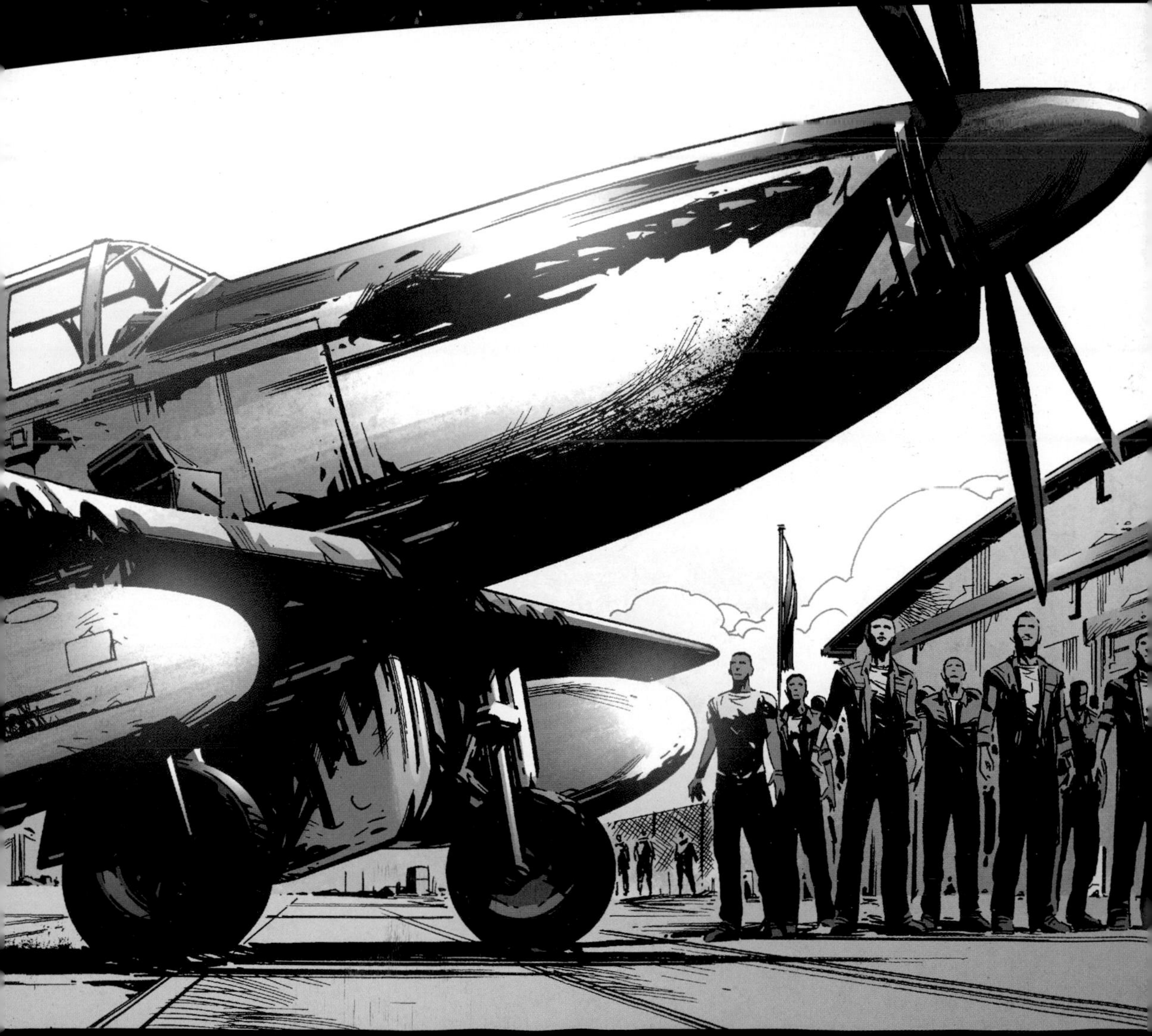

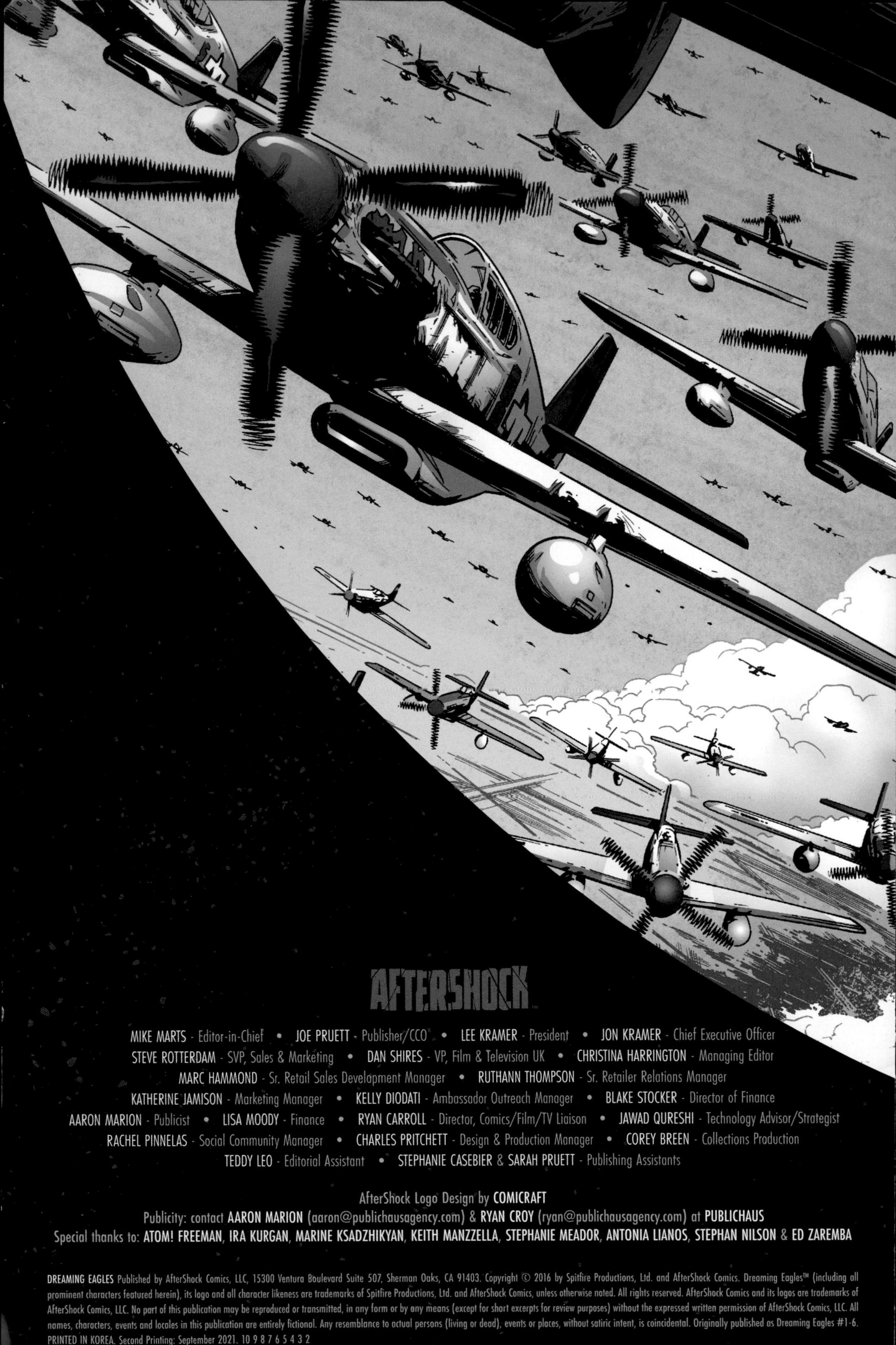

AFTERSHOCK

MIKE MARTS - Editor-in-Chief • JOE PRUETT - Publisher/CCO • LEE KRAMER - President • JON KRAMER - Chief Executive Officer
STEVE ROTTERDAM - SVP, Sales & Marketing • DAN SHIRES - VP, Film & Television UK • CHRISTINA HARRINGTON - Managing Editor
MARC HAMMOND - Sr. Retail Sales Development Manager • RUTHANN THOMPSON - Sr. Retailer Relations Manager
KATHERINE JAMISON - Marketing Manager • KELLY DIODATI - Ambassador Outreach Manager • BLAKE STOCKER - Director of Finance
AARON MARION - Publicist • LISA MOODY - Finance • RYAN CARROLL - Director, Comics/Film/TV Liaison • JAWAD QURESHI - Technology Advisor/Strategist
RACHEL PINNELAS - Social Community Manager • CHARLES PRITCHETT - Design & Production Manager • COREY BREEN - Collections Production
TEDDY LEO - Editorial Assistant • STEPHANIE CASEBIER & SARAH PRUETT - Publishing Assistants

AfterShock Logo Design by COMICRAFT
Publicity: contact AARON MARION (aaron@publichausagency.com) & RYAN CROY (ryan@publichausagency.com) at PUBLICHAUS
Special thanks to: ATOM! FREEMAN, IRA KURGAN, MARINE KSADZHIKYAN, KEITH MANZZELLA, STEPHANIE MEADOR, ANTONIA LIANOS, STEPHAN NILSON & ED ZAREMBA

PRINTED IN KOREA. Second Printing: September 2021. 10 9 8 7 6 5 4 3 2

1:WF CANNOT CONSECRATE

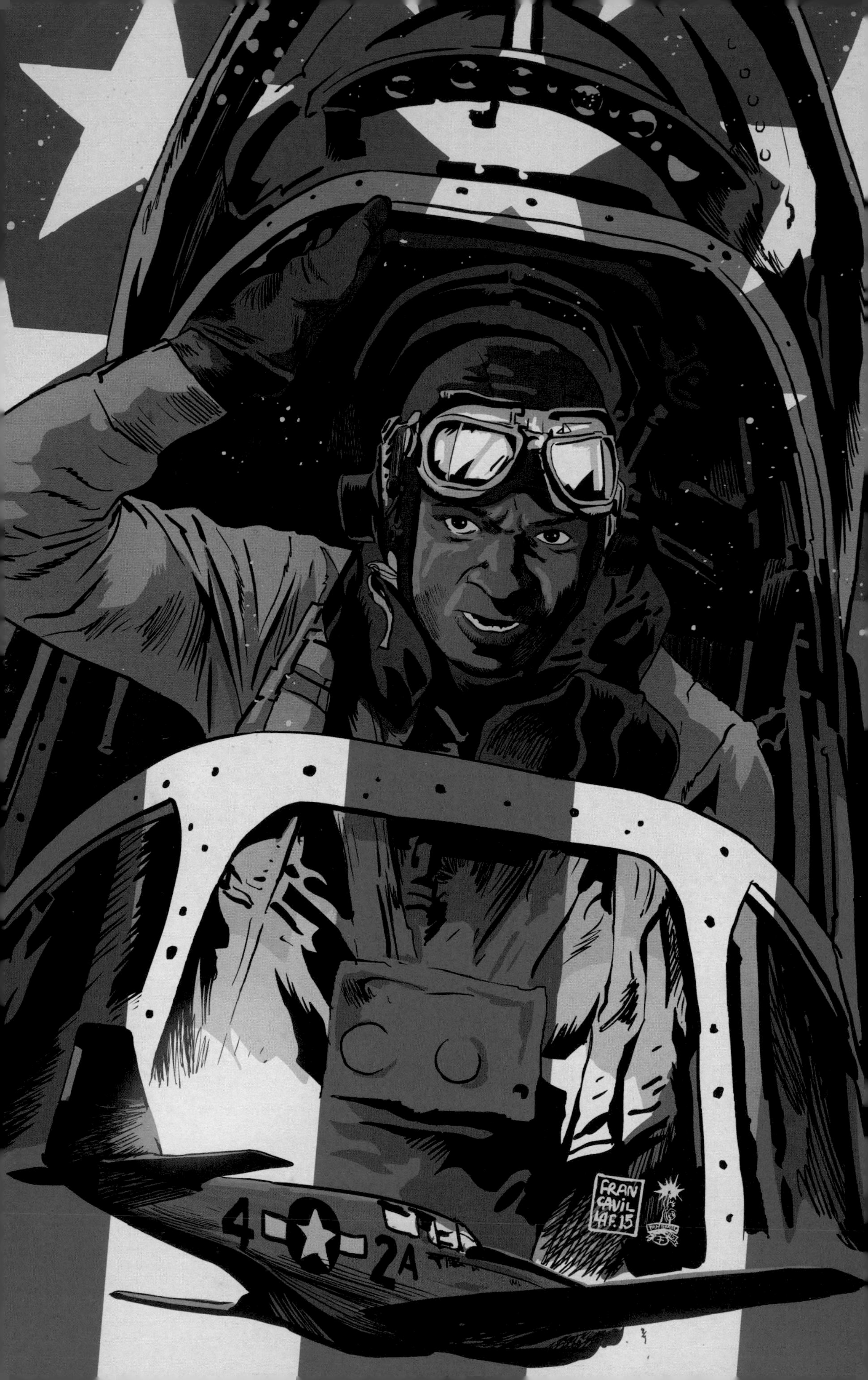
FRAN
CAVIL
14F.15
4
2A

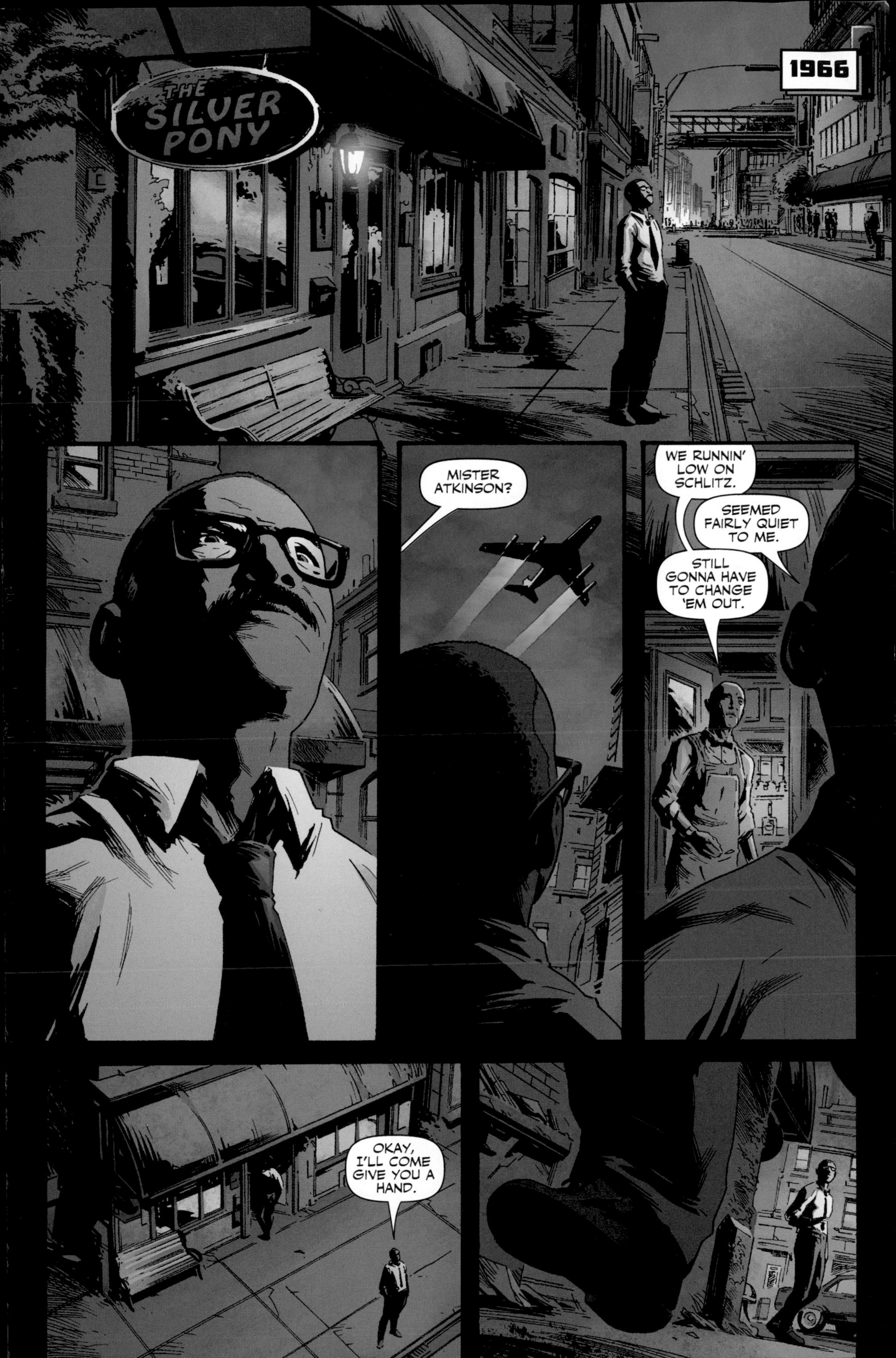
1966
THE SILVER PONY
MISTER ATKINSON?
WE RUNNIN' LOW ON SCHLITZ.
SEEMED FAIRLY QUIET TO ME.
STILL GONNA HAVE TO CHANGE 'EM OUT.
OKAY, I'LL COME GIVE YOU A HAND.

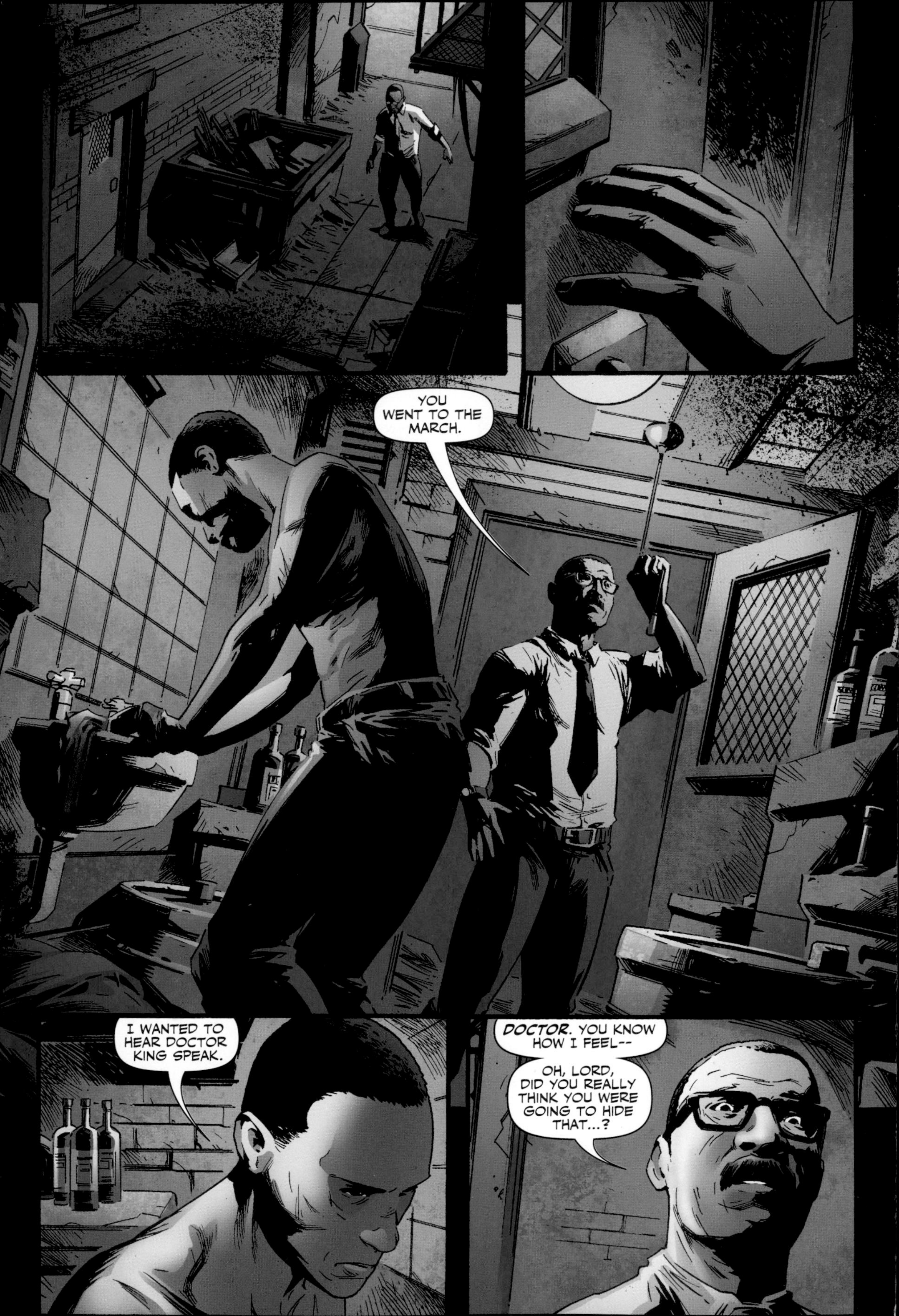
YOU WENT TO THE MARCH.
I WANTED TO HEAR DOCTOR KING SPEAK.
DOCTOR. YOU KNOW HOW I FEEL--
OH, LORD, DID YOU REALLY THINK YOU WERE GOING TO HIDE THAT...?

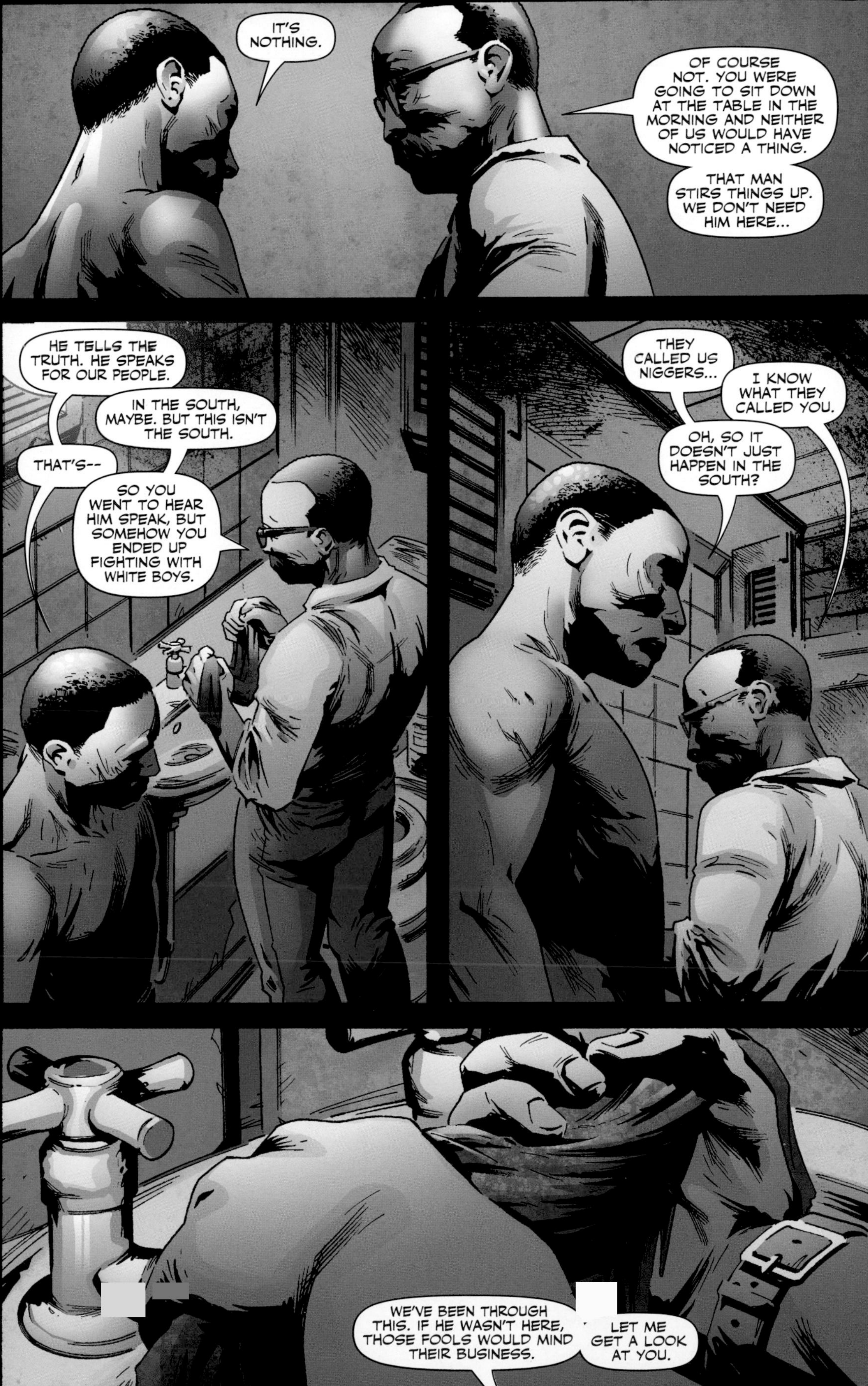
IT'S NOTHING.
OF COURSE NOT. YOU WERE GOING TO SIT DOWN AT THE TABLE IN THE MORNING AND NEITHER OF US WOULD HAVE NOTICED A THING.
THAT MAN STIRS THINGS UP. WE DON'T NEED HIM HERE...
HE TELLS THE TRUTH. HE SPEAKS FOR OUR PEOPLE.
IN THE SOUTH, MAYBE. BUT THIS ISN'T THE SOUTH.
THAT'S--
SO YOU WENT TO HEAR HIM SPEAK, BUT SOMEHOW YOU ENDED UP FIGHTING WITH WHITE BOYS.
THEY CALLED US NIGGERS...
I KNOW WHAT THEY CALLED YOU.
OH, SO IT DOESN'T JUST HAPPEN IN THE SOUTH?
WE'VE BEEN THROUGH THIS. IF HE WASN'T HERE, THOSE FOOLS WOULD MIND THEIR BUSINESS.
LET ME GET A LOOK AT YOU.

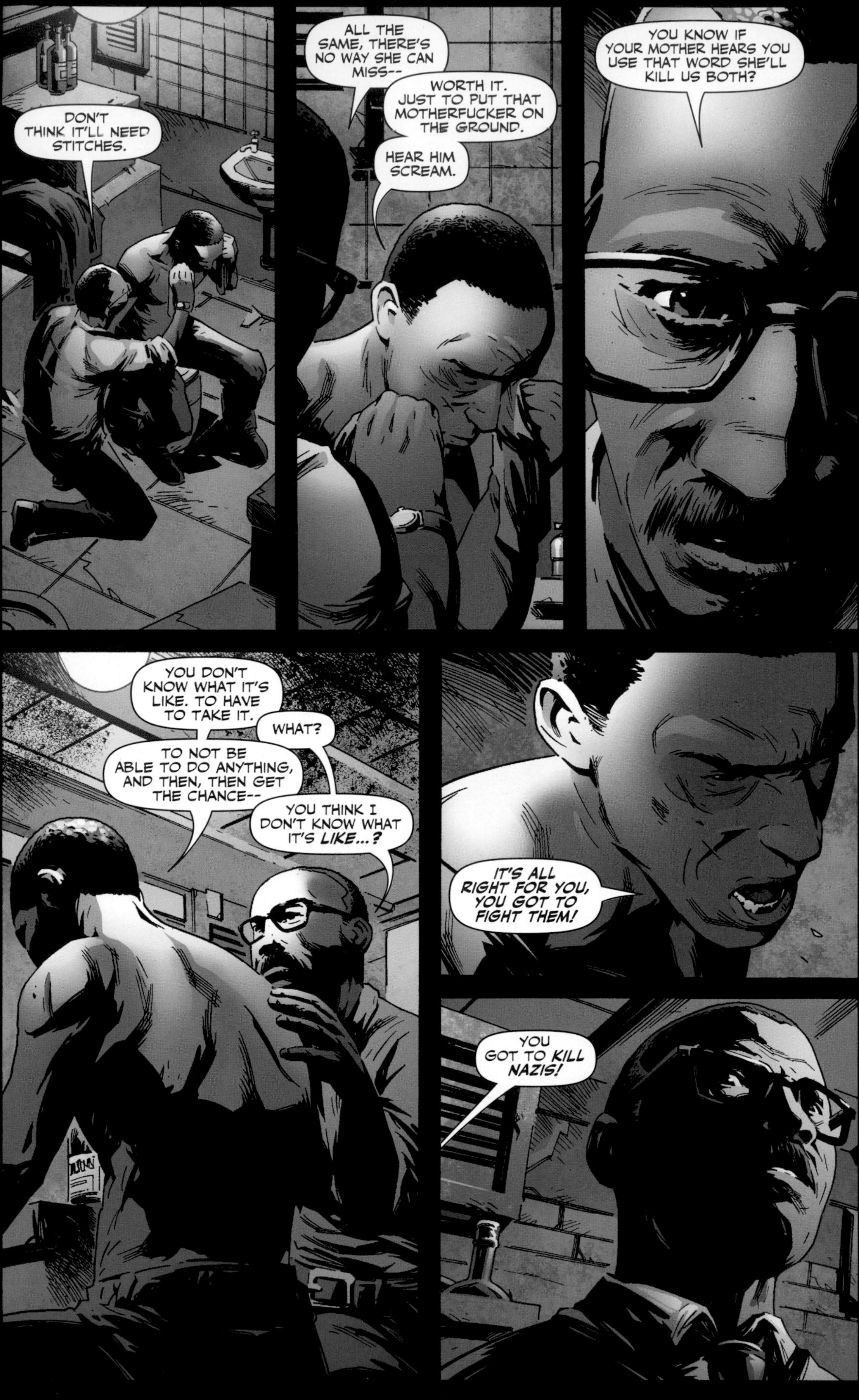
DON'T THINK IT'LL NEED STITCHES.
ALL THE SAME, THERE'S NO WAY SHE CAN MISS--
WORTH IT. JUST TO PUT THAT MOTHERFUCKER ON THE GROUND.
HEAR HIM SCREAM.
YOU KNOW IF YOUR MOTHER HEARS YOU USE THAT WORD SHE'LL KILL US BOTH?
YOU DON'T KNOW WHAT IT'S LIKE. TO HAVE TO TAKE IT.
WHAT?
TO NOT BE ABLE TO DO ANYTHING, AND THEN, THEN GET THE CHANCE--
YOU THINK I DON'T KNOW WHAT IT'S *LIKE...?*
IT'S ALL RIGHT FOR YOU, YOU GOT TO FIGHT THEM!
YOU GOT TO *KILL NAZIS!*

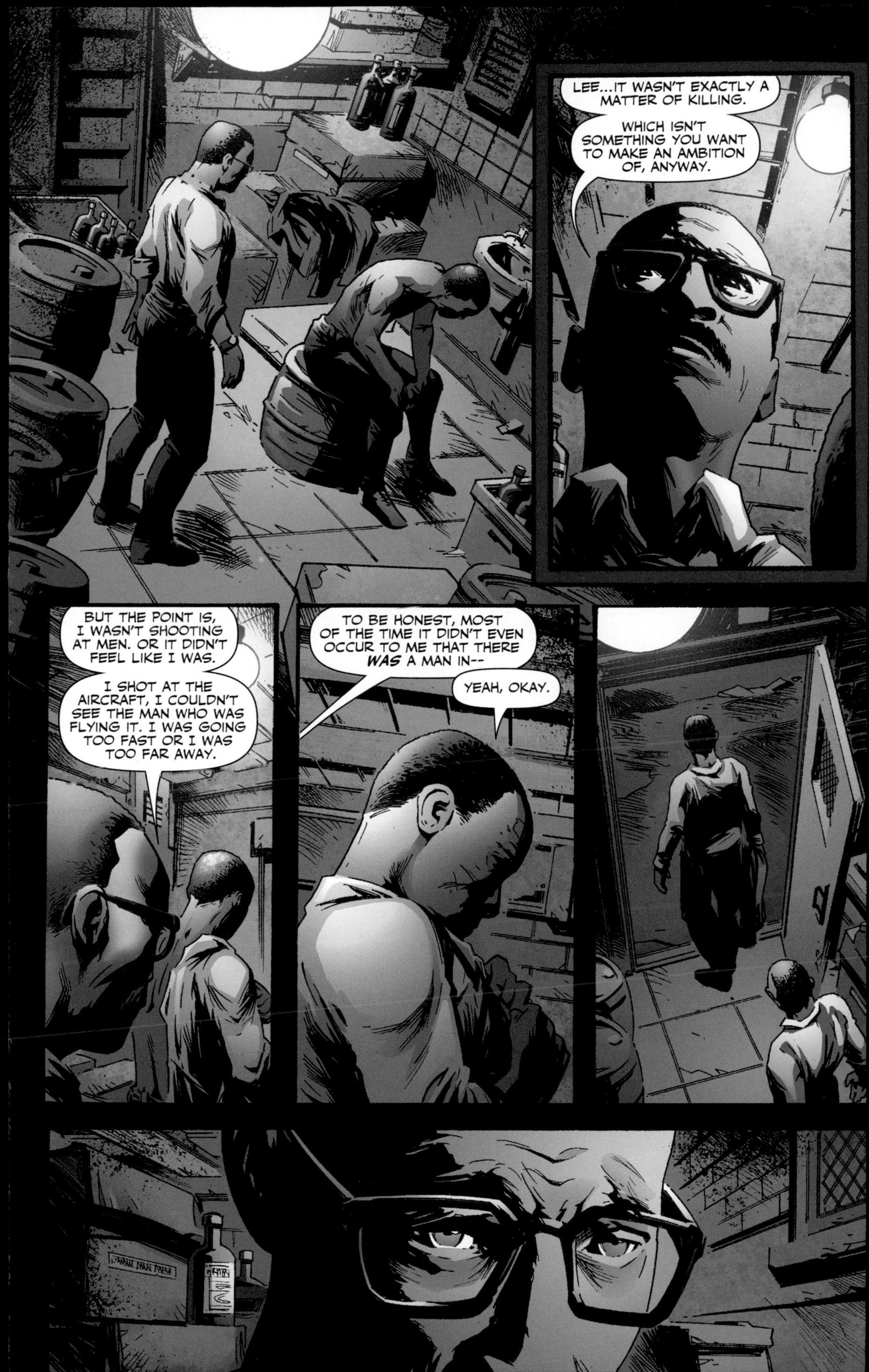
LEE...IT WASN'T EXACTLY A MATTER OF KILLING.
WHICH ISN'T SOMETHING YOU WANT TO MAKE AN AMBITION OF, ANYWAY.
BUT THE POINT IS, I WASN'T SHOOTING AT MEN. OR IT DIDN'T FEEL LIKE I WAS.
I SHOT AT THE AIRCRAFT, I COULDN'T SEE THE MAN WHO WAS FLYING IT. I WAS GOING TOO FAST OR I WAS TOO FAR AWAY.
TO BE HONEST, MOST OF THE TIME IT DIDN'T EVEN OCCUR TO ME THAT THERE *WAS* A MAN IN--
YEAH, OKAY.

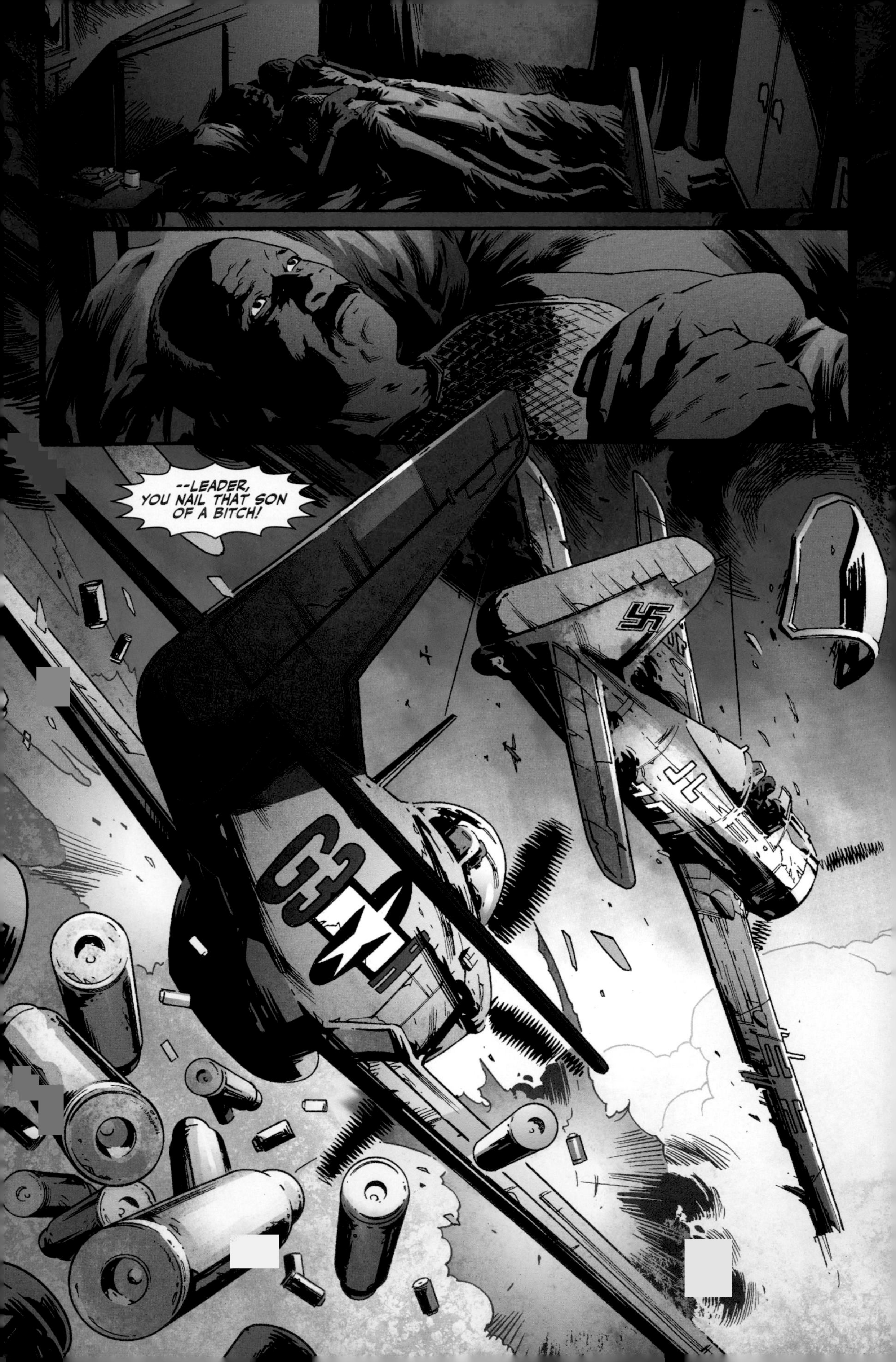
--LEADER, YOU NAIL THAT SON OF A BITCH!

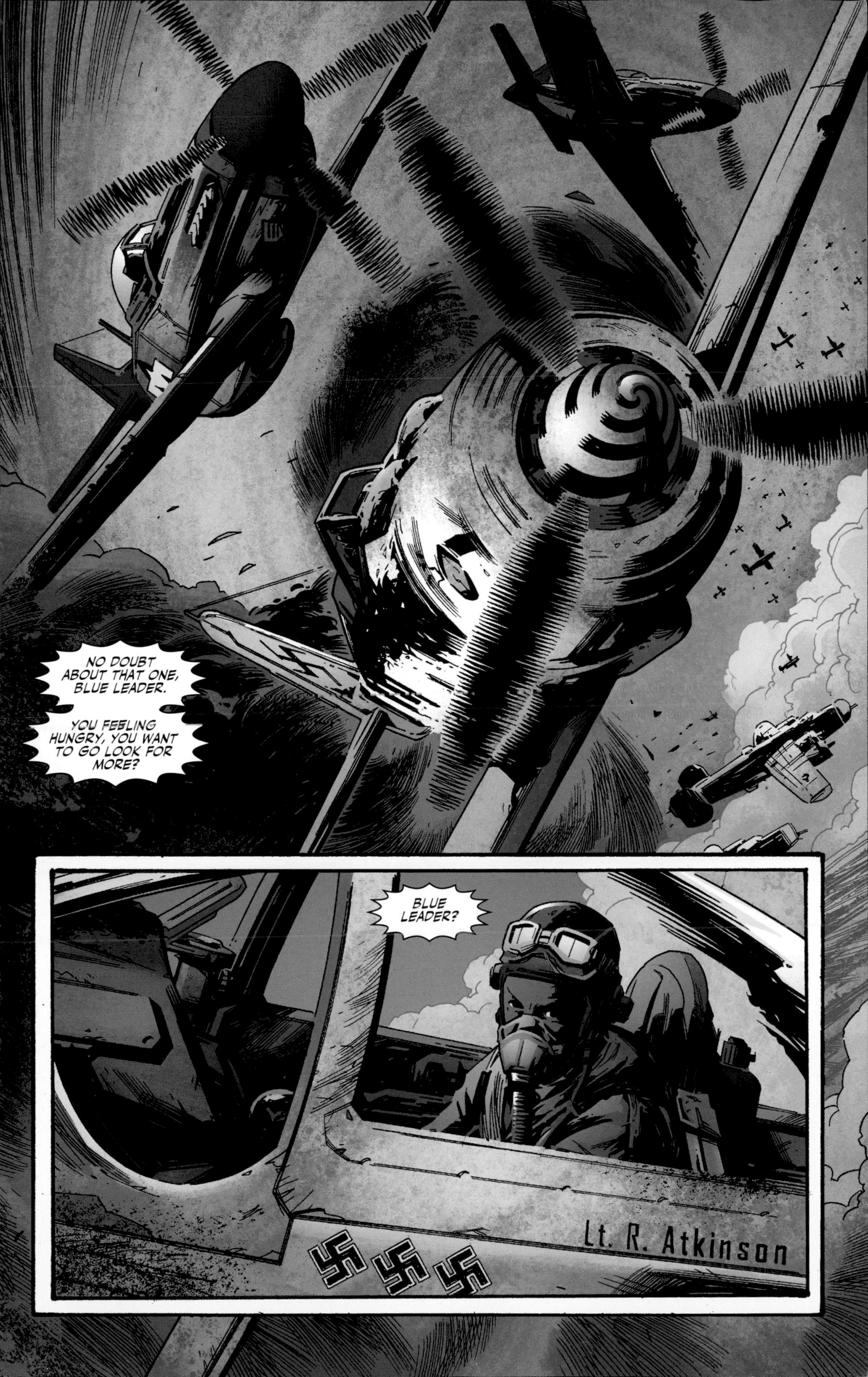
NO DOUBT ABOUT THAT ONE, BLUE LEADER.
YOU FEELING HUNGRY, YOU WANT TO GO LOOK FOR MORE?
BLUE LEADER?
Lt. R. Atkinson

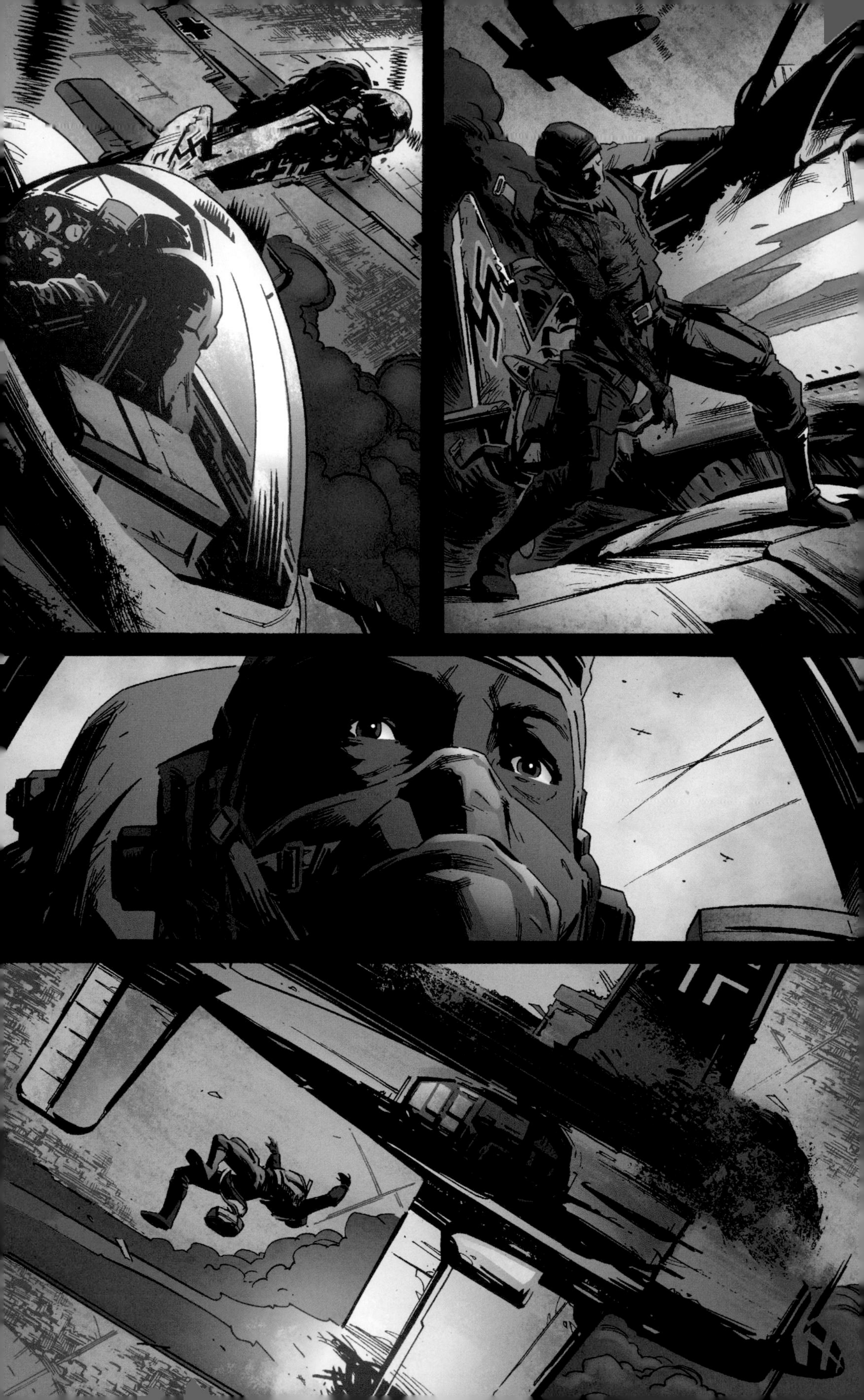

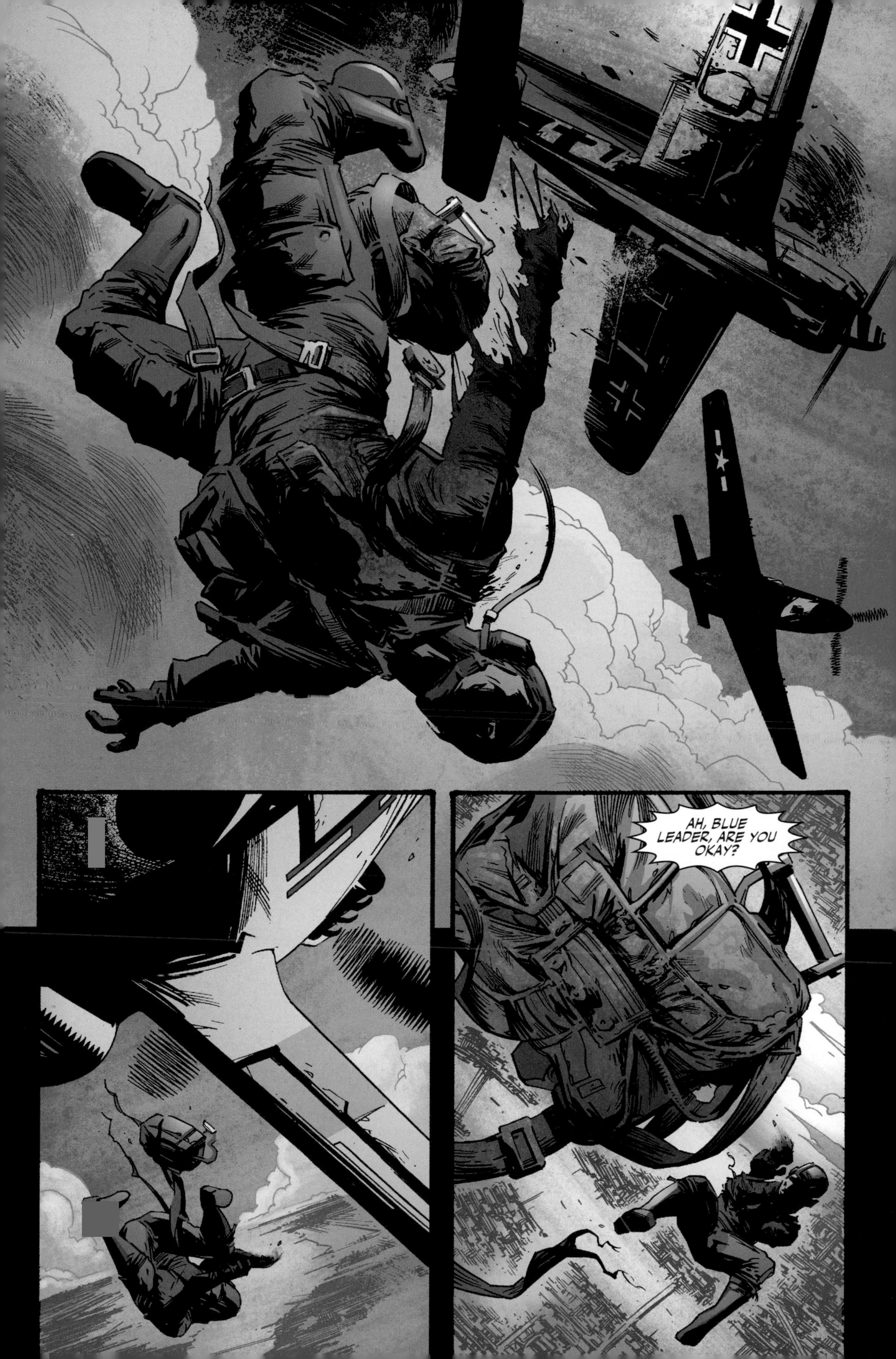
AH, BLUE LEADER, ARE YOU OKAY?

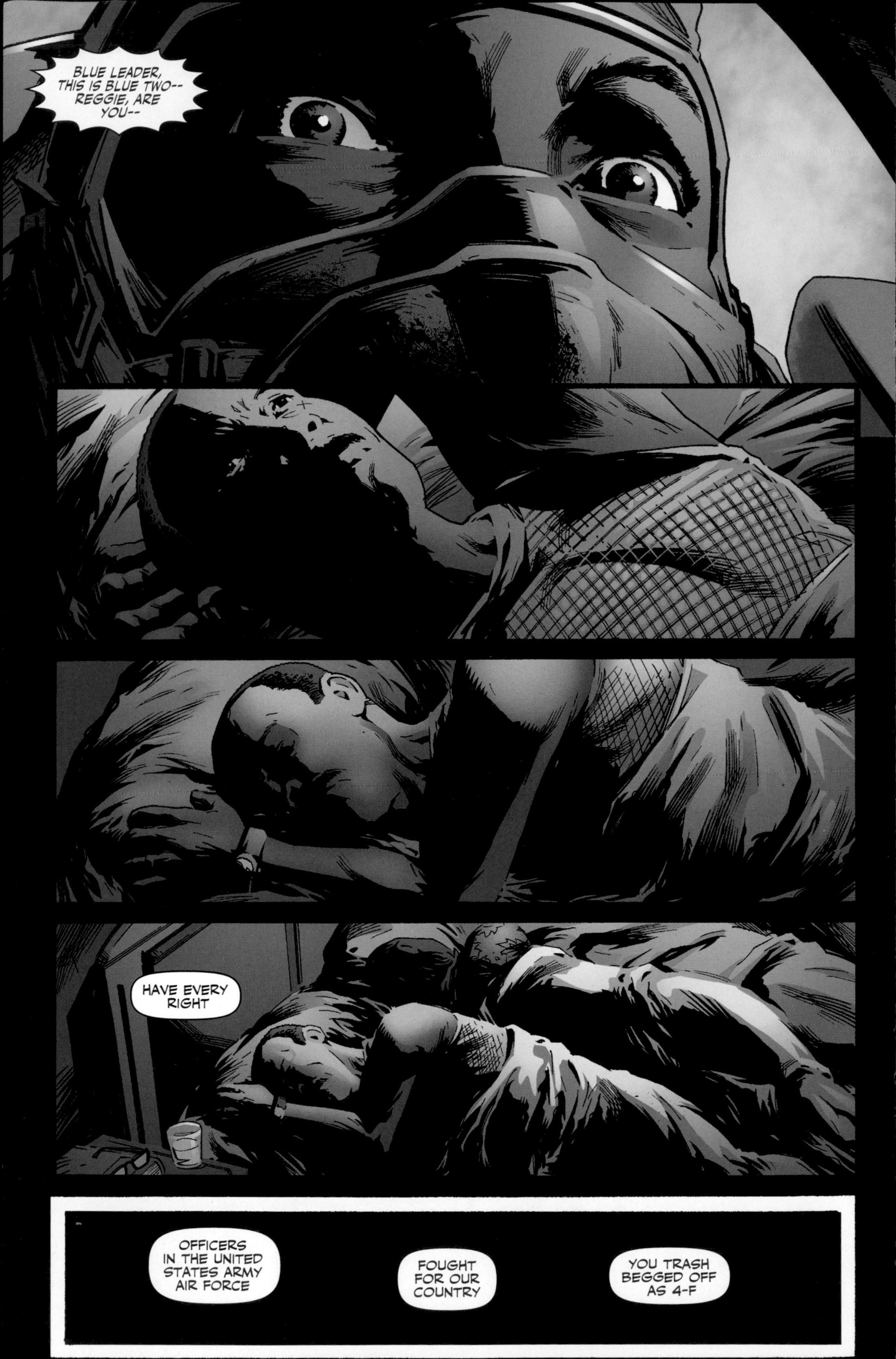
BLUE LEADER, THIS IS BLUE TWO-- REGGIE, ARE YOU--
HAVE EVERY RIGHT
OFFICERS IN THE UNITED STATES ARMY AIR FORCE
FOUGHT FOR OUR COUNTRY
YOU TRASH BEGGED OFF AS 4-F

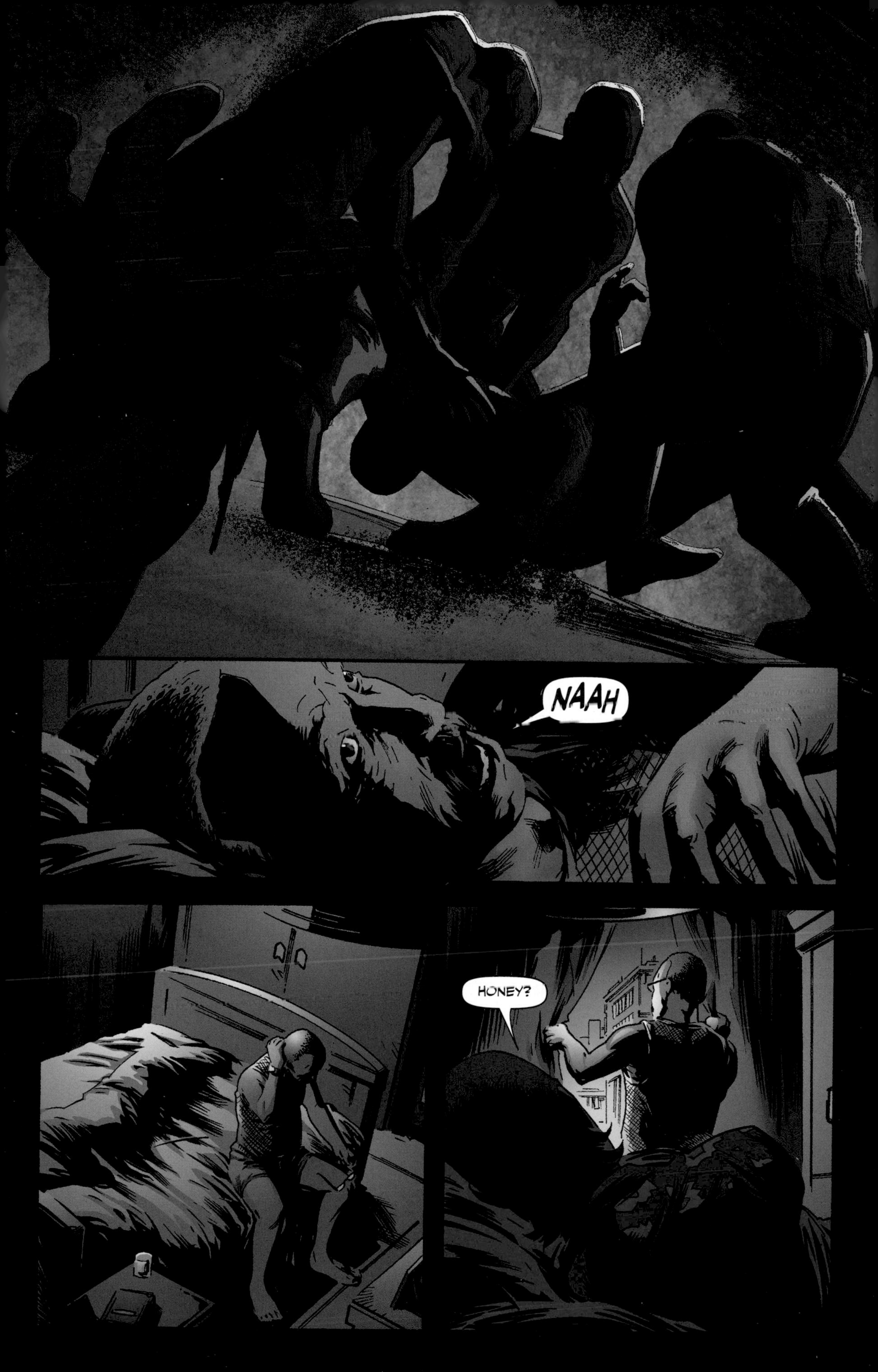
NAAH
HONEY?

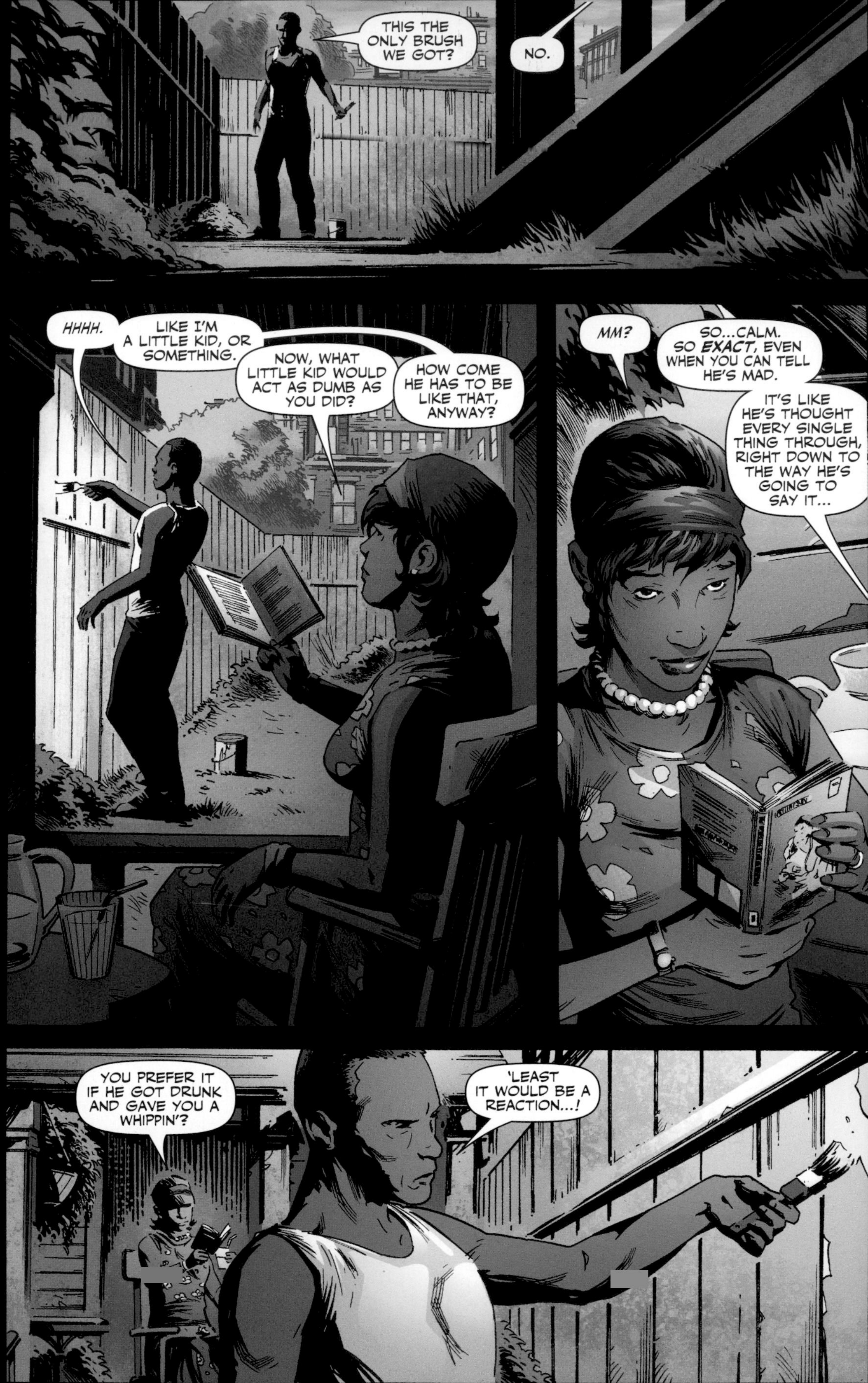
THIS THE ONLY BRUSH WE GOT?
NO.
HHHH.
LIKE I'M A LITTLE KID, OR SOMETHING.
NOW, WHAT LITTLE KID WOULD ACT AS DUMB AS YOU DID?
HOW COME HE HAS TO BE LIKE THAT, ANYWAY?
MM?
SO...CALM. SO EXACT, EVEN WHEN YOU CAN TELL HE'S MAD.
IT'S LIKE HE'S THOUGHT EVERY SINGLE THING THROUGH, RIGHT DOWN TO THE WAY HE'S GOING TO SAY IT...
YOU PREFER IT IF HE GOT DRUNK AND GAVE YOU A WHIPPIN'?
'LEAST IT WOULD BE A REACTION...!

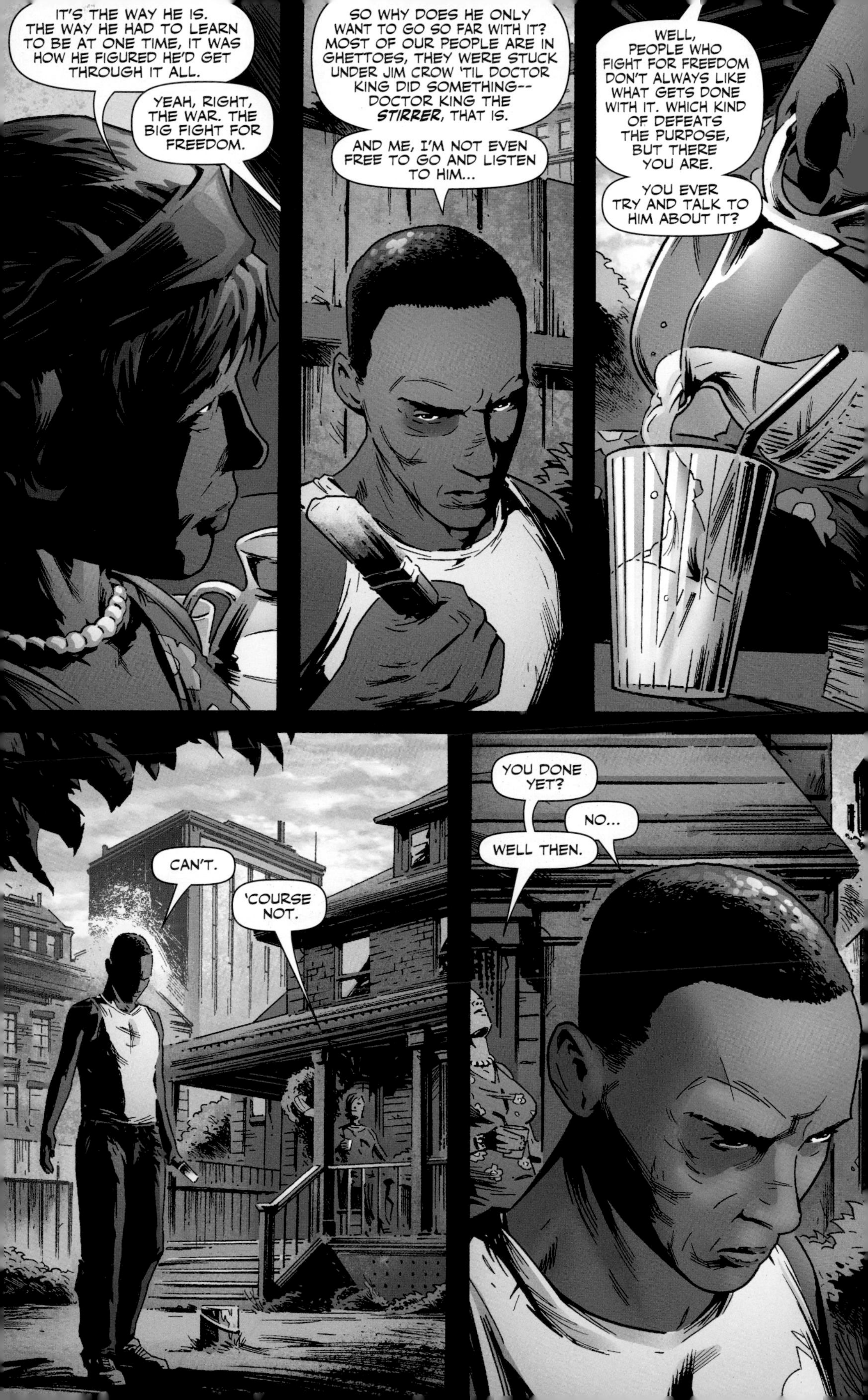
IT'S THE WAY HE IS. THE WAY HE HAD TO LEARN TO BE AT ONE TIME, IT WAS HOW HE FIGURED HE'D GET THROUGH IT ALL.
YEAH, RIGHT, THE WAR. THE BIG FIGHT FOR FREEDOM.
SO WHY DOES HE ONLY WANT TO GO SO FAR WITH IT? MOST OF OUR PEOPLE ARE IN GHETTOES, THEY WERE STUCK UNDER JIM CROW 'TIL DOCTOR KING DID SOMETHING-- DOCTOR KING THE STIRRER, THAT IS.
AND ME, I'M NOT EVEN FREE TO GO AND LISTEN TO HIM...
WELL, PEOPLE WHO FIGHT FOR FREEDOM DON'T ALWAYS LIKE WHAT GETS DONE WITH IT. WHICH KIND OF DEFEATS THE PURPOSE, BUT THERE YOU ARE.
YOU EVER TRY AND TALK TO HIM ABOUT IT?
CAN'T.
'COURSE NOT.
YOU DONE YET?
NO...
WELL THEN.

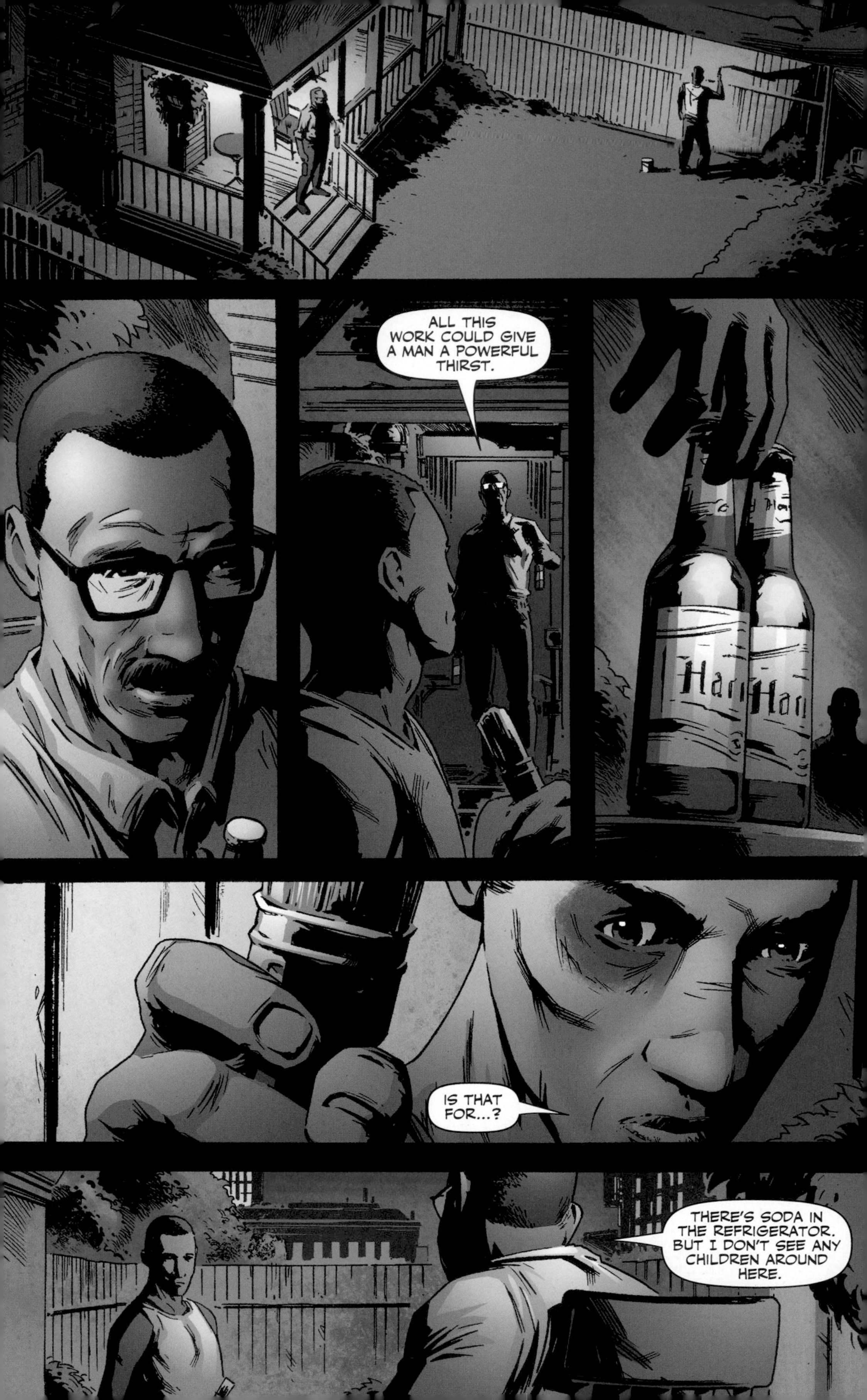
ALL THIS WORK COULD GIVE A MAN A POWERFUL THIRST.
IS THAT FOR...?
THERE'S SODA IN THE REFRIGERATOR. BUT I DON'T SEE ANY CHILDREN AROUND HERE.

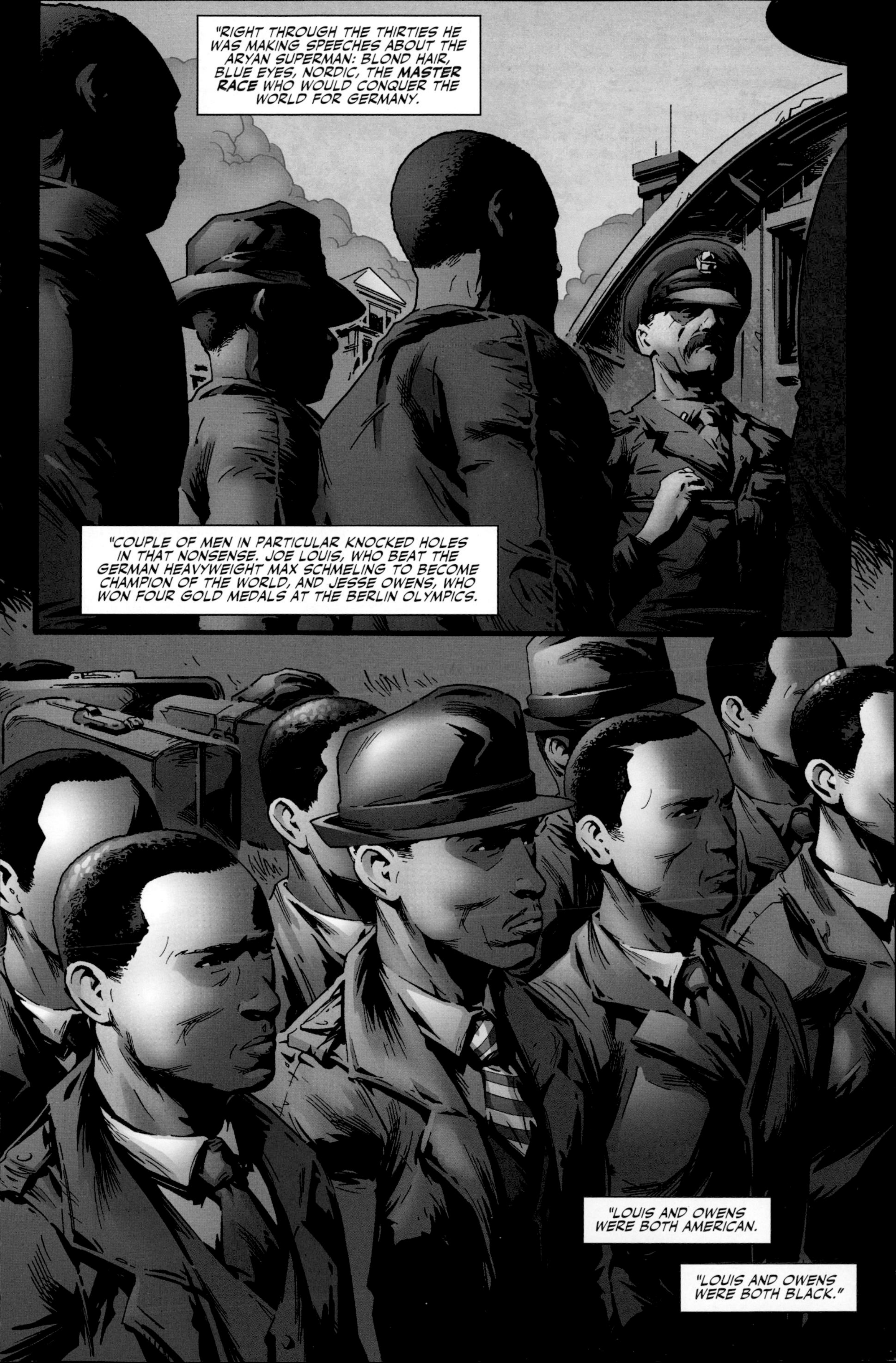
"RIGHT THROUGH THE THIRTIES HE WAS MAKING SPEECHES ABOUT THE ARYAN SUPERMAN: BLOND HAIR, BLUE EYES, NORDIC, THE **MASTER RACE** WHO WOULD CONQUER THE WORLD FOR GERMANY.
"COUPLE OF MEN IN PARTICULAR KNOCKED HOLES IN THAT NONSENSE. JOE LOUIS, WHO BEAT THE GERMAN HEAVYWEIGHT MAX SCHMELING TO BECOME CHAMPION OF THE WORLD, AND JESSE OWENS, WHO WON FOUR GOLD MEDALS AT THE BERLIN OLYMPICS.
"LOUIS AND OWENS WERE BOTH AMERICAN.
"LOUIS AND OWENS WERE BOTH BLACK."

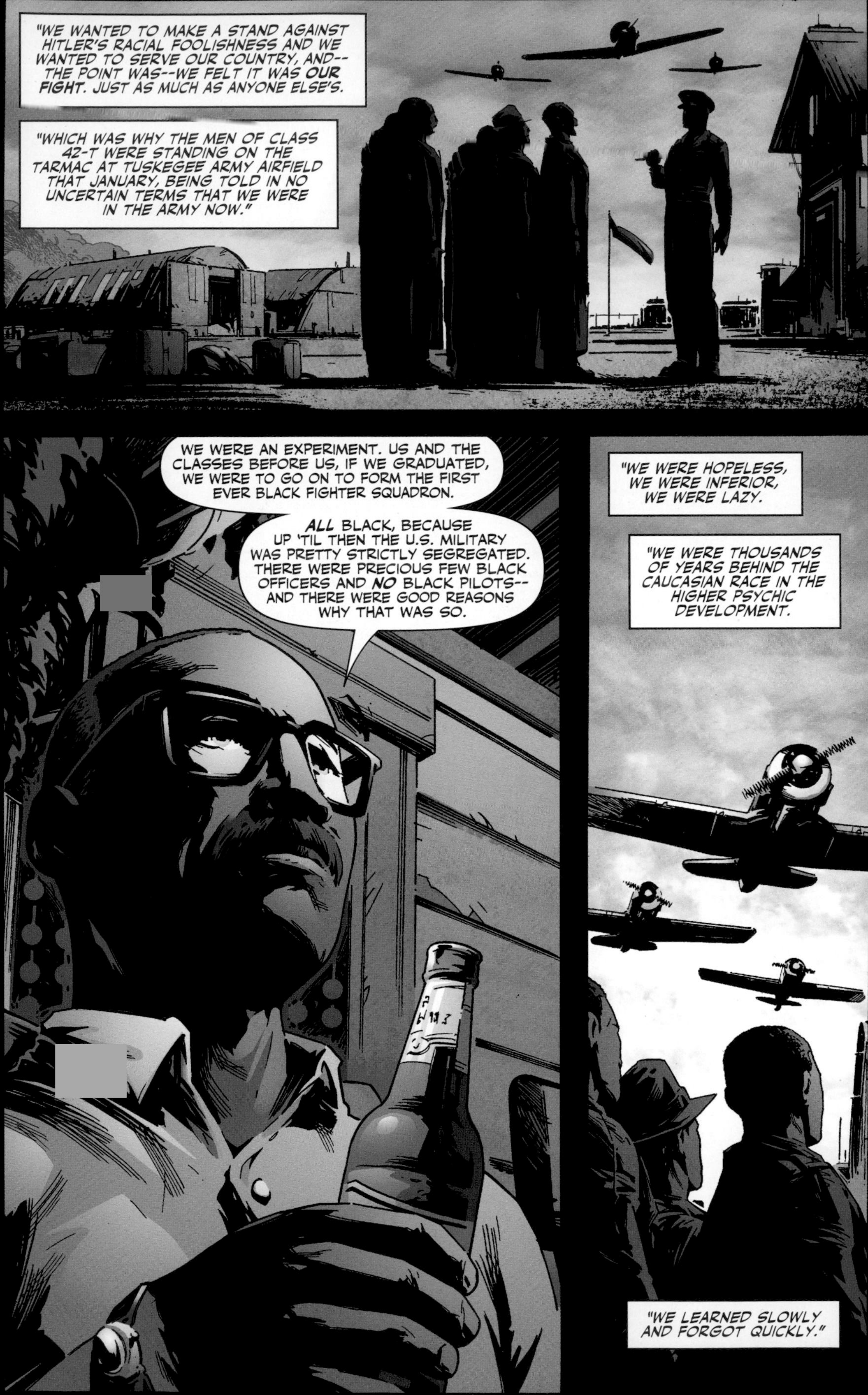
"WE WANTED TO MAKE A STAND AGAINST HITLER'S RACIAL FOOLISHNESS AND WE WANTED TO SERVE OUR COUNTRY, AND-- THE POINT WAS--WE FELT IT WAS **OUR FIGHT**. JUST AS MUCH AS ANYONE ELSE'S.
"WHICH WAS WHY THE MEN OF CLASS 42-T WERE STANDING ON THE TARMAC AT TUSKEGEE ARMY AIRFIELD THAT JANUARY, BEING TOLD IN NO UNCERTAIN TERMS THAT WE WERE IN THE ARMY NOW."
WE WERE AN EXPERIMENT. US AND THE CLASSES BEFORE US, IF WE GRADUATED, WE WERE TO GO ON TO FORM THE FIRST EVER BLACK FIGHTER SQUADRON.
ALL BLACK, BECAUSE UP 'TIL THEN THE U.S. MILITARY WAS PRETTY STRICTLY SEGREGATED. THERE WERE PRECIOUS FEW BLACK OFFICERS AND ***NO*** BLACK PILOTS-- AND THERE WERE GOOD REASONS WHY THAT WAS SO.
"WE WERE HOPELESS, WE WERE INFERIOR, WE WERE LAZY.
"WE WERE THOUSANDS OF YEARS BEHIND THE CAUCASIAN RACE IN THE HIGHER PSYCHIC DEVELOPMENT.
"WE LEARNED SLOWLY AND FORGOT QUICKLY."

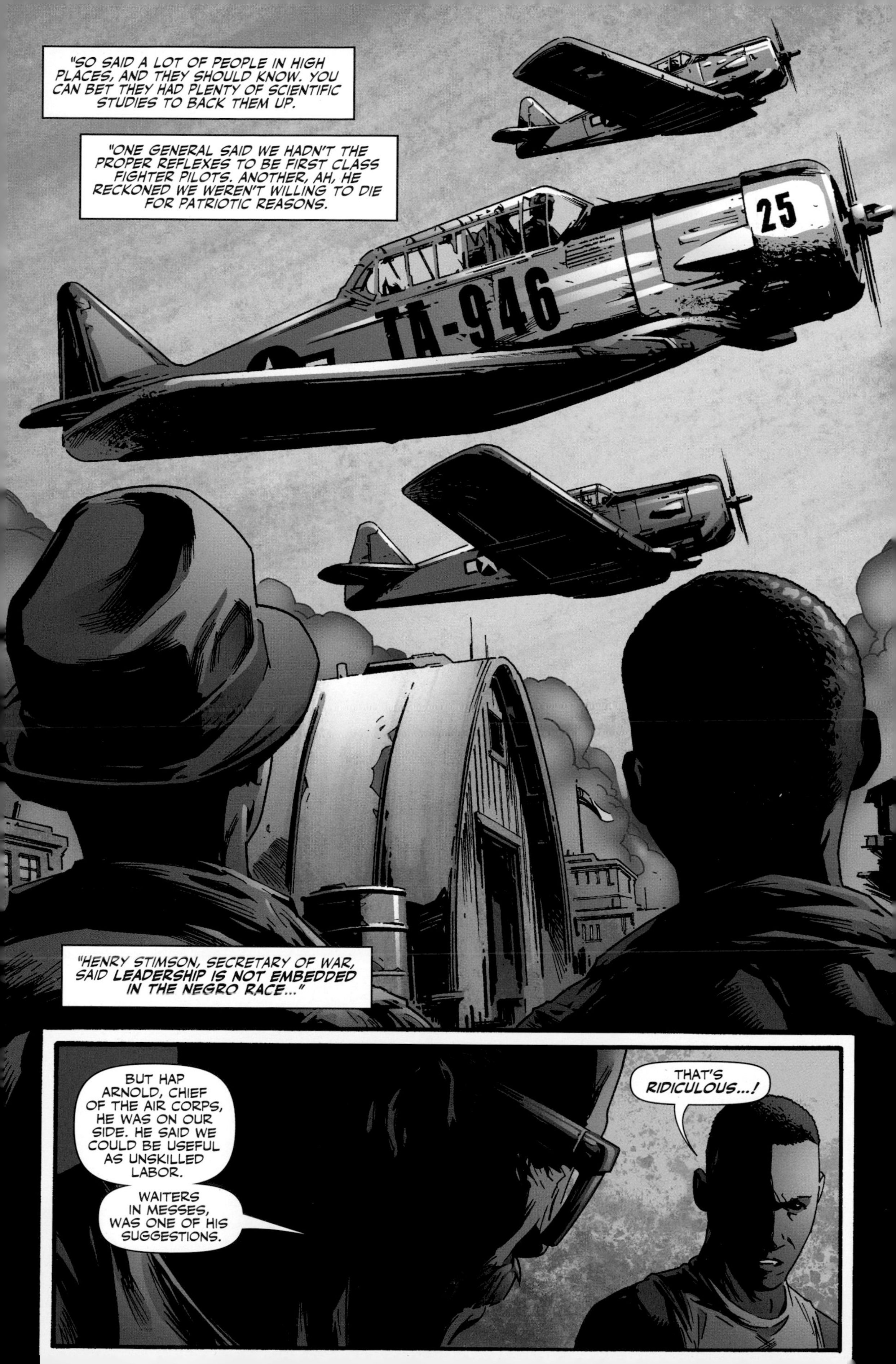
"SO SAID A LOT OF PEOPLE IN HIGH PLACES, AND THEY SHOULD KNOW. YOU CAN BET THEY HAD PLENTY OF SCIENTIFIC STUDIES TO BACK THEM UP.
"ONE GENERAL SAID WE HADN'T THE PROPER REFLEXES TO BE FIRST CLASS FIGHTER PILOTS. ANOTHER, AH, HE RECKONED WE WEREN'T WILLING TO DIE FOR PATRIOTIC REASONS.
25
TA-946
"HENRY STIMSON, SECRETARY OF WAR, SAID **LEADERSHIP IS NOT EMBEDDED IN THE NEGRO RACE**..."
BUT HAP ARNOLD, CHIEF OF THE AIR CORPS, HE WAS ON OUR SIDE. HE SAID WE COULD BE USEFUL AS UNSKILLED LABOR.
WAITERS IN MESSES, WAS ONE OF HIS SUGGESTIONS.
THAT'S ***RIDICULOUS...!***

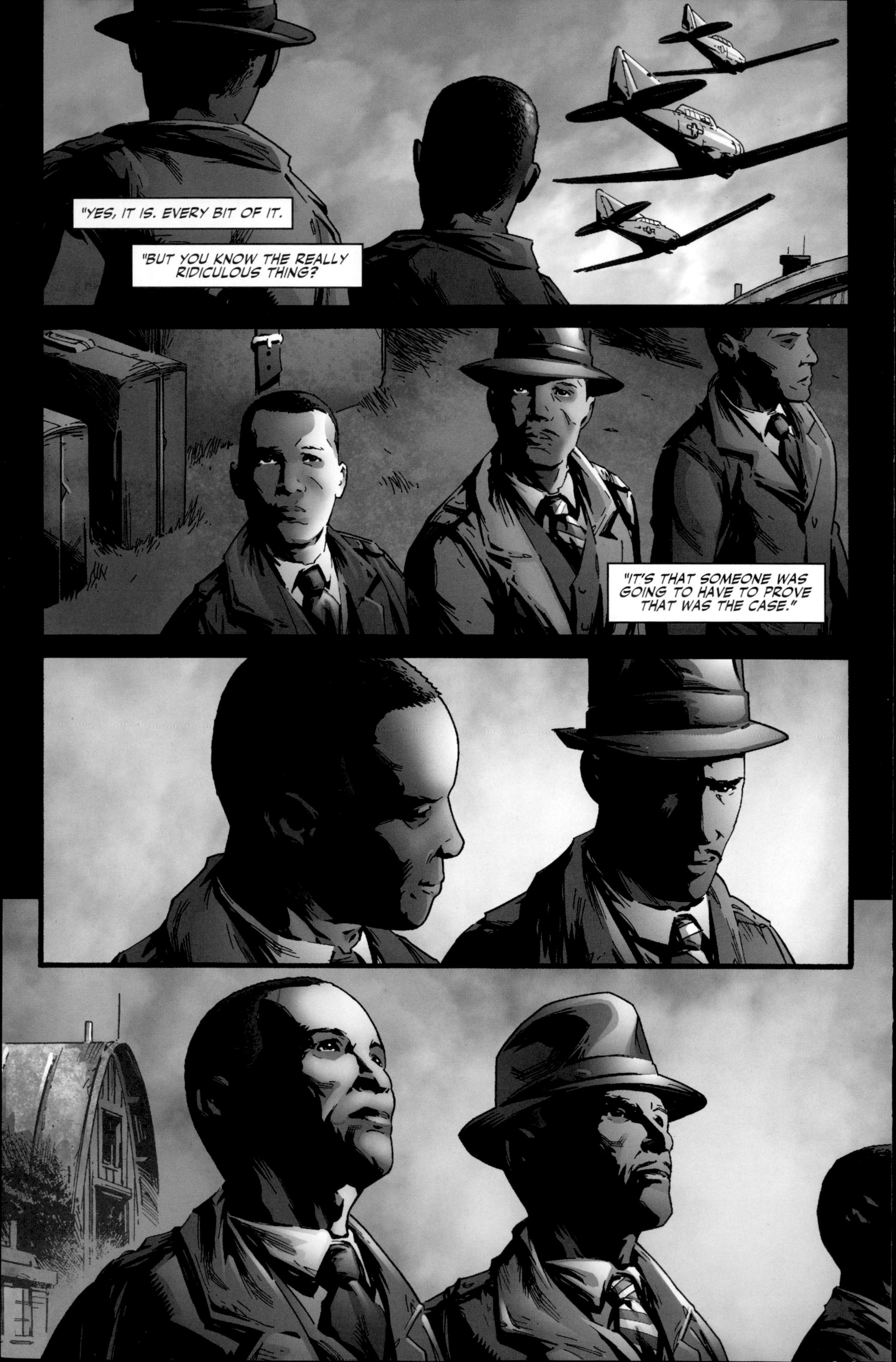
"YES, IT IS. EVERY BIT OF IT.
"BUT YOU KNOW THE REALLY RIDICULOUS THING?
"IT'S THAT SOMEONE WAS GOING TO HAVE TO PROVE THAT WAS THE CASE."

2 : SUNWARD I'VE CLIMBED

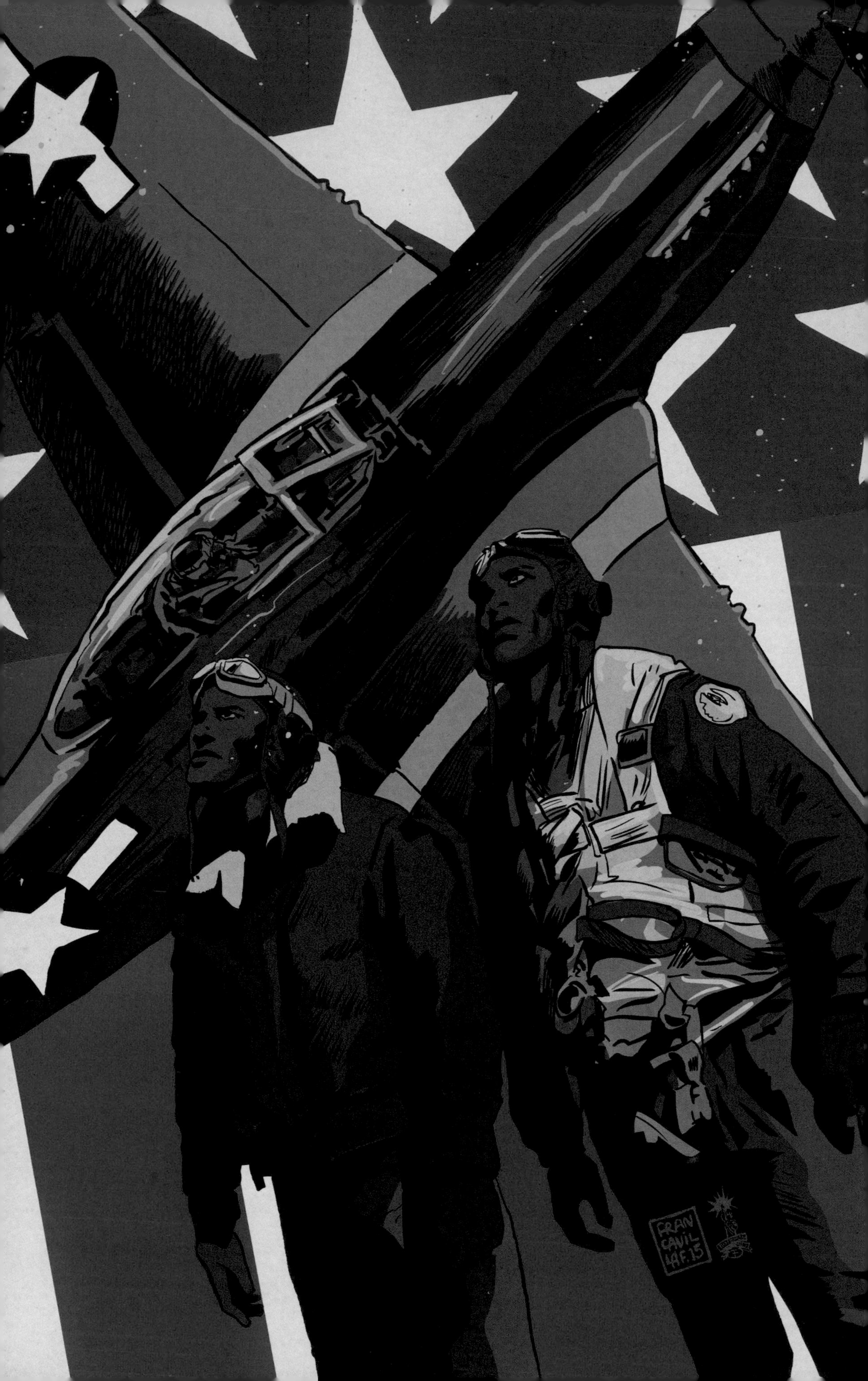
FRAN
CAVIL
14F.15

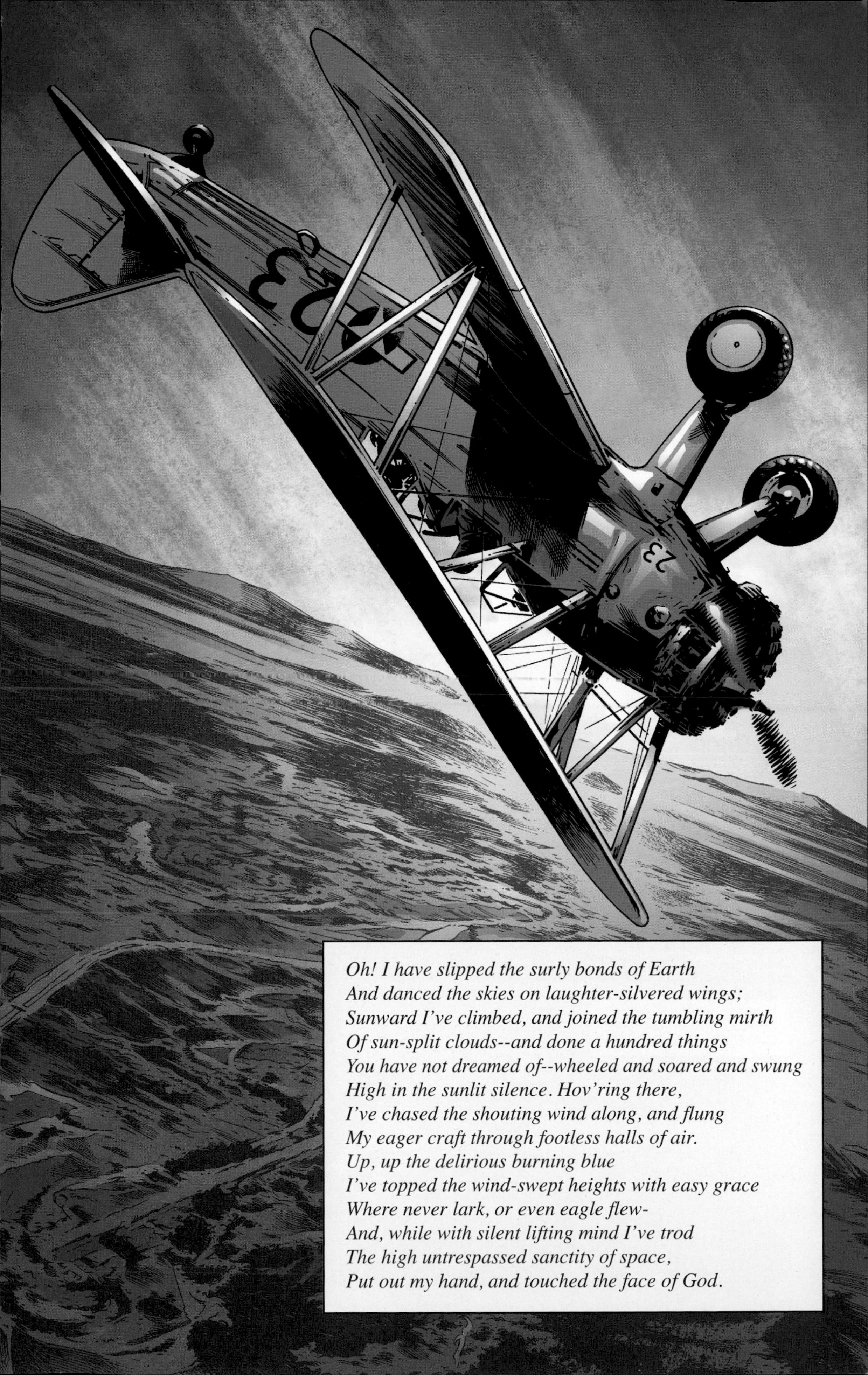
23
23
Oh! I have slipped the surly bonds of Earth
And danced the skies on laughter-silvered wings;
Sunward I've climbed, and joined the tumbling mirth
Of sun-split clouds--and done a hundred things
You have not dreamed of--wheeled and soared and swung
High in the sunlit silence. Hov'ring there,
I've chased the shouting wind along, and flung
My eager craft through footless halls of air.
Up, up the delirious burning blue
I've topped the wind-swept heights with easy grace
Where never lark, or even eagle flew-
And, while with silent lifting mind I've trod
The high untrespassed sanctity of space,
Put out my hand, and touched the face of God.

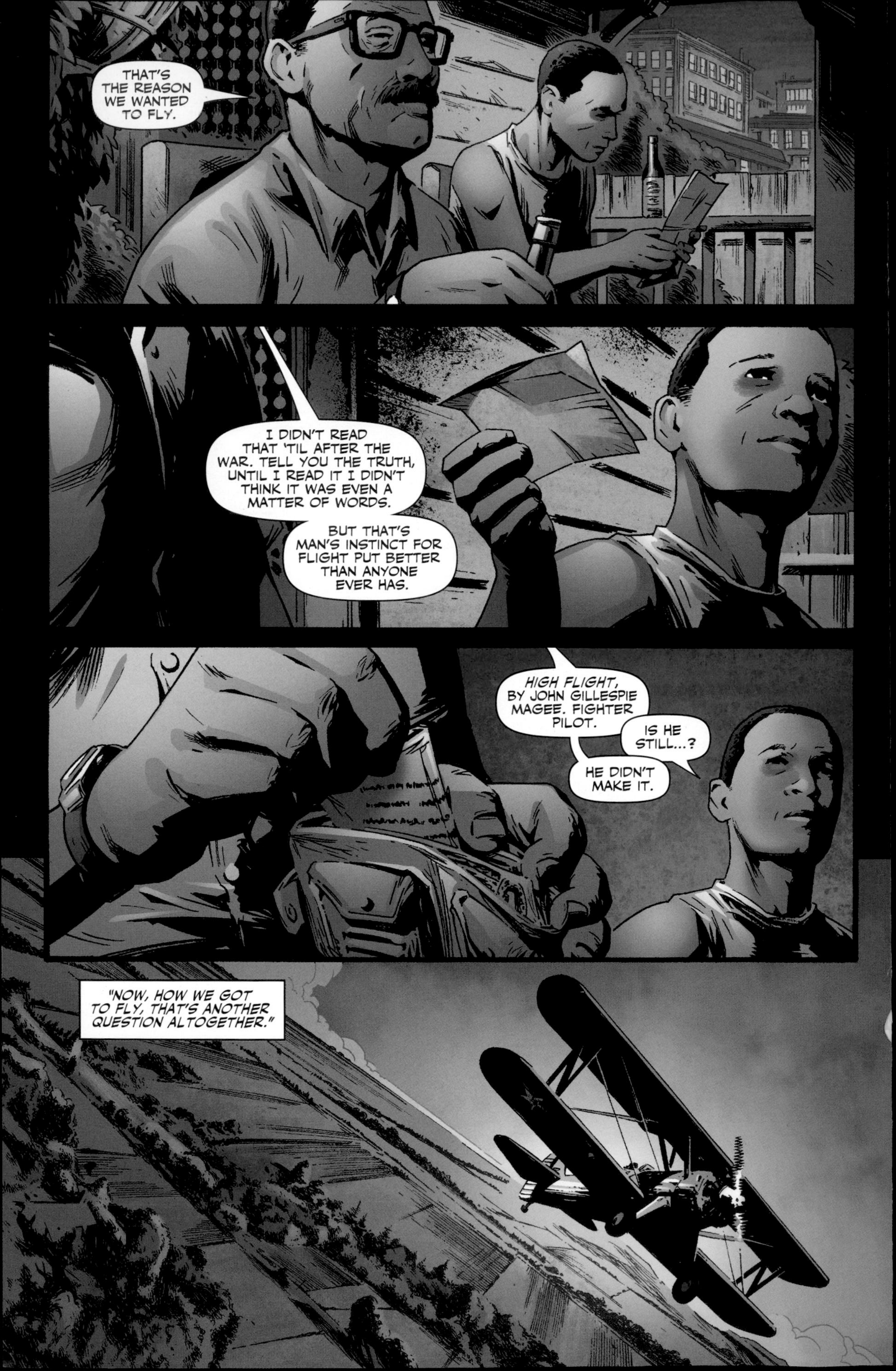
THAT'S THE REASON WE WANTED TO FLY.
I DIDN'T READ THAT 'TIL AFTER THE WAR. TELL YOU THE TRUTH, UNTIL I READ IT I DIDN'T THINK IT WAS EVEN A MATTER OF WORDS.
BUT THAT'S MAN'S INSTINCT FOR FLIGHT PUT BETTER THAN ANYONE EVER HAS.
HIGH FLIGHT, BY JOHN GILLESPIE MAGEE. FIGHTER PILOT.
IS HE STILL...?
HE DIDN'T MAKE IT.
"NOW, HOW WE GOT TO FLY, THAT'S ANOTHER QUESTION ALTOGETHER."

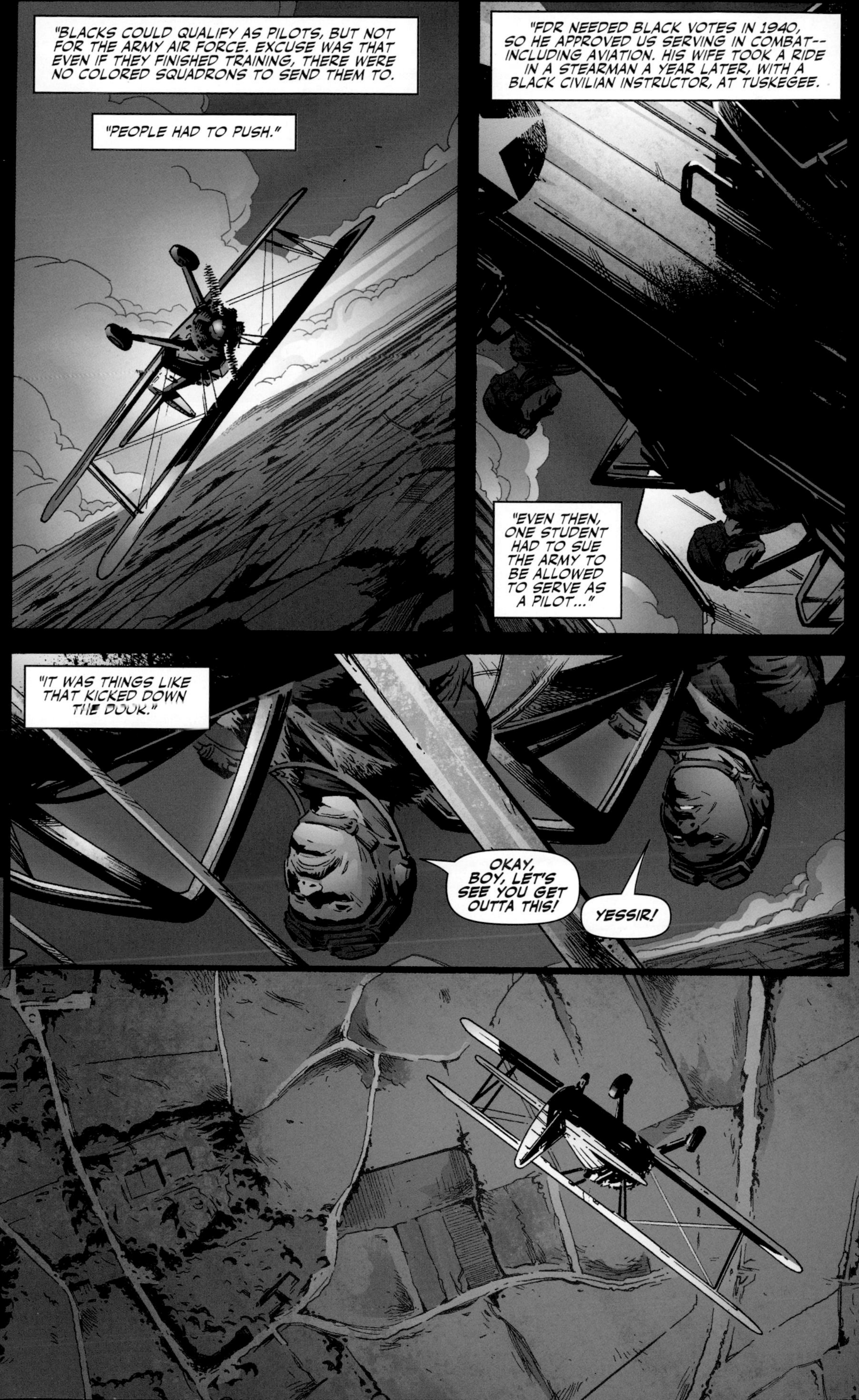
"BLACKS COULD QUALIFY AS PILOTS, BUT NOT FOR THE ARMY AIR FORCE. EXCUSE WAS THAT EVEN IF THEY FINISHED TRAINING, THERE WERE NO COLORED SQUADRONS TO SEND THEM TO.
"PEOPLE HAD TO PUSH."
"FDR NEEDED BLACK VOTES IN 1940, SO HE APPROVED US SERVING IN COMBAT-- INCLUDING AVIATION. HIS WIFE TOOK A RIDE IN A STEARMAN A YEAR LATER, WITH A BLACK CIVILIAN INSTRUCTOR, AT TUSKEGEE.
"EVEN THEN, ONE STUDENT HAD TO SUE THE ARMY TO BE ALLOWED TO SERVE AS A PILOT..."
"IT WAS THINGS LIKE THAT KICKED DOWN THE DOOR."
OKAY, BOY, LET'S SEE YOU GET OUTTA THIS!
YESSIR!

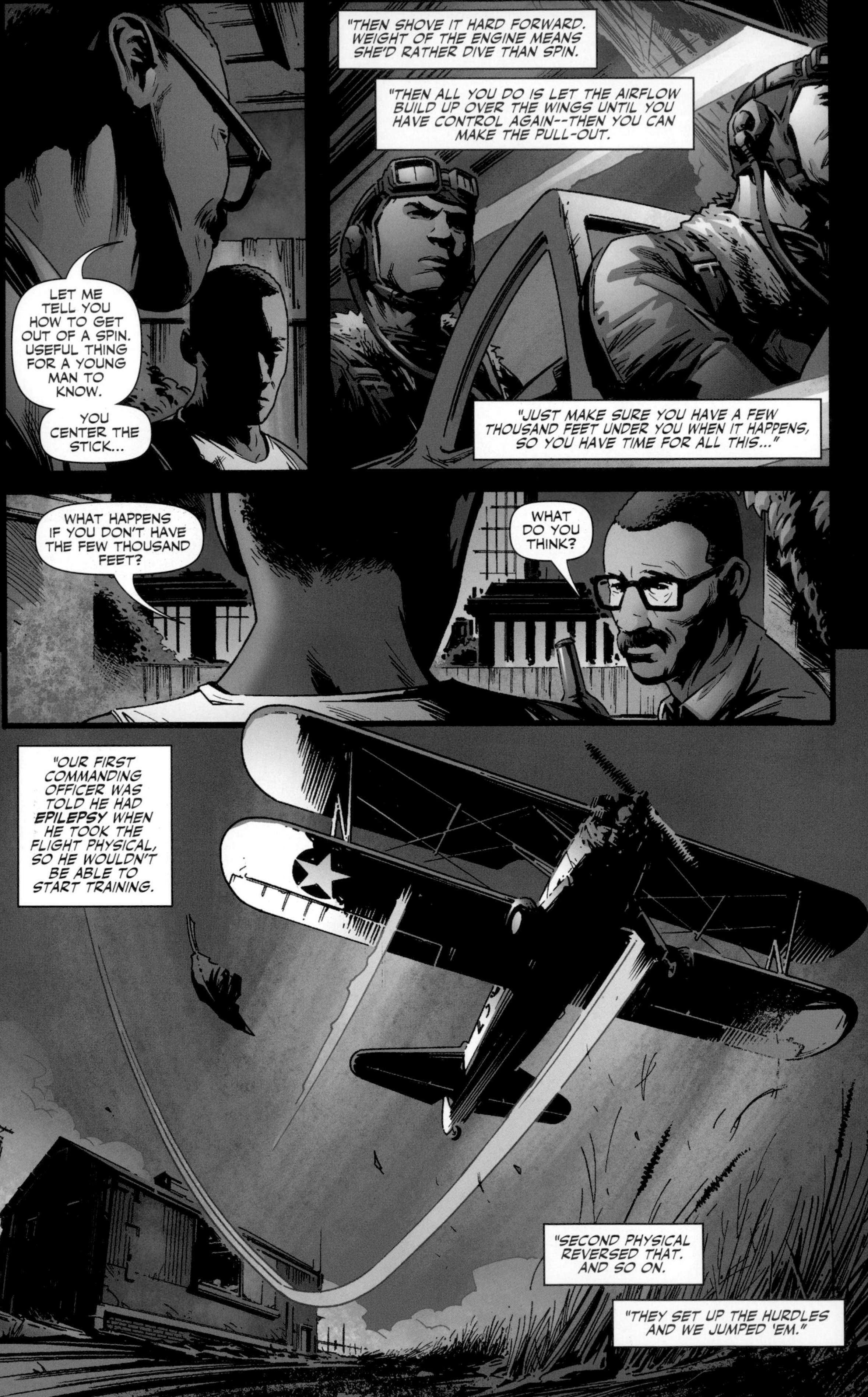
LET ME TELL YOU HOW TO GET OUT OF A SPIN. USEFUL THING FOR A YOUNG MAN TO KNOW.
YOU CENTER THE STICK...
"THEN SHOVE IT HARD FORWARD. WEIGHT OF THE ENGINE MEANS SHE'D RATHER DIVE THAN SPIN.
"THEN ALL YOU DO IS LET THE AIRFLOW BUILD UP OVER THE WINGS UNTIL YOU HAVE CONTROL AGAIN--THEN YOU CAN MAKE THE PULL-OUT.
"JUST MAKE SURE YOU HAVE A FEW THOUSAND FEET UNDER YOU WHEN IT HAPPENS, SO YOU HAVE TIME FOR ALL THIS..."
WHAT HAPPENS IF YOU DON'T HAVE THE FEW THOUSAND FEET?
WHAT DO YOU THINK?
"OUR FIRST COMMANDING OFFICER WAS TOLD HE HAD EPILEPSY WHEN HE TOOK THE FLIGHT PHYSICAL, SO HE WOULDN'T BE ABLE TO START TRAINING.
"SECOND PHYSICAL REVERSED THAT. AND SO ON.
"THEY SET UP THE HURDLES AND WE JUMPED 'EM."

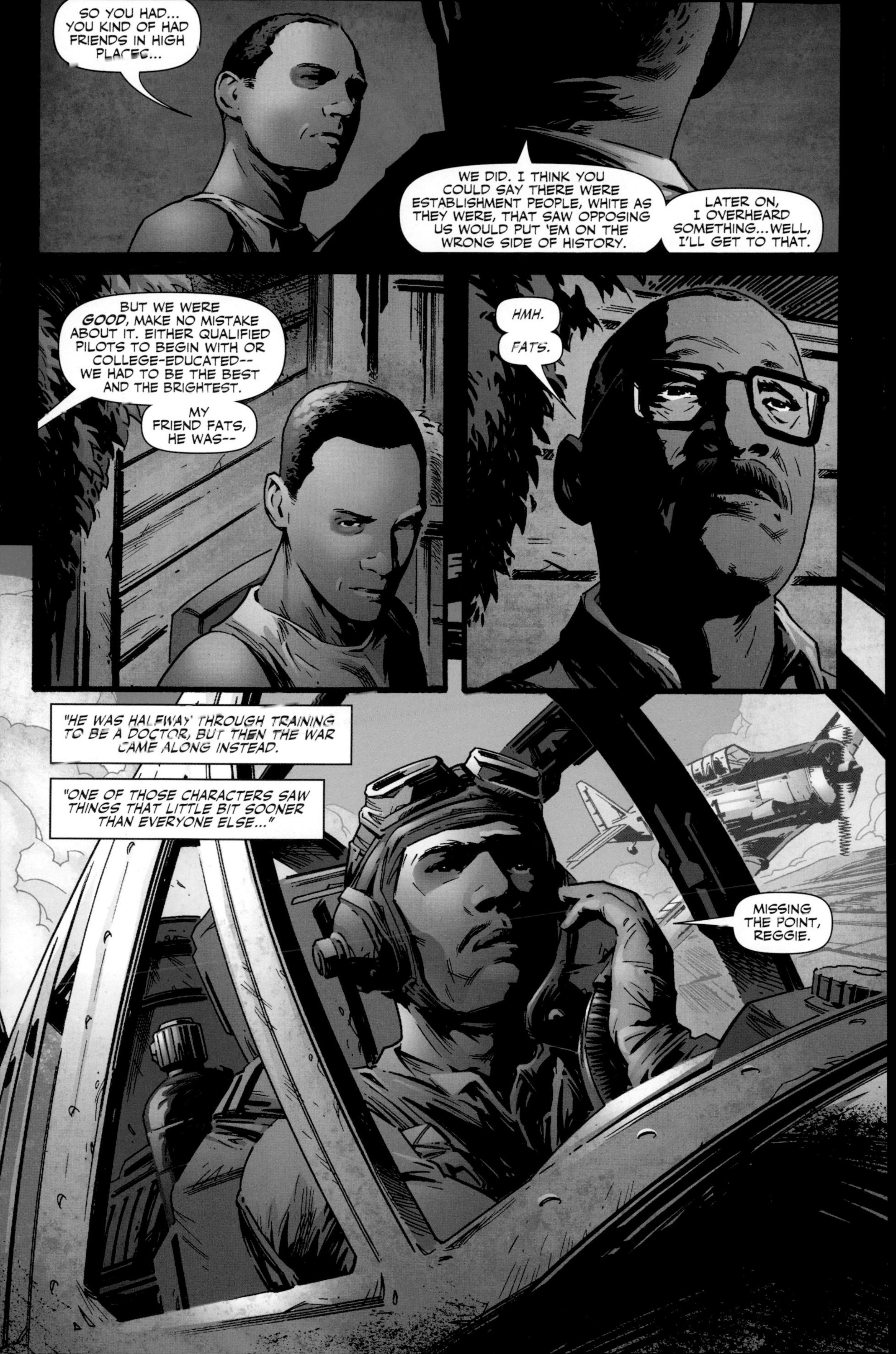
SO YOU HAD... YOU KIND OF HAD FRIENDS IN HIGH PLACES...
WE DID. I THINK YOU COULD SAY THERE WERE ESTABLISHMENT PEOPLE, WHITE AS THEY WERE, THAT SAW OPPOSING US WOULD PUT 'EM ON THE WRONG SIDE OF HISTORY.
LATER ON, I OVERHEARD SOMETHING...WELL, I'LL GET TO THAT.
BUT WE WERE *GOOD*, MAKE NO MISTAKE ABOUT IT. EITHER QUALIFIED PILOTS TO BEGIN WITH OR COLLEGE-EDUCATED-- WE HAD TO BE THE BEST AND THE BRIGHTEST.
MY FRIEND FATS, HE WAS--
HMH.
FATS.
"HE WAS HALFWAY THROUGH TRAINING TO BE A DOCTOR, BUT THEN THE WAR CAME ALONG INSTEAD.
"ONE OF THOSE CHARACTERS SAW THINGS THAT LITTLE BIT SOONER THAN EVERYONE ELSE..."
MISSING THE POINT, REGGIE.

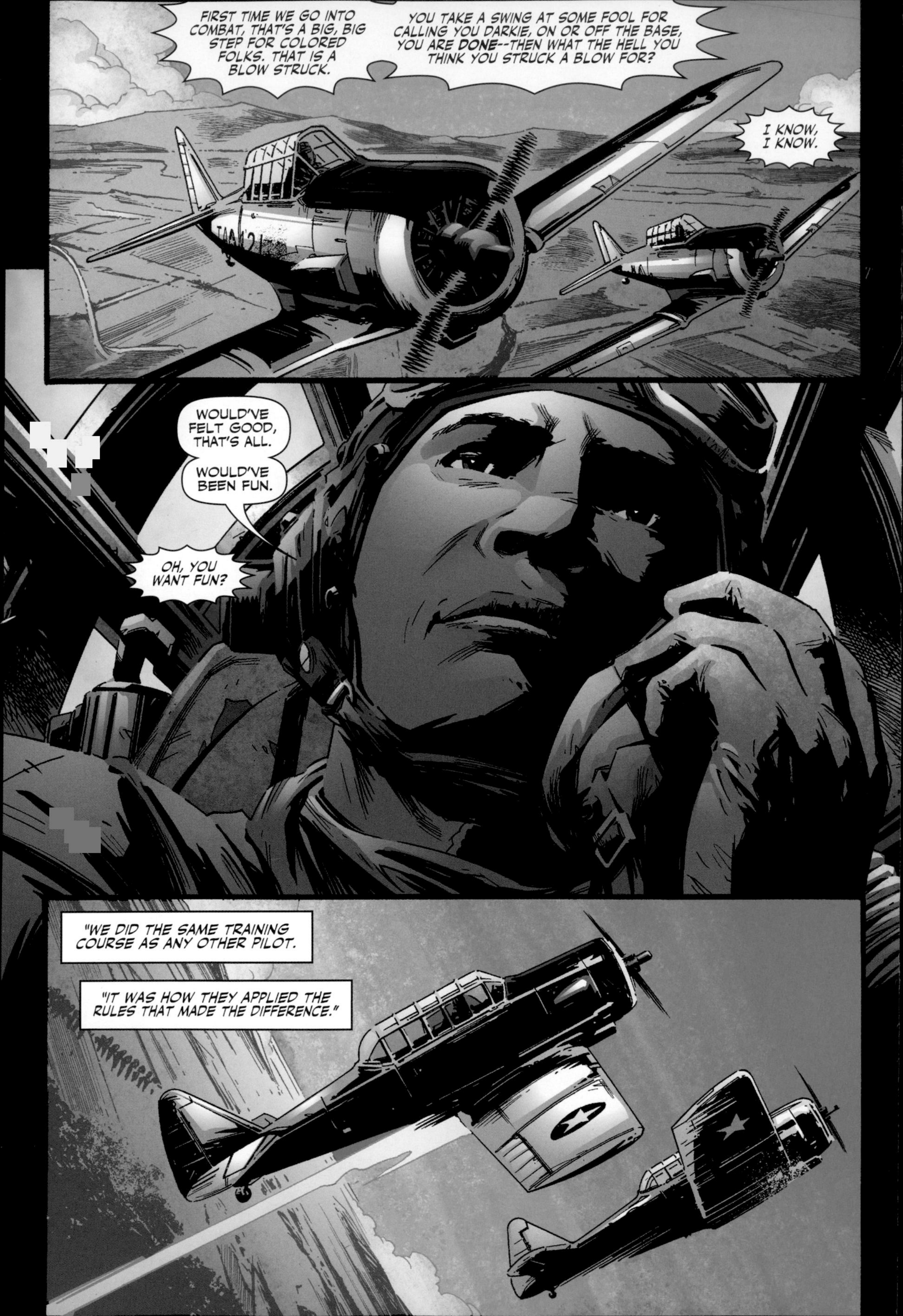
FIRST TIME WE GO INTO COMBAT, THAT'S A BIG, BIG STEP FOR COLORED FOLKS. THAT IS A BLOW STRUCK.
YOU TAKE A SWING AT SOME FOOL FOR CALLING YOU DARKIE, ON OR OFF THE BASE, YOU ARE DONE--THEN WHAT THE HELL YOU THINK YOU STRUCK A BLOW FOR?
I KNOW, I KNOW.
WOULD'VE FELT GOOD, THAT'S ALL.
WOULD'VE BEEN FUN.
OH, YOU WANT FUN?
"WE DID THE SAME TRAINING COURSE AS ANY OTHER PILOT.
"IT WAS HOW THEY APPLIED THE RULES THAT MADE THE DIFFERENCE."

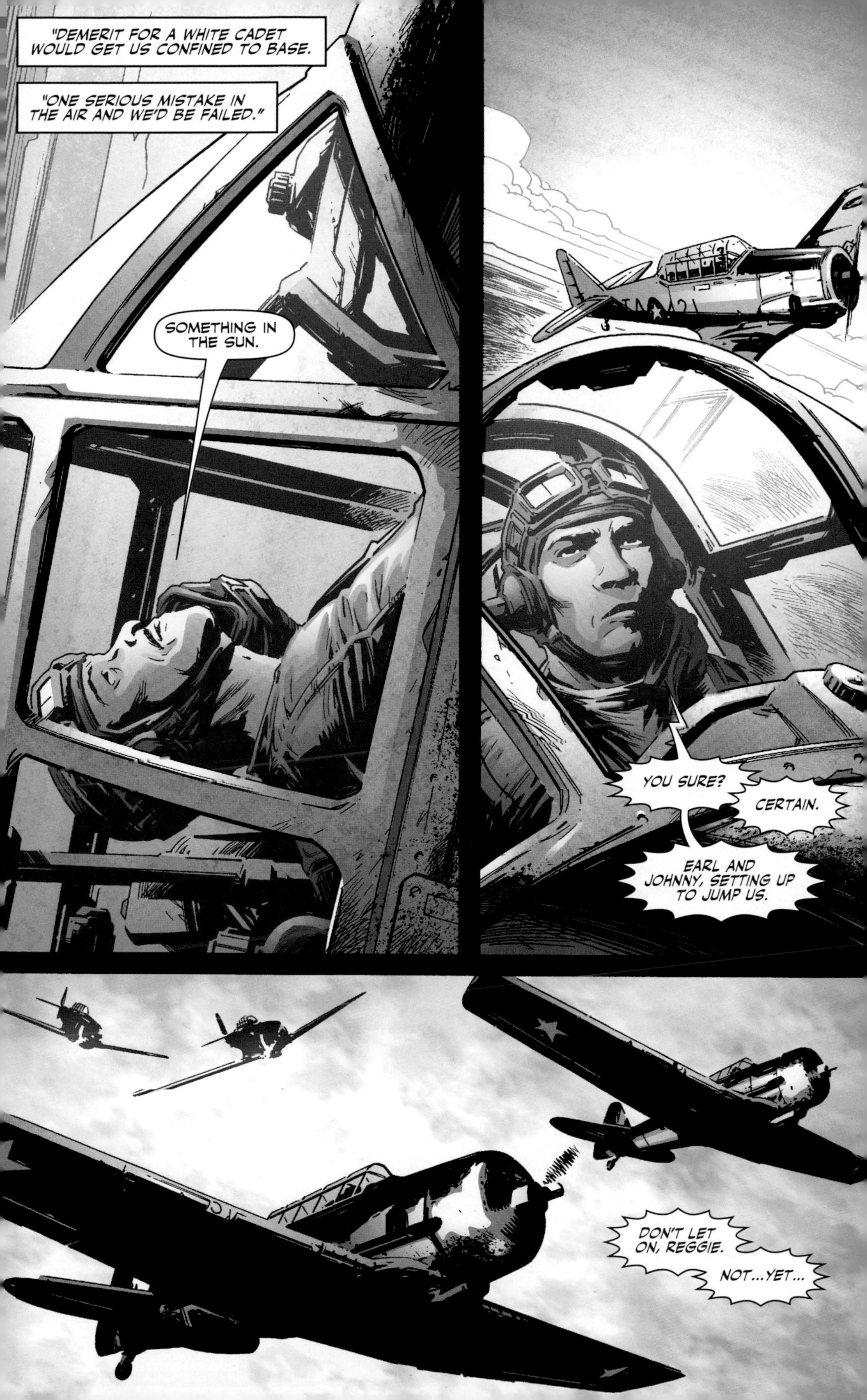
"DEMERIT FOR A WHITE CADET WOULD GET US CONFINED TO BASE.
"ONE SERIOUS MISTAKE IN THE AIR AND WE'D BE FAILED."
SOMETHING IN THE SUN.
YOU SURE?
CERTAIN.
EARL AND JOHNNY, SETTING UP TO JUMP US.
DON'T LET ON, REGGIE.
NOT...YET...

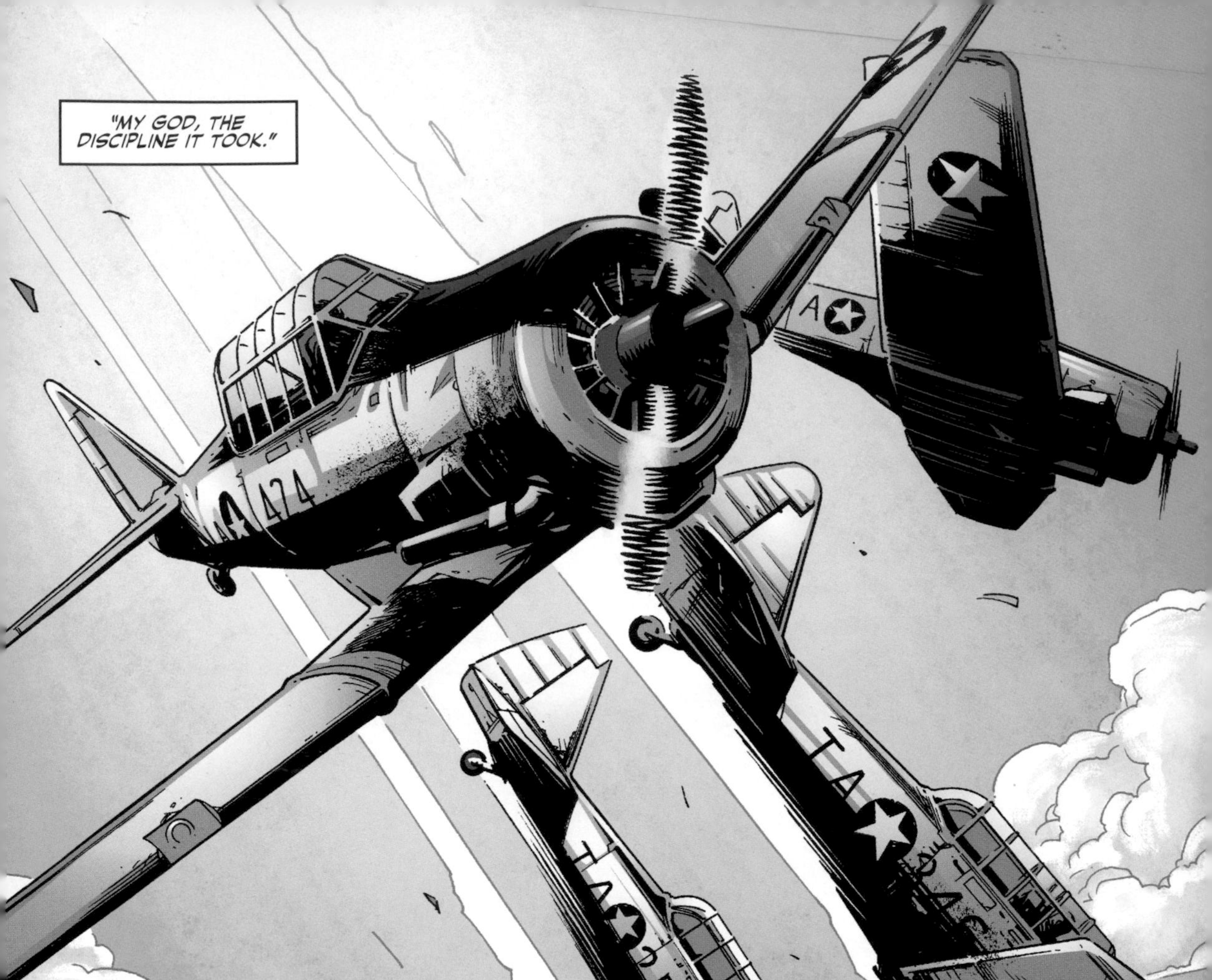
"MY GOD, THE DISCIPLINE IT TOOK."

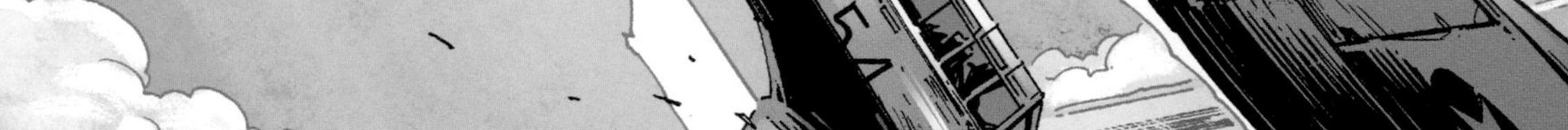
NICE TRY, BOYS.
"TIGHT. EXACT. NO MARGIN FOR ERROR.
"AND WE WERE GIVEN EVERY CHANCE TO FAIL."

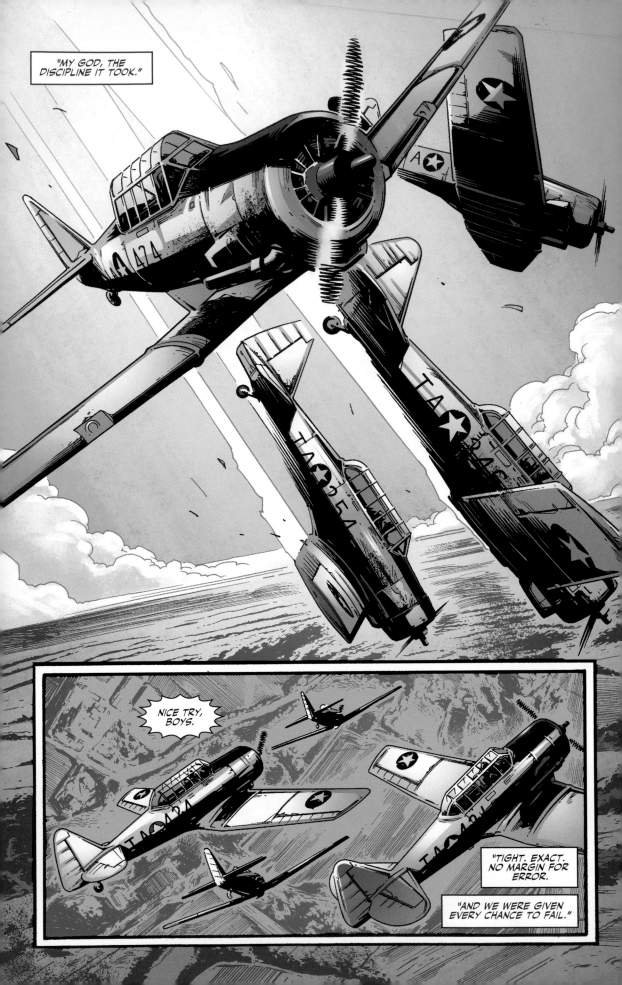

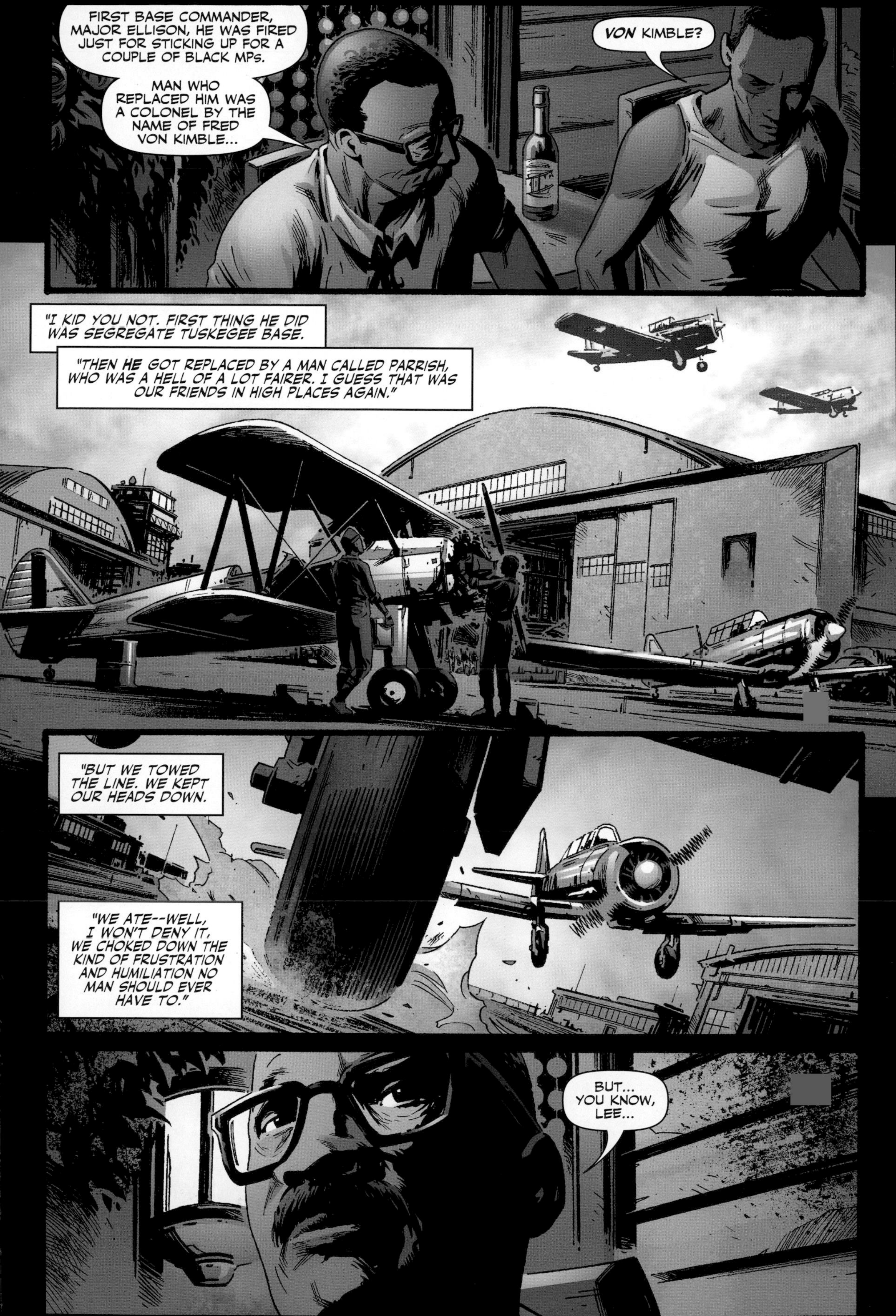
FIRST BASE COMMANDER, MAJOR ELLISON, HE WAS FIRED JUST FOR STICKING UP FOR A COUPLE OF BLACK MPs.
MAN WHO REPLACED HIM WAS A COLONEL BY THE NAME OF FRED VON KIMBLE...
VON KIMBLE?
"I KID YOU NOT. FIRST THING HE DID WAS SEGREGATE TUSKEGEE BASE.
"THEN HE GOT REPLACED BY A MAN CALLED PARRISH, WHO WAS A HELL OF A LOT FAIRER. I GUESS THAT WAS OUR FRIENDS IN HIGH PLACES AGAIN."
"BUT WE TOWED THE LINE. WE KEPT OUR HEADS DOWN.
"WE ATE--WELL, I WON'T DENY IT, WE CHOKED DOWN THE KIND OF FRUSTRATION AND HUMILIATION NO MAN SHOULD EVER HAVE TO."
BUT... YOU KNOW, LEE...

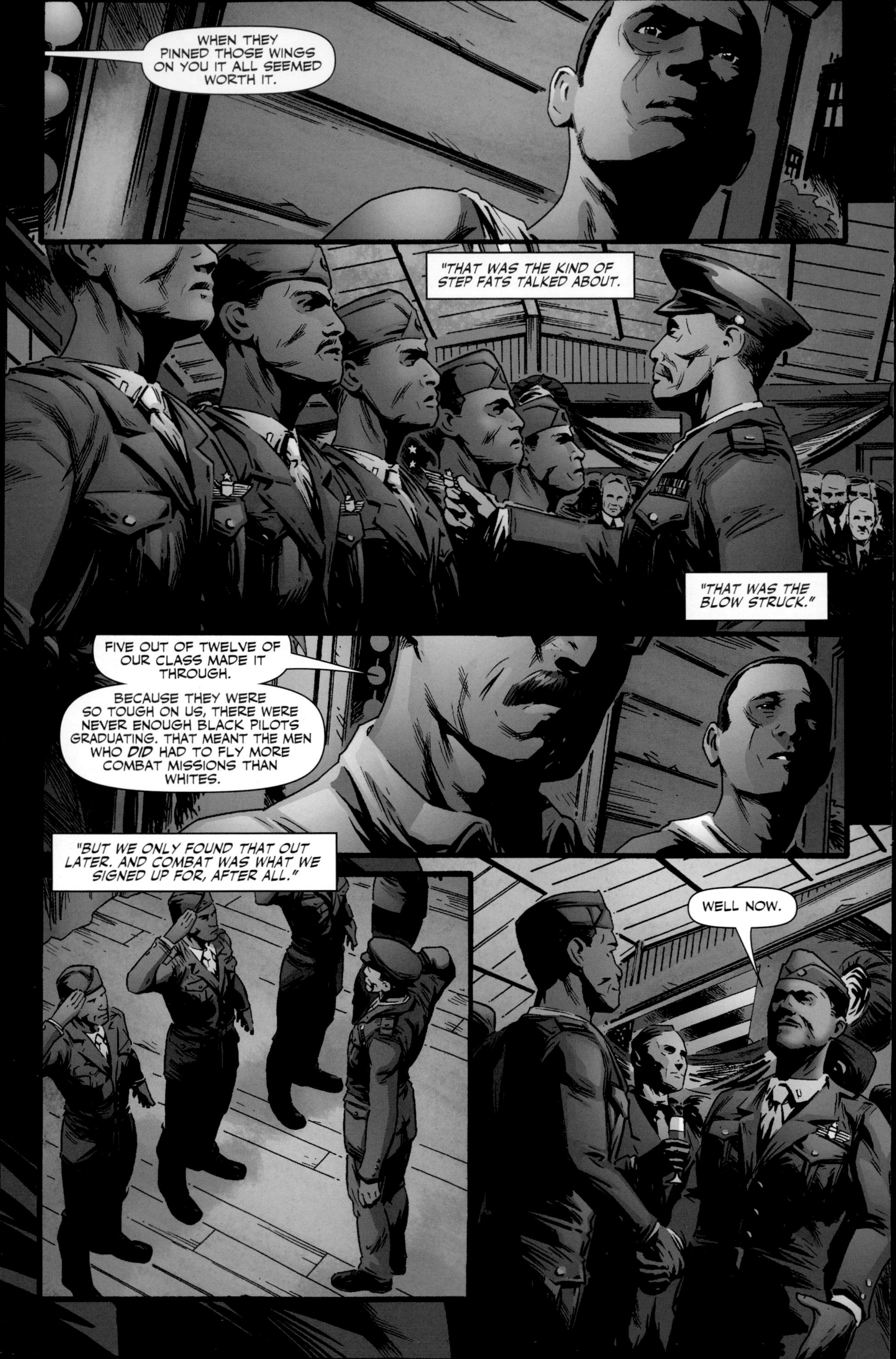
WHEN THEY PINNED THOSE WINGS ON YOU IT ALL SEEMED WORTH IT.
"THAT WAS THE KIND OF STEP FATS TALKED ABOUT.
"THAT WAS THE BLOW STRUCK."
FIVE OUT OF TWELVE OF OUR CLASS MADE IT THROUGH.
BECAUSE THEY WERE SO TOUGH ON US, THERE WERE NEVER ENOUGH BLACK PILOTS GRADUATING. THAT MEANT THE MEN WHO *DID* HAD TO FLY MORE COMBAT MISSIONS THAN WHITES.
"BUT WE ONLY FOUND THAT OUT LATER. AND COMBAT WAS WHAT WE SIGNED UP FOR, AFTER ALL."
WELL NOW.

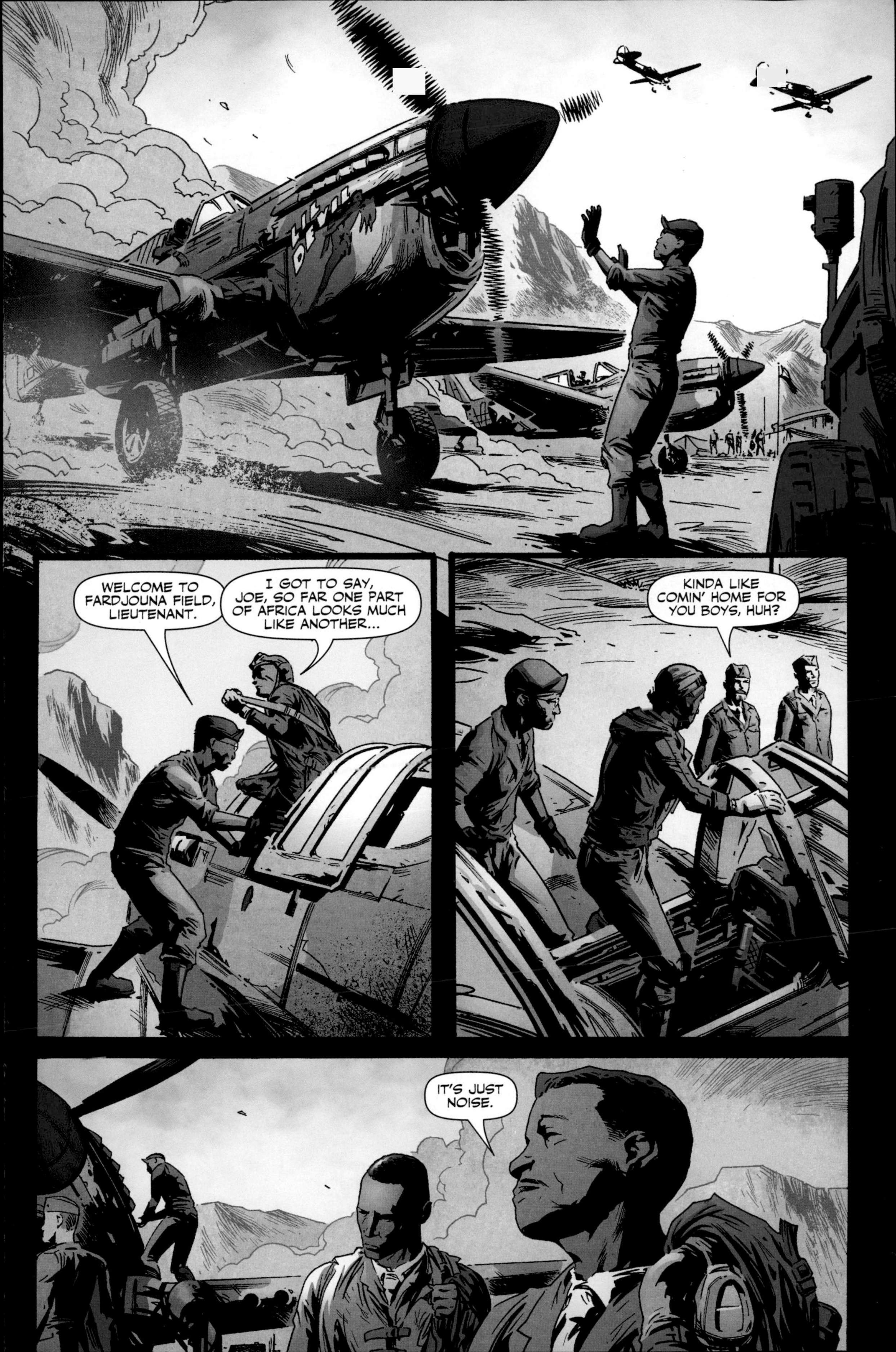
WELCOME TO FARDJOUNA FIELD, LIEUTENANT.
I GOT TO SAY, JOE, SO FAR ONE PART OF AFRICA LOOKS MUCH LIKE ANOTHER...
KINDA LIKE COMIN' HOME FOR YOU BOYS, HUH?
IT'S JUST NOISE.

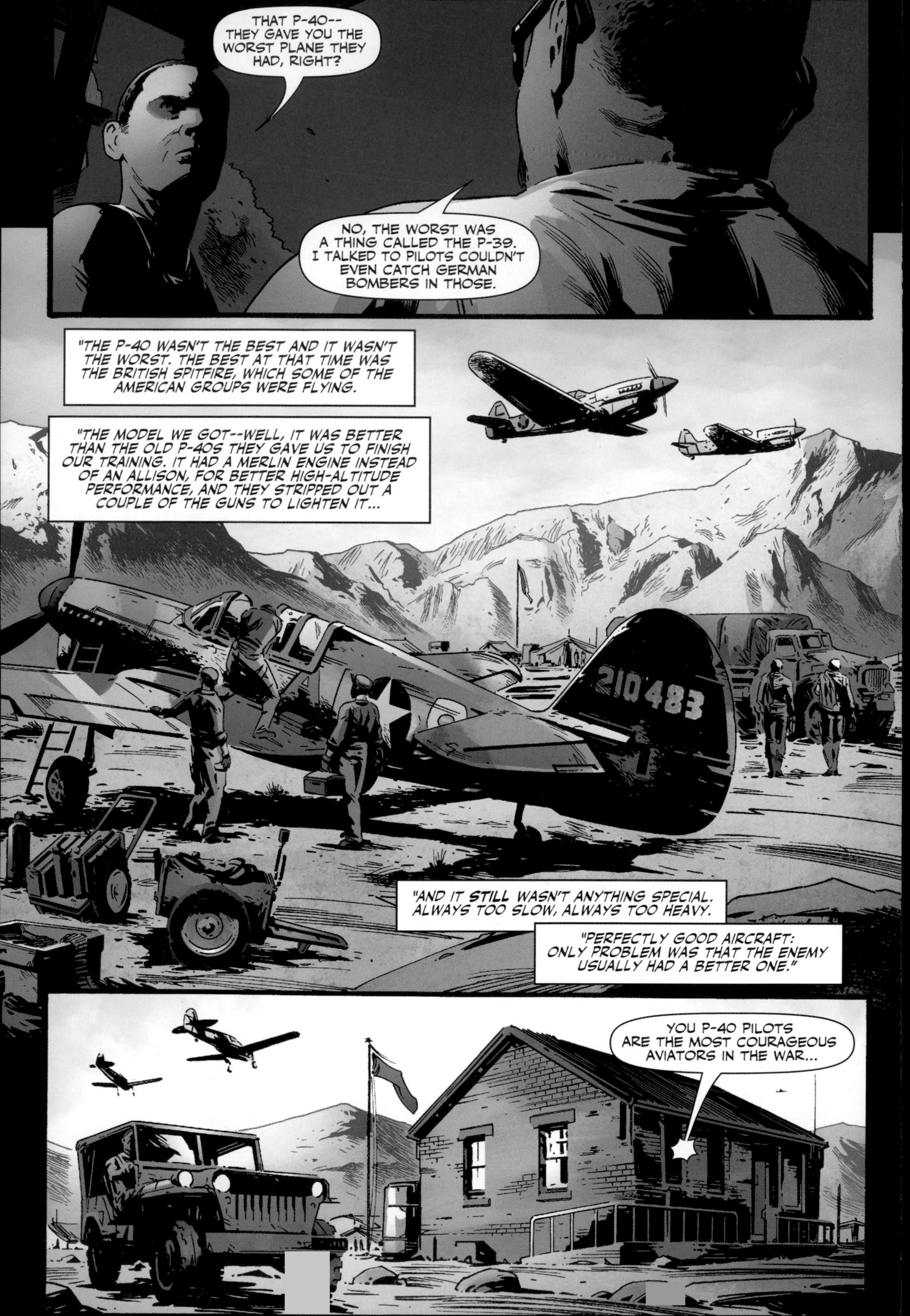

THAT P-40-- THEY GAVE YOU THE WORST PLANE THEY HAD, RIGHT?
NO, THE WORST WAS A THING CALLED THE P-39. I TALKED TO PILOTS COULDN'T EVEN CATCH GERMAN BOMBERS IN THOSE.
"THE P-40 WASN'T THE BEST AND IT WASN'T THE WORST. THE BEST AT THAT TIME WAS THE BRITISH SPITFIRE, WHICH SOME OF THE AMERICAN GROUPS WERE FLYING.
"THE MODEL WE GOT--WELL, IT WAS BETTER THAN THE OLD P-40S THEY GAVE US TO FINISH OUR TRAINING. IT HAD A MERLIN ENGINE INSTEAD OF AN ALLISON, FOR BETTER HIGH-ALTITUDE PERFORMANCE, AND THEY STRIPPED OUT A COUPLE OF THE GUNS TO LIGHTEN IT...
210483
"AND IT **STILL** WASN'T ANYTHING SPECIAL. ALWAYS TOO SLOW, ALWAYS TOO HEAVY.
"PERFECTLY GOOD AIRCRAFT: ONLY PROBLEM WAS THAT THE ENEMY USUALLY HAD A BETTER ONE."
YOU P-40 PILOTS ARE THE MOST COURAGEOUS AVIATORS IN THE WAR...

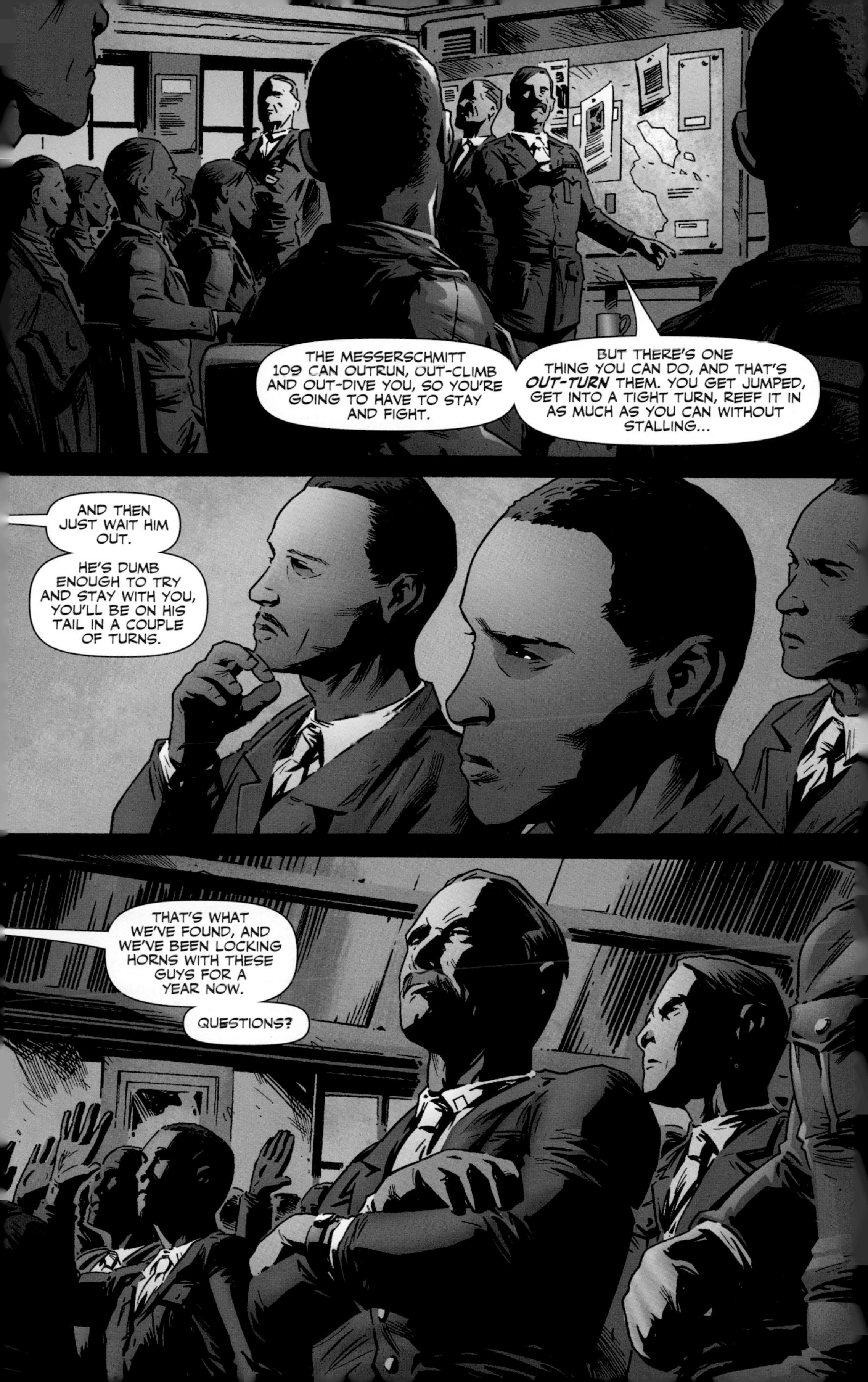
THE MESSERSCHMITT 109 CAN OUTRUN, OUT-CLIMB AND OUT-DIVE YOU, SO YOU'RE GOING TO HAVE TO STAY AND FIGHT.
BUT THERE'S ONE THING YOU CAN DO, AND THAT'S *OUT-TURN* THEM. YOU GET JUMPED, GET INTO A TIGHT TURN, REEF IT IN AS MUCH AS YOU CAN WITHOUT STALLING...
AND THEN JUST WAIT HIM OUT.
HE'S DUMB ENOUGH TO TRY AND STAY WITH YOU, YOU'LL BE ON HIS TAIL IN A COUPLE OF TURNS.
THAT'S WHAT WE'VE FOUND, AND WE'VE BEEN LOCKING HORNS WITH THESE GUYS FOR A YEAR NOW.
QUESTIONS?

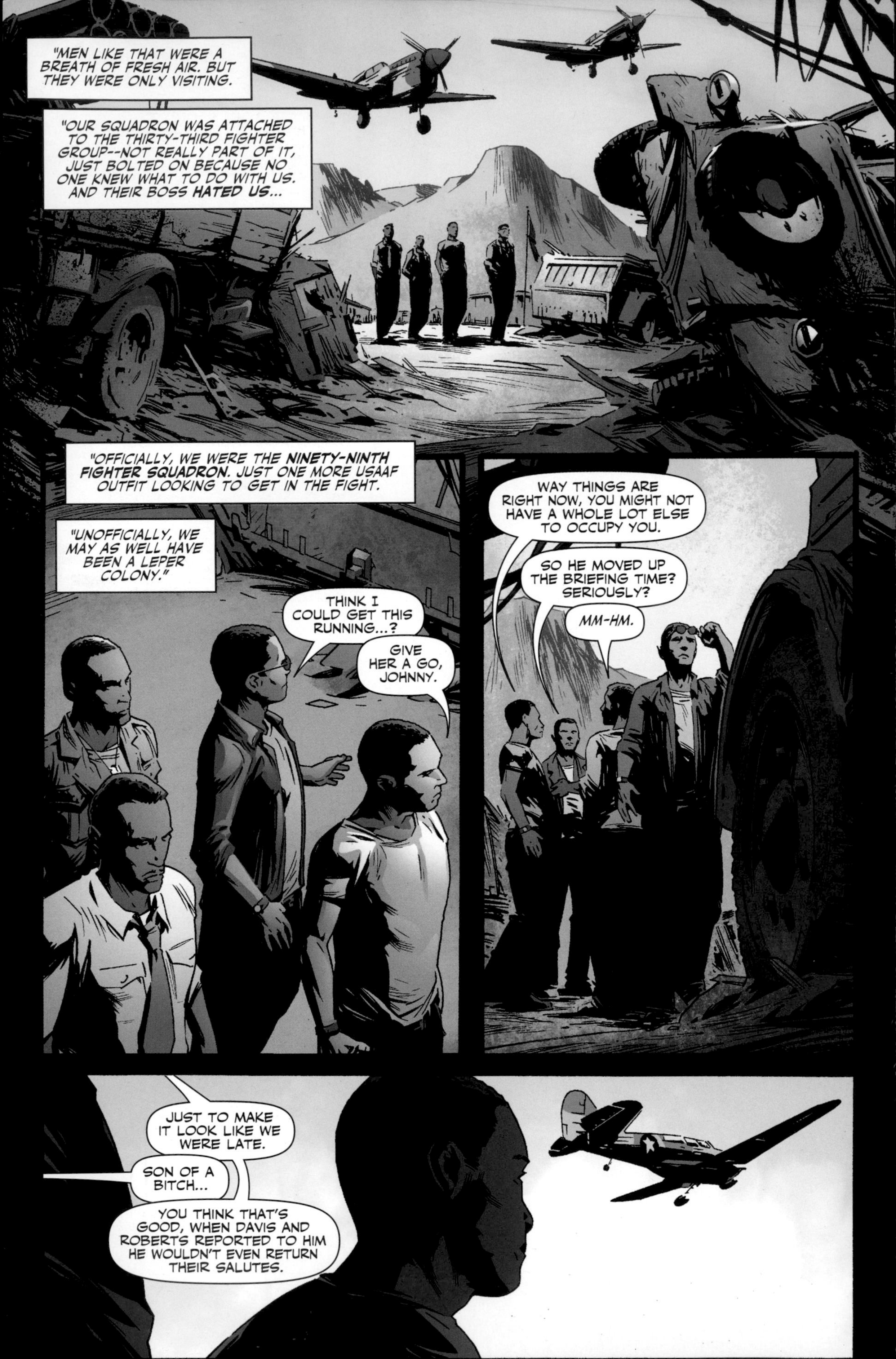
"MEN LIKE THAT WERE A BREATH OF FRESH AIR. BUT THEY WERE ONLY VISITING.
"OUR SQUADRON WAS ATTACHED TO THE THIRTY-THIRD FIGHTER GROUP--NOT REALLY PART OF IT, JUST BOLTED ON BECAUSE NO ONE KNEW WHAT TO DO WITH US. AND THEIR BOSS **HATED US**...
"OFFICIALLY, WE WERE THE **NINETY-NINTH FIGHTER SQUADRON**. JUST ONE MORE USAAF OUTFIT LOOKING TO GET IN THE FIGHT.
"UNOFFICIALLY, WE MAY AS WELL HAVE BEEN A LEPER COLONY."
THINK I COULD GET THIS RUNNING...?
GIVE HER A GO, JOHNNY.
WAY THINGS ARE RIGHT NOW, YOU MIGHT NOT HAVE A WHOLE LOT ELSE TO OCCUPY YOU.
SO HE MOVED UP THE BRIEFING TIME? SERIOUSLY?
MM-HM.
JUST TO MAKE IT LOOK LIKE WE WERE LATE.
SON OF A BITCH...
YOU THINK THAT'S GOOD, WHEN DAVIS AND ROBERTS REPORTED TO HIM HE WOULDN'T EVEN RETURN THEIR SALUTES.

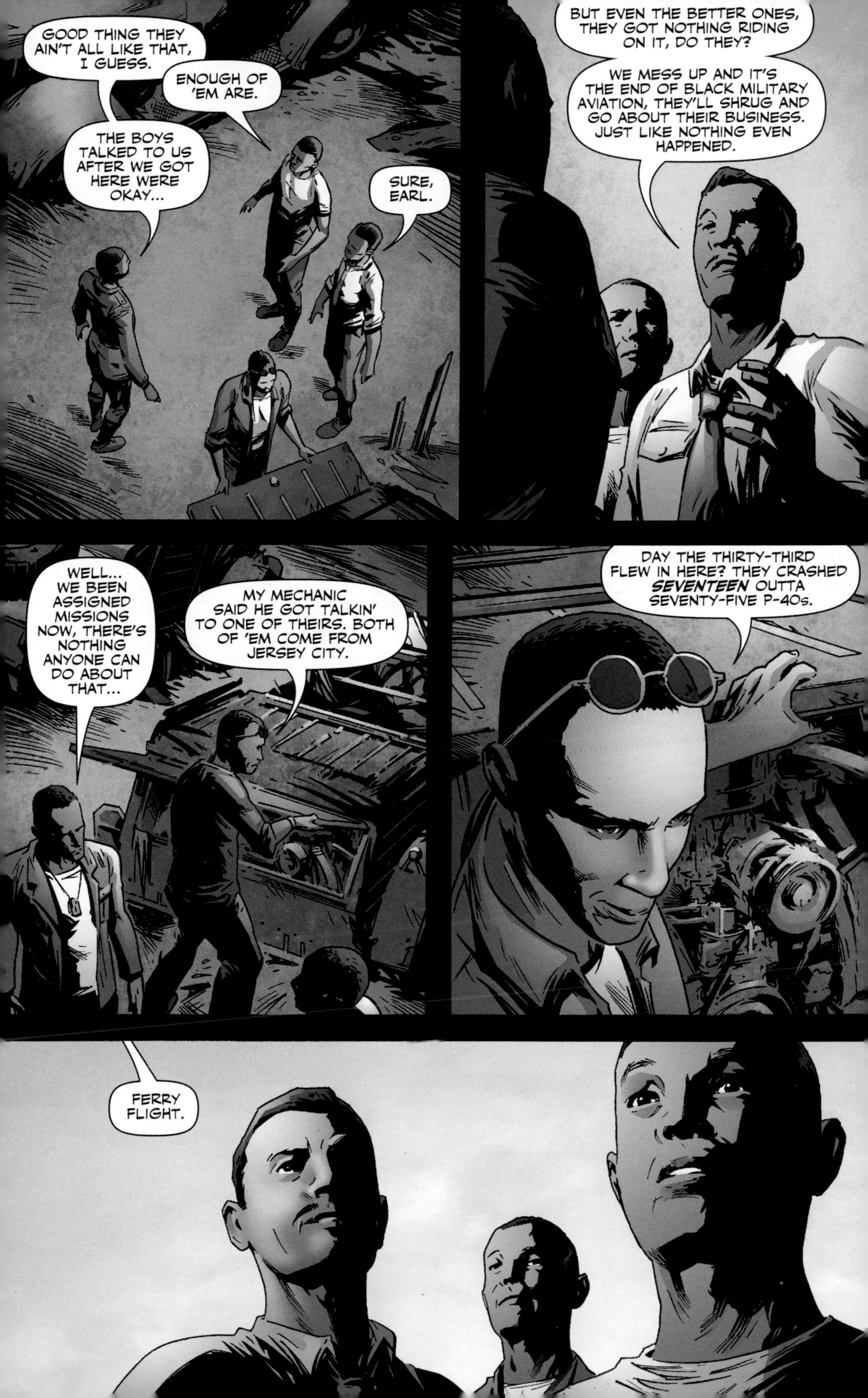
GOOD THING THEY AIN'T ALL LIKE THAT, I GUESS.
ENOUGH OF 'EM ARE.
THE BOYS TALKED TO US AFTER WE GOT HERE WERE OKAY...
SURE, EARL.
BUT EVEN THE BETTER ONES, THEY GOT NOTHING RIDING ON IT, DO THEY?
WE MESS UP AND IT'S THE END OF BLACK MILITARY AVIATION, THEY'LL SHRUG AND GO ABOUT THEIR BUSINESS. JUST LIKE NOTHING EVEN HAPPENED.
WELL... WE BEEN ASSIGNED MISSIONS NOW, THERE'S NOTHING ANYONE CAN DO ABOUT THAT...
MY MECHANIC SAID HE GOT TALKIN' TO ONE OF THEIRS. BOTH OF 'EM COME FROM JERSEY CITY.
DAY THE THIRTY-THIRD FLEW IN HERE? THEY CRASHED ***SEVENTEEN*** OUTTA SEVENTY-FIVE P-40s.
FERRY FLIGHT.

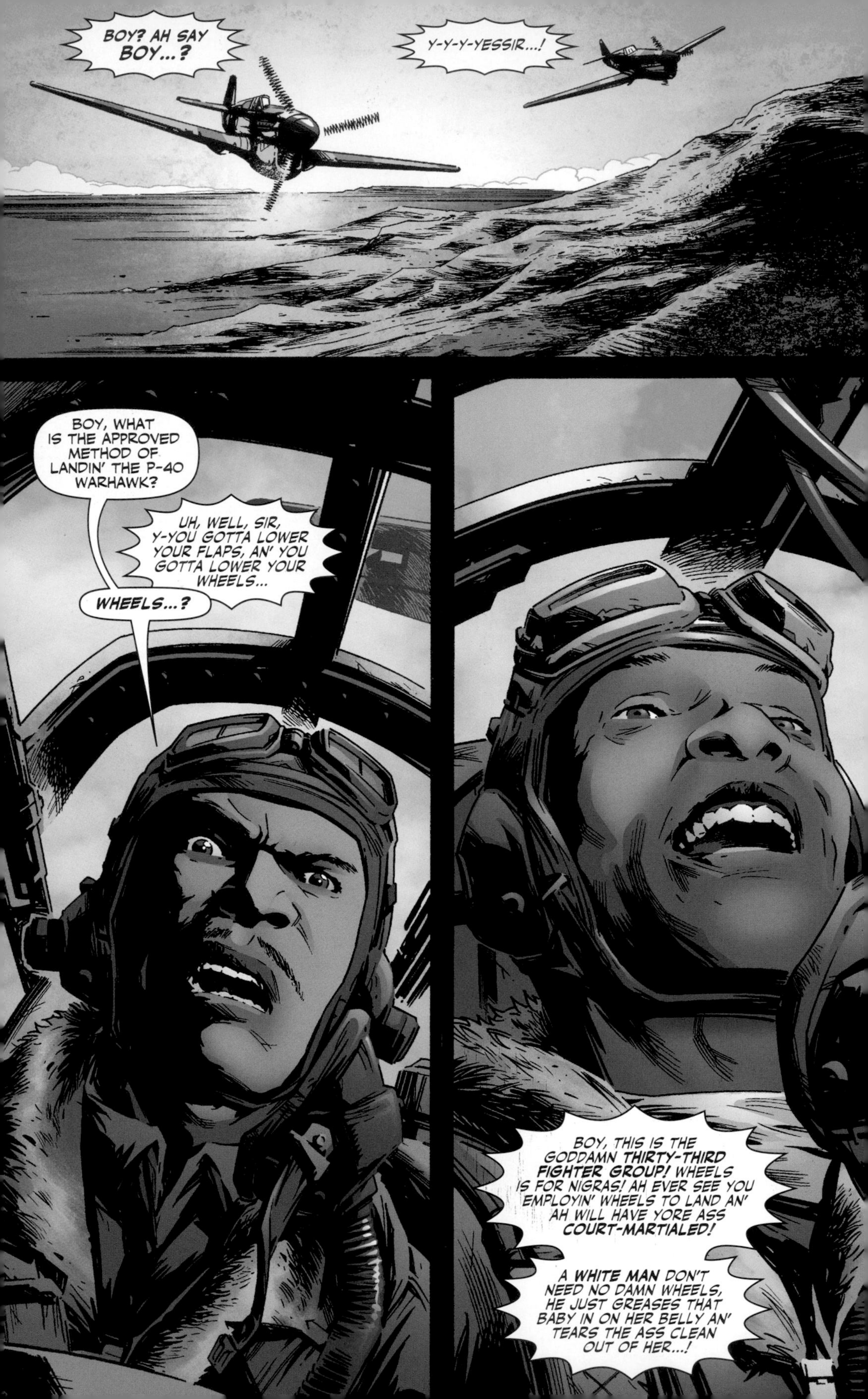
BOY? AH SAY BOY...?
Y-Y-Y-YESSIR...!
BOY, WHAT IS THE APPROVED METHOD OF LANDIN' THE P-40 WARHAWK?
UH, WELL, SIR, Y-YOU GOTTA LOWER YOUR FLAPS, AN' YOU GOTTA LOWER YOUR WHEELS...
WHEELS...?
BOY, THIS IS THE GODDAMN THIRTY-THIRD FIGHTER GROUP! WHEELS IS FOR NIGRAS! AH EVER SEE YOU EMPLOYIN' WHEELS TO LAND AN' AH WILL HAVE YORE ASS COURT-MARTIALED!
A WHITE MAN DON'T NEED NO DAMN WHEELS, HE JUST GREASES THAT BABY IN ON HER BELLY AN' TEARS THE ASS CLEAN OUT OF HER...!

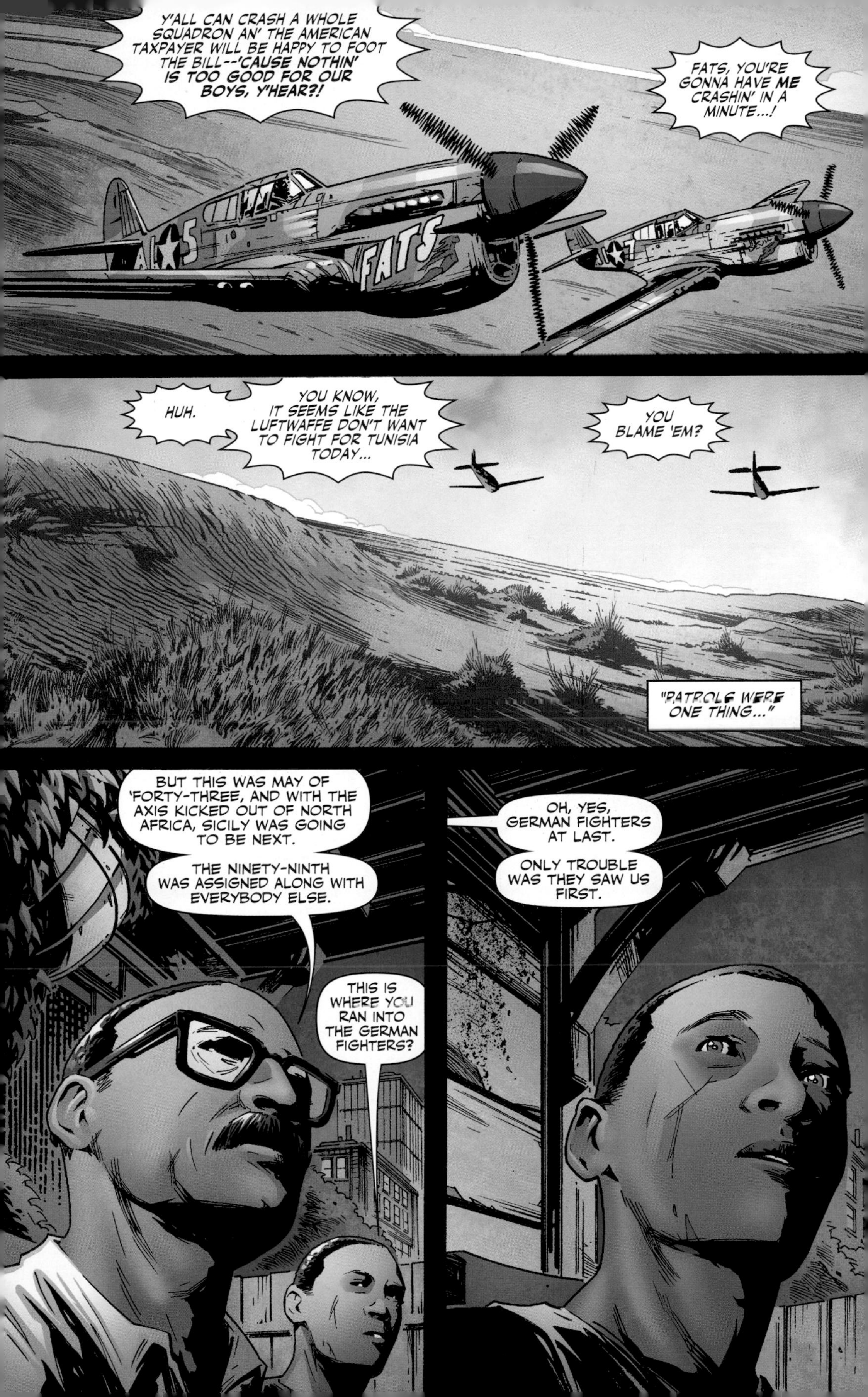
Y'ALL CAN CRASH A WHOLE SQUADRON AN' THE AMERICAN TAXPAYER WILL BE HAPPY TO FOOT THE BILL--'CAUSE NOTHIN' IS TOO GOOD FOR OUR BOYS, Y'HEAR?!
FATS, YOU'RE GONNA HAVE ME CRASHIN' IN A MINUTE...!
FATS
HUH.
YOU KNOW, IT SEEMS LIKE THE LUFTWAFFE DON'T WANT TO FIGHT FOR TUNISIA TODAY...
YOU BLAME 'EM?
"PATROLS WERE ONE THING..."
BUT THIS WAS MAY OF 'FORTY-THREE, AND WITH THE AXIS KICKED OUT OF NORTH AFRICA, SICILY WAS GOING TO BE NEXT.
THE NINETY-NINTH WAS ASSIGNED ALONG WITH EVERYBODY ELSE.
THIS IS WHERE YOU RAN INTO THE GERMAN FIGHTERS?
OH, YES, GERMAN FIGHTERS AT LAST.
ONLY TROUBLE WAS THEY SAW US FIRST.

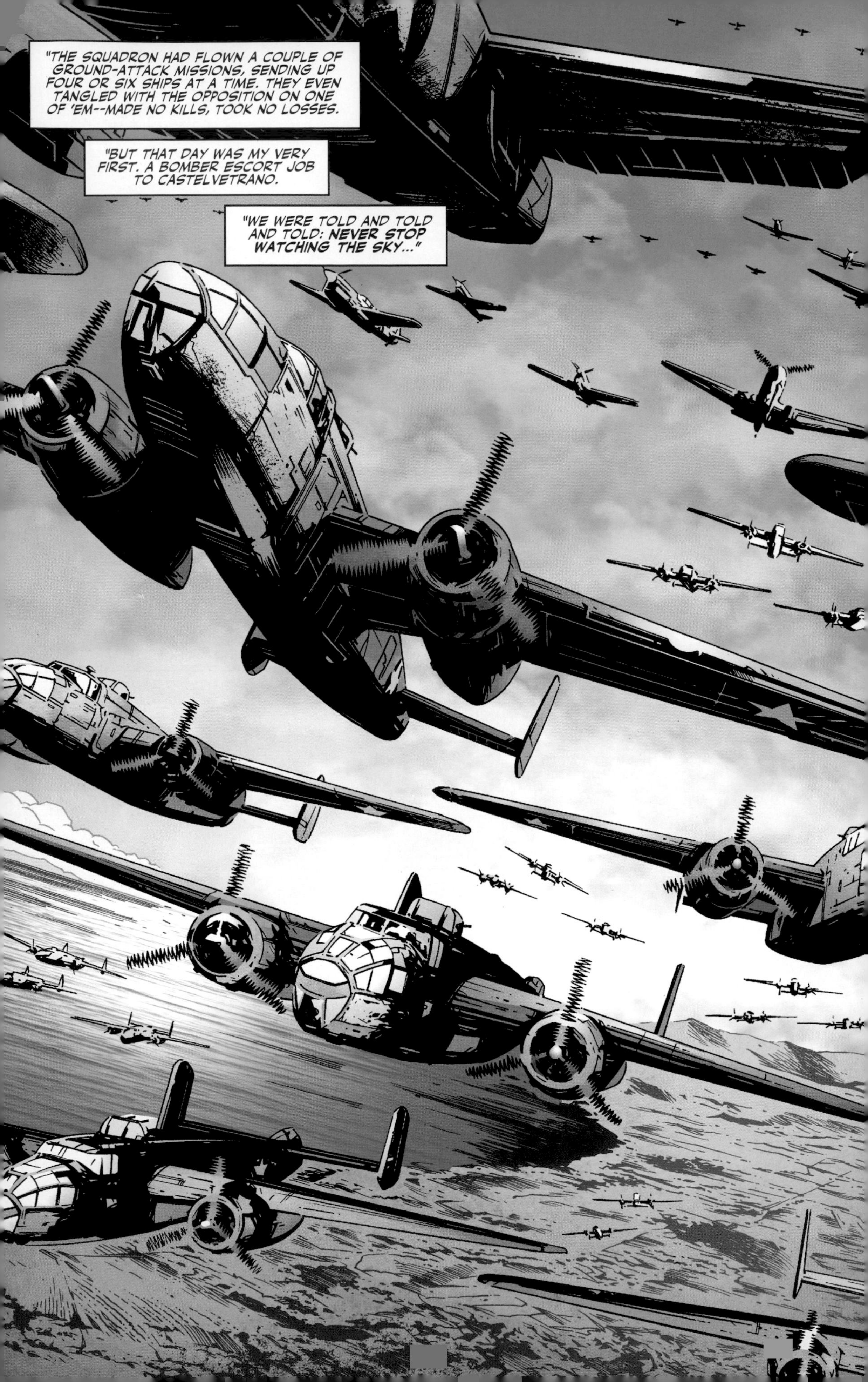
"THE SQUADRON HAD FLOWN A COUPLE OF GROUND-ATTACK MISSIONS, SENDING UP FOUR OR SIX SHIPS AT A TIME. THEY EVEN TANGLED WITH THE OPPOSITION ON ONE OF 'EM--MADE NO KILLS, TOOK NO LOSSES.
"BUT THAT DAY WAS MY VERY FIRST. A BOMBER ESCORT JOB TO CASTELVETRANO.
"WE WERE TOLD AND TOLD AND TOLD: NEVER STOP WATCHING THE SKY..."

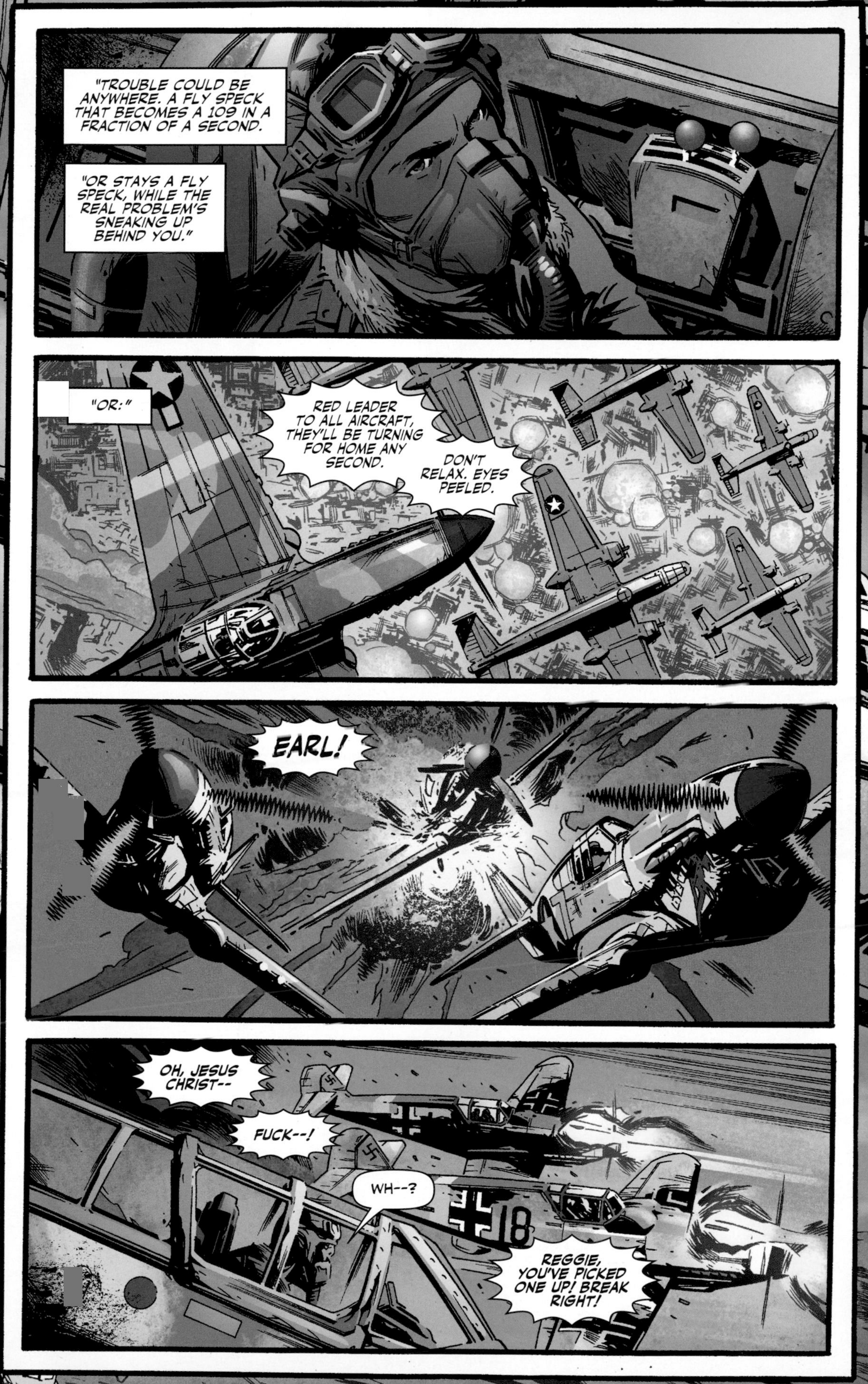
"TROUBLE COULD BE ANYWHERE. A FLY SPECK THAT BECOMES A 109 IN A FRACTION OF A SECOND.
"OR STAYS A FLY SPECK, WHILE THE REAL PROBLEM'S SNEAKING UP BEHIND YOU."
"OR:"
RED LEADER TO ALL AIRCRAFT, THEY'LL BE TURNING FOR HOME ANY SECOND.
DON'T RELAX. EYES PEELED.
EARL!
OH, JESUS CHRIST--
FUCK--!
WH--?
REGGIE, YOU'VE PICKED ONE UP! BREAK RIGHT!

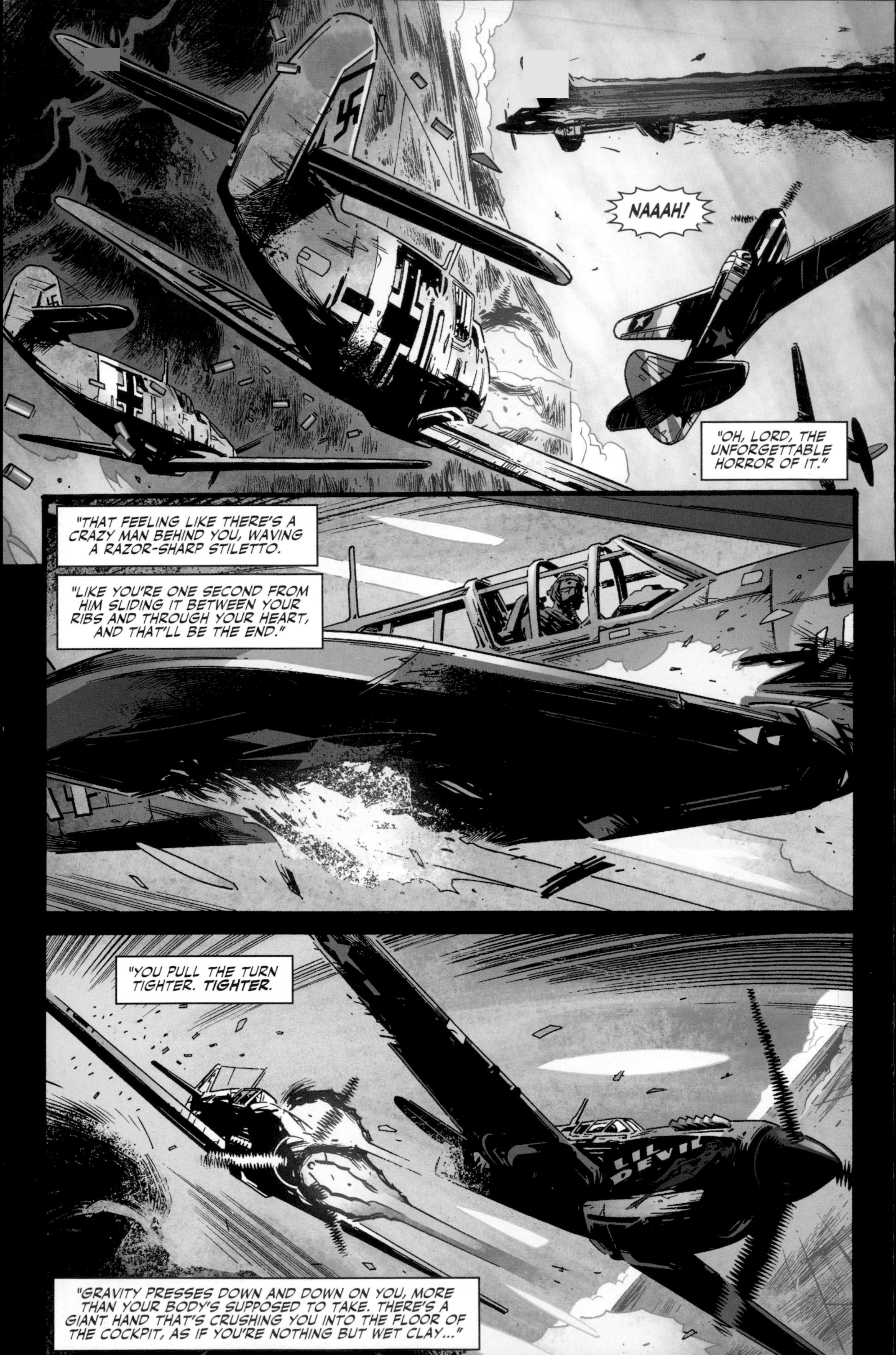
NAAAH!
"OH, LORD, THE UNFORGETTABLE HORROR OF IT."
"THAT FEELING LIKE THERE'S A CRAZY MAN BEHIND YOU, WAVING A RAZOR-SHARP STILETTO.
"LIKE YOU'RE ONE SECOND FROM HIM SLIDING IT BETWEEN YOUR RIBS AND THROUGH YOUR HEART, AND THAT'LL BE THE END."
"YOU PULL THE TURN TIGHTER. TIGHTER.
LIL DEVIL
"GRAVITY PRESSES DOWN AND DOWN ON YOU, MORE THAN YOUR BODY'S SUPPOSED TO TAKE. THERE'S A GIANT HAND THAT'S CRUSHING YOU INTO THE FLOOR OF THE COCKPIT, AS IF YOU'RE NOTHING BUT WET CLAY..."

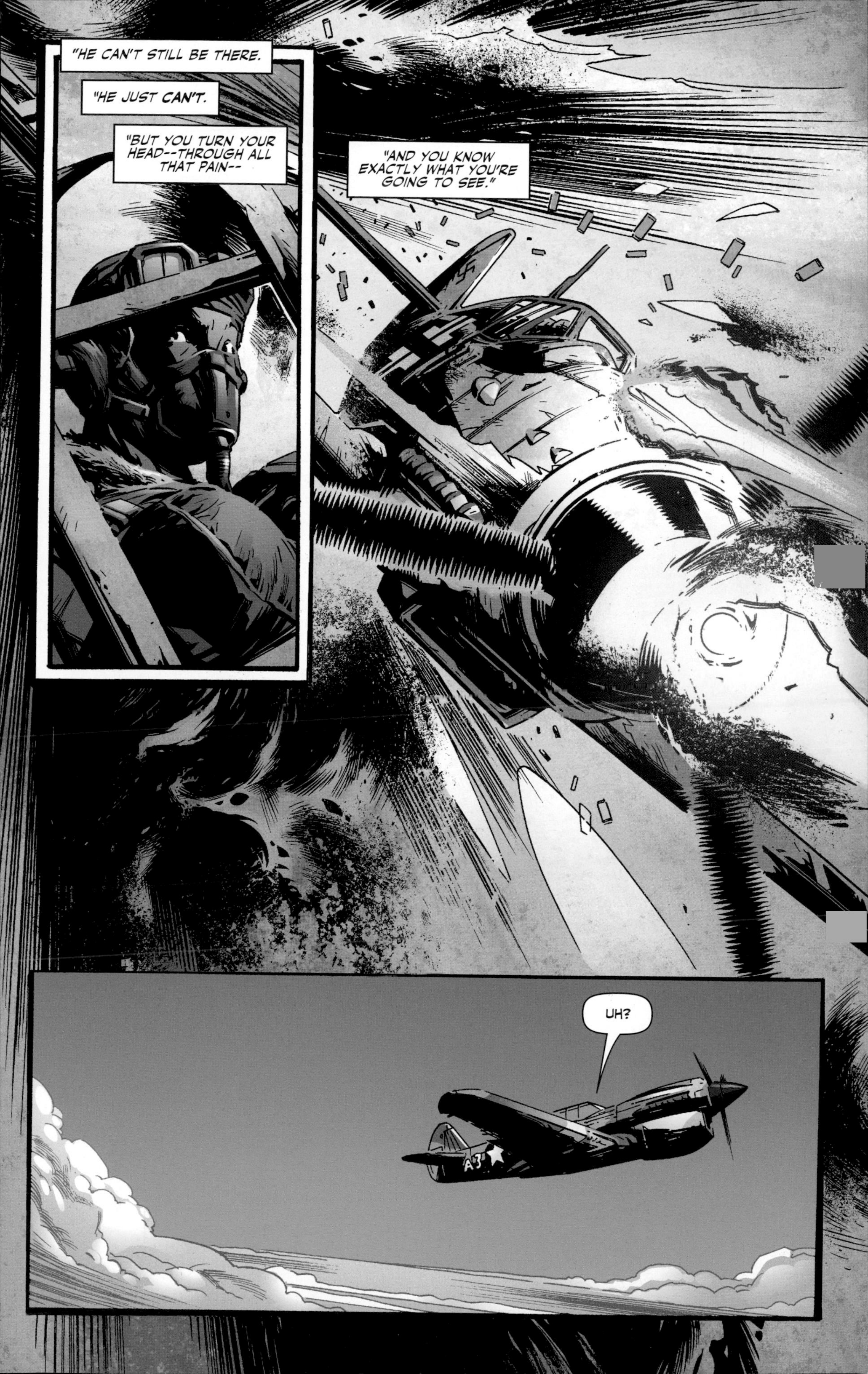
"HE CAN'T STILL BE THERE.
"HE JUST CAN'T.
"BUT YOU TURN YOUR HEAD--THROUGH ALL THAT PAIN--
"AND YOU KNOW EXACTLY WHAT YOU'RE GOING TO SEE."
UH?
A3

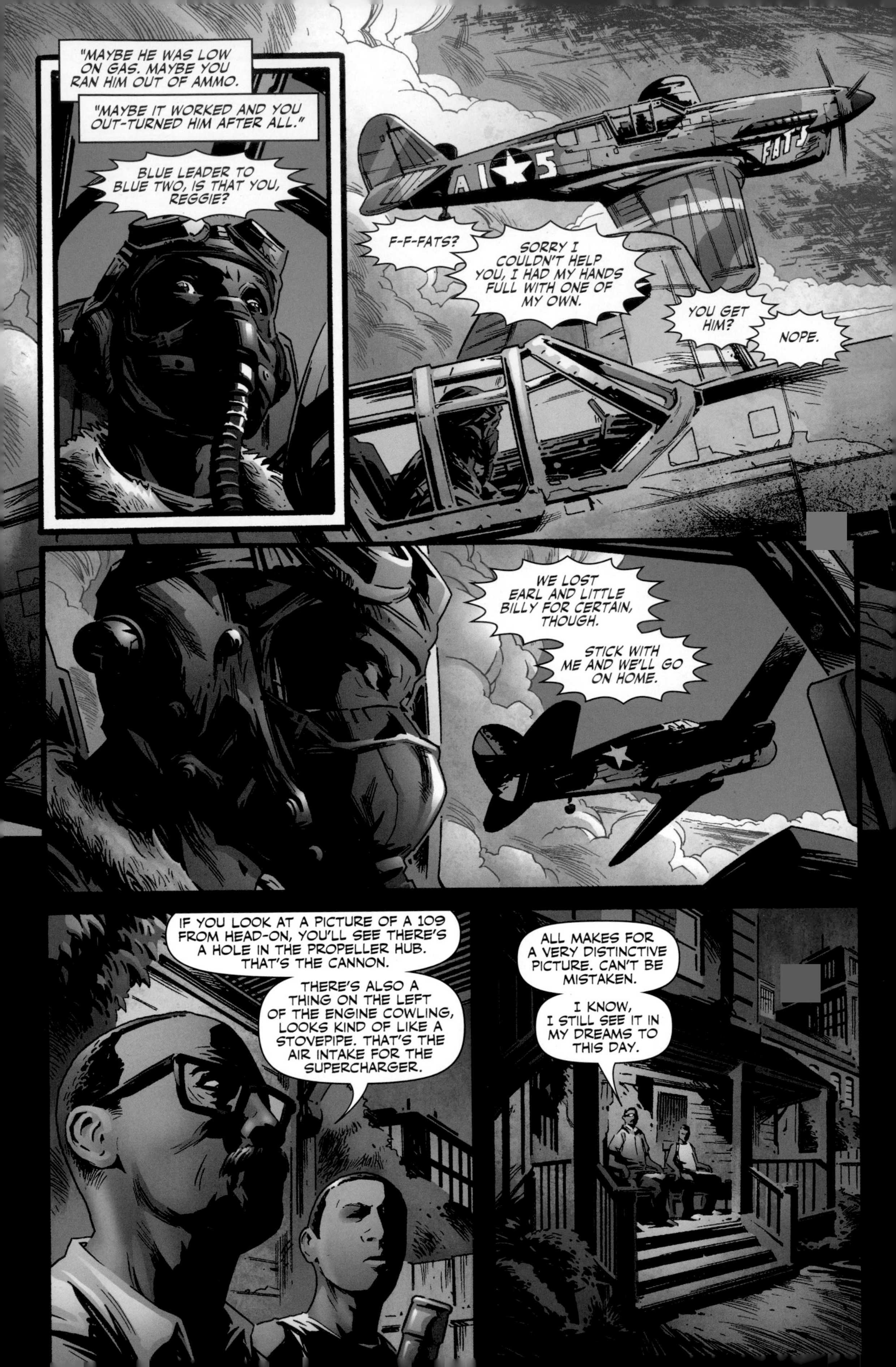
"MAYBE HE WAS LOW ON GAS. MAYBE YOU RAN HIM OUT OF AMMO.
"MAYBE IT WORKED AND YOU OUT-TURNED HIM AFTER ALL."
BLUE LEADER TO BLUE TWO, IS THAT YOU, REGGIE?
A1 ★ 5
FATS
F-F-FATS?
SORRY I COULDN'T HELP YOU, I HAD MY HANDS FULL WITH ONE OF MY OWN.
YOU GET HIM?
NOPE.
WE LOST EARL AND LITTLE BILLY FOR CERTAIN, THOUGH.
STICK WITH ME AND WE'LL GO ON HOME.
IF YOU LOOK AT A PICTURE OF A 109 FROM HEAD-ON, YOU'LL SEE THERE'S A HOLE IN THE PROPELLER HUB. THAT'S THE CANNON.
THERE'S ALSO A THING ON THE LEFT OF THE ENGINE COWLING, LOOKS KIND OF LIKE A STOVEPIPE. THAT'S THE AIR INTAKE FOR THE SUPERCHARGER.
ALL MAKES FOR A VERY DISTINCTIVE PICTURE. CAN'T BE MISTAKEN.
I KNOW, I STILL SEE IT IN MY DREAMS TO THIS DAY.

3 : VESUVIUS

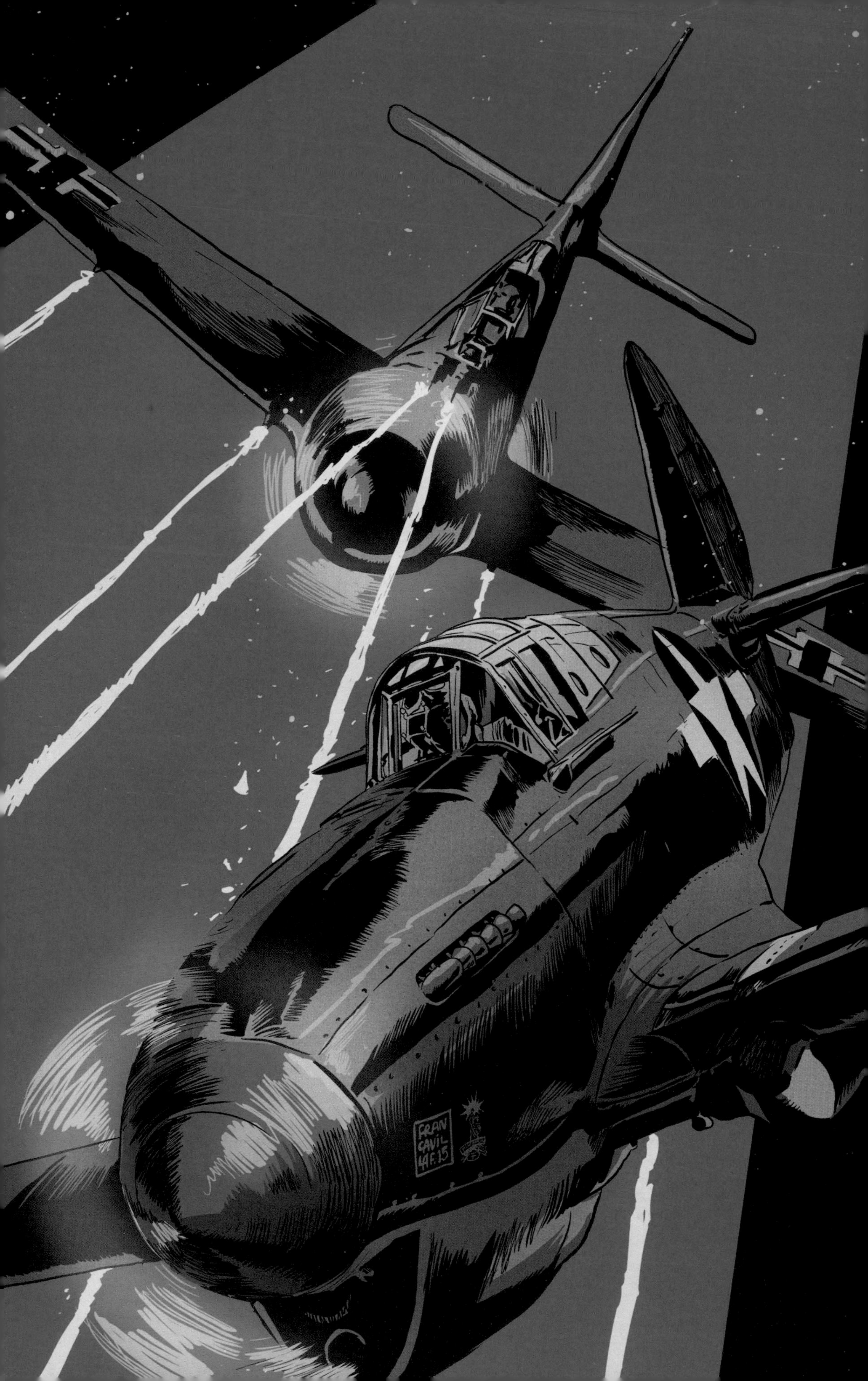

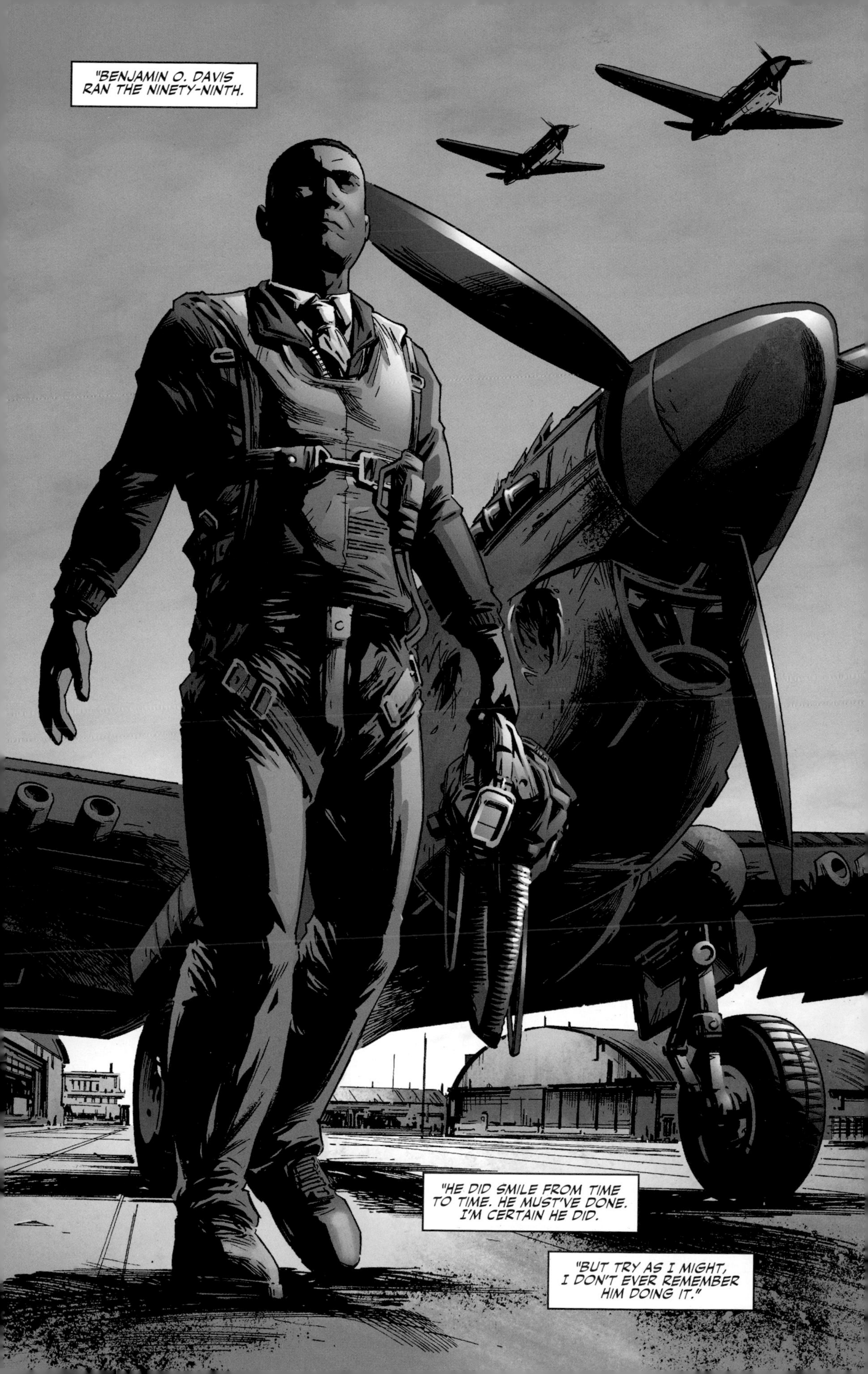
"BENJAMIN O. DAVIS RAN THE NINETY-NINTH.
"HE DID SMILE FROM TIME TO TIME. HE MUST'VE DONE. I'M CERTAIN HE DID.
"BUT TRY AS I MIGHT, I DON'T EVER REMEMBER HIM DOING IT."

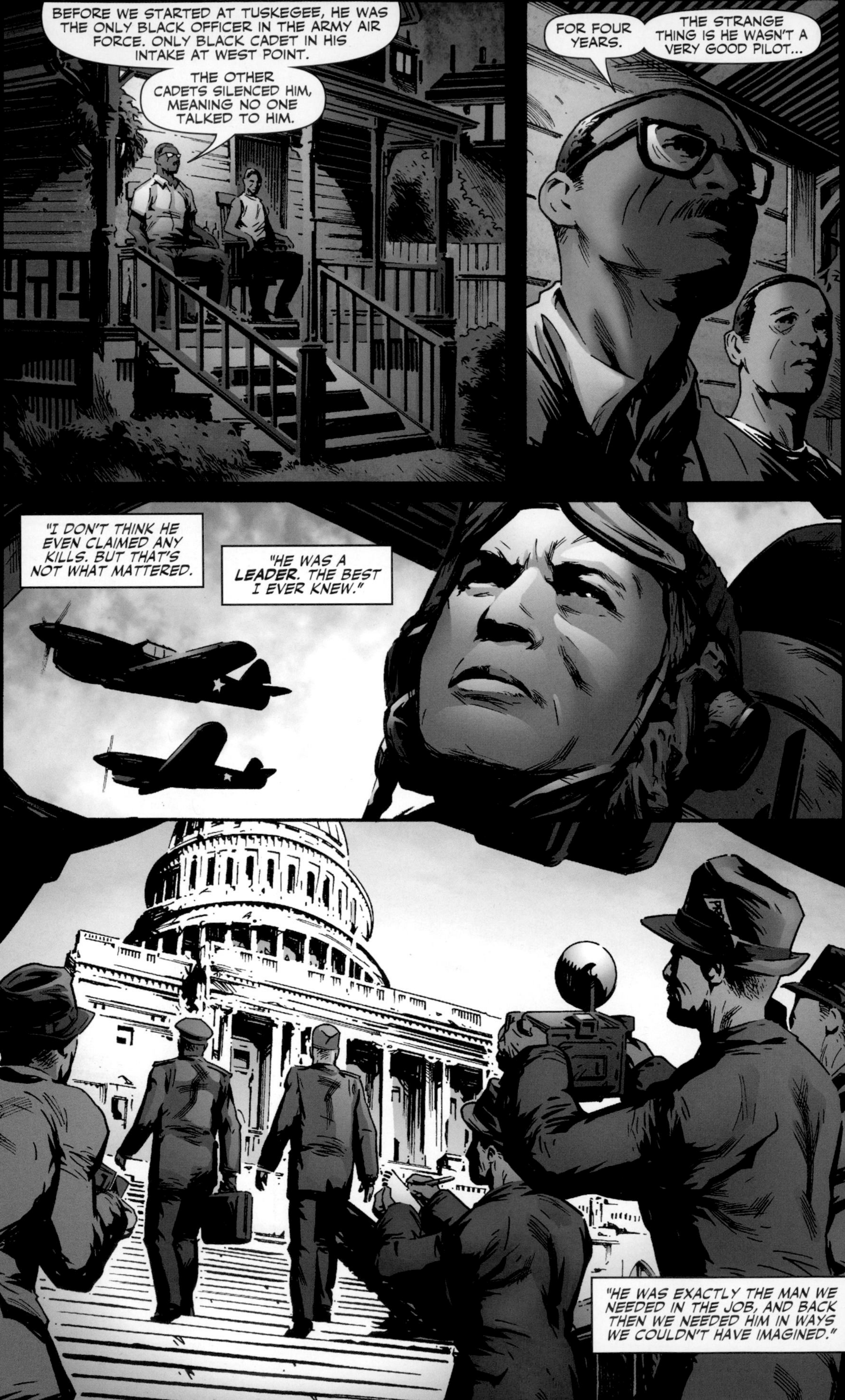
BEFORE WE STARTED AT TUSKEGEE, HE WAS THE ONLY BLACK OFFICER IN THE ARMY AIR FORCE. ONLY BLACK CADET IN HIS INTAKE AT WEST POINT.
THE OTHER CADETS SILENCED HIM, MEANING NO ONE TALKED TO HIM.
FOR FOUR YEARS.
THE STRANGE THING IS HE WASN'T A VERY GOOD PILOT...
"I DON'T THINK HE EVEN CLAIMED ANY KILLS. BUT THAT'S NOT WHAT MATTERED.
"HE WAS A LEADER. THE BEST I EVER KNEW."
"HE WAS EXACTLY THE MAN WE NEEDED IN THE JOB, AND BACK THEN WE NEEDED HIM IN WAYS WE COULDN'T HAVE IMAGINED."

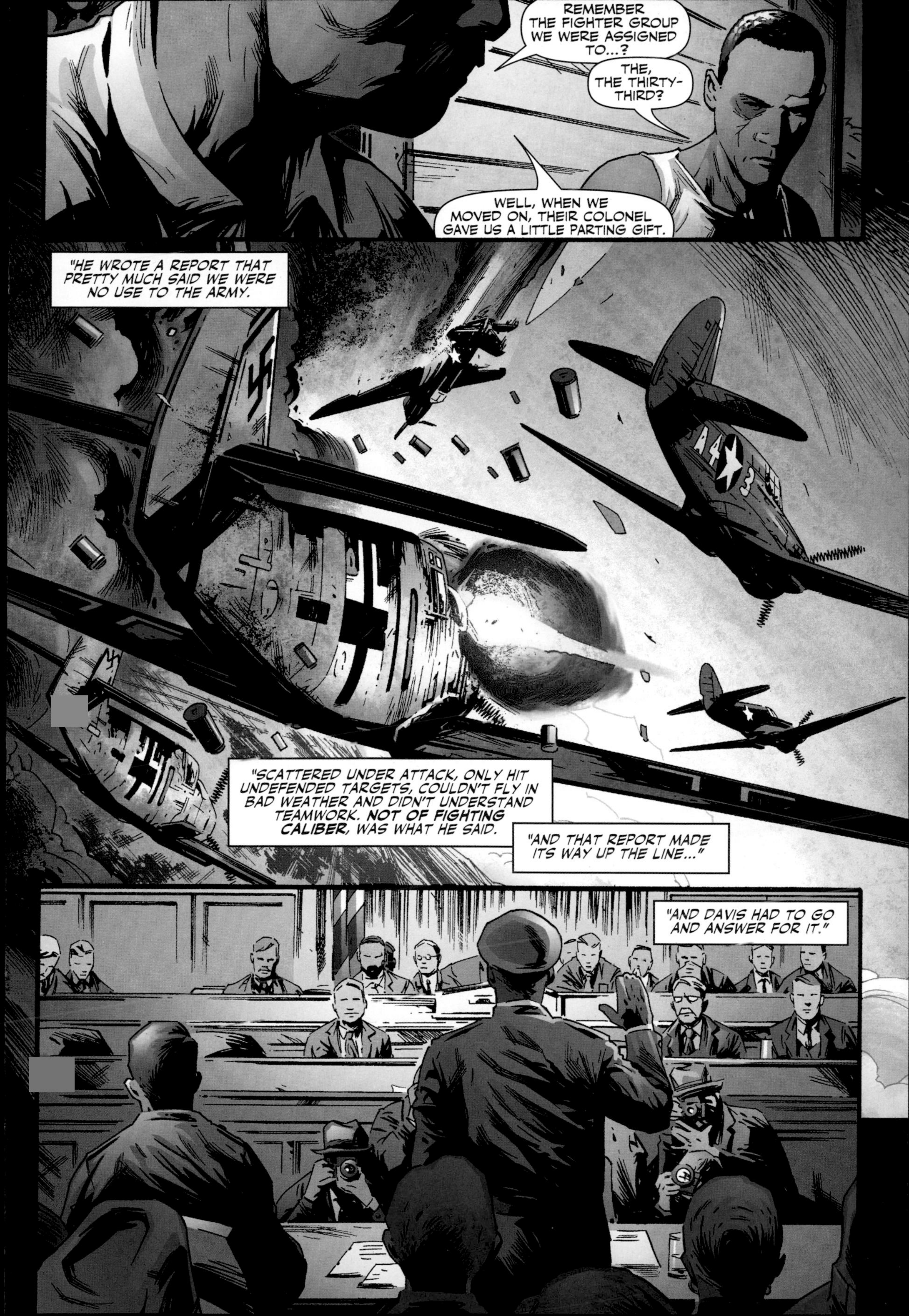
REMEMBER THE FIGHTER GROUP WE WERE ASSIGNED TO...?
THE, THE THIRTY-THIRD?
WELL, WHEN WE MOVED ON, THEIR COLONEL GAVE US A LITTLE PARTING GIFT.
"HE WROTE A REPORT THAT PRETTY MUCH SAID WE WERE NO USE TO THE ARMY.
A4 3
"SCATTERED UNDER ATTACK, ONLY HIT UNDEFENDED TARGETS, COULDN'T FLY IN BAD WEATHER AND DIDN'T UNDERSTAND TEAMWORK. NOT OF FIGHTING CALIBER, WAS WHAT HE SAID.
"AND THAT REPORT MADE ITS WAY UP THE LINE..."
"AND DAVIS HAD TO GO AND ANSWER FOR IT."

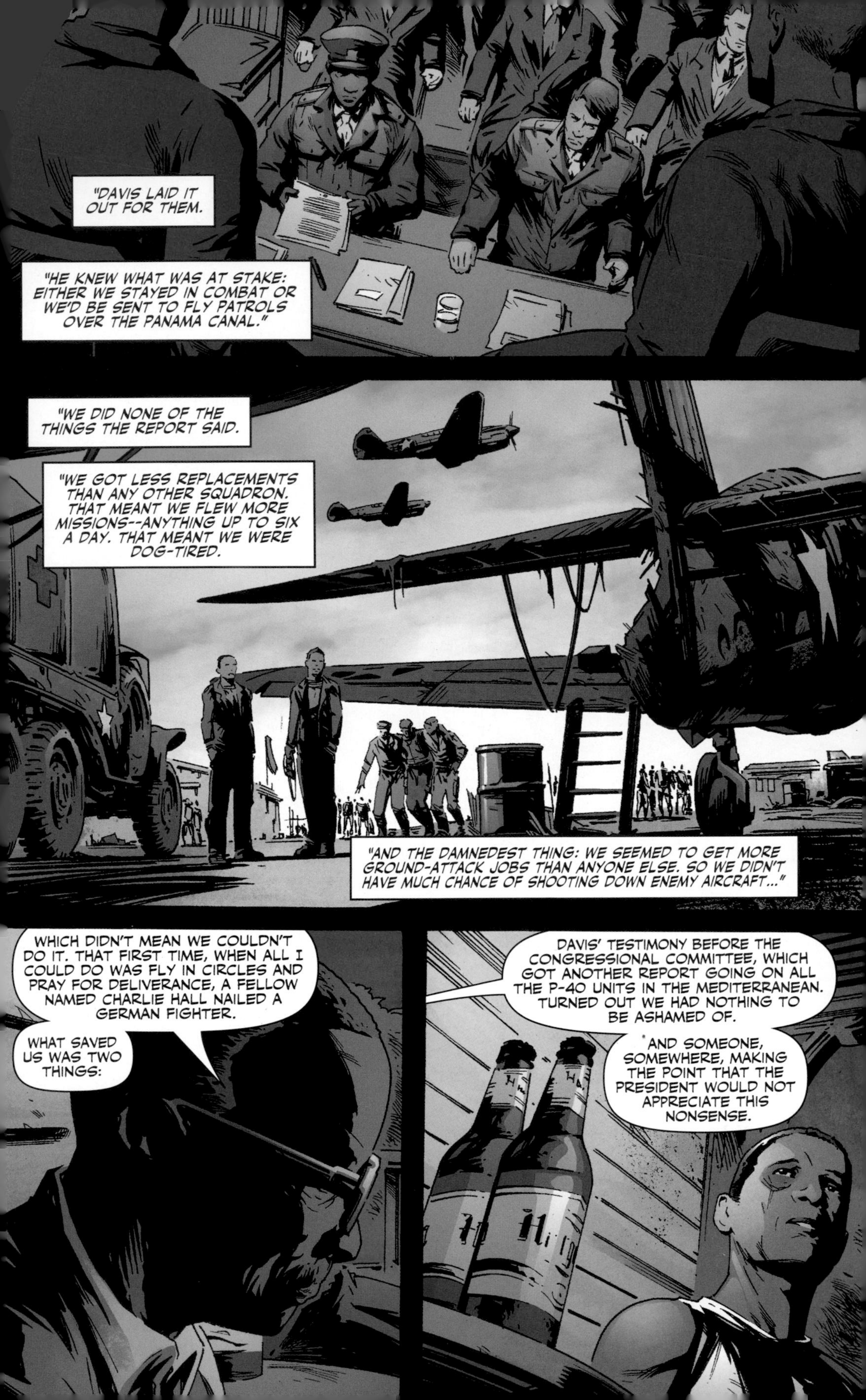
"DAVIS LAID IT OUT FOR THEM.
"HE KNEW WHAT WAS AT STAKE: EITHER WE STAYED IN COMBAT OR WE'D BE SENT TO FLY PATROLS OVER THE PANAMA CANAL."
"WE DID NONE OF THE THINGS THE REPORT SAID.
"WE GOT LESS REPLACEMENTS THAN ANY OTHER SQUADRON. THAT MEANT WE FLEW MORE MISSIONS--ANYTHING UP TO SIX A DAY. THAT MEANT WE WERE DOG-TIRED.
"AND THE DAMNEDEST THING: WE SEEMED TO GET MORE GROUND-ATTACK JOBS THAN ANYONE ELSE. SO WE DIDN'T HAVE MUCH CHANCE OF SHOOTING DOWN ENEMY AIRCRAFT..."
WHICH DIDN'T MEAN WE COULDN'T DO IT. THAT FIRST TIME, WHEN ALL I COULD DO WAS FLY IN CIRCLES AND PRAY FOR DELIVERANCE, A FELLOW NAMED CHARLIE HALL NAILED A GERMAN FIGHTER.
WHAT SAVED US WAS TWO THINGS:
DAVIS' TESTIMONY BEFORE THE CONGRESSIONAL COMMITTEE, WHICH GOT ANOTHER REPORT GOING ON ALL THE P-40 UNITS IN THE MEDITERRANEAN. TURNED OUT WE HAD NOTHING TO BE ASHAMED OF.
AND SOMEONE, SOMEWHERE, MAKING THE POINT THAT THE PRESIDENT WOULD NOT APPRECIATE THIS NONSENSE.

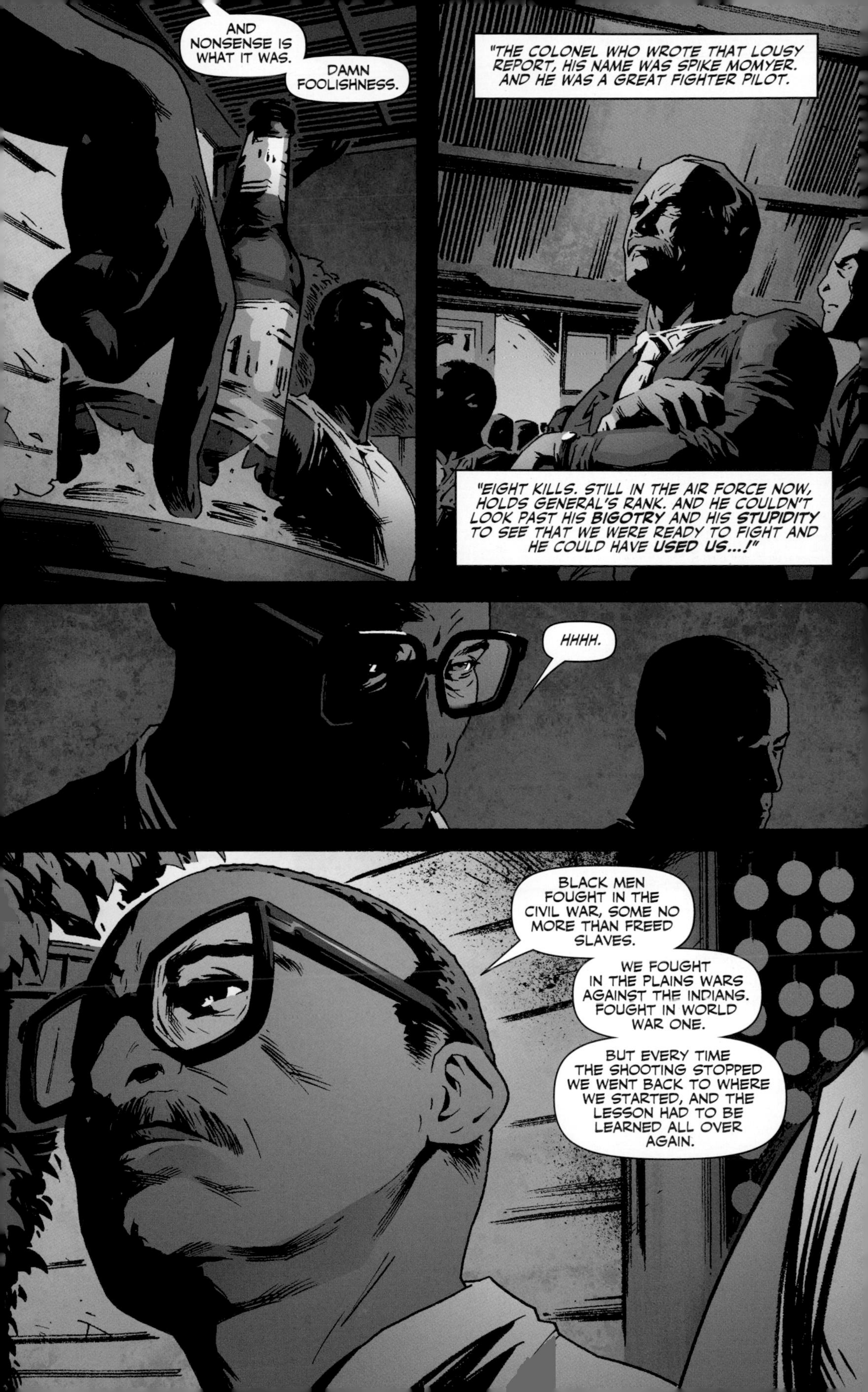
AND NONSENSE IS WHAT IT WAS.
DAMN FOOLISHNESS.
"THE COLONEL WHO WROTE THAT LOUSY REPORT, HIS NAME WAS SPIKE MOMYER. AND HE WAS A GREAT FIGHTER PILOT.
"EIGHT KILLS. STILL IN THE AIR FORCE NOW, HOLDS GENERAL'S RANK. AND HE COULDN'T LOOK PAST HIS BIGOTRY AND HIS STUPIDITY TO SEE THAT WE WERE READY TO FIGHT AND HE COULD HAVE USED US...!"
HHHH.
BLACK MEN FOUGHT IN THE CIVIL WAR, SOME NO MORE THAN FREED SLAVES.
WE FOUGHT IN THE PLAINS WARS AGAINST THE INDIANS. FOUGHT IN WORLD WAR ONE.
BUT EVERY TIME THE SHOOTING STOPPED WE WENT BACK TO WHERE WE STARTED, AND THE LESSON HAD TO BE LEARNED ALL OVER AGAIN.

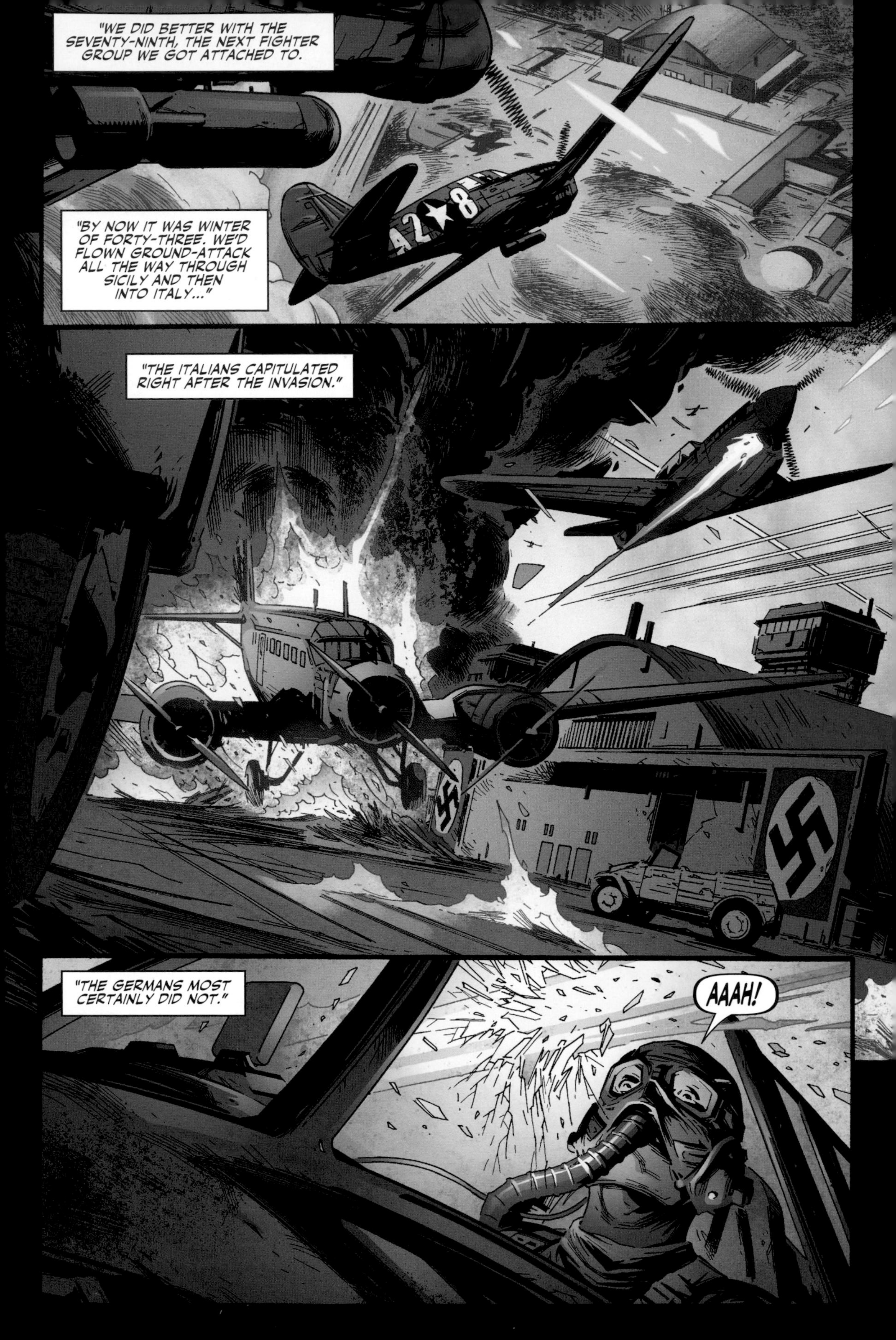
"WE DID BETTER WITH THE SEVENTY-NINTH, THE NEXT FIGHTER GROUP WE GOT ATTACHED TO.
42 8
"BY NOW IT WAS WINTER OF FORTY-THREE. WE'D FLOWN GROUND-ATTACK ALL THE WAY THROUGH SICILY AND THEN INTO ITALY..."
"THE ITALIANS CAPITULATED RIGHT AFTER THE INVASION."
"THE GERMANS MOST CERTAINLY DID NOT."
AAAH!

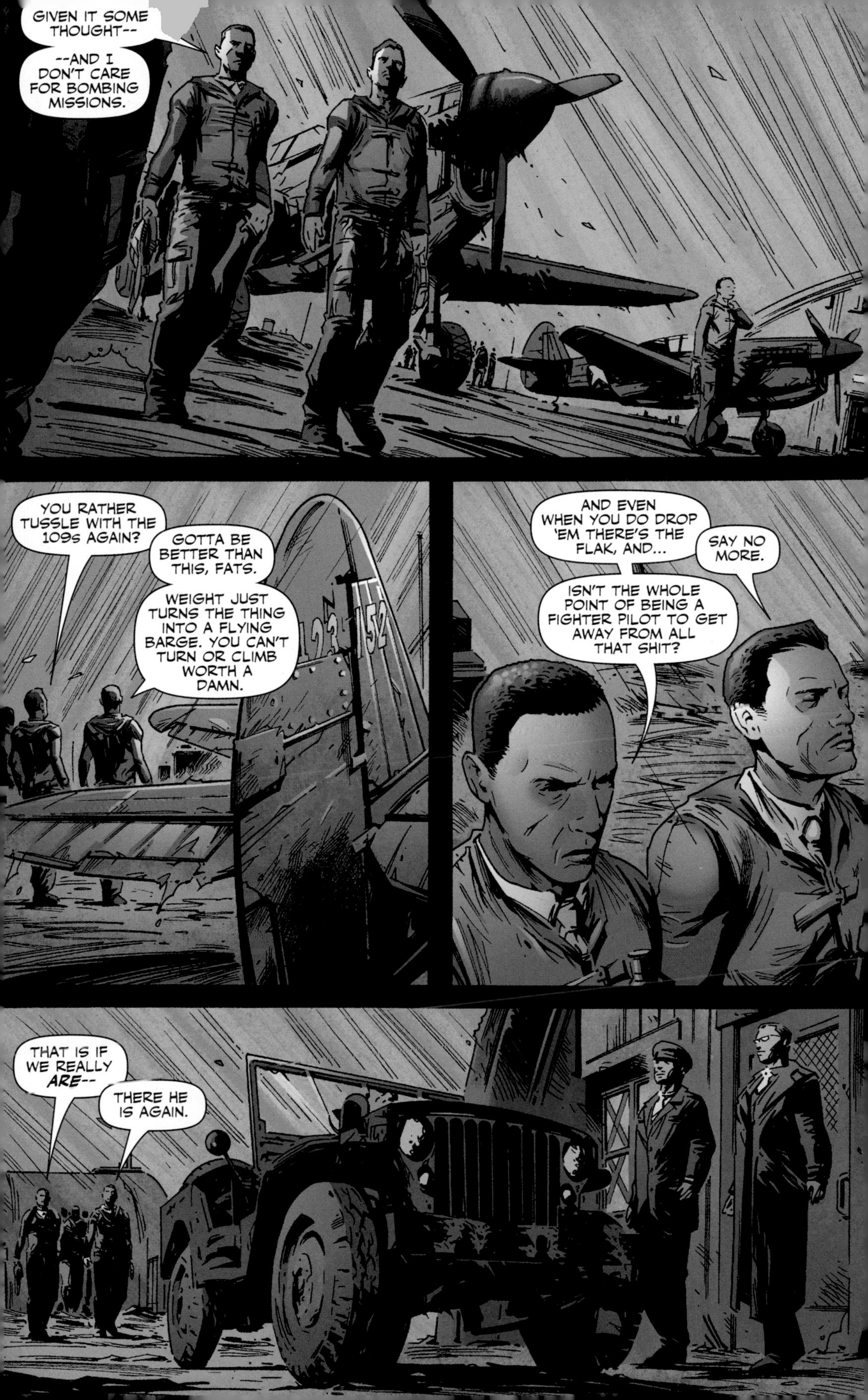
GIVEN IT SOME THOUGHT--
--AND I DON'T CARE FOR BOMBING MISSIONS.
YOU RATHER TUSSLE WITH THE 109s AGAIN?
GOTTA BE BETTER THAN THIS, FATS.
WEIGHT JUST TURNS THE THING INTO A FLYING BARGE. YOU CAN'T TURN OR CLIMB WORTH A DAMN.
AND EVEN WHEN YOU DO DROP 'EM THERE'S THE FLAK, AND...
SAY NO MORE.
ISN'T THE WHOLE POINT OF BEING A FIGHTER PILOT TO GET AWAY FROM ALL THAT SHIT?
THAT IS IF WE REALLY *ARE*--
THERE HE IS AGAIN.

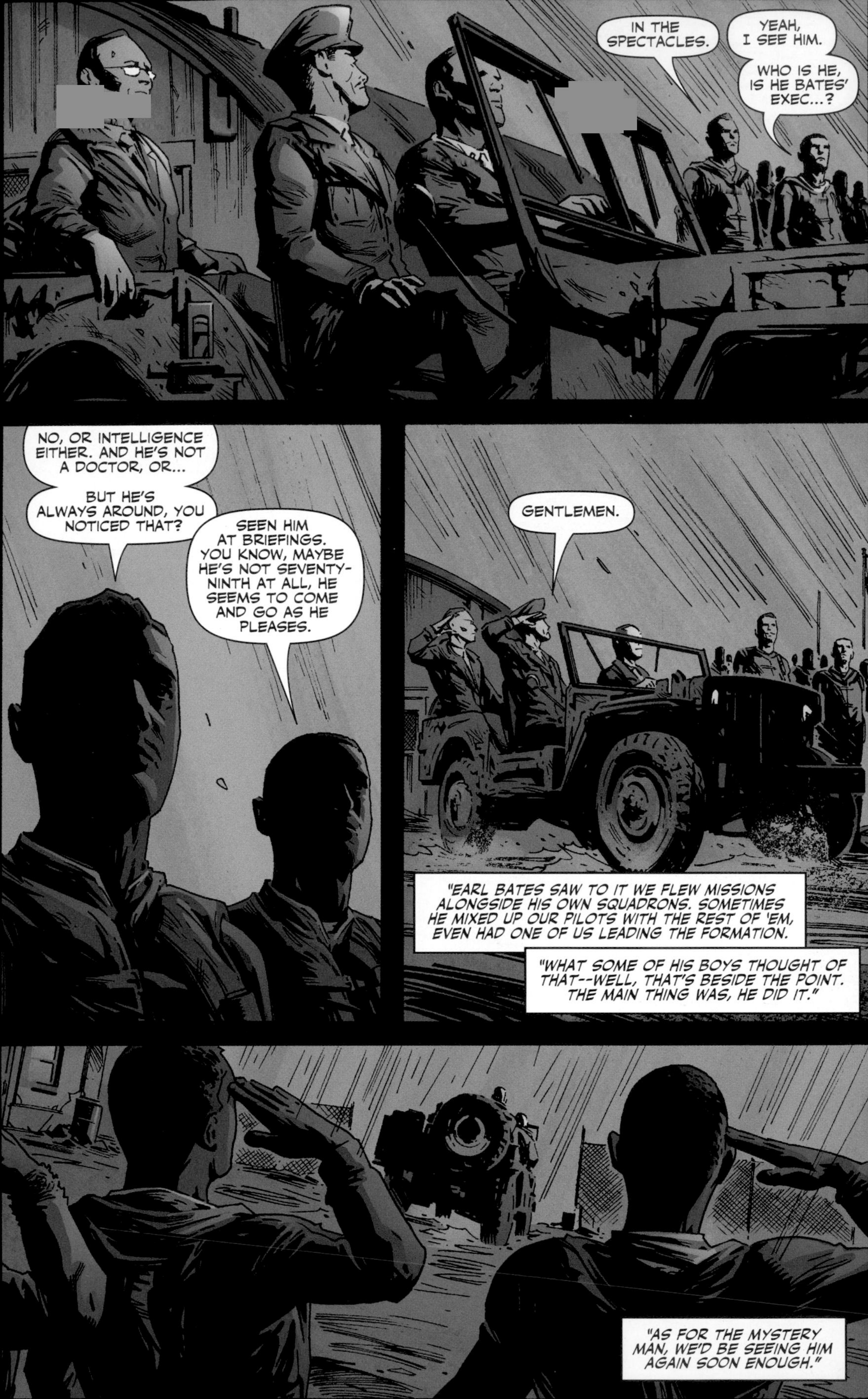
IN THE SPECTACLES.
YEAH, I SEE HIM.
WHO IS HE, IS HE BATES' EXEC...?
NO, OR INTELLIGENCE EITHER. AND HE'S NOT A DOCTOR, OR...
BUT HE'S ALWAYS AROUND, YOU NOTICED THAT?
SEEN HIM AT BRIEFINGS. YOU KNOW, MAYBE HE'S NOT SEVENTY-NINTH AT ALL, HE SEEMS TO COME AND GO AS HE PLEASES.
GENTLEMEN.
"EARL BATES SAW TO IT WE FLEW MISSIONS ALONGSIDE HIS OWN SQUADRONS. SOMETIMES HE MIXED UP OUR PILOTS WITH THE REST OF 'EM, EVEN HAD ONE OF US LEADING THE FORMATION.
"WHAT SOME OF HIS BOYS THOUGHT OF THAT--WELL, THAT'S BESIDE THE POINT. THE MAIN THING WAS, HE DID IT."
"AS FOR THE MYSTERY MAN, WE'D BE SEEING HIM AGAIN SOON ENOUGH."

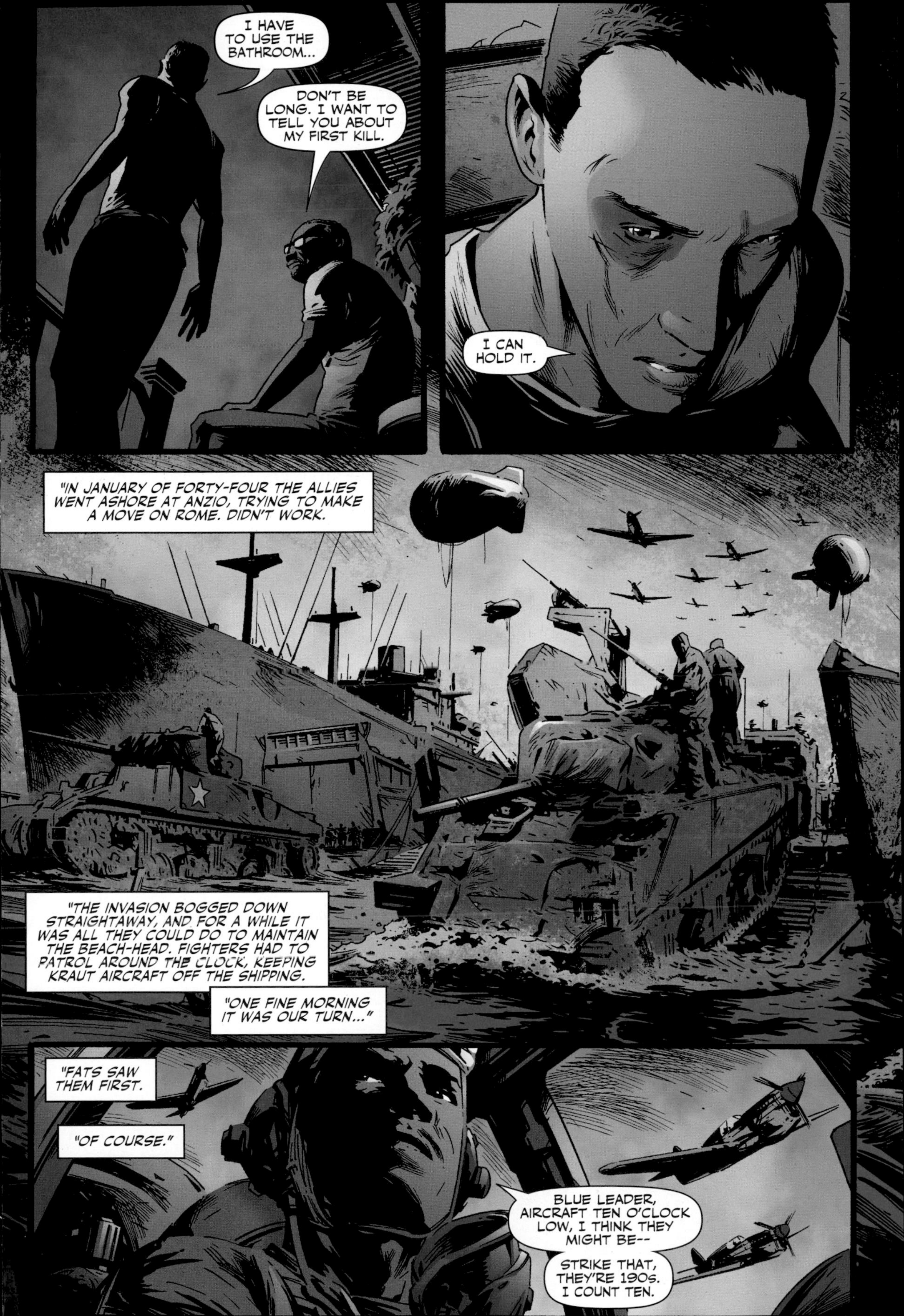
I HAVE TO USE THE BATHROOM...
DON'T BE LONG. I WANT TO TELL YOU ABOUT MY FIRST KILL.
I CAN HOLD IT.
"IN JANUARY OF FORTY-FOUR THE ALLIES WENT ASHORE AT ANZIO, TRYING TO MAKE A MOVE ON ROME. DIDN'T WORK.
"THE INVASION BOGGED DOWN STRAIGHTAWAY, AND FOR A WHILE IT WAS ALL THEY COULD DO TO MAINTAIN THE BEACH-HEAD. FIGHTERS HAD TO PATROL AROUND THE CLOCK, KEEPING KRAUT AIRCRAFT OFF THE SHIPPING.
"ONE FINE MORNING IT WAS OUR TURN..."
"FATS SAW THEM FIRST.
"OF COURSE."
BLUE LEADER, AIRCRAFT TEN O'CLOCK LOW, I THINK THEY MIGHT BE--
STRIKE THAT, THEY'RE 190s. I COUNT TEN.

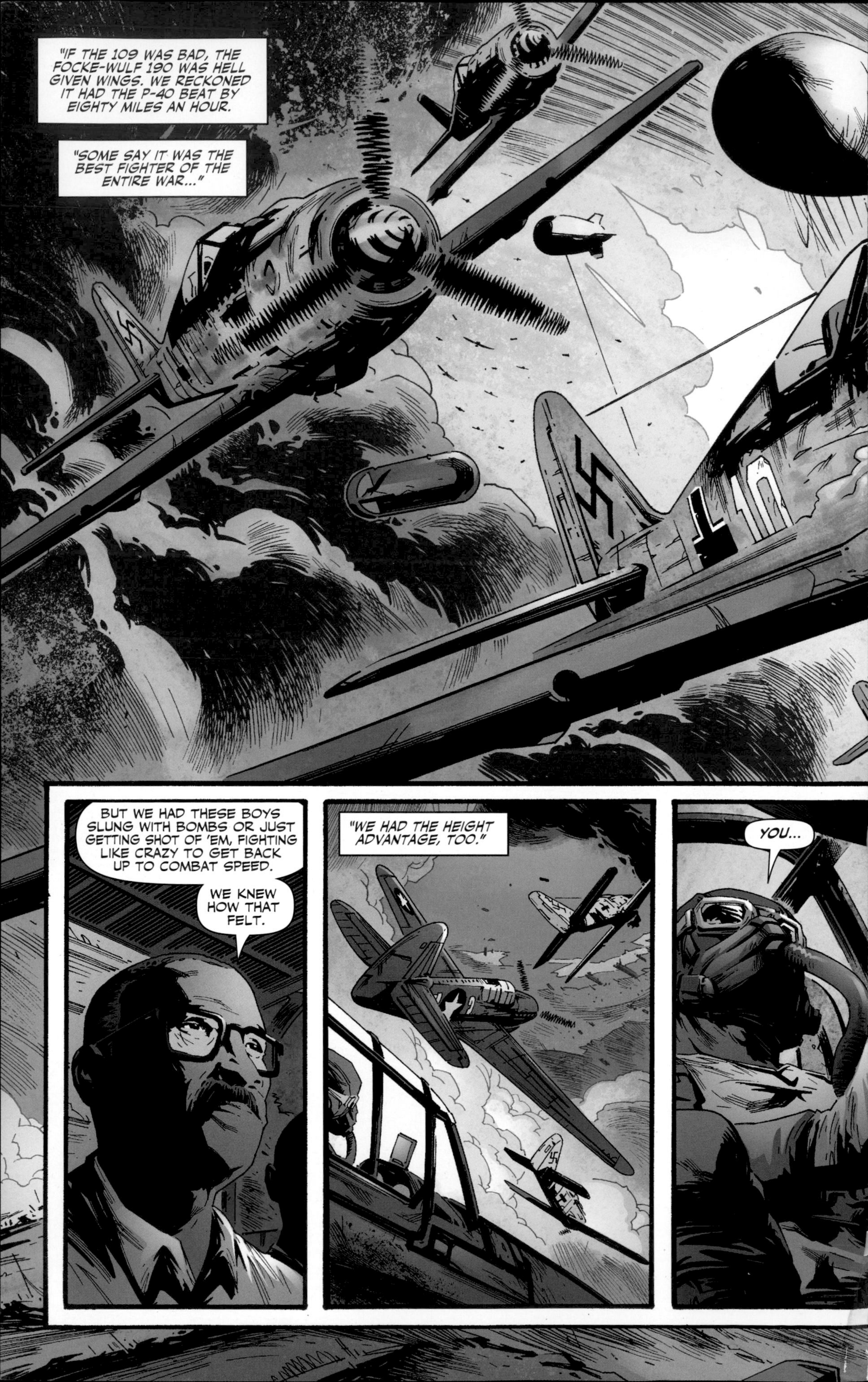
"IF THE 109 WAS BAD, THE FOCKE-WULF 190 WAS HELL GIVEN WINGS. WE RECKONED IT HAD THE P-40 BEAT BY EIGHTY MILES AN HOUR.
"SOME SAY IT WAS THE BEST FIGHTER OF THE ENTIRE WAR..."
BUT WE HAD THESE BOYS SLUNG WITH BOMBS OR JUST GETTING SHOT OF 'EM, FIGHTING LIKE CRAZY TO GET BACK UP TO COMBAT SPEED.
WE KNEW HOW THAT FELT.
"WE HAD THE HEIGHT ADVANTAGE, TOO."
YOU...

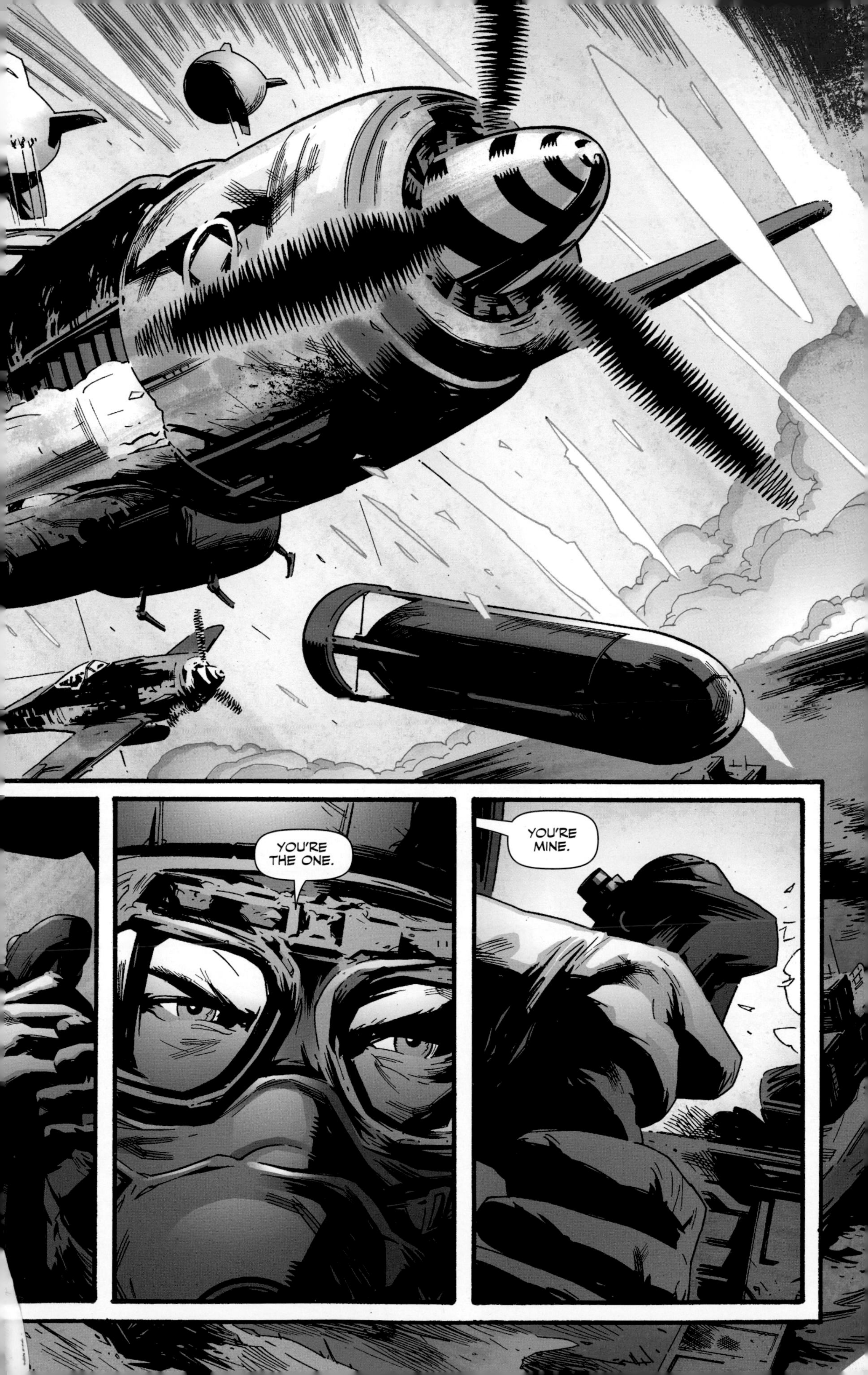
YOU'RE THE ONE.
YOU'RE MINE.

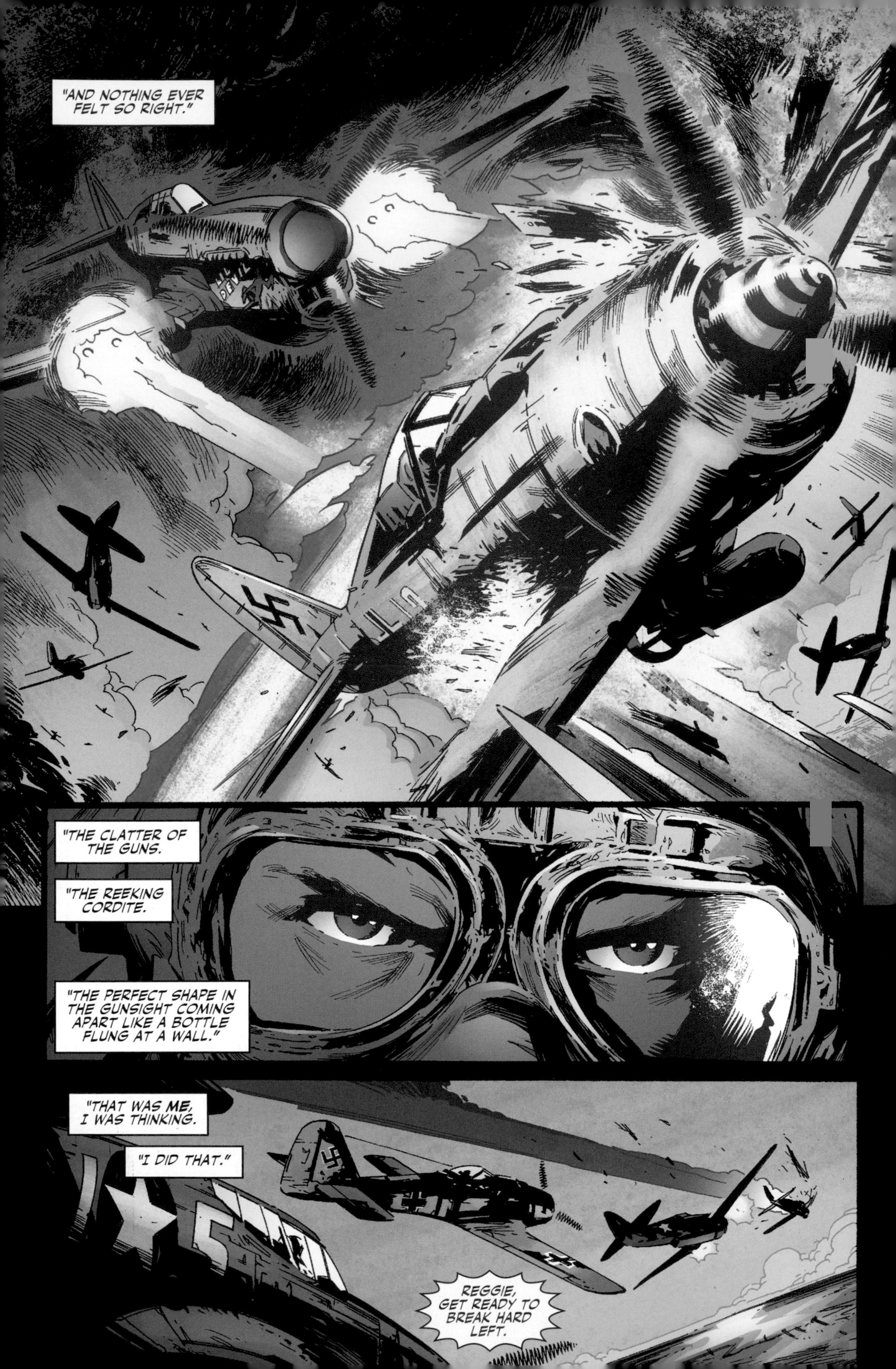
"AND NOTHING EVER FELT SO RIGHT."
"THE CLATTER OF THE GUNS.
"THE REEKING CORDITE.
"THE PERFECT SHAPE IN THE GUNSIGHT COMING APART LIKE A BOTTLE FLUNG AT A WALL."
"THAT WAS ME, I WAS THINKING.
"I DID THAT."
REGGIE, GET READY TO BREAK HARD LEFT.

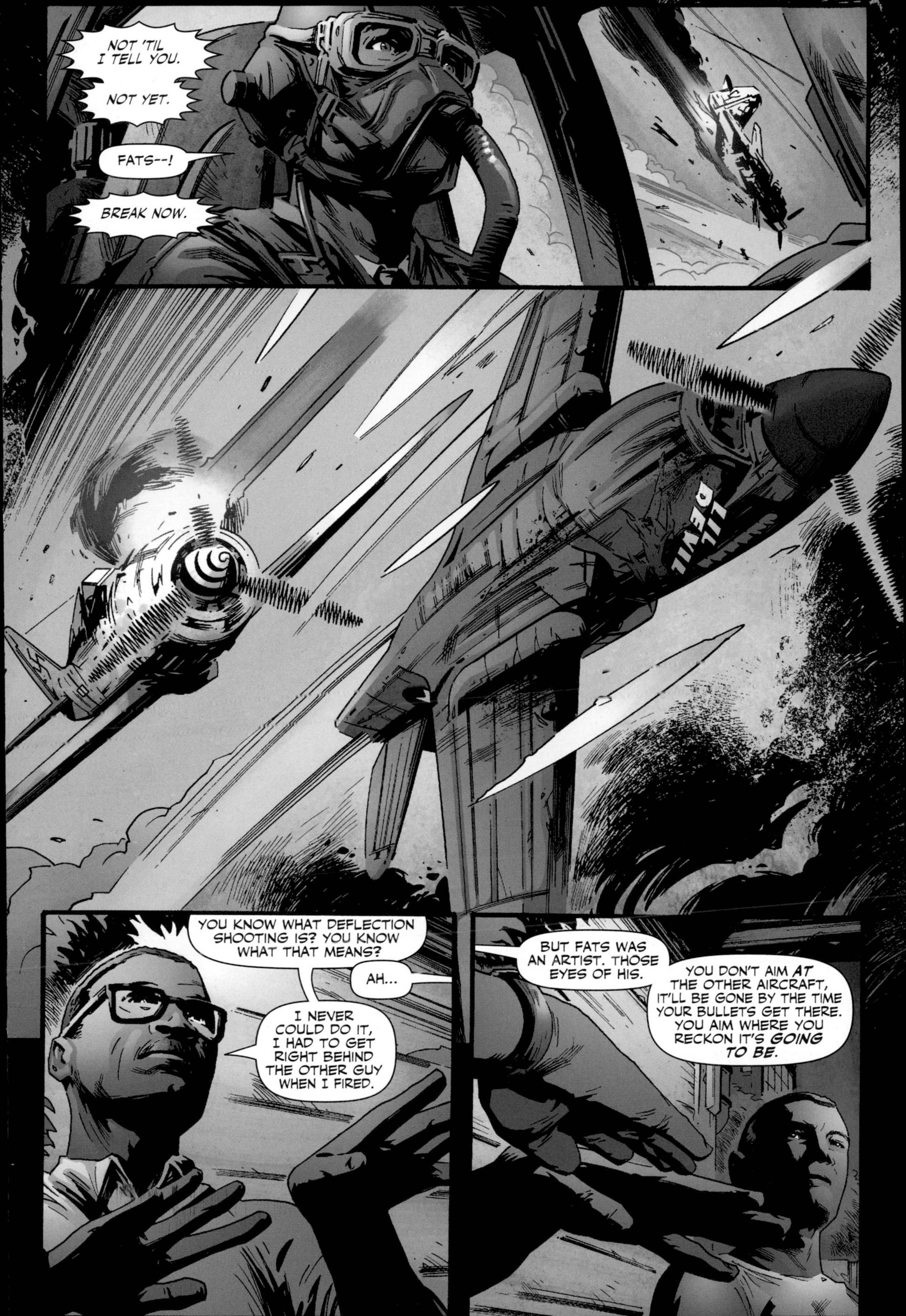
NOT 'TIL I TELL YOU.
NOT YET.
FATS--!
BREAK NOW.
DEVIL
YOU KNOW WHAT DEFLECTION SHOOTING IS? YOU KNOW WHAT THAT MEANS?
AH...
I NEVER COULD DO IT, I HAD TO GET RIGHT BEHIND THE OTHER GUY WHEN I FIRED.
BUT FATS WAS AN ARTIST. THOSE EYES OF HIS.
YOU DON'T AIM AT THE OTHER AIRCRAFT, IT'LL BE GONE BY THE TIME YOUR BULLETS GET THERE. YOU AIM WHERE YOU RECKON IT'S GOING TO BE.

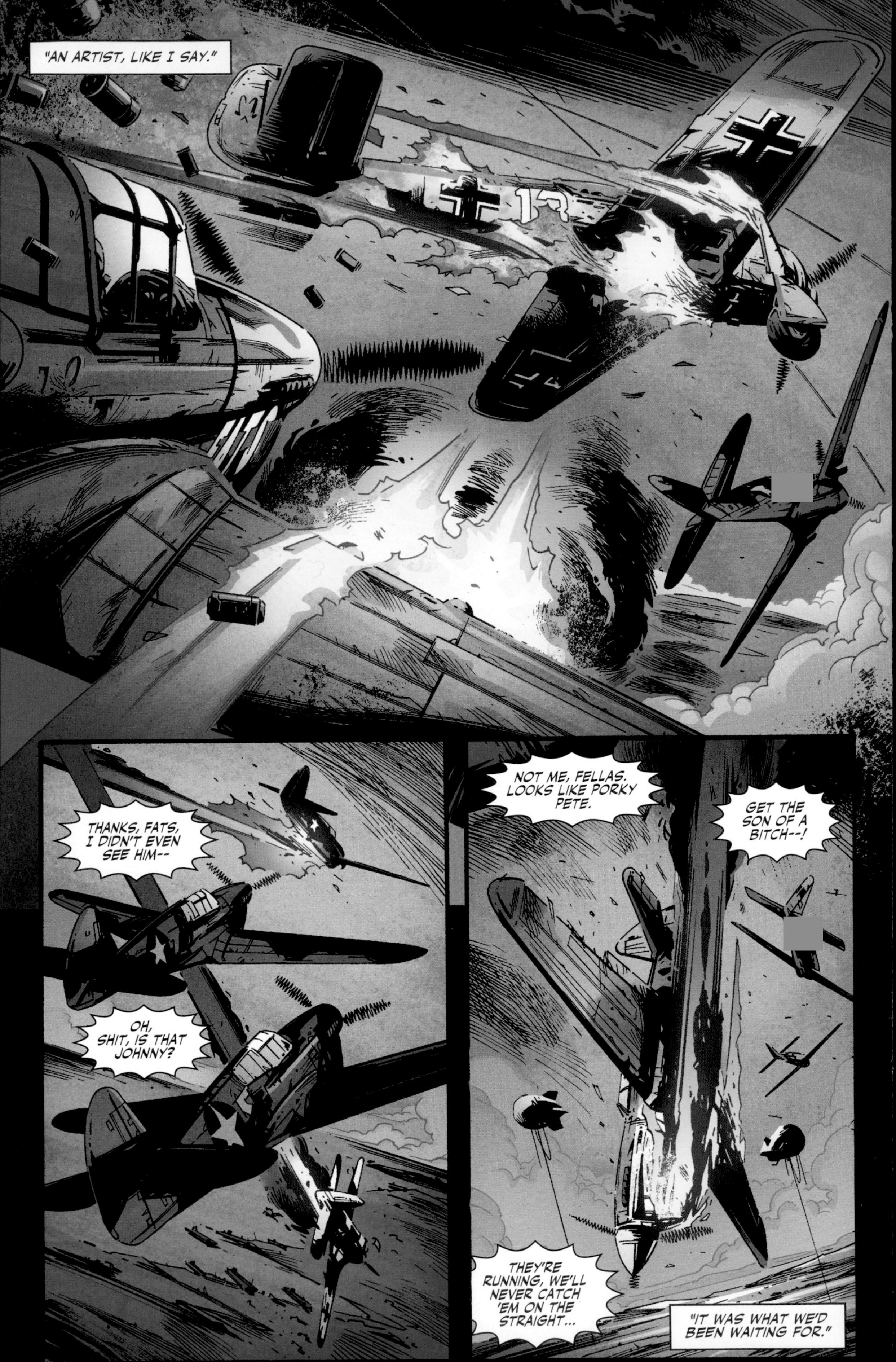
"AN ARTIST, LIKE I SAY."
THANKS, FATS, I DIDN'T EVEN SEE HIM--
OH, SHIT, IS THAT JOHNNY?
NOT ME, FELLAS. LOOKS LIKE PORKY PETE.
GET THE SON OF A BITCH--!
THEY'RE RUNNING, WE'LL NEVER CATCH 'EM ON THE STRAIGHT...
"IT WAS WHAT WE'D BEEN WAITING FOR."

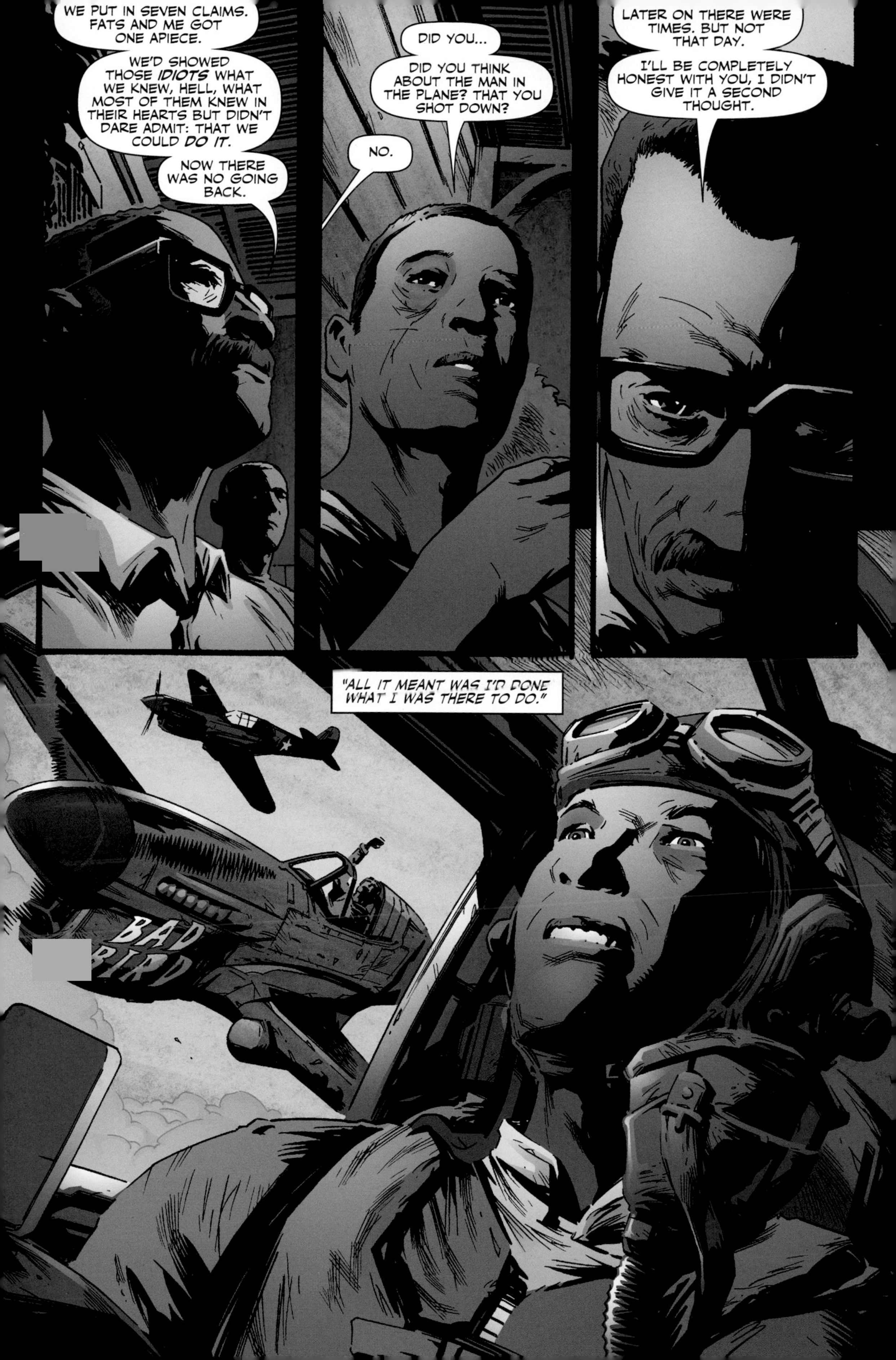
WE PUT IN SEVEN CLAIMS. FATS AND ME GOT ONE APIECE.
WE'D SHOWED THOSE *IDIOTS* WHAT WE KNEW, HELL, WHAT MOST OF THEM KNEW IN THEIR HEARTS BUT DIDN'T DARE ADMIT: THAT WE COULD *DO IT*.
NOW THERE WAS NO GOING BACK.
DID YOU...
DID YOU THINK ABOUT THE MAN IN THE PLANE? THAT YOU SHOT DOWN?
NO.
LATER ON THERE WERE TIMES. BUT NOT THAT DAY.
I'LL BE COMPLETELY HONEST WITH YOU, I DIDN'T GIVE IT A SECOND THOUGHT.
"ALL IT MEANT WAS I'D DONE WHAT I WAS THERE TO DO."
BAD BIRD

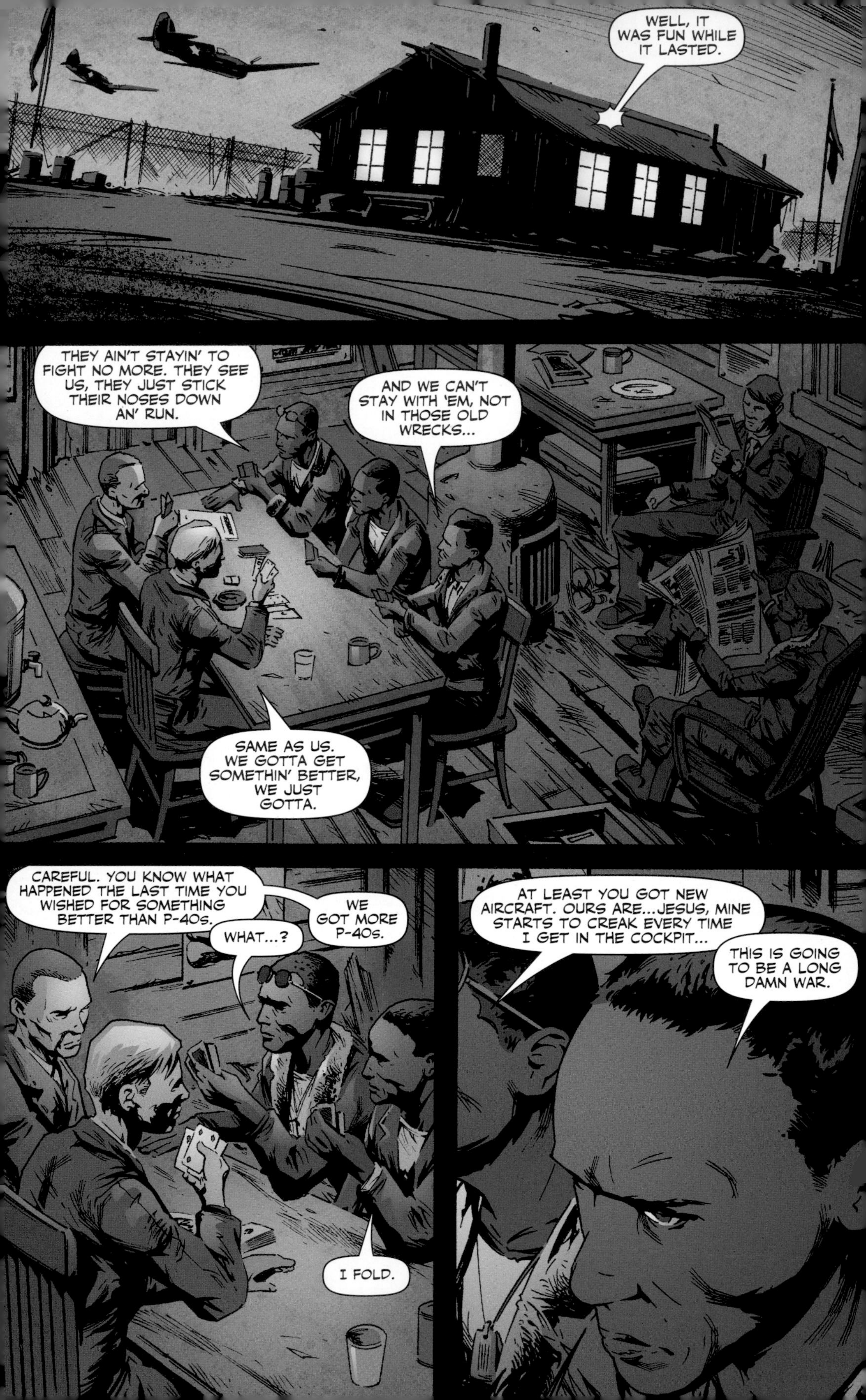
WELL, IT WAS FUN WHILE IT LASTED.
THEY AIN'T STAYIN' TO FIGHT NO MORE. THEY SEE US, THEY JUST STICK THEIR NOSES DOWN AN' RUN.
AND WE CAN'T STAY WITH 'EM, NOT IN THOSE OLD WRECKS...
SAME AS US. WE GOTTA GET SOMETHIN' BETTER, WE JUST GOTTA.
CAREFUL. YOU KNOW WHAT HAPPENED THE LAST TIME YOU WISHED FOR SOMETHING BETTER THAN P-40s.
WHAT...?
WE GOT MORE P-40s.
I FOLD.
AT LEAST YOU GOT NEW AIRCRAFT. OURS ARE...JESUS, MINE STARTS TO CREAK EVERY TIME I GET IN THE COCKPIT...
THIS IS GOING TO BE A LONG DAMN WAR.

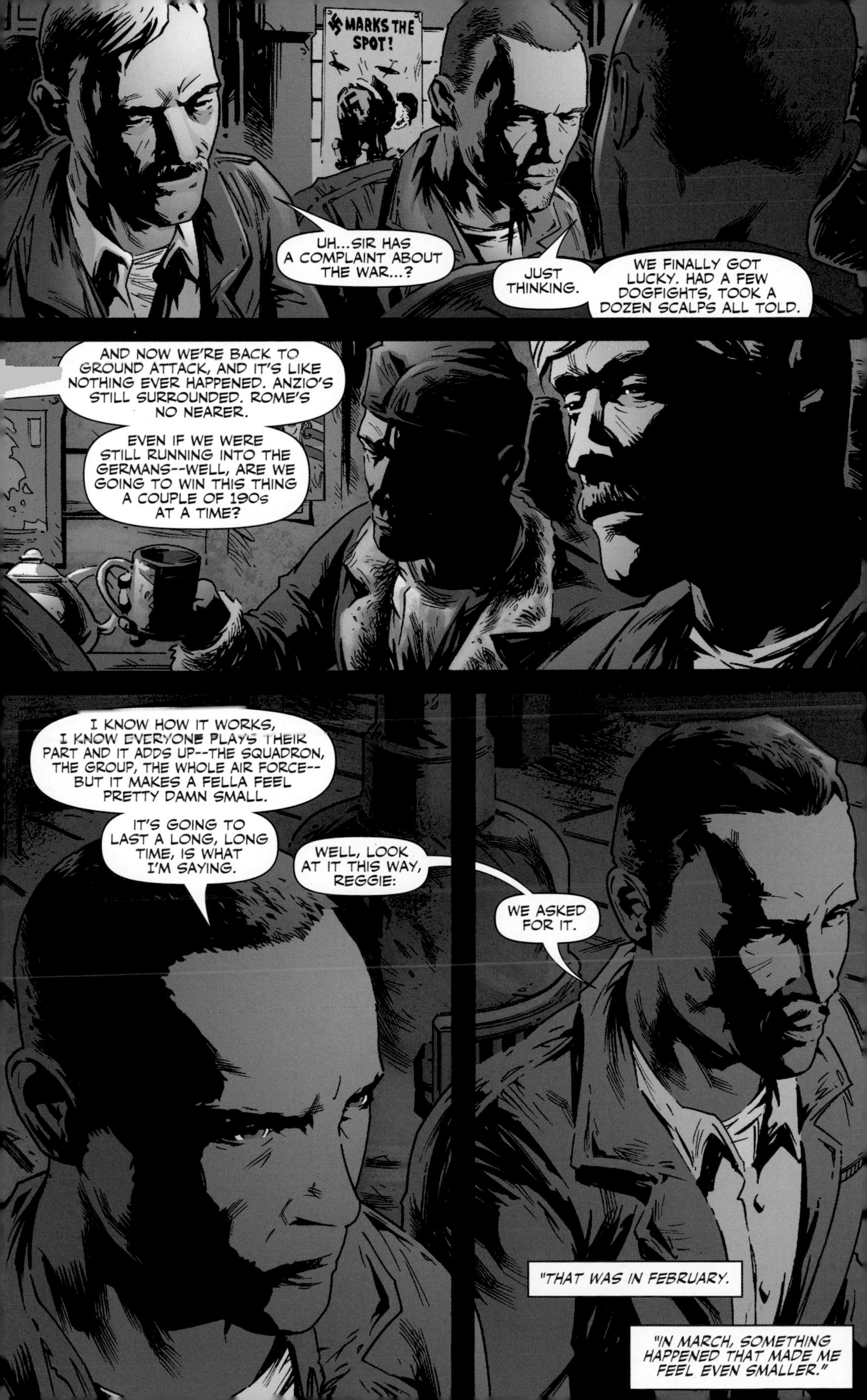
MARKS THE SPOT!
UH...SIR HAS A COMPLAINT ABOUT THE WAR...?
JUST THINKING.
WE FINALLY GOT LUCKY. HAD A FEW DOGFIGHTS, TOOK A DOZEN SCALPS ALL TOLD.
AND NOW WE'RE BACK TO GROUND ATTACK, AND IT'S LIKE NOTHING EVER HAPPENED. ANZIO'S STILL SURROUNDED. ROME'S NO NEARER.
EVEN IF WE WERE STILL RUNNING INTO THE GERMANS--WELL, ARE WE GOING TO WIN THIS THING A COUPLE OF 190s AT A TIME?
I KNOW HOW IT WORKS, I KNOW EVERYONE PLAYS THEIR PART AND IT ADDS UP--THE SQUADRON, THE GROUP, THE WHOLE AIR FORCE--BUT IT MAKES A FELLA FEEL PRETTY DAMN SMALL.
IT'S GOING TO LAST A LONG, LONG TIME, IS WHAT I'M SAYING.
WELL, LOOK AT IT THIS WAY, REGGIE:
WE ASKED FOR IT.
"THAT WAS IN FEBRUARY.
"IN MARCH, SOMETHING HAPPENED THAT MADE ME FEEL EVEN SMALLER."

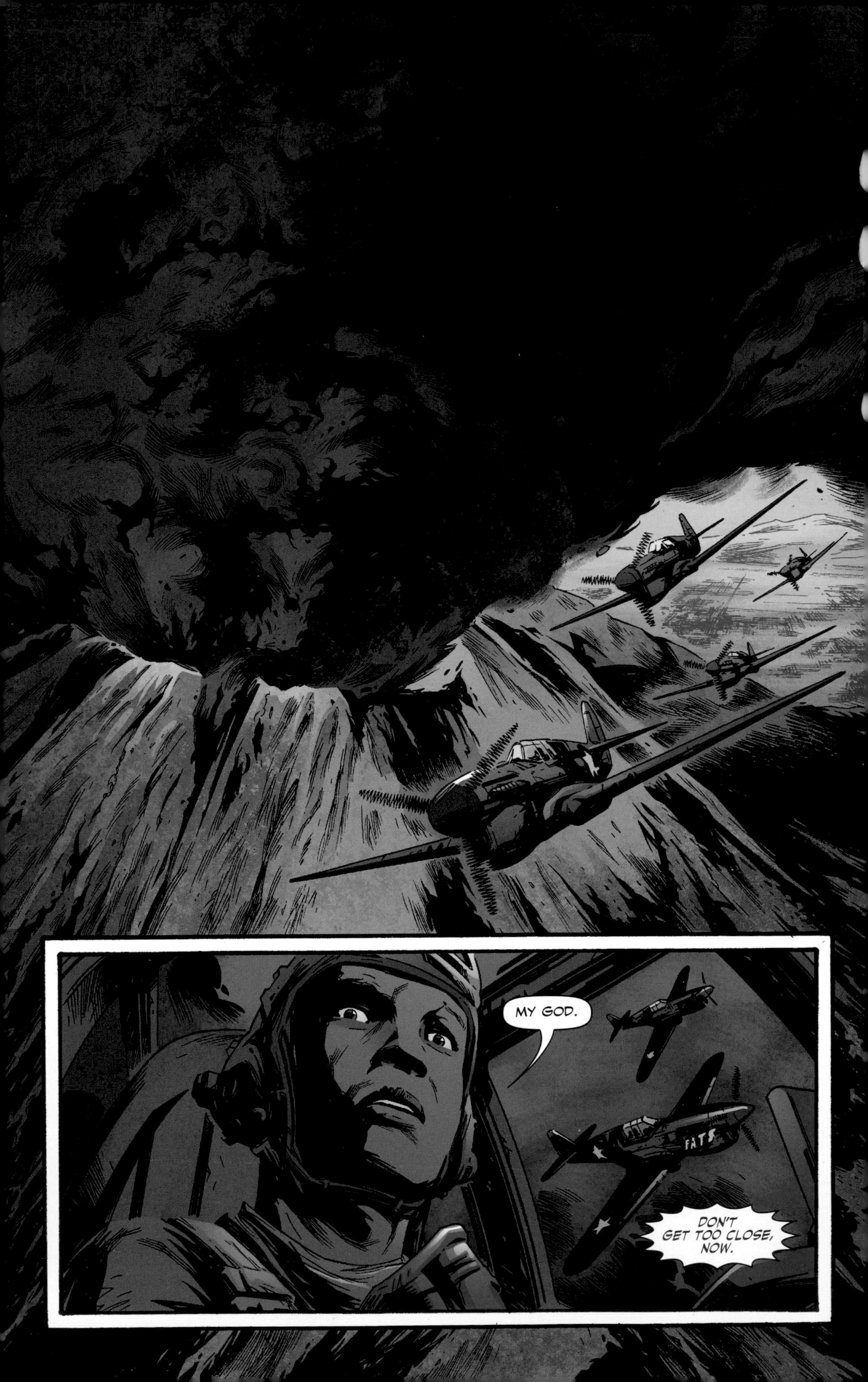
MY GOD.
DON'T GET TOO CLOSE, NOW.

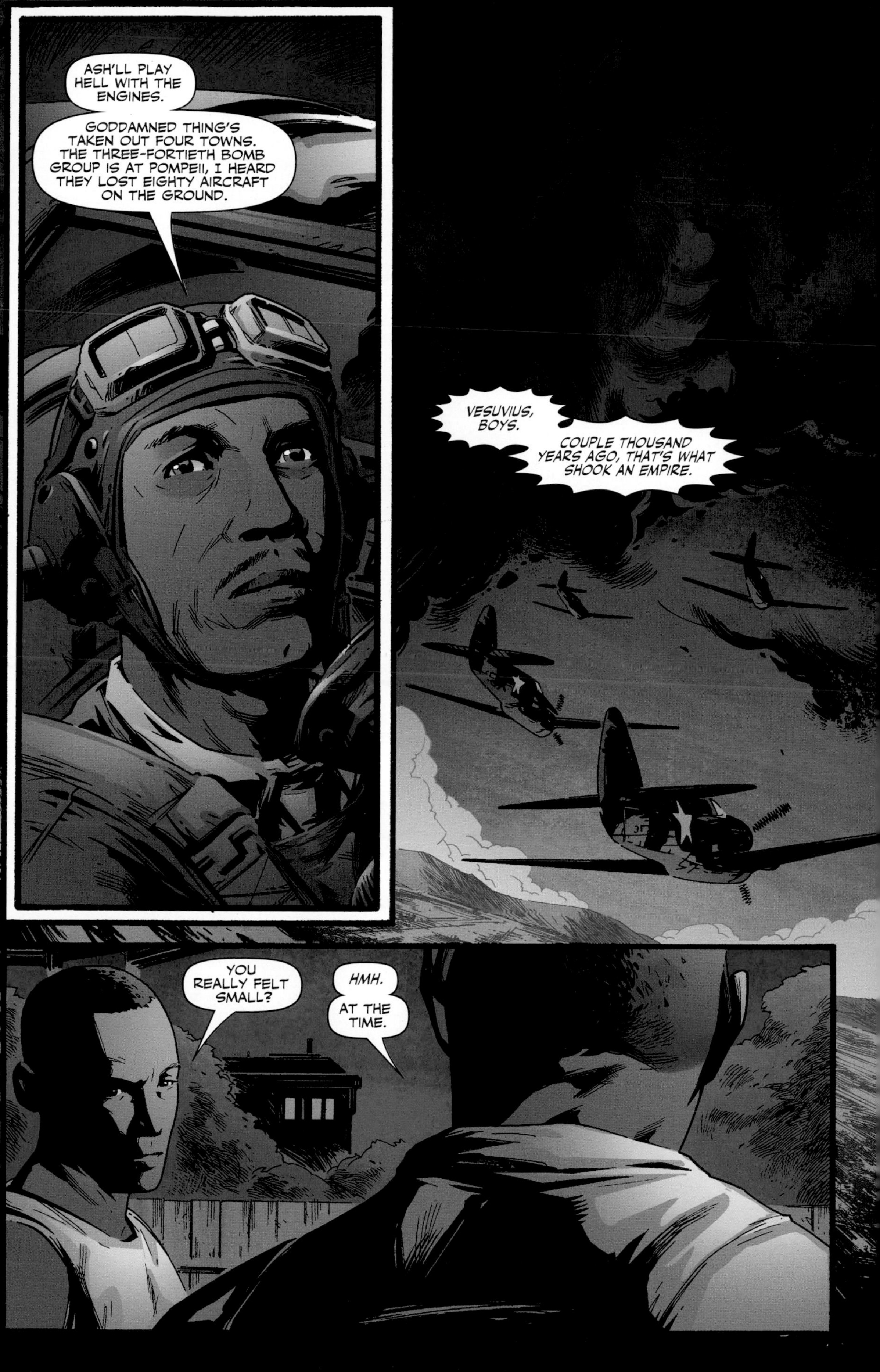
ASH'LL PLAY HELL WITH THE ENGINES.
GODDAMNED THING'S TAKEN OUT FOUR TOWNS. THE THREE-FORTIETH BOMB GROUP IS AT POMPEII, I HEARD THEY LOST EIGHTY AIRCRAFT ON THE GROUND.
VESUVIUS, BOYS.
COUPLE THOUSAND YEARS AGO, THAT'S WHAT SHOOK AN EMPIRE.
YOU REALLY FELT SMALL?
HMH.
AT THE TIME.

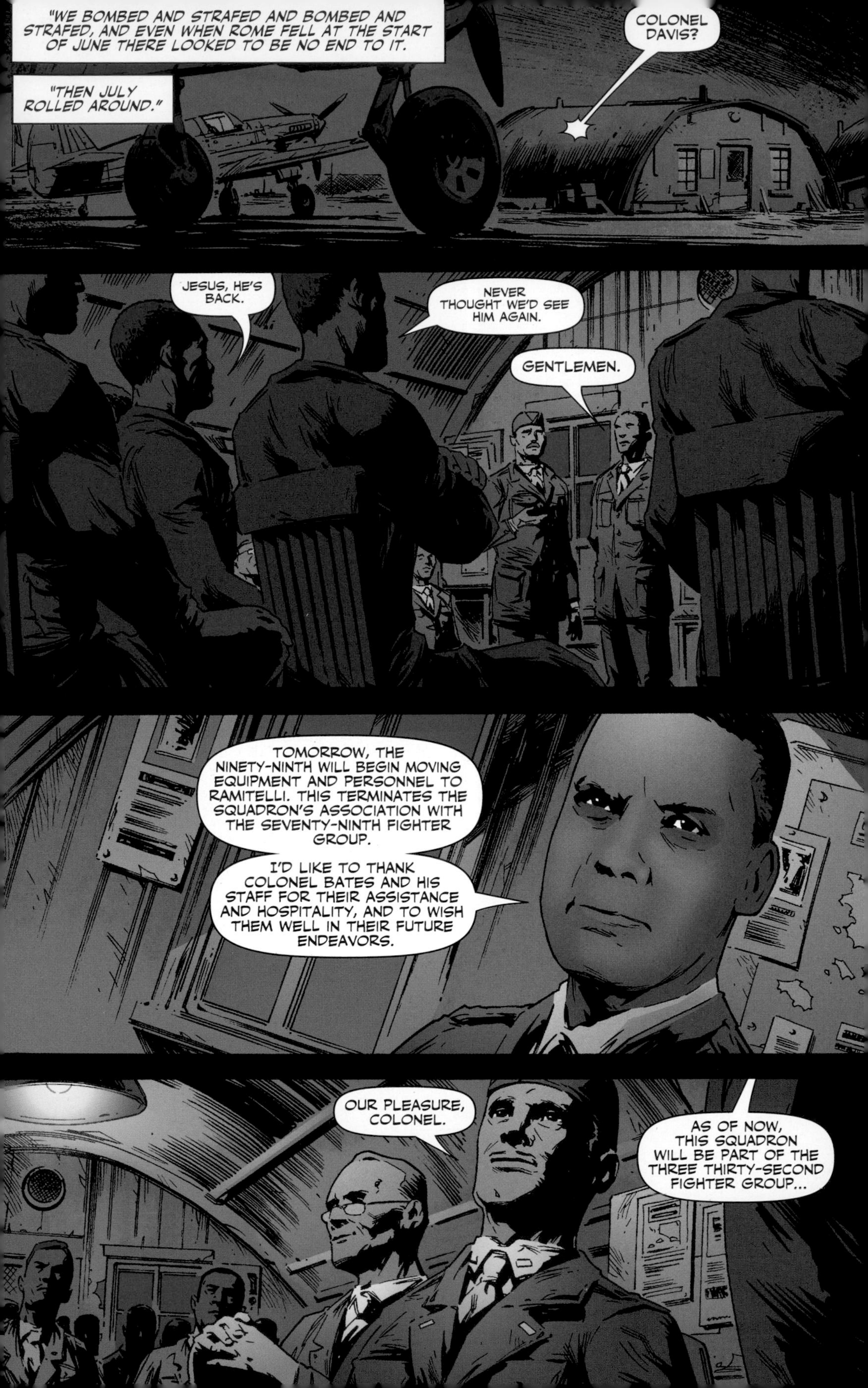
"WE BOMBED AND STRAFED AND BOMBED AND STRAFED, AND EVEN WHEN ROME FELL AT THE START OF JUNE THERE LOOKED TO BE NO END TO IT.
"THEN JULY ROLLED AROUND."
COLONEL DAVIS?
JESUS, HE'S BACK.
NEVER THOUGHT WE'D SEE HIM AGAIN.
GENTLEMEN.
TOMORROW, THE NINETY-NINTH WILL BEGIN MOVING EQUIPMENT AND PERSONNEL TO RAMITELLI. THIS TERMINATES THE SQUADRON'S ASSOCIATION WITH THE SEVENTY-NINTH FIGHTER GROUP.
I'D LIKE TO THANK COLONEL BATES AND HIS STAFF FOR THEIR ASSISTANCE AND HOSPITALITY, AND TO WISH THEM WELL IN THEIR FUTURE ENDEAVORS.
OUR PLEASURE, COLONEL.
AS OF NOW, THIS SQUADRON WILL BE PART OF THE THREE THIRTY-SECOND FIGHTER GROUP...

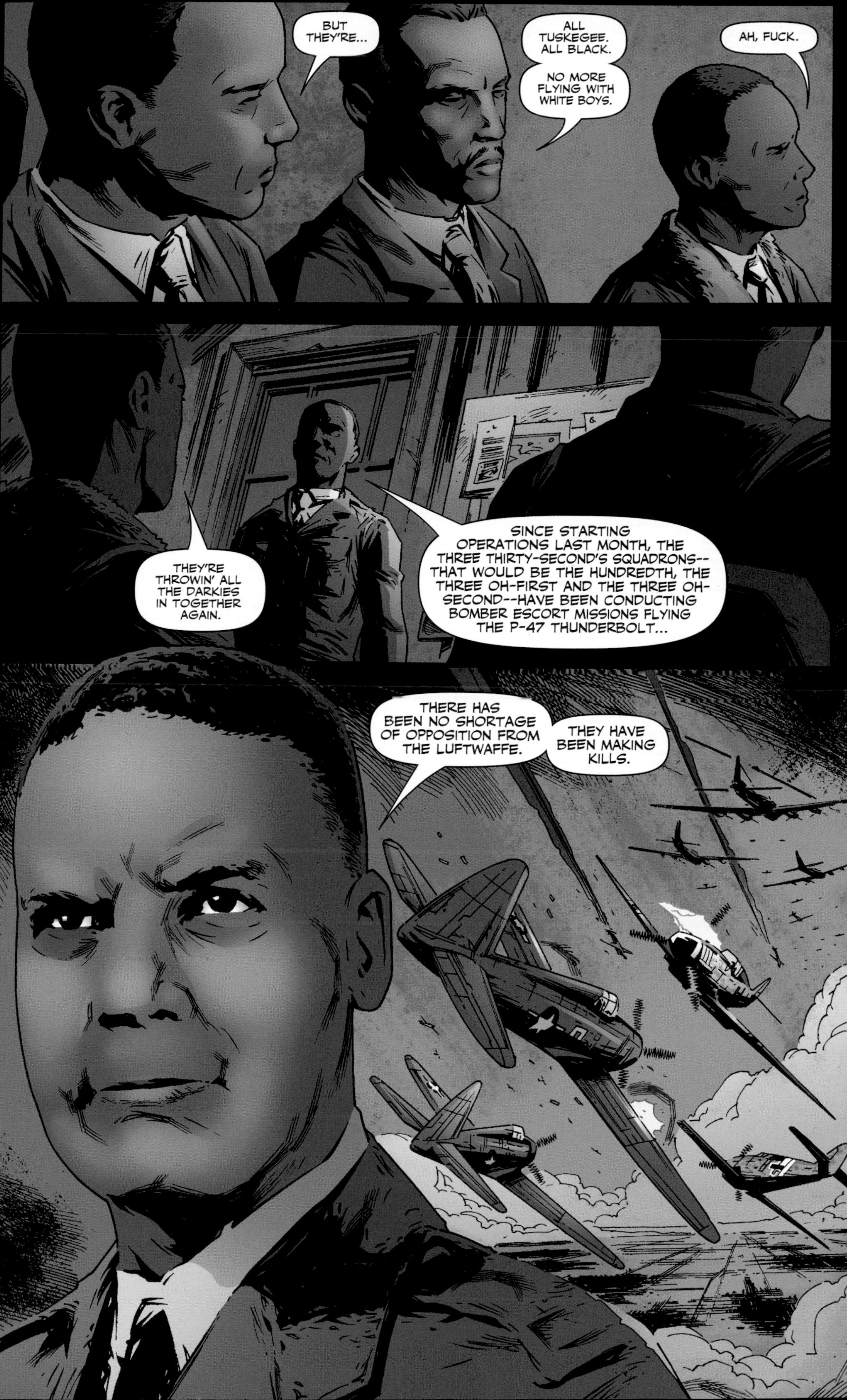
BUT THEY'RE...
ALL TUSKEGEE. ALL BLACK.
NO MORE FLYING WITH WHITE BOYS.
AH, FUCK.
THEY'RE THROWIN' ALL THE DARKIES IN TOGETHER AGAIN.
SINCE STARTING OPERATIONS LAST MONTH, THE THREE THIRTY-SECOND'S SQUADRONS--THAT WOULD BE THE HUNDREDTH, THE THREE OH-FIRST AND THE THREE OH-SECOND--HAVE BEEN CONDUCTING BOMBER ESCORT MISSIONS FLYING THE P-47 THUNDERBOLT...
THERE HAS BEEN NO SHORTAGE OF OPPOSITION FROM THE LUFTWAFFE.
THEY HAVE BEEN MAKING KILLS.

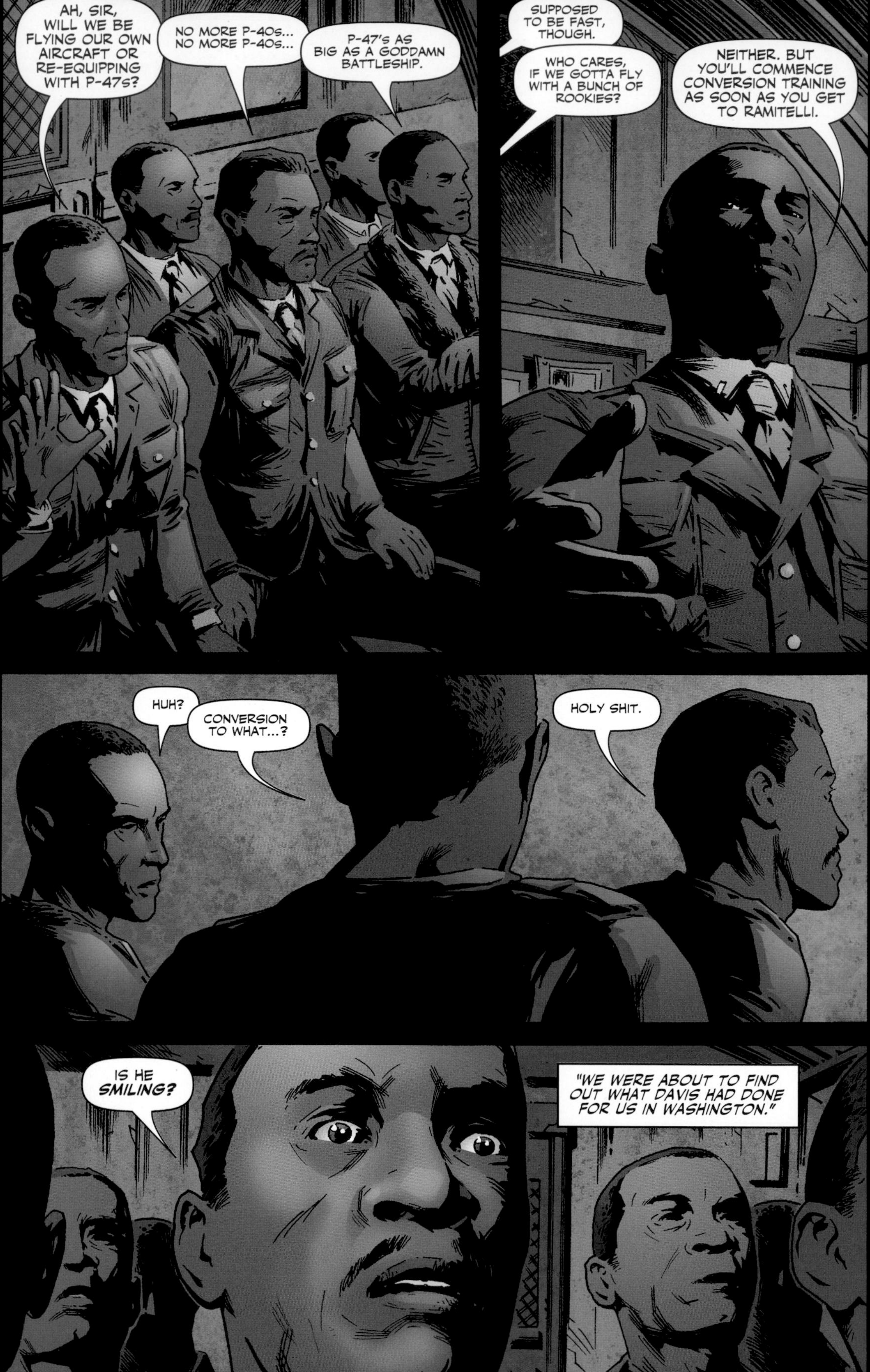
AH, SIR, WILL WE BE FLYING OUR OWN AIRCRAFT OR RE-EQUIPPING WITH P-47s?
NO MORE P-40s... NO MORE P-40s...
P-47's AS BIG AS A GODDAMN BATTLESHIP.
SUPPOSED TO BE FAST, THOUGH.
WHO CARES, IF WE GOTTA FLY WITH A BUNCH OF ROOKIES?
NEITHER. BUT YOU'LL COMMENCE CONVERSION TRAINING AS SOON AS YOU GET TO RAMITELLI.
HUH?
CONVERSION TO WHAT...?
HOLY SHIT.
IS HE *SMILING?*
"WE WERE ABOUT TO FIND OUT WHAT DAVIS HAD DONE FOR US IN WASHINGTON."

4: A HORSE AND A HALF

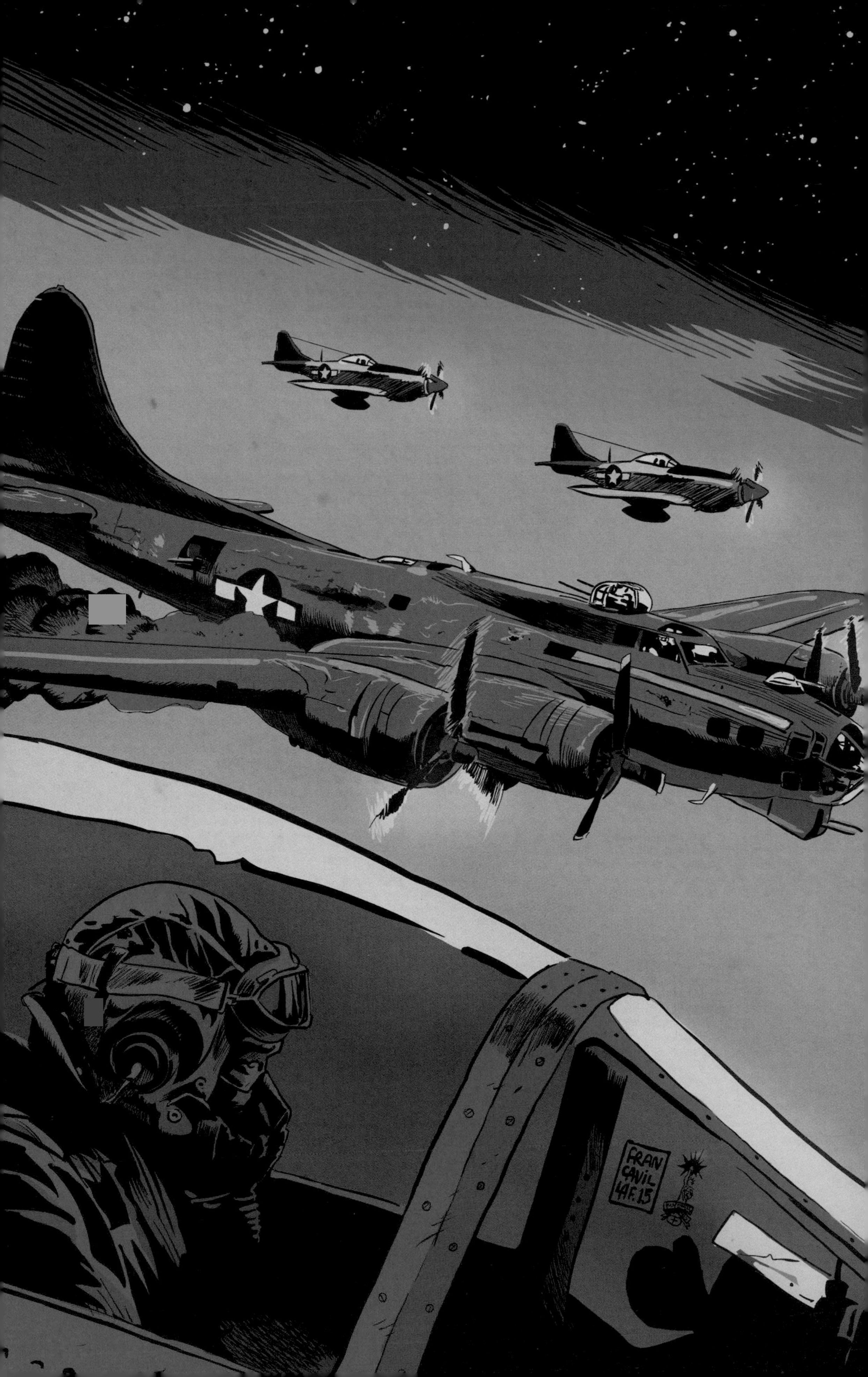

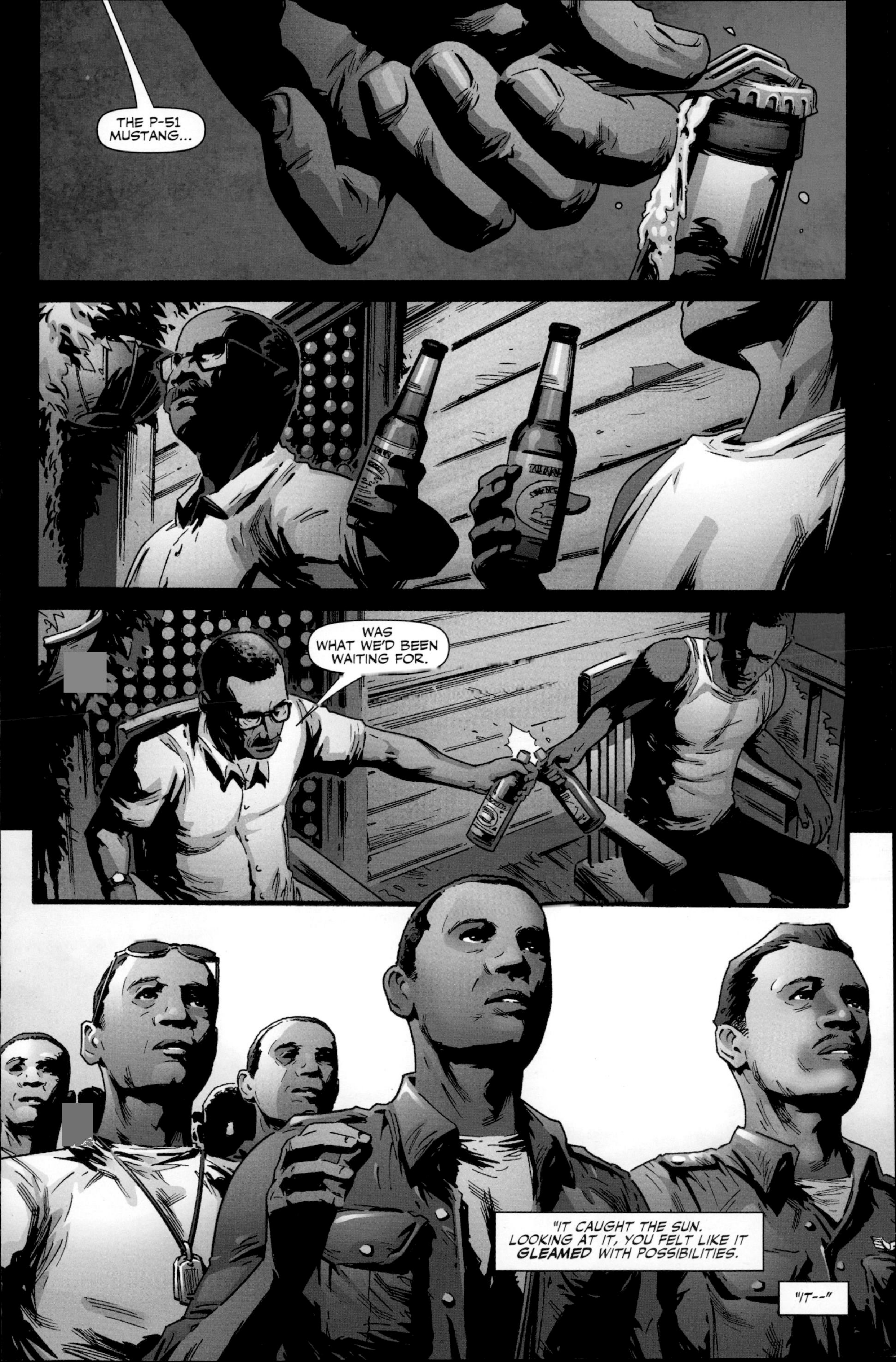
THE P-51 MUSTANG...
WAS WHAT WE'D BEEN WAITING FOR.
"IT CAUGHT THE SUN. LOOKING AT IT, YOU FELT LIKE IT **GLEAMED** WITH POSSIBILITIES.
"IT--"

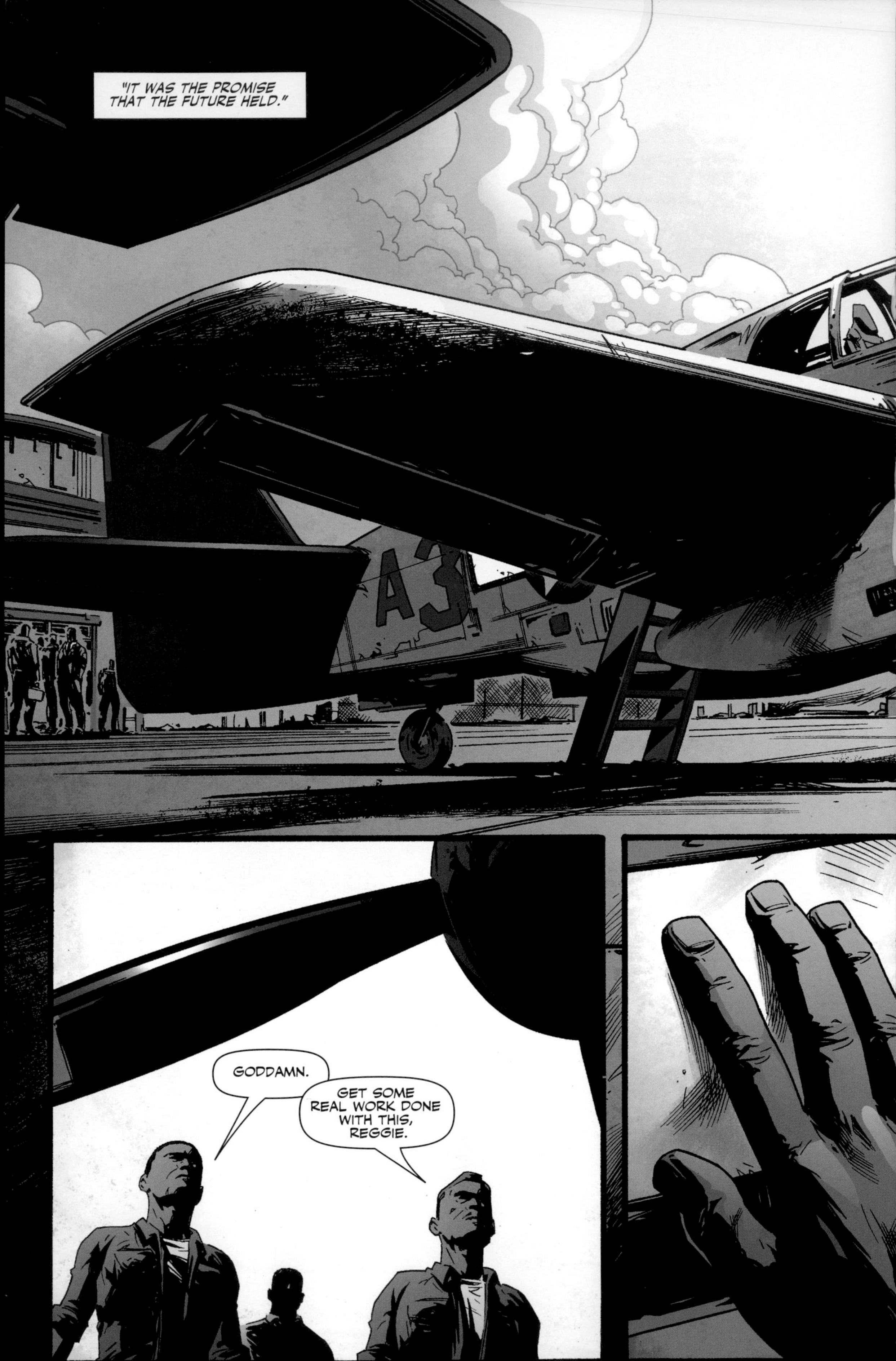
"IT WAS THE PROMISE THAT THE FUTURE HELD."
A3
GODDAMN.
GET SOME REAL WORK DONE WITH THIS, REGGIE.

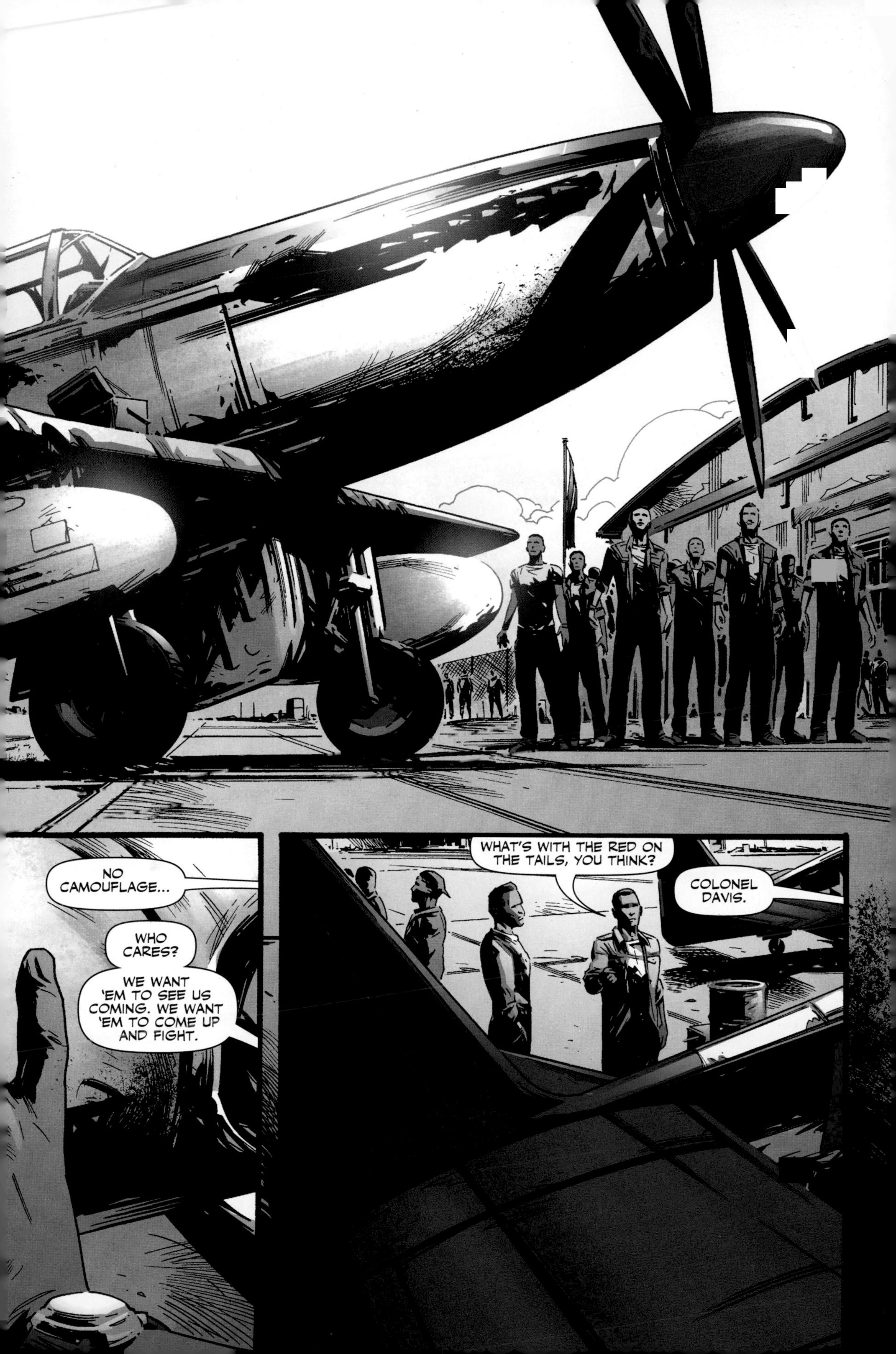
NO CAMOUFLAGE...
WHO CARES?
WE WANT 'EM TO SEE US COMING. WE WANT 'EM TO COME UP AND FIGHT.
WHAT'S WITH THE RED ON THE TAILS, YOU THINK?
COLONEL DAVIS.

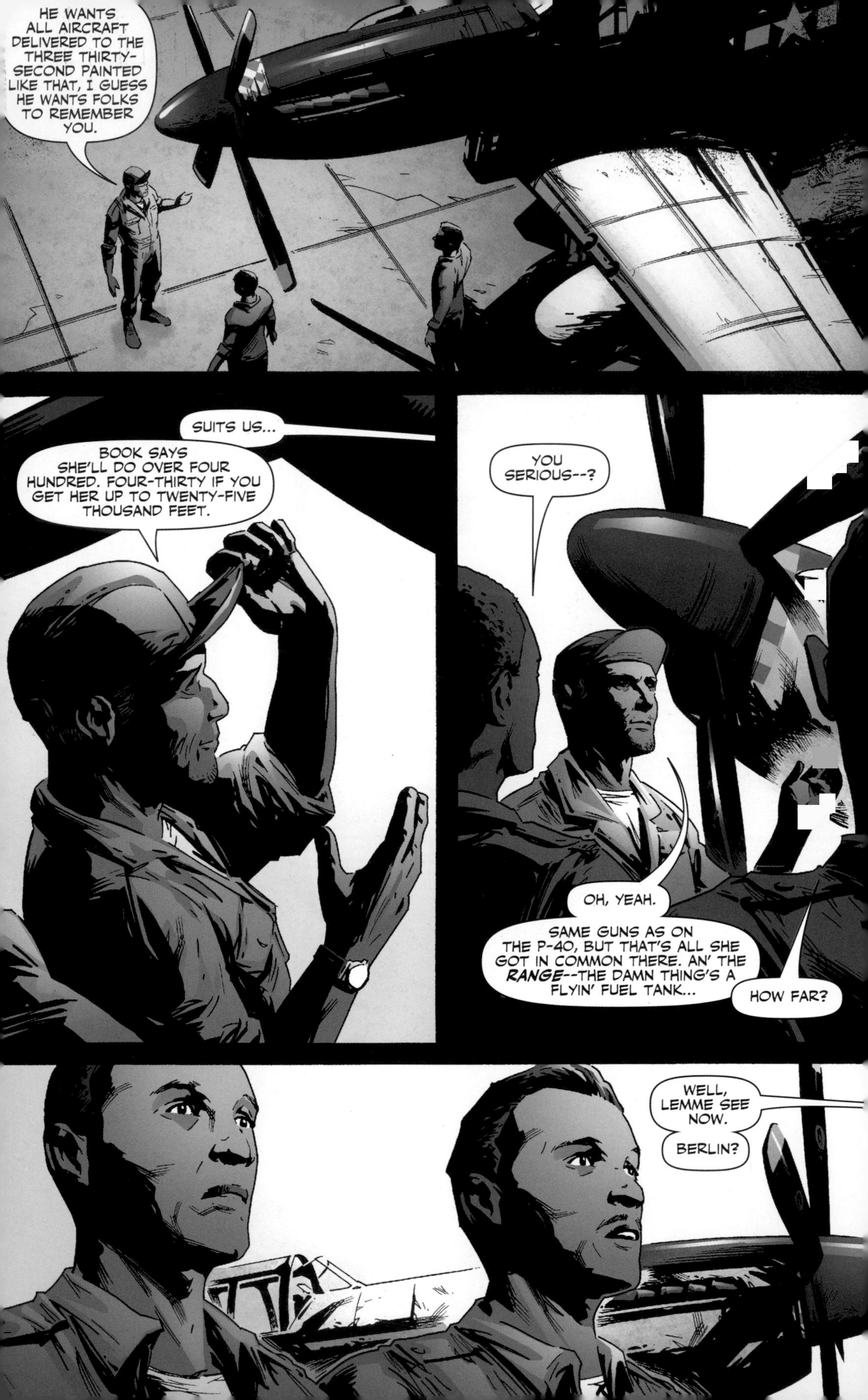
HE WANTS ALL AIRCRAFT DELIVERED TO THE THREE THIRTY-SECOND PAINTED LIKE THAT, I GUESS HE WANTS FOLKS TO REMEMBER YOU.
SUITS US...
BOOK SAYS SHE'LL DO OVER FOUR HUNDRED. FOUR-THIRTY IF YOU GET HER UP TO TWENTY-FIVE THOUSAND FEET.
YOU SERIOUS--?
OH, YEAH.
SAME GUNS AS ON THE P-40, BUT THAT'S ALL SHE GOT IN COMMON THERE. AN' THE RANGE--THE DAMN THING'S A FLYIN' FUEL TANK...
HOW FAR?
WELL, LEMME SEE NOW.
BERLIN?

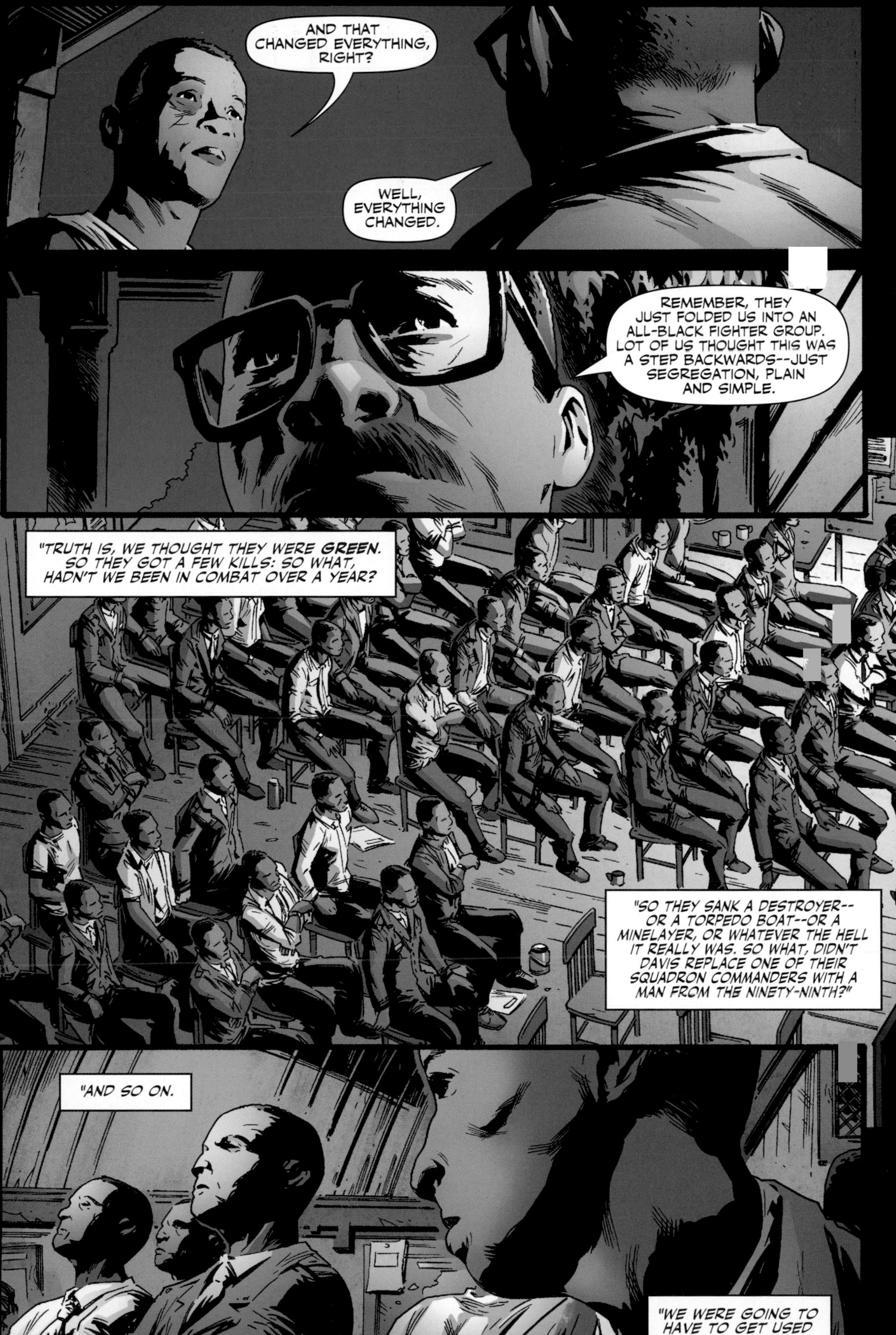
AND THAT CHANGED EVERYTHING, RIGHT?
WELL, EVERYTHING CHANGED.
REMEMBER, THEY JUST FOLDED US INTO AN ALL-BLACK FIGHTER GROUP. LOT OF US THOUGHT THIS WAS A STEP BACKWARDS--JUST SEGREGATION, PLAIN AND SIMPLE.
"TRUTH IS, WE THOUGHT THEY WERE GREEN. SO THEY GOT A FEW KILLS: SO WHAT, HADN'T WE BEEN IN COMBAT OVER A YEAR?
"SO THEY SANK A DESTROYER--OR A TORPEDO BOAT--OR A MINELAYER, OR WHATEVER THE HELL IT REALLY WAS. SO WHAT, DIDN'T DAVIS REPLACE ONE OF THEIR SQUADRON COMMANDERS WITH A MAN FROM THE NINETY-NINTH?"
"AND SO ON.
"WE WERE GOING TO HAVE TO GET USED TO EACH OTHER."

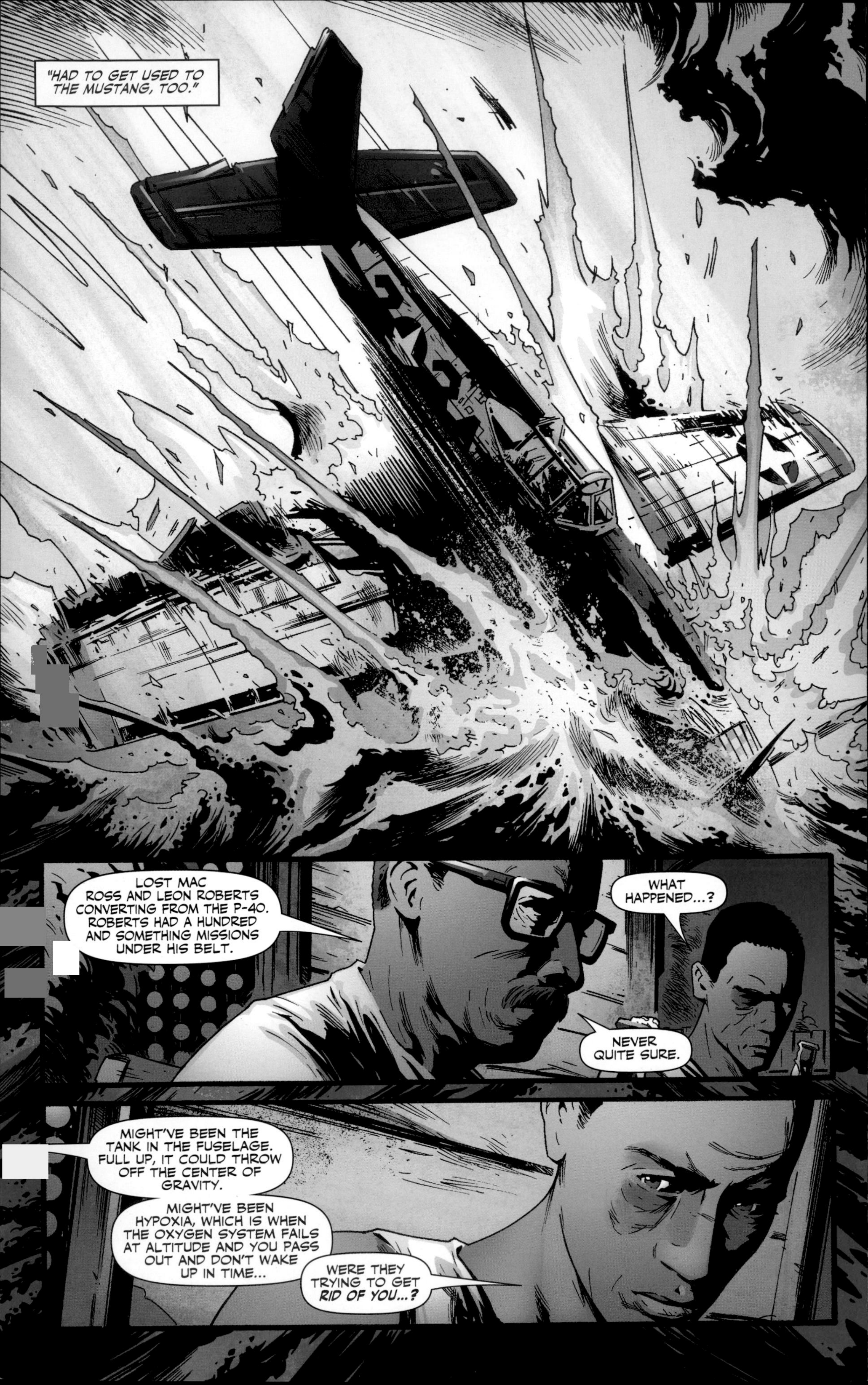
"HAD TO GET USED TO THE MUSTANG, TOO."
LOST MAC ROSS AND LEON ROBERTS CONVERTING FROM THE P-40. ROBERTS HAD A HUNDRED AND SOMETHING MISSIONS UNDER HIS BELT.
WHAT HAPPENED...?
NEVER QUITE SURE.
MIGHT'VE BEEN THE TANK IN THE FUSELAGE. FULL UP, IT COULD THROW OFF THE CENTER OF GRAVITY.
MIGHT'VE BEEN HYPOXIA, WHICH IS WHEN THE OXYGEN SYSTEM FAILS AT ALTITUDE AND YOU PASS OUT AND DON'T WAKE UP IN TIME...
WERE THEY TRYING TO GET *RID OF YOU...?*

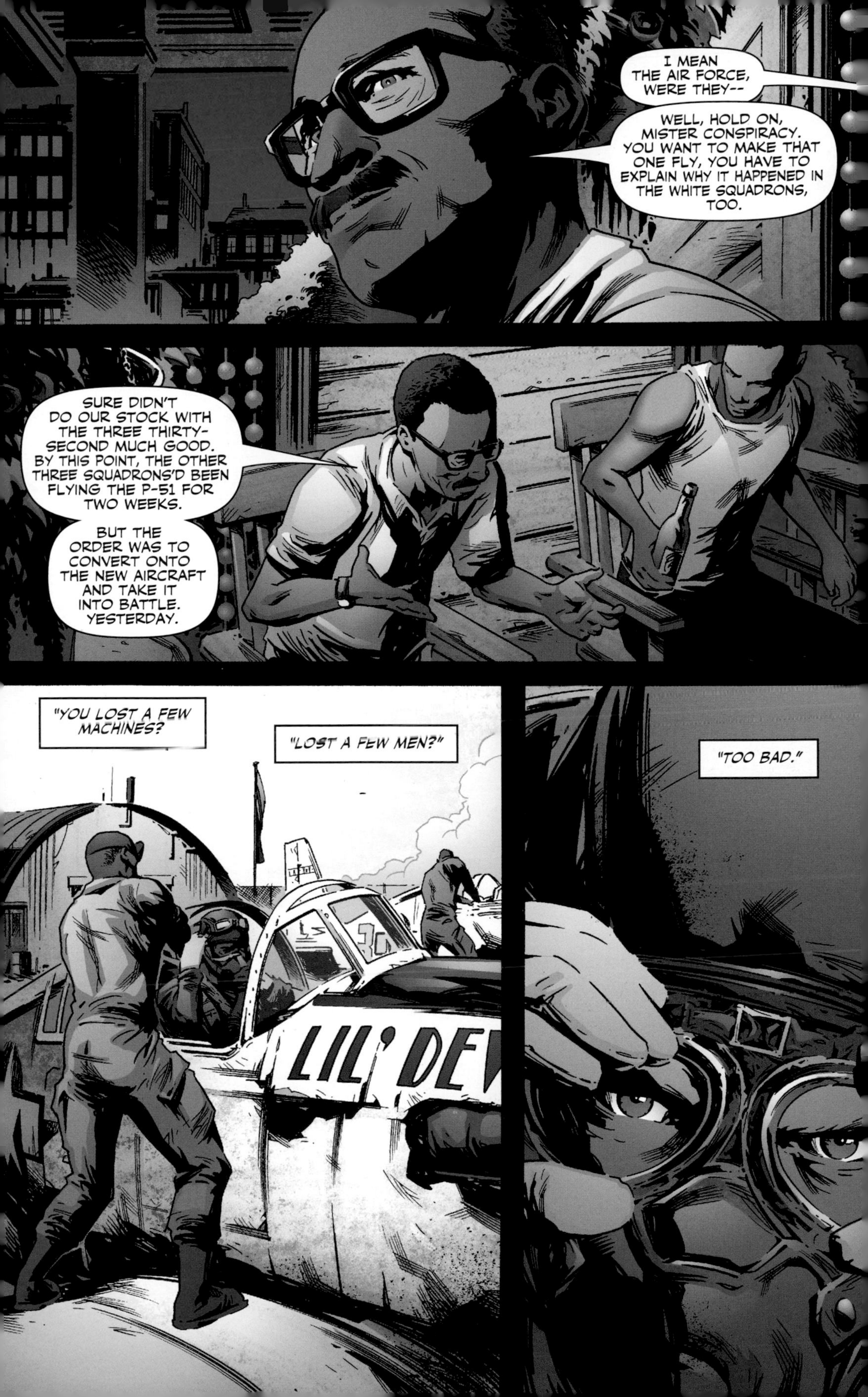
I MEAN THE AIR FORCE, WERE THEY--
WELL, HOLD ON, MISTER CONSPIRACY. YOU WANT TO MAKE THAT ONE FLY, YOU HAVE TO EXPLAIN WHY IT HAPPENED IN THE WHITE SQUADRONS, TOO.
SURE DIDN'T DO OUR STOCK WITH THE THREE THIRTY-SECOND MUCH GOOD. BY THIS POINT, THE OTHER THREE SQUADRONS'D BEEN FLYING THE P-51 FOR TWO WEEKS.
BUT THE ORDER WAS TO CONVERT ONTO THE NEW AIRCRAFT AND TAKE IT INTO BATTLE. YESTERDAY.
"YOU LOST A FEW MACHINES?
"LOST A FEW MEN?"
LIL' DEV
"TOO BAD."

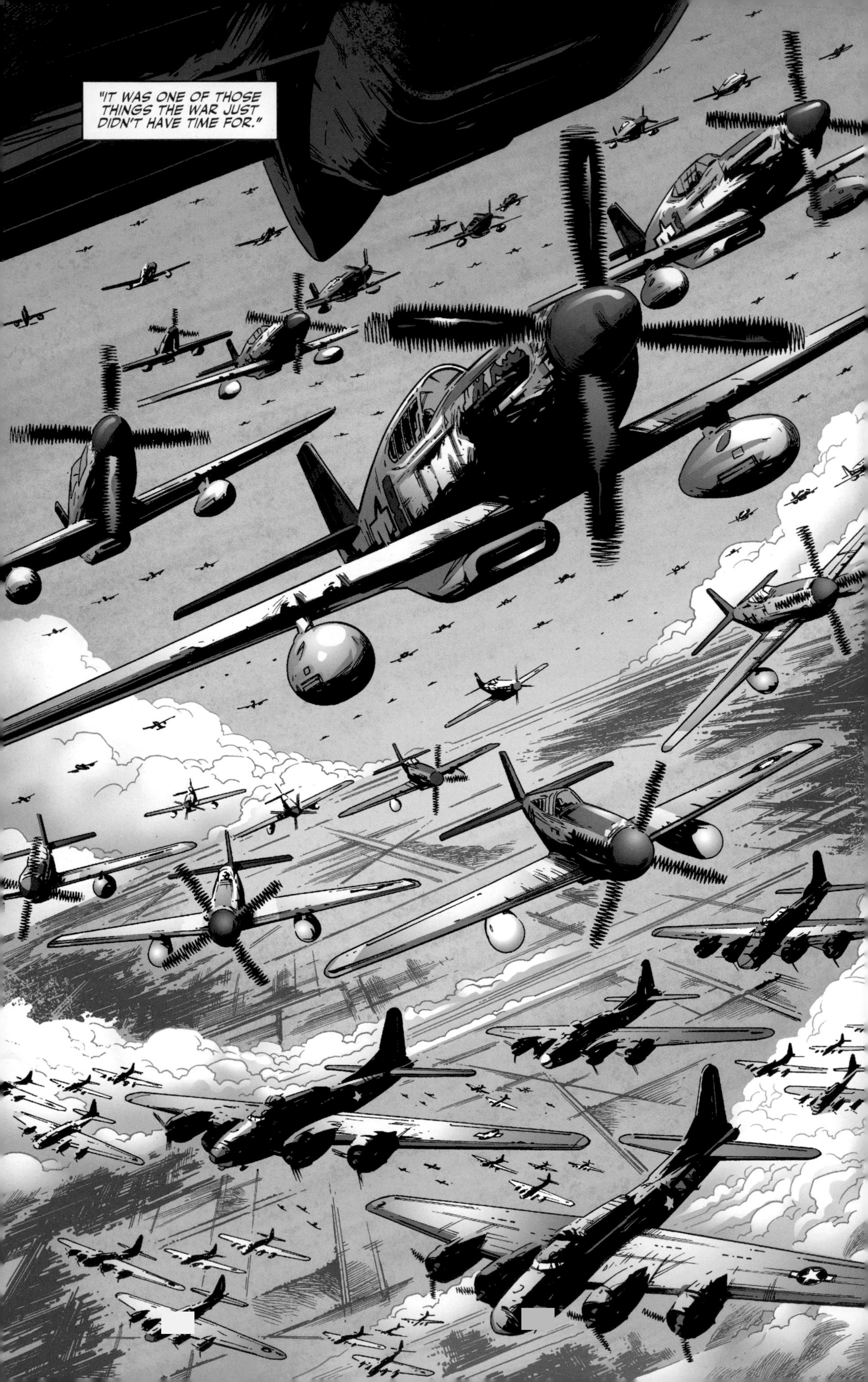
"IT WAS ONE OF THOSE THINGS THE WAR JUST DIDN'T HAVE TIME FOR."

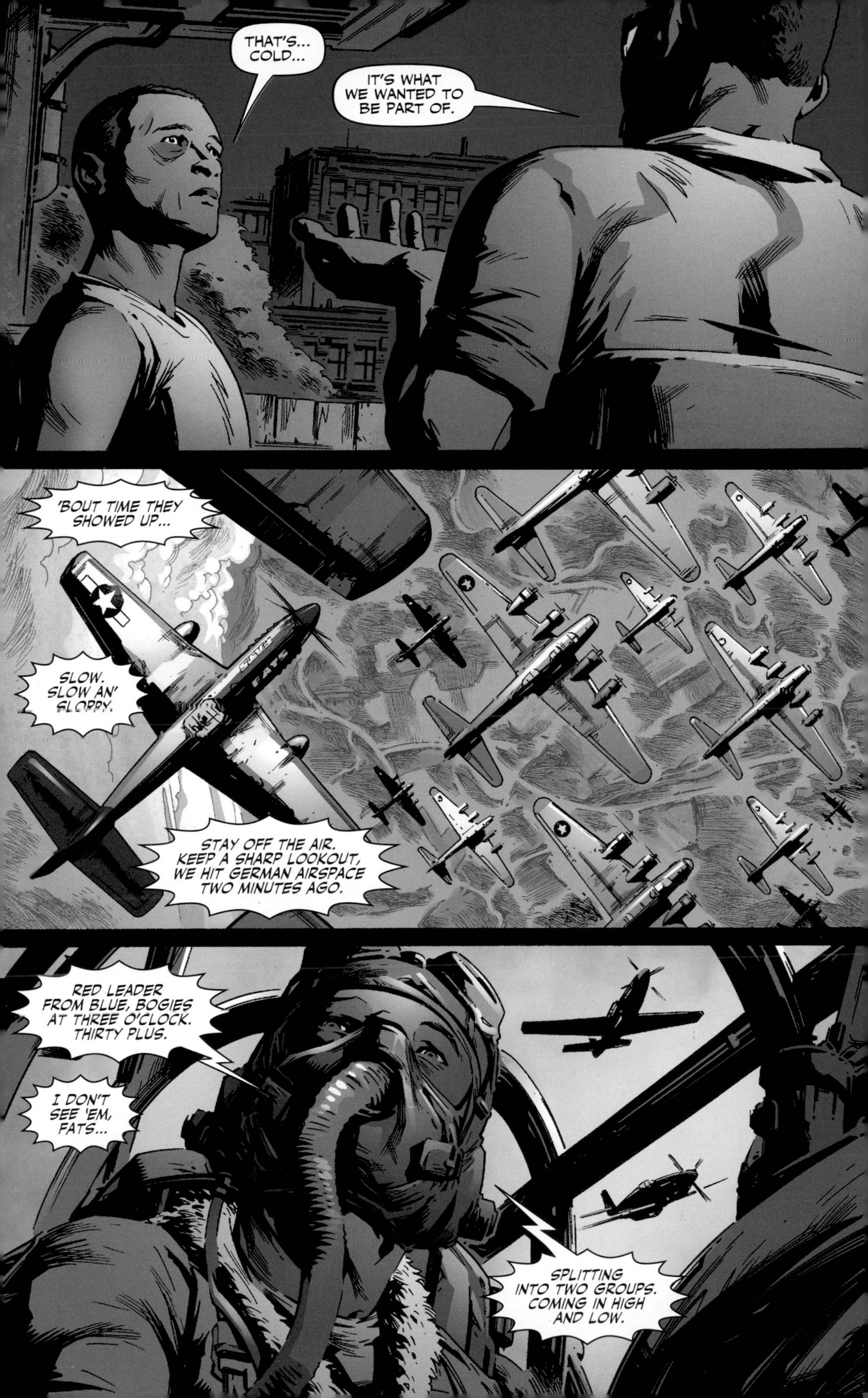
THAT'S... COLD...
IT'S WHAT WE WANTED TO BE PART OF.
'BOUT TIME THEY SHOWED UP...
SLOW. SLOW AN' SLOPPY.
STAY OFF THE AIR. KEEP A SHARP LOOKOUT, WE HIT GERMAN AIRSPACE TWO MINUTES AGO.
RED LEADER FROM BLUE, BOGIES AT THREE O'CLOCK. THIRTY PLUS.
I DON'T SEE 'EM, FATS...
SPLITTING INTO TWO GROUPS. COMING IN HIGH AND LOW.

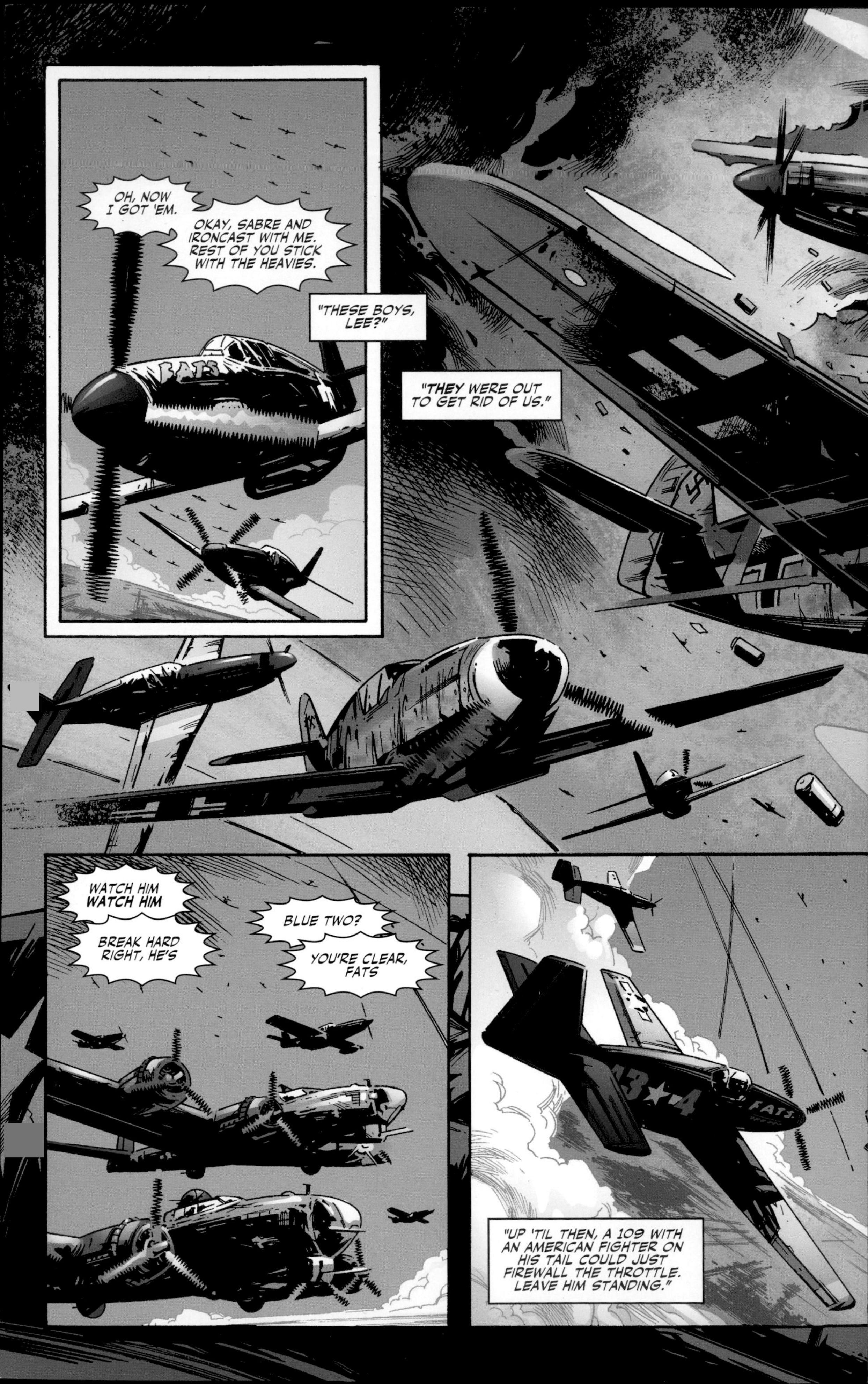
OH, NOW I GOT 'EM.
OKAY, SABRE AND IRONCAST WITH ME. REST OF YOU STICK WITH THE HEAVIES.
"THESE BOYS, LEE?"
"THEY WERE OUT TO GET RID OF US."
FATS
WATCH HIM WATCH HIM
BREAK HARD RIGHT, HE'S
BLUE TWO?
YOU'RE CLEAR, FATS
"UP 'TIL THEN, A 109 WITH AN AMERICAN FIGHTER ON HIS TAIL COULD JUST FIREWALL THE THROTTLE. LEAVE HIM STANDING."

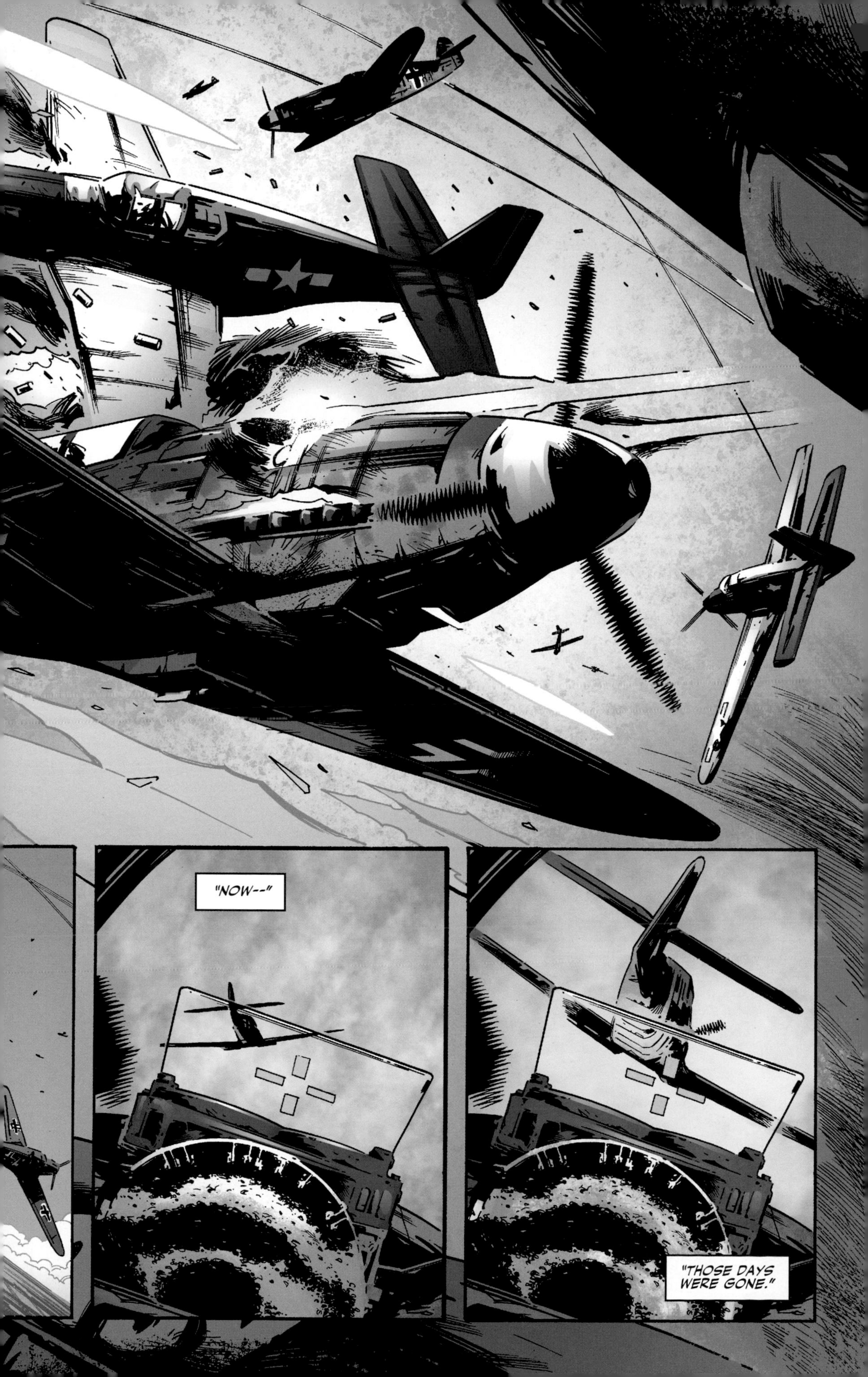
"NOW--"
"THOSE DAYS WERE GONE."

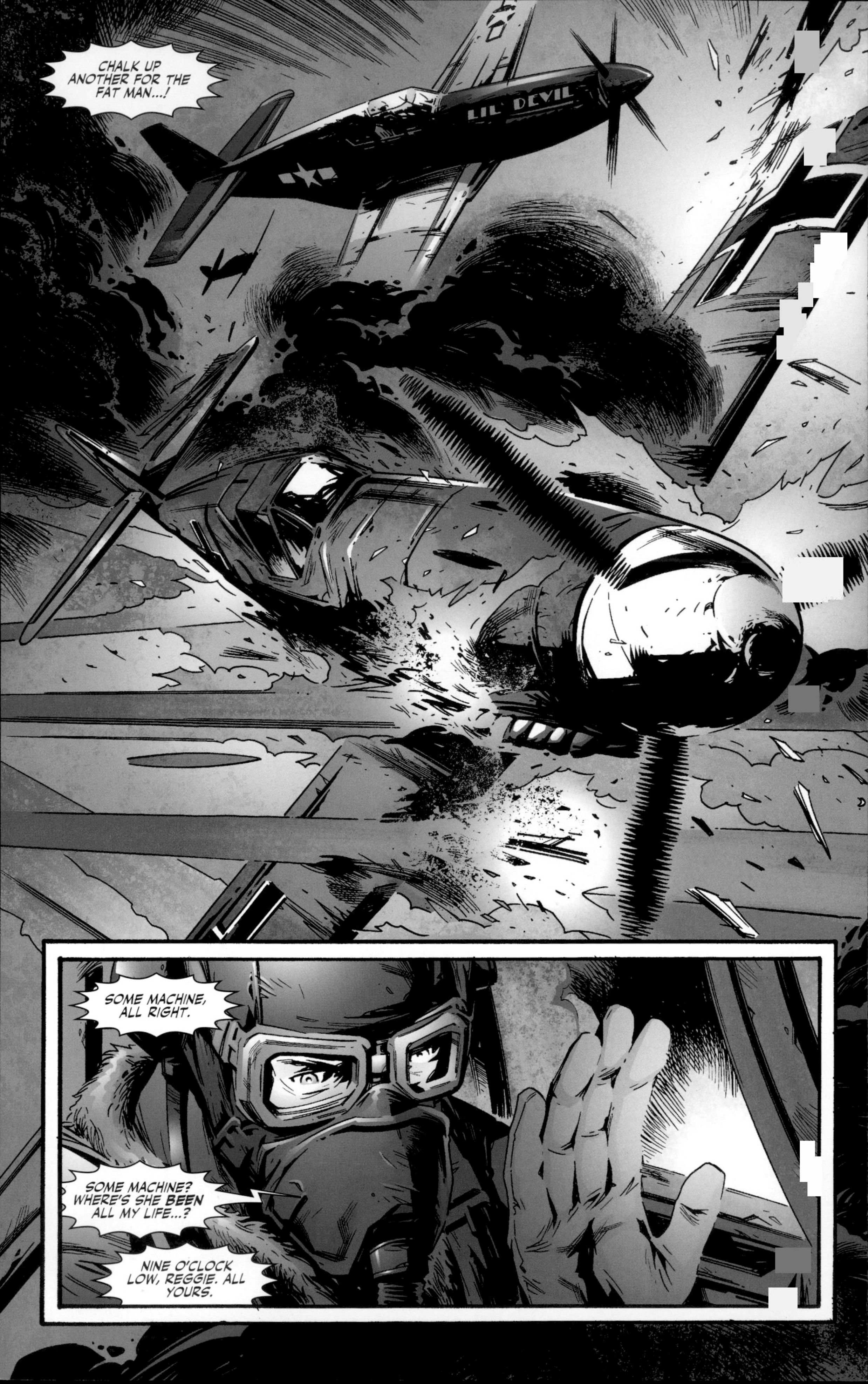
CHALK UP ANOTHER FOR THE FAT MAN...!
LIL' DEVIL
SOME MACHINE, ALL RIGHT.
SOME MACHINE? WHERE'S SHE BEEN ALL MY LIFE...?
NINE O'CLOCK LOW, REGGIE. ALL YOURS.

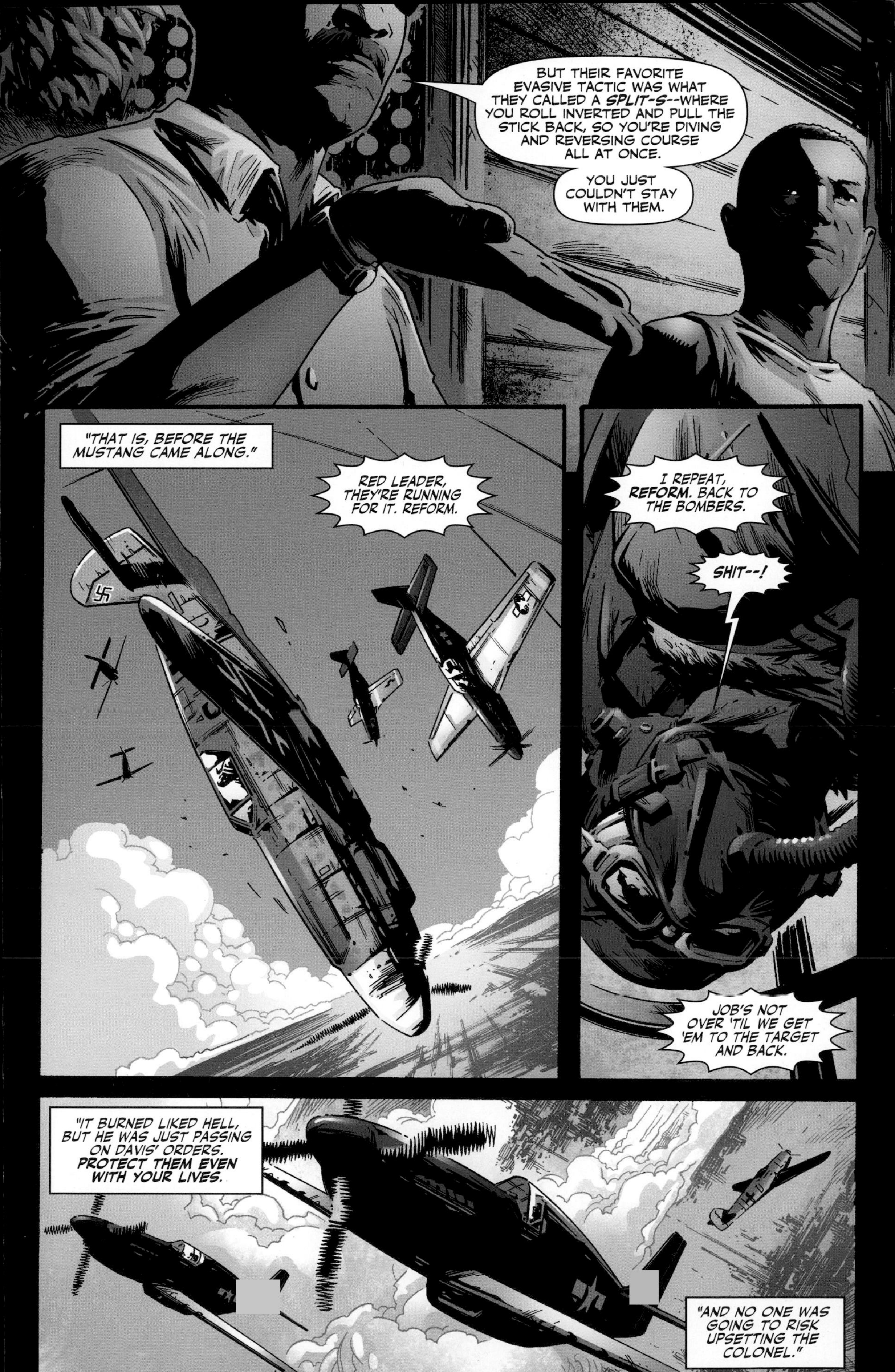
BUT THEIR FAVORITE EVASIVE TACTIC WAS WHAT THEY CALLED A SPLIT-S--WHERE YOU ROLL INVERTED AND PULL THE STICK BACK, SO YOU'RE DIVING AND REVERSING COURSE ALL AT ONCE.
YOU JUST COULDN'T STAY WITH THEM.
"THAT IS, BEFORE THE MUSTANG CAME ALONG."
RED LEADER, THEY'RE RUNNING FOR IT. REFORM.
I REPEAT, REFORM. BACK TO THE BOMBERS.
SHIT--!
JOB'S NOT OVER 'TIL WE GET 'EM TO THE TARGET AND BACK.
"IT BURNED LIKED HELL, BUT HE WAS JUST PASSING ON DAVIS' ORDERS. PROTECT THEM EVEN WITH YOUR LIVES.
"AND NO ONE WAS GOING TO RISK UPSETTING THE COLONEL."

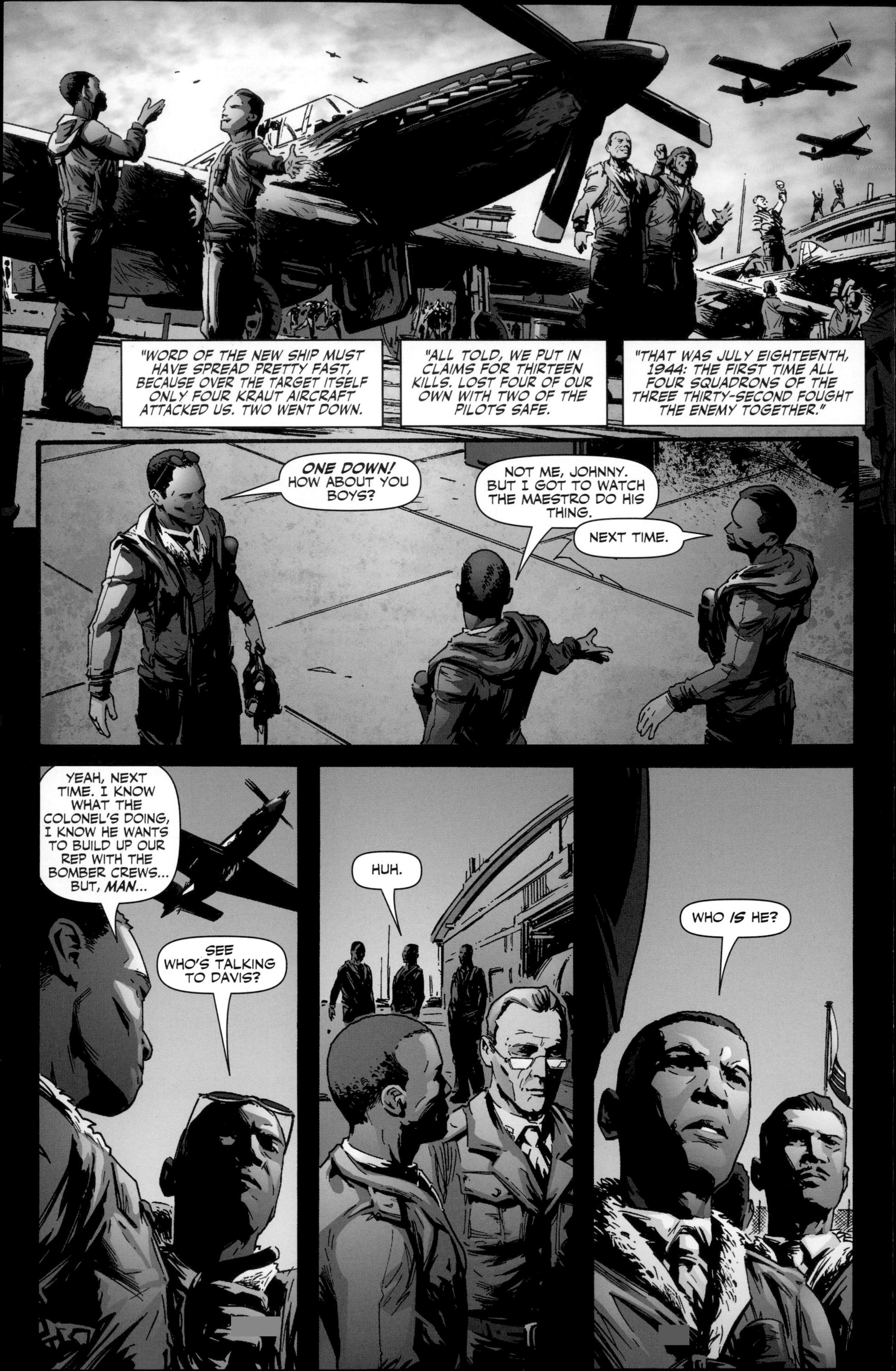
"WORD OF THE NEW SHIP MUST HAVE SPREAD PRETTY FAST, BECAUSE OVER THE TARGET ITSELF ONLY FOUR KRAUT AIRCRAFT ATTACKED US. TWO WENT DOWN.
"ALL TOLD, WE PUT IN CLAIMS FOR THIRTEEN KILLS. LOST FOUR OF OUR OWN WITH TWO OF THE PILOTS SAFE.
"THAT WAS JULY EIGHTEENTH, 1944: THE FIRST TIME ALL FOUR SQUADRONS OF THE THREE THIRTY-SECOND FOUGHT THE ENEMY TOGETHER."
ONE DOWN! HOW ABOUT YOU BOYS?
NOT ME, JOHNNY. BUT I GOT TO WATCH THE MAESTRO DO HIS THING.
NEXT TIME.
YEAH, NEXT TIME. I KNOW WHAT THE COLONEL'S DOING, I KNOW HE WANTS TO BUILD UP OUR REP WITH THE BOMBER CREWS... BUT, MAN...
SEE WHO'S TALKING TO DAVIS?
HUH.
WHO IS HE?

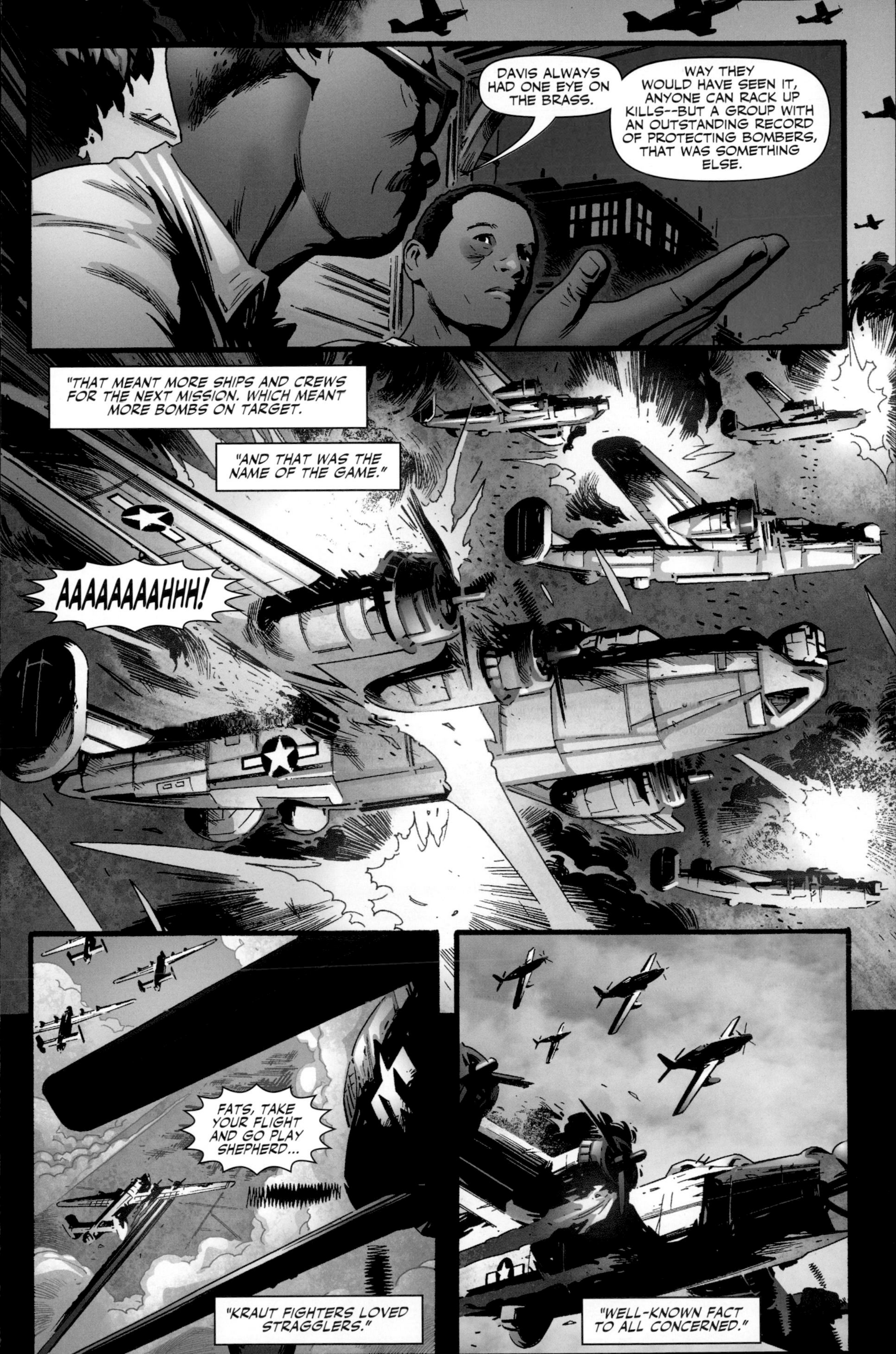
DAVIS ALWAYS HAD ONE EYE ON THE BRASS.
WAY THEY WOULD HAVE SEEN IT, ANYONE CAN RACK UP KILLS--BUT A GROUP WITH AN OUTSTANDING RECORD OF PROTECTING BOMBERS, THAT WAS SOMETHING ELSE.
"THAT MEANT MORE SHIPS AND CREWS FOR THE NEXT MISSION. WHICH MEANT MORE BOMBS ON TARGET.
"AND THAT WAS THE NAME OF THE GAME."
AAAAAAAAHHH!
FATS, TAKE YOUR FLIGHT AND GO PLAY SHEPHERD...
"KRAUT FIGHTERS LOVED STRAGGLERS."
"WELL-KNOWN FACT TO ALL CONCERNED."

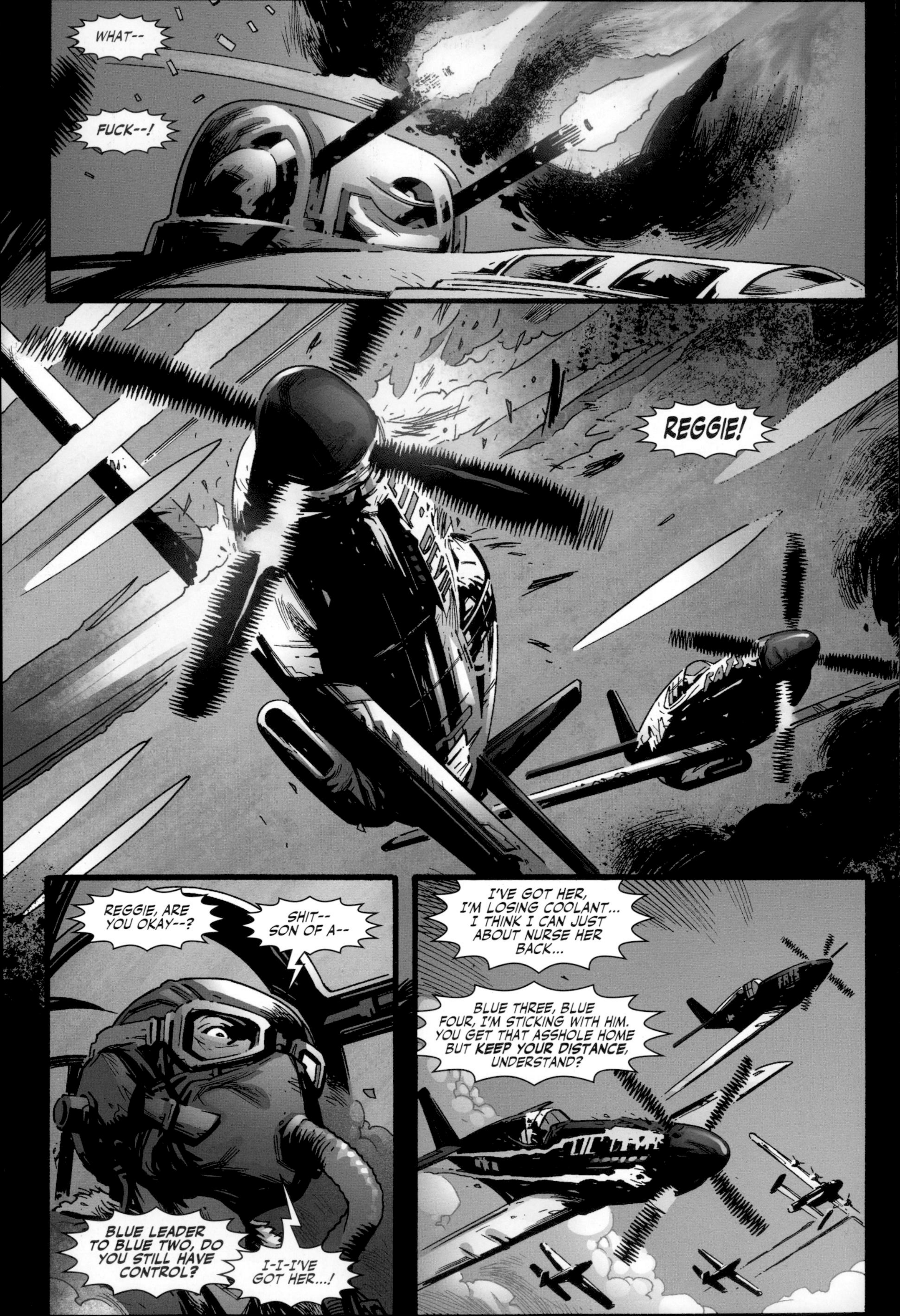
WHAT--
FUCK--!
REGGIE!
REGGIE, ARE YOU OKAY--?
SHIT-- SON OF A--
BLUE LEADER TO BLUE TWO, DO YOU STILL HAVE CONTROL?
I-I-I'VE GOT HER...!
I'VE GOT HER, I'M LOSING COOLANT... I THINK I CAN JUST ABOUT NURSE HER BACK...
BLUE THREE, BLUE FOUR, I'M STICKING WITH HIM. YOU GET THAT ASSHOLE HOME BUT KEEP YOUR DISTANCE, UNDERSTAND?

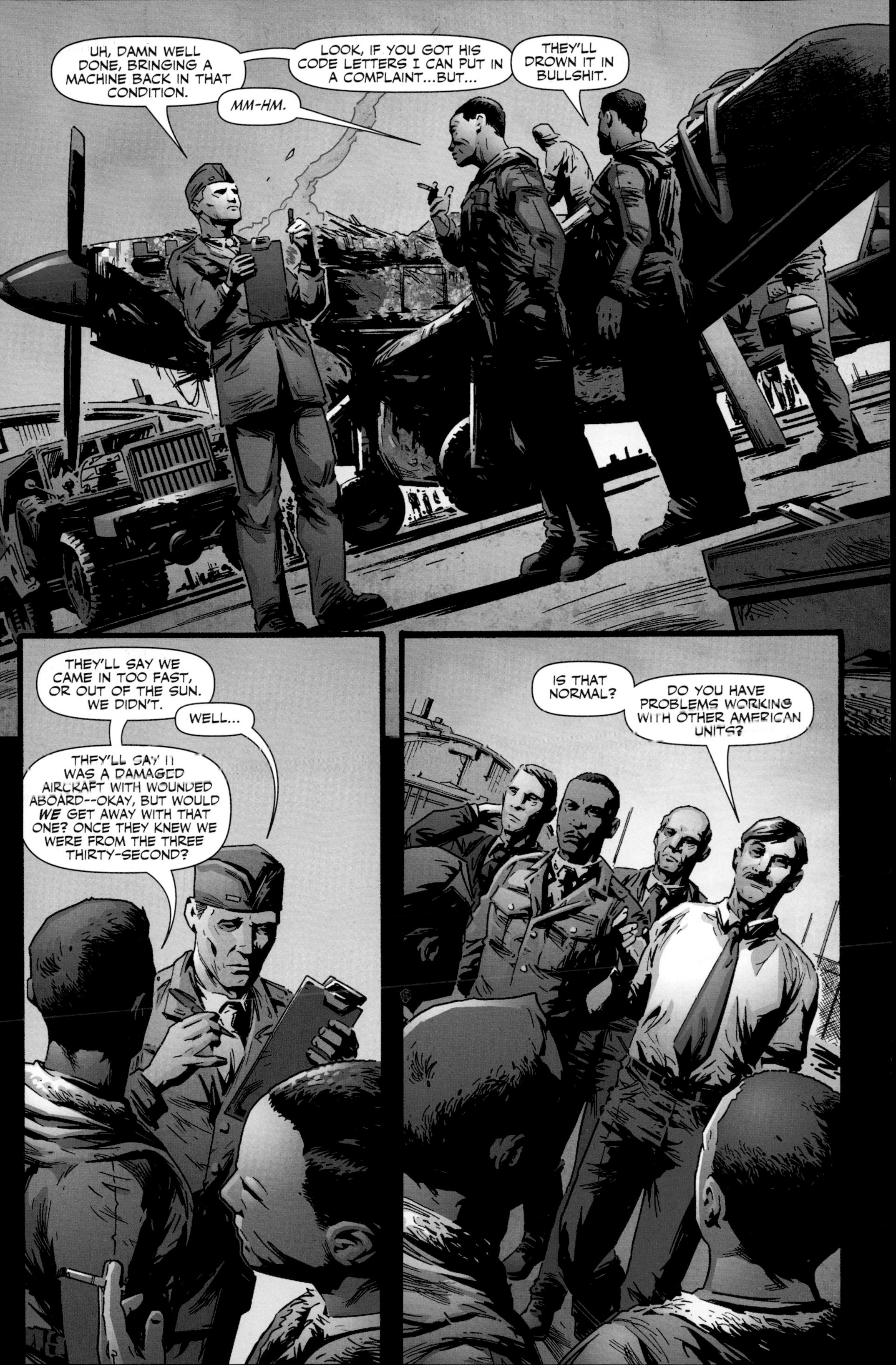
UH, DAMN WELL DONE, BRINGING A MACHINE BACK IN THAT CONDITION.
LOOK, IF YOU GOT HIS CODE LETTERS I CAN PUT IN A COMPLAINT...BUT...
MM-HM.
THEY'LL DROWN IT IN BULLSHIT.
THEY'LL SAY WE CAME IN TOO FAST, OR OUT OF THE SUN. WE DIDN'T.
WELL...
THEY'LL SAY IT WAS A DAMAGED AIRCRAFT WITH WOUNDED ABOARD--OKAY, BUT WOULD WE GET AWAY WITH THAT ONE? ONCE THEY KNEW WE WERE FROM THE THREE THIRTY-SECOND?
IS THAT NORMAL?
DO YOU HAVE PROBLEMS WORKING WITH OTHER AMERICAN UNITS?

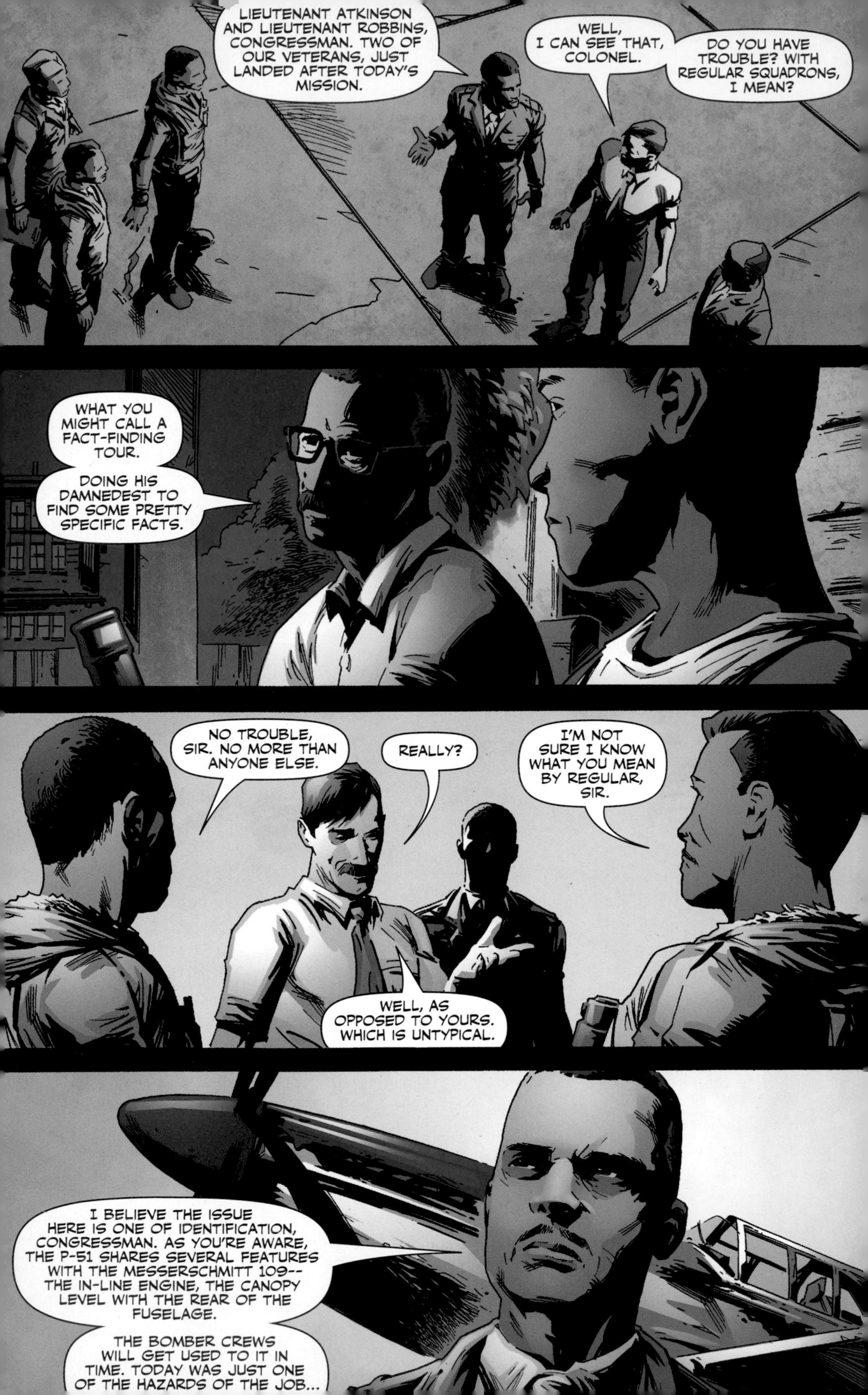
LIEUTENANT ATKINSON AND LIEUTENANT ROBBINS, CONGRESSMAN. TWO OF OUR VETERANS, JUST LANDED AFTER TODAY'S MISSION.
WELL, I CAN SEE THAT, COLONEL.
DO YOU HAVE TROUBLE? WITH REGULAR SQUADRONS, I MEAN?
WHAT YOU MIGHT CALL A FACT-FINDING TOUR.
DOING HIS DAMNEDEST TO FIND SOME PRETTY SPECIFIC FACTS.
NO TROUBLE, SIR. NO MORE THAN ANYONE ELSE.
REALLY?
I'M NOT SURE I KNOW WHAT YOU MEAN BY REGULAR, SIR.
WELL, AS OPPOSED TO YOURS. WHICH IS UNTYPICAL.
I BELIEVE THE ISSUE HERE IS ONE OF IDENTIFICATION, CONGRESSMAN. AS YOU'RE AWARE, THE P-51 SHARES SEVERAL FEATURES WITH THE MESSERSCHMITT 109-- THE IN-LINE ENGINE, THE CANOPY LEVEL WITH THE REAR OF THE FUSELAGE.
THE BOMBER CREWS WILL GET USED TO IT IN TIME. TODAY WAS JUST ONE OF THE HAZARDS OF THE JOB...

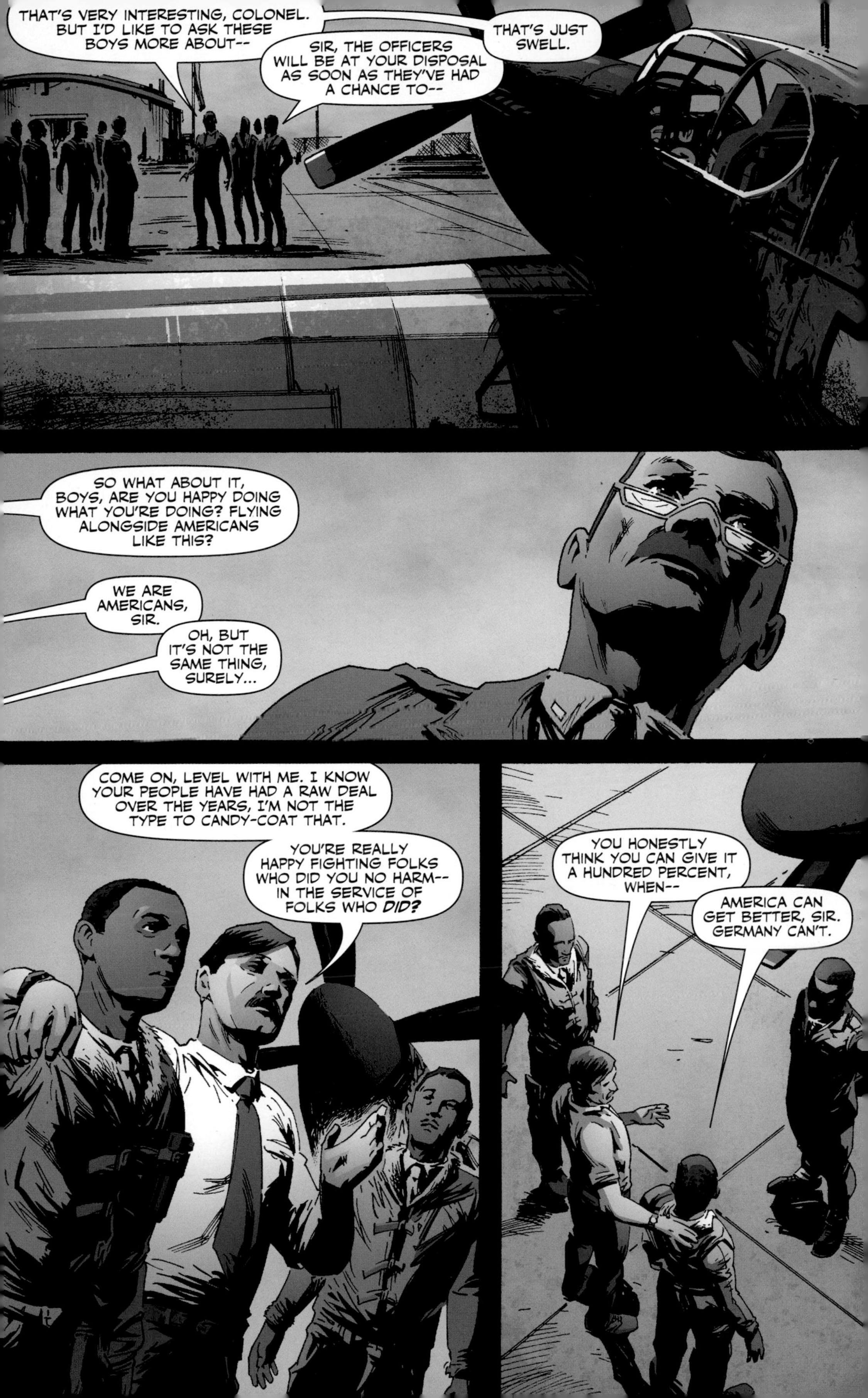
THAT'S VERY INTERESTING, COLONEL. BUT I'D LIKE TO ASK THESE BOYS MORE ABOUT--
SIR, THE OFFICERS WILL BE AT YOUR DISPOSAL AS SOON AS THEY'VE HAD A CHANCE TO--
THAT'S JUST SWELL.
SO WHAT ABOUT IT, BOYS, ARE YOU HAPPY DOING WHAT YOU'RE DOING? FLYING ALONGSIDE AMERICANS LIKE THIS?
WE ARE AMERICANS, SIR.
OH, BUT IT'S NOT THE SAME THING, SURELY...
COME ON, LEVEL WITH ME. I KNOW YOUR PEOPLE HAVE HAD A RAW DEAL OVER THE YEARS, I'M NOT THE TYPE TO CANDY-COAT THAT.
YOU'RE REALLY HAPPY FIGHTING FOLKS WHO DID YOU NO HARM-- IN THE SERVICE OF FOLKS WHO *DID?*
YOU HONESTLY THINK YOU CAN GIVE IT A HUNDRED PERCENT, WHEN--
AMERICA CAN GET BETTER, SIR. GERMANY CAN'T.

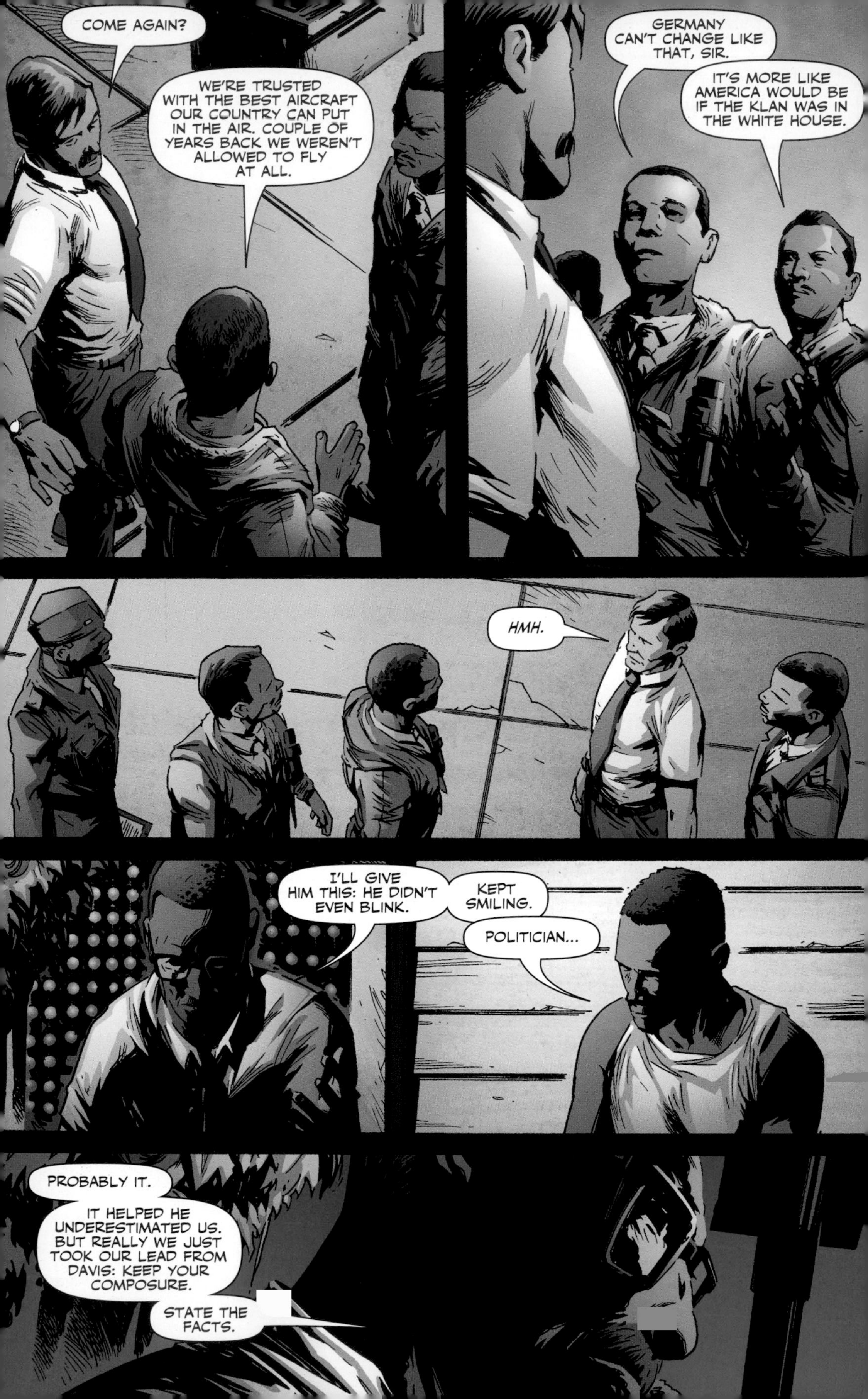
COME AGAIN?
WE'RE TRUSTED WITH THE BEST AIRCRAFT OUR COUNTRY CAN PUT IN THE AIR. COUPLE OF YEARS BACK WE WEREN'T ALLOWED TO FLY AT ALL.
GERMANY CAN'T CHANGE LIKE THAT, SIR.
IT'S MORE LIKE AMERICA WOULD BE IF THE KLAN WAS IN THE WHITE HOUSE.
HMH.
I'LL GIVE HIM THIS: HE DIDN'T EVEN BLINK.
KEPT SMILING.
POLITICIAN...
PROBABLY IT.
IT HELPED HE UNDERESTIMATED US. BUT REALLY WE JUST TOOK OUR LEAD FROM DAVIS: KEEP YOUR COMPOSURE.
STATE THE FACTS.

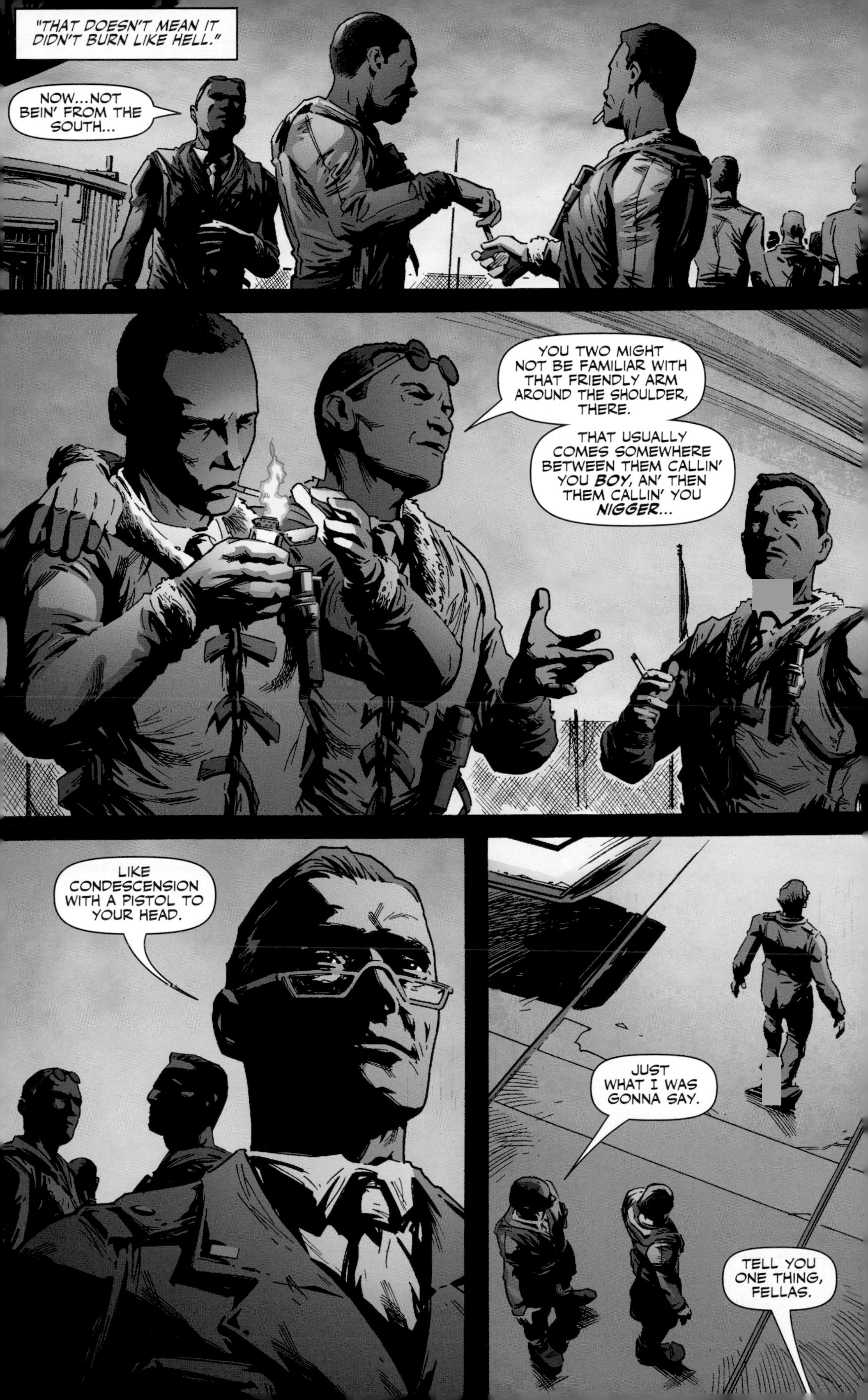
"THAT DOESN'T MEAN IT DIDN'T BURN LIKE HELL."
NOW...NOT BEIN' FROM THE SOUTH...
YOU TWO MIGHT NOT BE FAMILIAR WITH THAT FRIENDLY ARM AROUND THE SHOULDER, THERE.
THAT USUALLY COMES SOMEWHERE BETWEEN THEM CALLIN' YOU *BOY*, AN' THEN THEM CALLIN' YOU *NIGGER*...
LIKE CONDESCENSION WITH A PISTOL TO YOUR HEAD.
JUST WHAT I WAS GONNA SAY.
TELL YOU ONE THING, FELLAS.

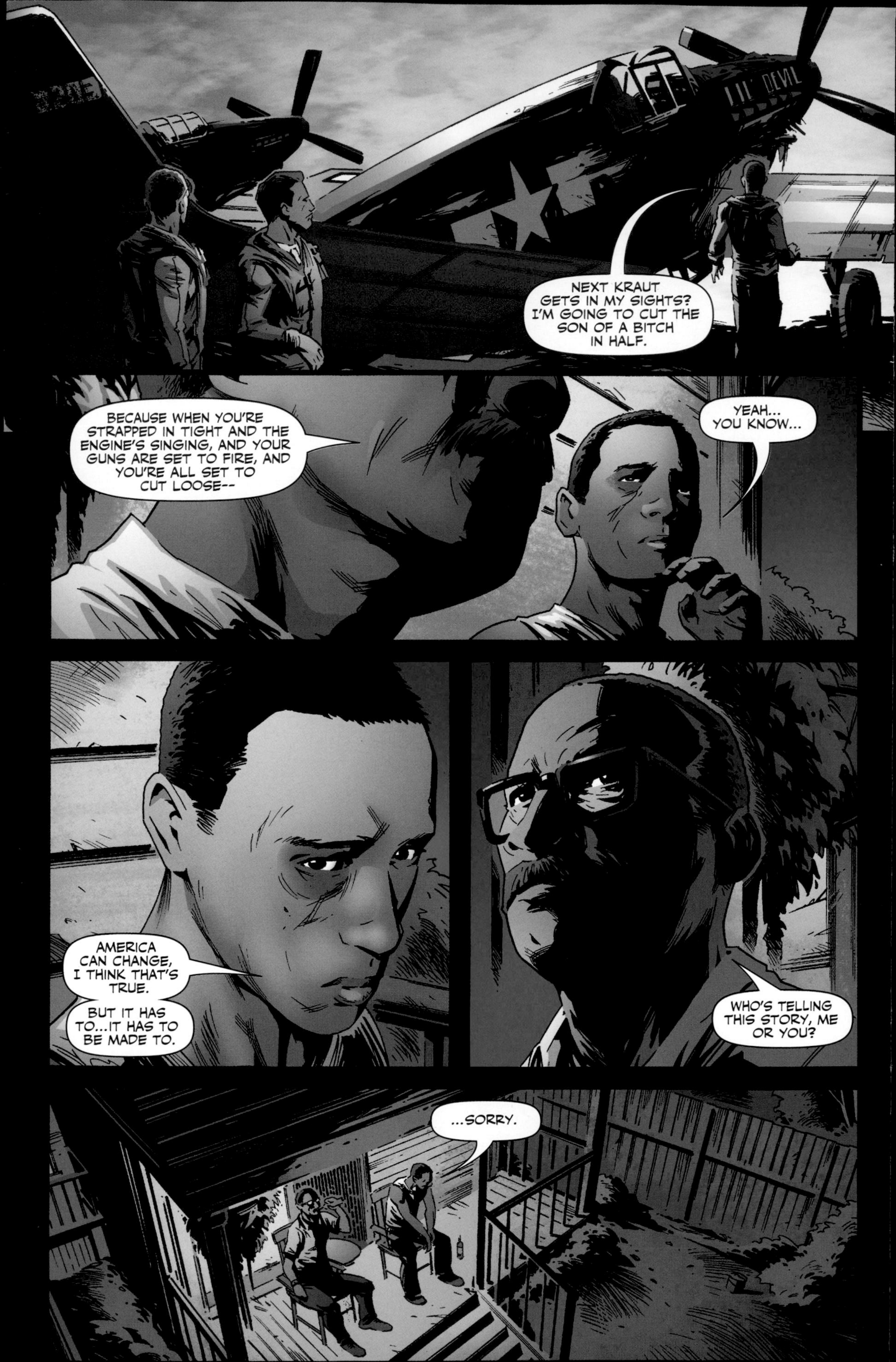
LIL' DEVIL
NEXT KRAUT GETS IN MY SIGHTS? I'M GOING TO CUT THE SON OF A BITCH IN HALF.
BECAUSE WHEN YOU'RE STRAPPED IN TIGHT AND THE ENGINE'S SINGING, AND YOUR GUNS ARE SET TO FIRE, AND YOU'RE ALL SET TO CUT LOOSE--
YEAH... YOU KNOW...
AMERICA CAN CHANGE, I THINK THAT'S TRUE.
BUT IT HAS TO...IT HAS TO BE MADE TO.
WHO'S TELLING THIS STORY, ME OR YOU?
...SORRY.

5 : RIDING HERD

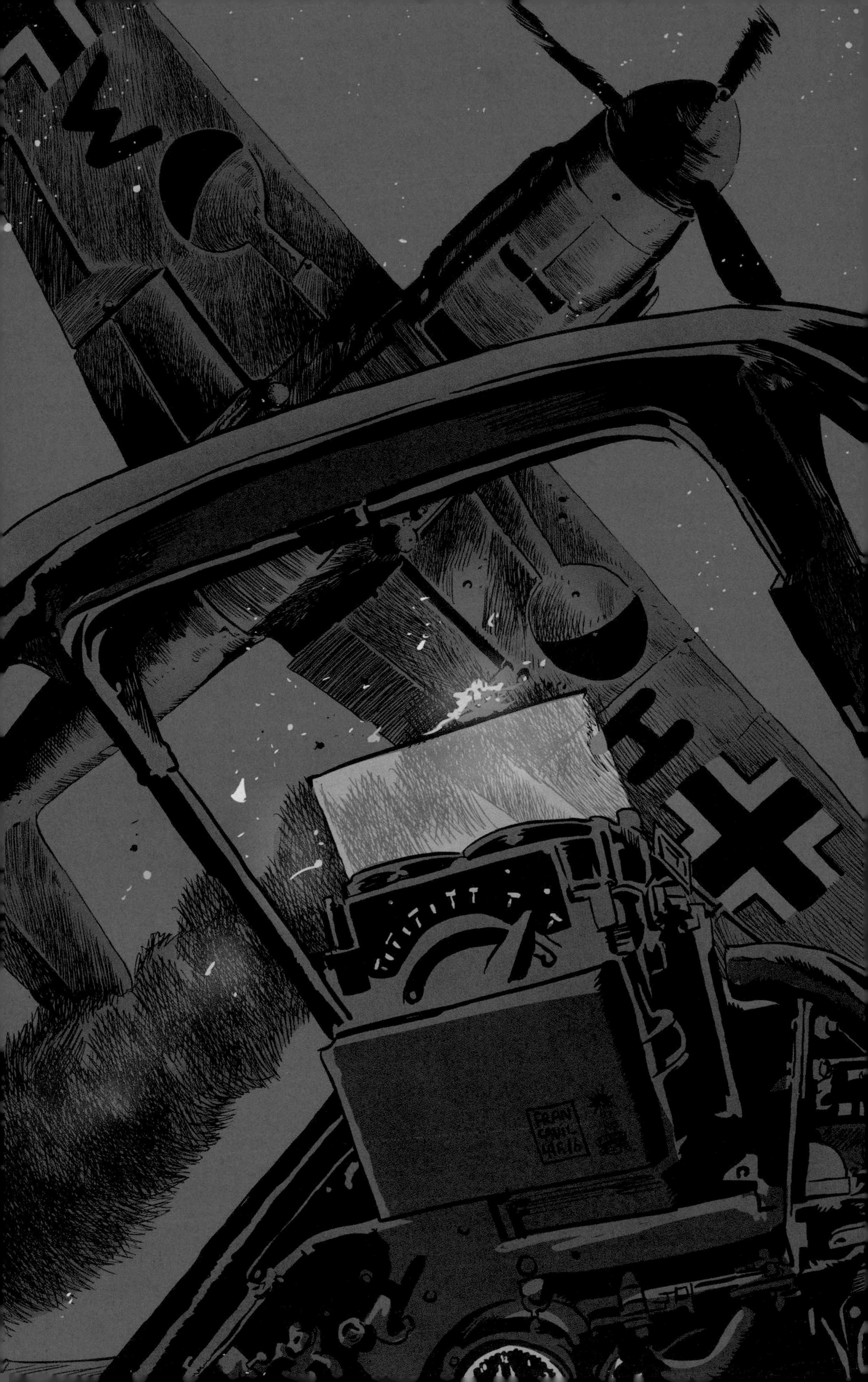

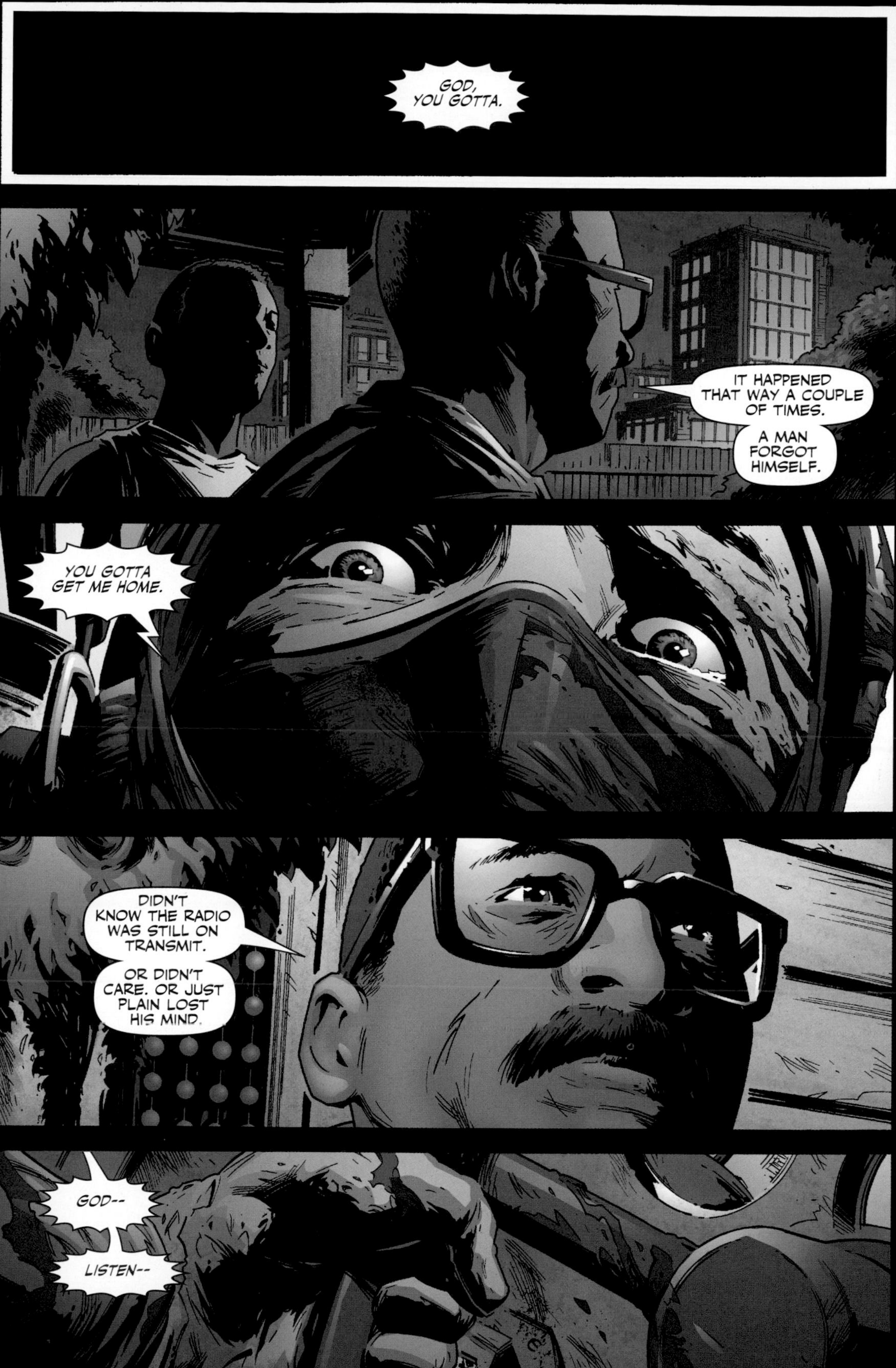
GOD, YOU GOTTA.
IT HAPPENED THAT WAY A COUPLE OF TIMES.
A MAN FORGOT HIMSELF.
YOU GOTTA GET ME HOME.
DIDN'T KNOW THE RADIO WAS STILL ON TRANSMIT.
OR DIDN'T CARE. OR JUST PLAIN LOST HIS MIND.
GOD--
LISTEN--

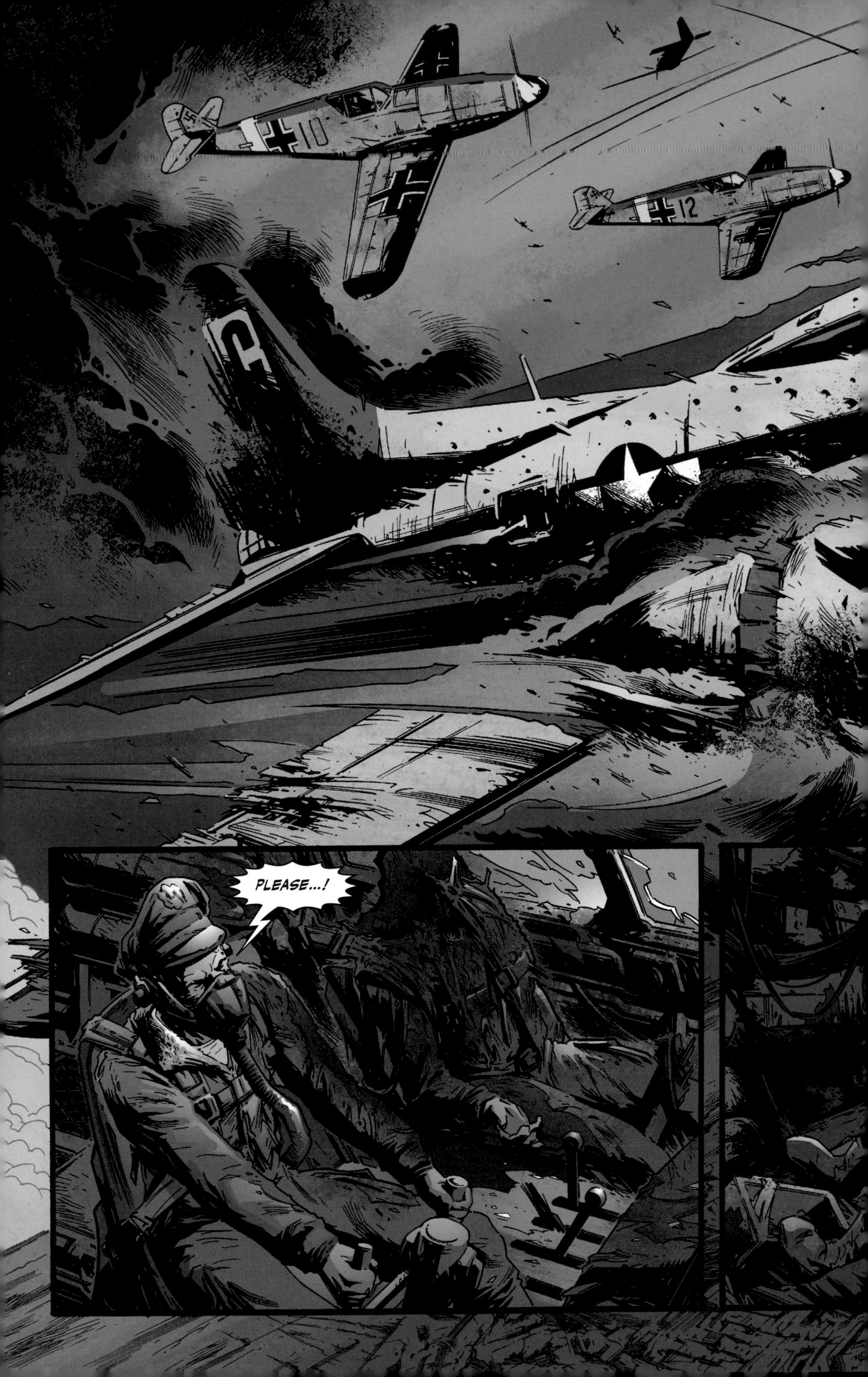
PLEASE...!

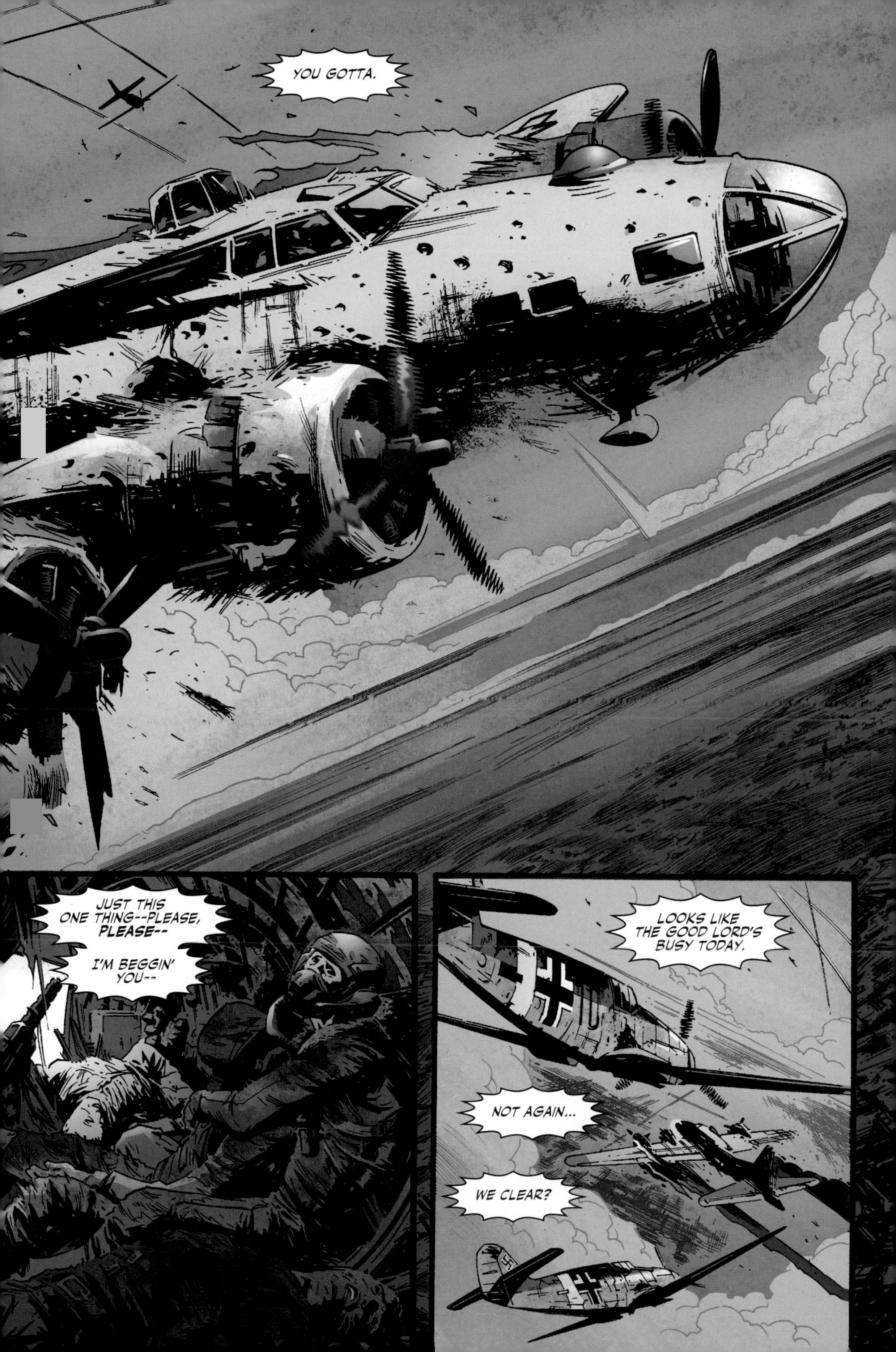
YOU GOTTA.
JUST THIS ONE THING--PLEASE, PLEASE--
I'M BEGGIN' YOU--
LOOKS LIKE THE GOOD LORD'S BUSY TODAY.
NOT AGAIN...
WE CLEAR?

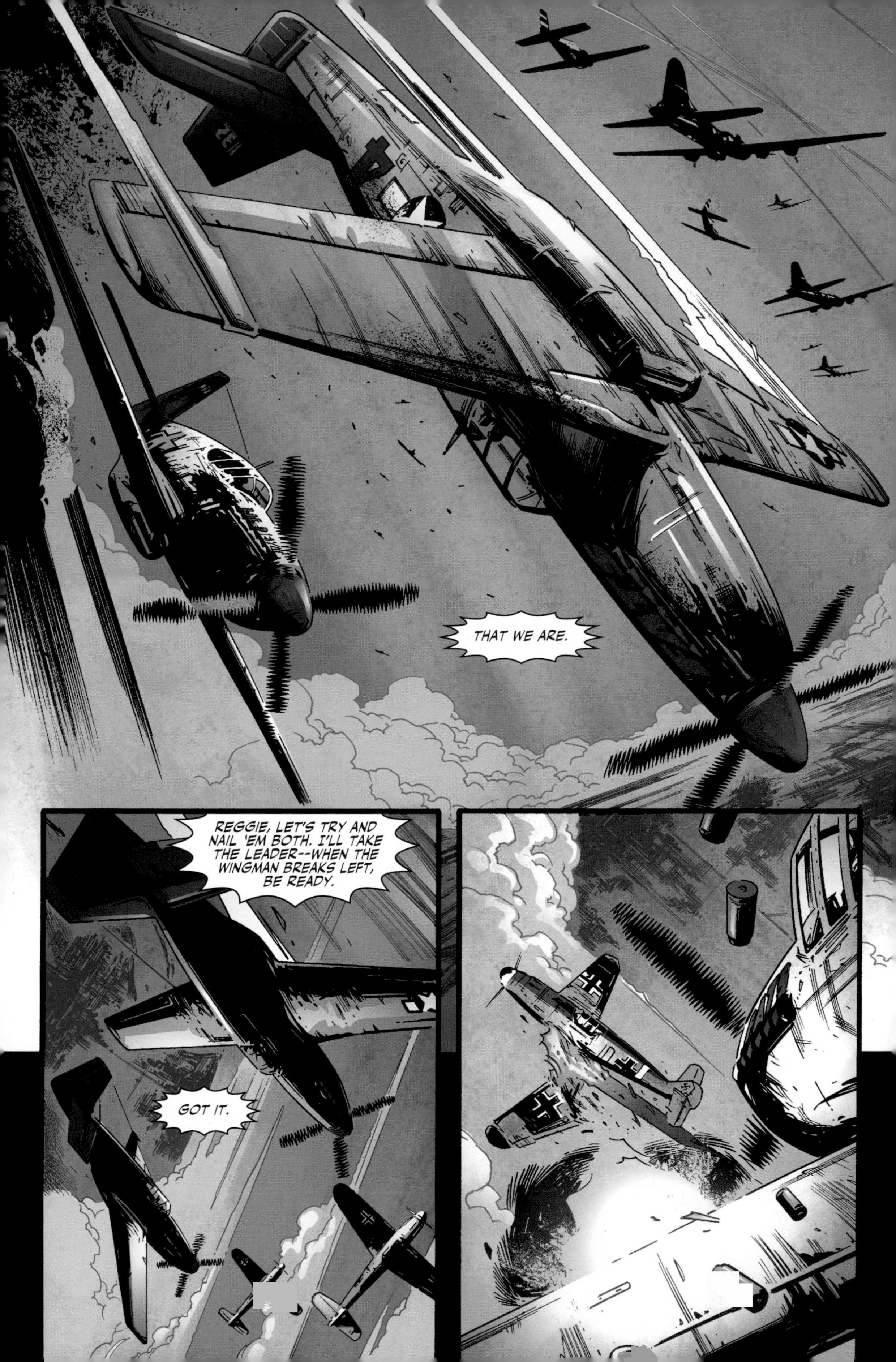
THAT WE ARE.
REGGIE, LET'S TRY AND NAIL 'EM BOTH. I'LL TAKE THE LEADER--WHEN THE WINGMAN BREAKS LEFT, BE READY.
GOT IT.

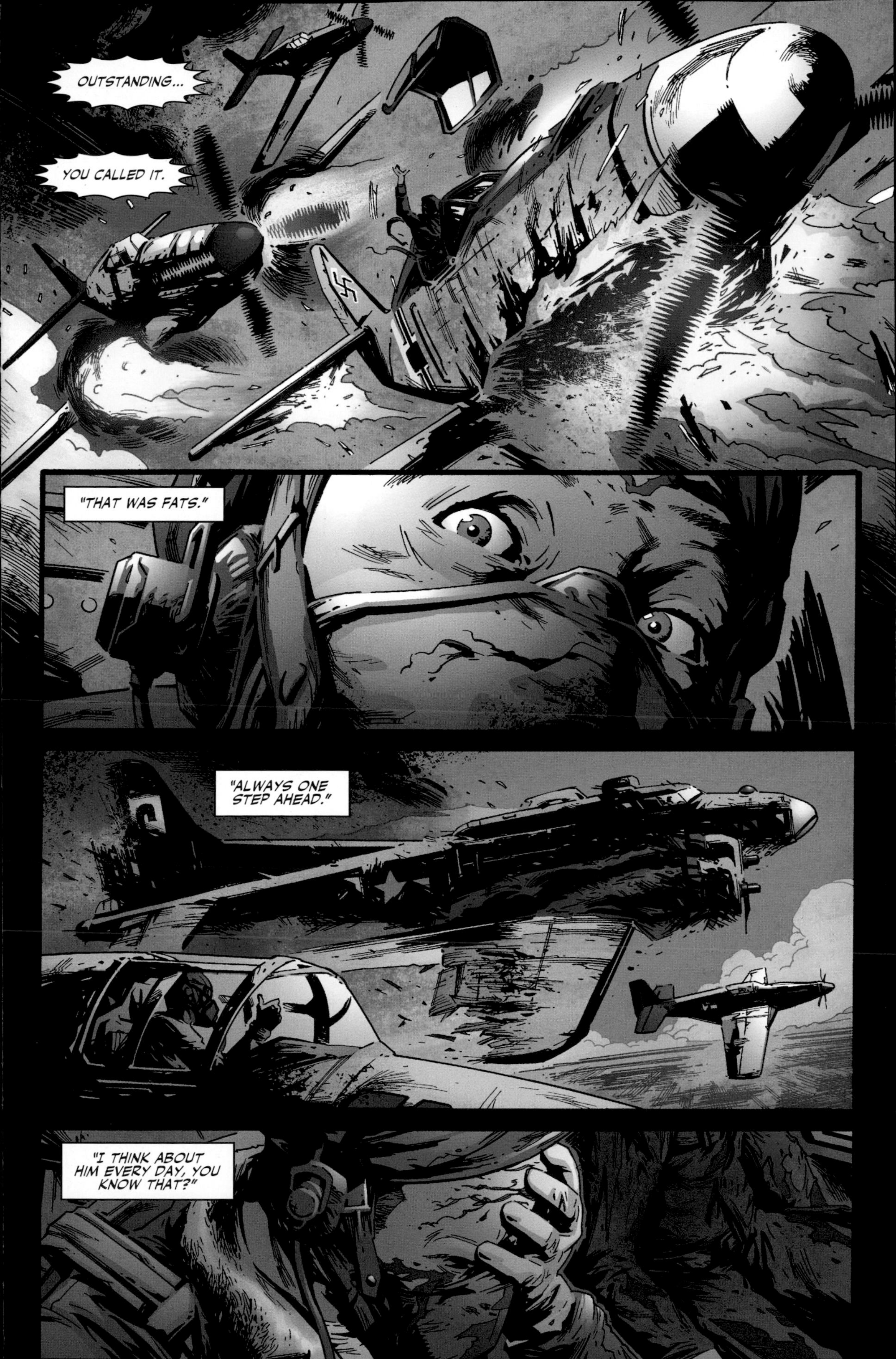
OUTSTANDING...
YOU CALLED IT.
"THAT WAS FATS."
"ALWAYS ONE STEP AHEAD."
"I THINK ABOUT HIM EVERY DAY, YOU KNOW THAT?"

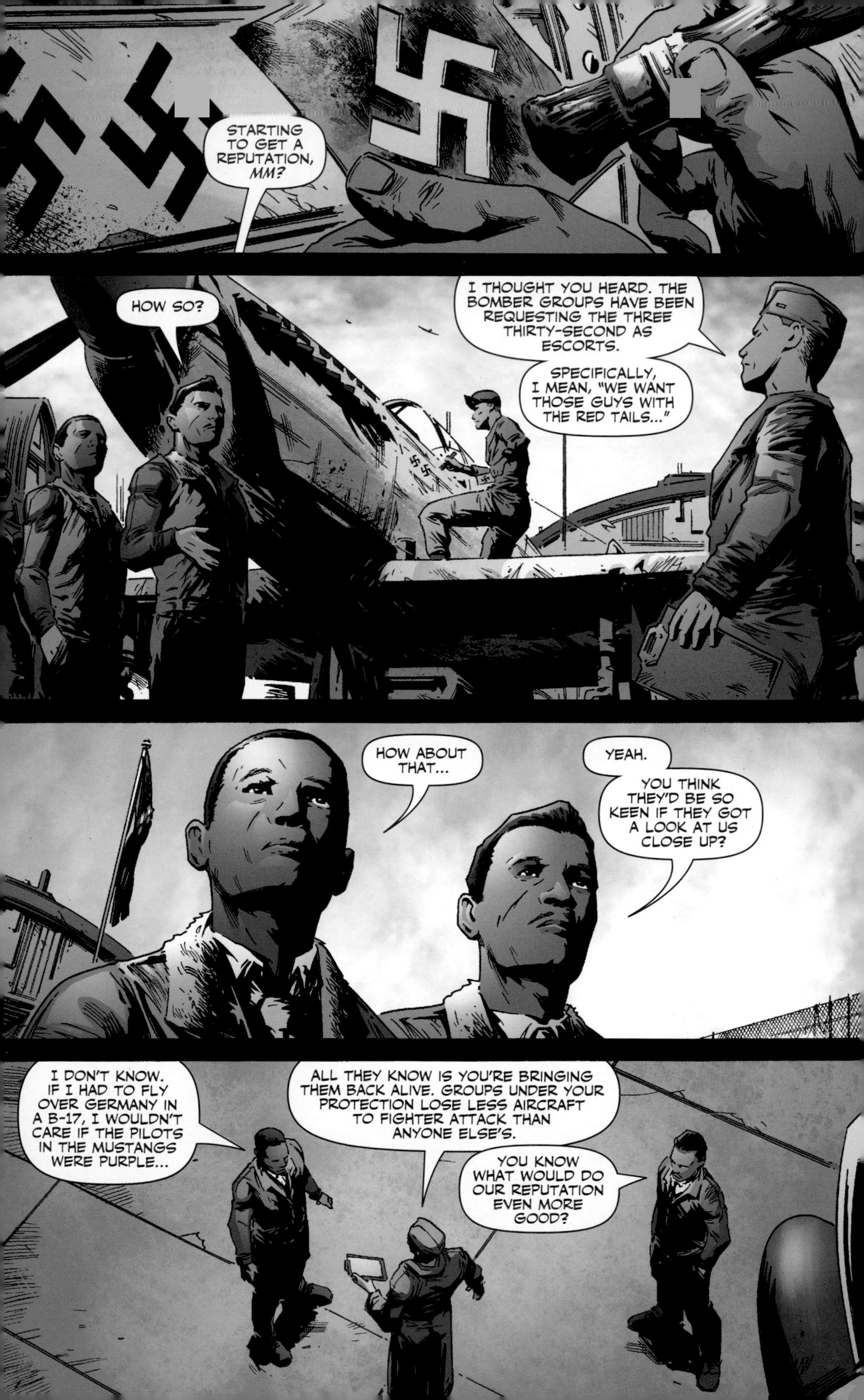
STARTING TO GET A REPUTATION, *MM?*
HOW SO?
I THOUGHT YOU HEARD. THE BOMBER GROUPS HAVE BEEN REQUESTING THE THREE THIRTY-SECOND AS ESCORTS.
SPECIFICALLY, I MEAN, "WE WANT THOSE GUYS WITH THE RED TAILS..."
HOW ABOUT THAT...
YEAH.
YOU THINK THEY'D BE SO KEEN IF THEY GOT A LOOK AT US CLOSE UP?
I DON'T KNOW. IF I HAD TO FLY OVER GERMANY IN A B-17, I WOULDN'T CARE IF THE PILOTS IN THE MUSTANGS WERE PURPLE...
ALL THEY KNOW IS YOU'RE BRINGING THEM BACK ALIVE. GROUPS UNDER YOUR PROTECTION LOSE LESS AIRCRAFT TO FIGHTER ATTACK THAN ANYONE ELSE'S.
YOU KNOW WHAT WOULD DO OUR REPUTATION EVEN MORE GOOD?

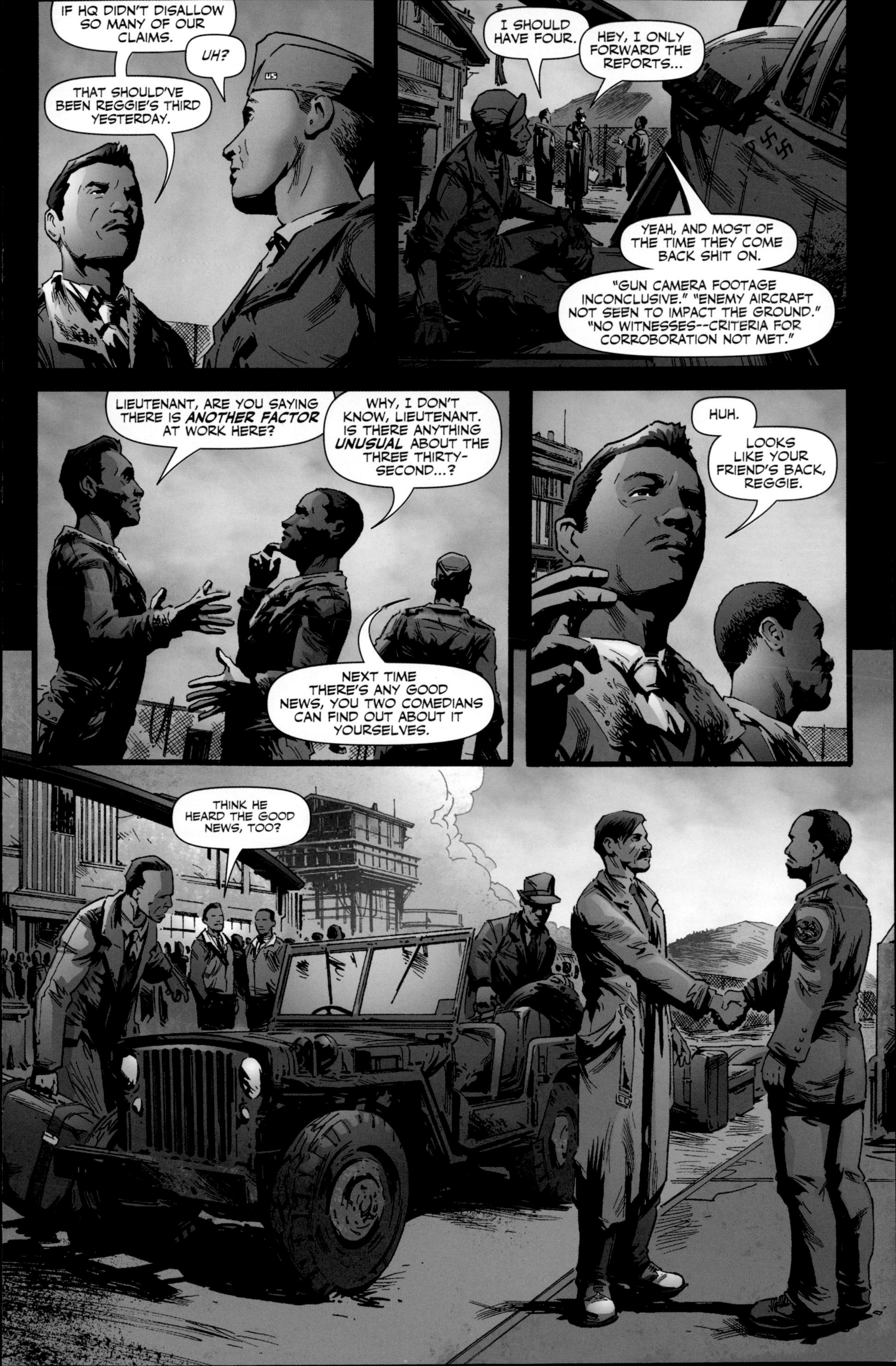
IF HQ DIDN'T DISALLOW SO MANY OF OUR CLAIMS.
UH?
THAT SHOULD'VE BEEN REGGIE'S THIRD YESTERDAY.
I SHOULD HAVE FOUR.
HEY, I ONLY FORWARD THE REPORTS...
YEAH, AND MOST OF THE TIME THEY COME BACK SHIT ON.
"GUN CAMERA FOOTAGE INCONCLUSIVE." "ENEMY AIRCRAFT NOT SEEN TO IMPACT THE GROUND." "NO WITNESSES--CRITERIA FOR CORROBORATION NOT MET."
LIEUTENANT, ARE YOU SAYING THERE IS ANOTHER FACTOR AT WORK HERE?
WHY, I DON'T KNOW, LIEUTENANT. IS THERE ANYTHING UNUSUAL ABOUT THE THREE THIRTY-SECOND...?
NEXT TIME THERE'S ANY GOOD NEWS, YOU TWO COMEDIANS CAN FIND OUT ABOUT IT YOURSELVES.
HUH.
LOOKS LIKE YOUR FRIEND'S BACK, REGGIE.
THINK HE HEARD THE GOOD NEWS, TOO?

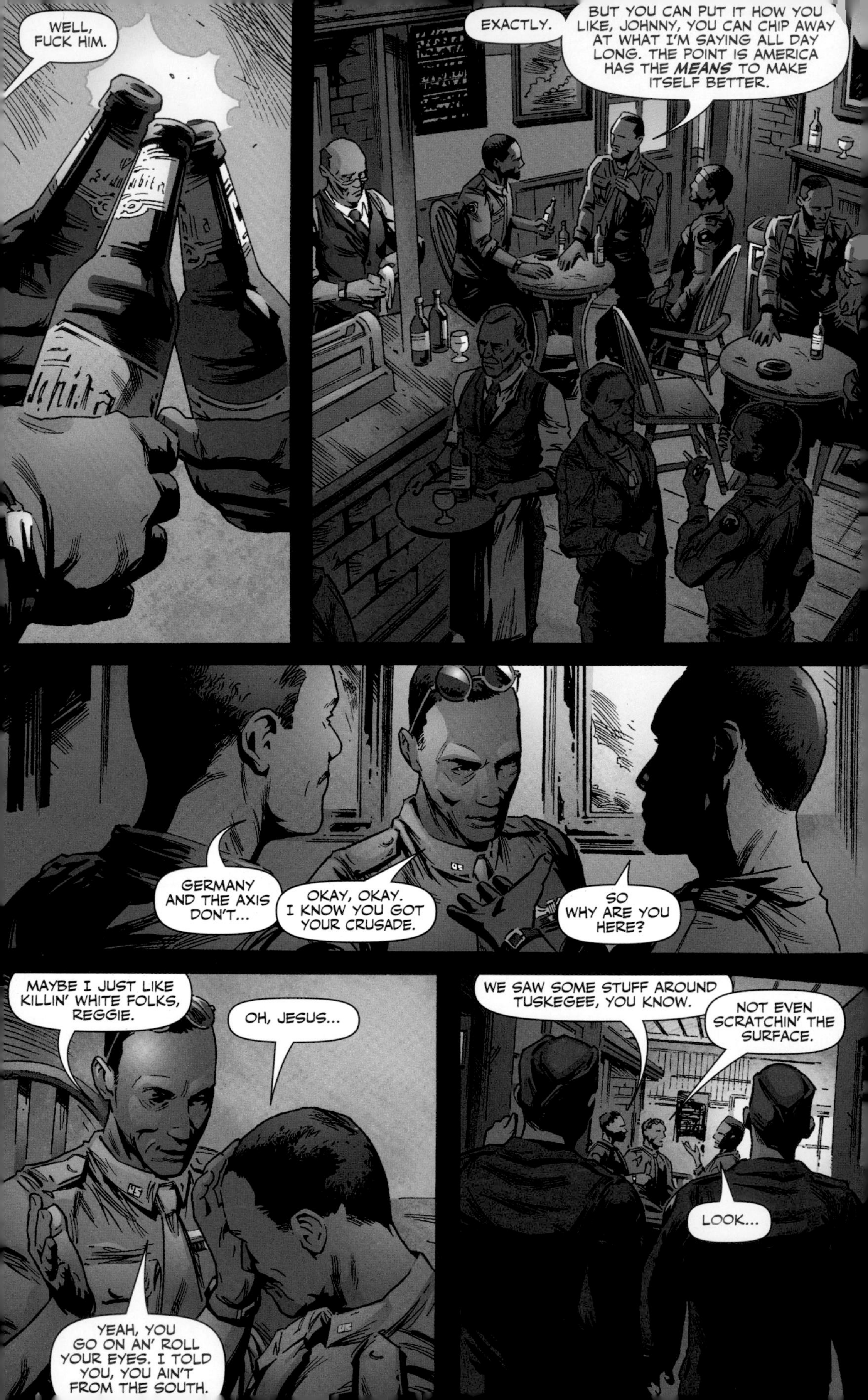
WELL, FUCK HIM.
EXACTLY.
BUT YOU CAN PUT IT HOW YOU LIKE, JOHNNY, YOU CAN CHIP AWAY AT WHAT I'M SAYING ALL DAY LONG. THE POINT IS AMERICA HAS THE *MEANS* TO MAKE ITSELF BETTER.
GERMANY AND THE AXIS DON'T...
OKAY, OKAY. I KNOW YOU GOT YOUR CRUSADE.
SO WHY ARE YOU HERE?
MAYBE I JUST LIKE KILLIN' WHITE FOLKS, REGGIE.
OH, JESUS...
YEAH, YOU GO ON AN' ROLL YOUR EYES. I TOLD YOU, YOU AIN'T FROM THE SOUTH.
WE SAW SOME STUFF AROUND TUSKEGEE, YOU KNOW.
NOT EVEN SCRATCHIN' THE SURFACE.
LOOK...

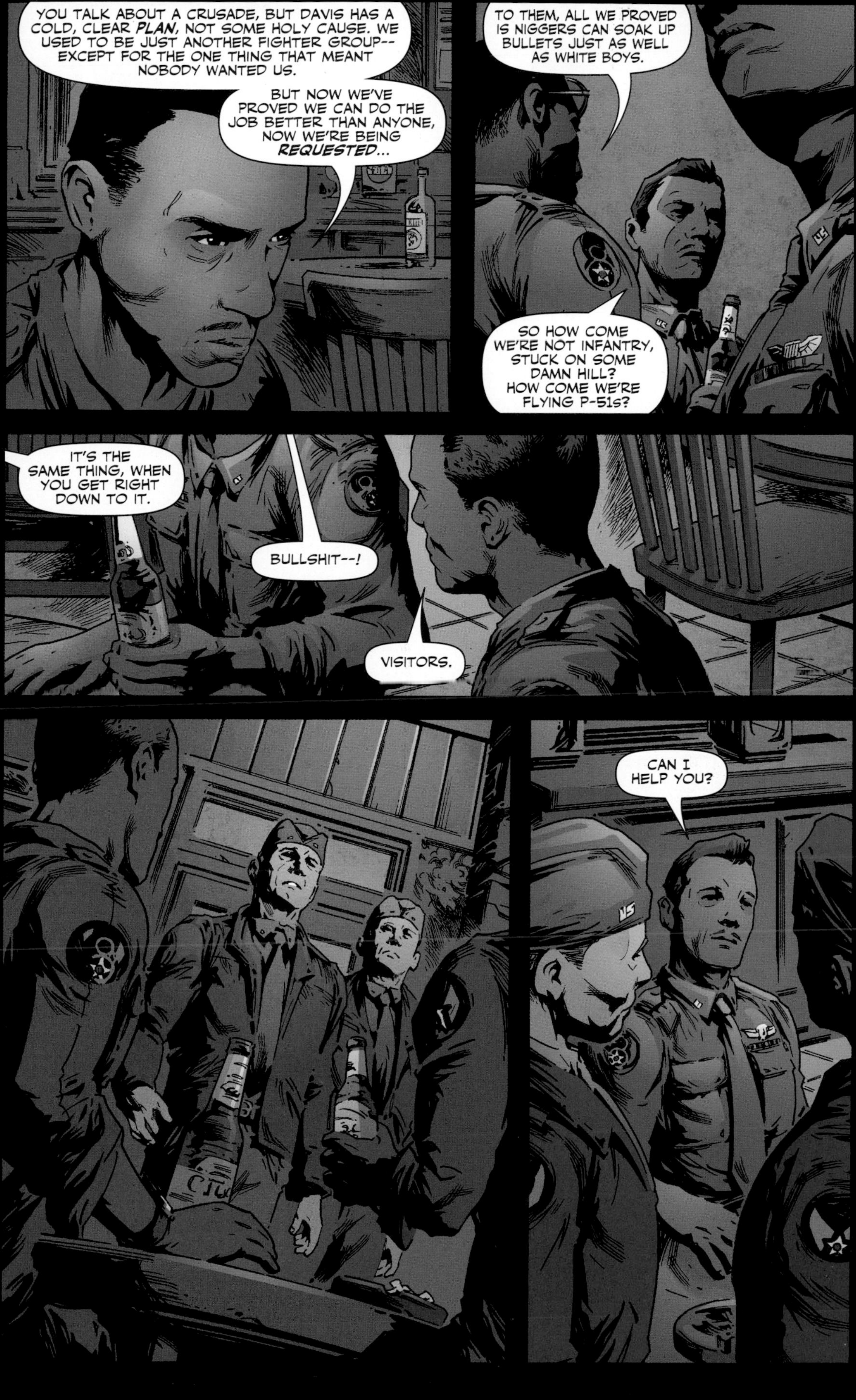
YOU TALK ABOUT A CRUSADE, BUT DAVIS HAS A COLD, CLEAR PLAN, NOT SOME HOLY CAUSE. WE USED TO BE JUST ANOTHER FIGHTER GROUP-- EXCEPT FOR THE ONE THING THAT MEANT NOBODY WANTED US.
BUT NOW WE'VE PROVED WE CAN DO THE JOB BETTER THAN ANYONE, NOW WE'RE BEING REQUESTED...
TO THEM, ALL WE PROVED IS NIGGERS CAN SOAK UP BULLETS JUST AS WELL AS WHITE BOYS.
SO HOW COME WE'RE NOT INFANTRY, STUCK ON SOME DAMN HILL? HOW COME WE'RE FLYING P-51s?
IT'S THE SAME THING, WHEN YOU GET RIGHT DOWN TO IT.
BULLSHIT--!
VISITORS.
CAN I HELP YOU?

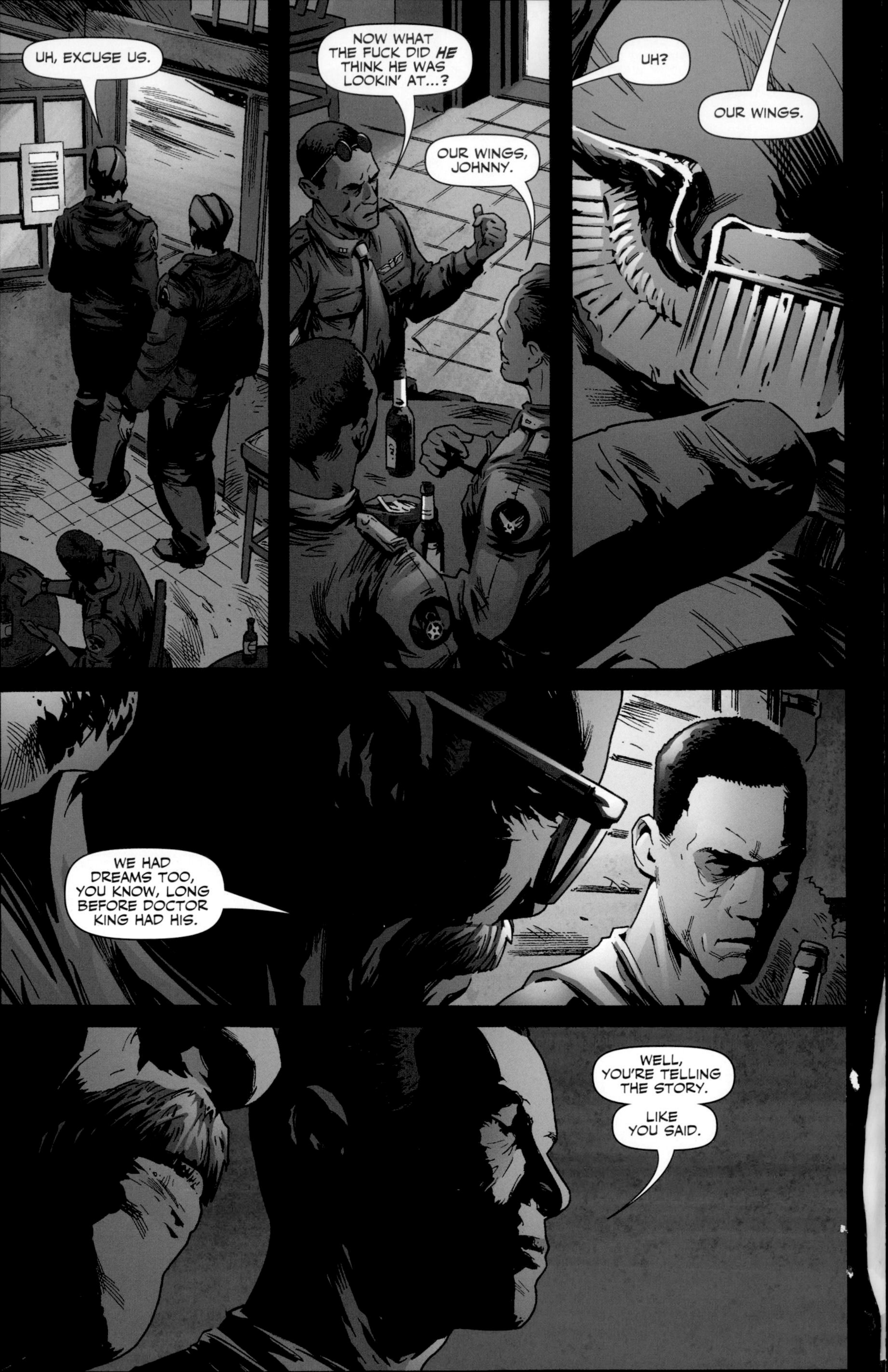
UH, EXCUSE US.
NOW WHAT THE FUCK DID HE THINK HE WAS LOOKIN' AT...?
OUR WINGS, JOHNNY.
UH?
OUR WINGS.
WE HAD DREAMS TOO, YOU KNOW, LONG BEFORE DOCTOR KING HAD HIS.
WELL, YOU'RE TELLING THE STORY.
LIKE YOU SAID.

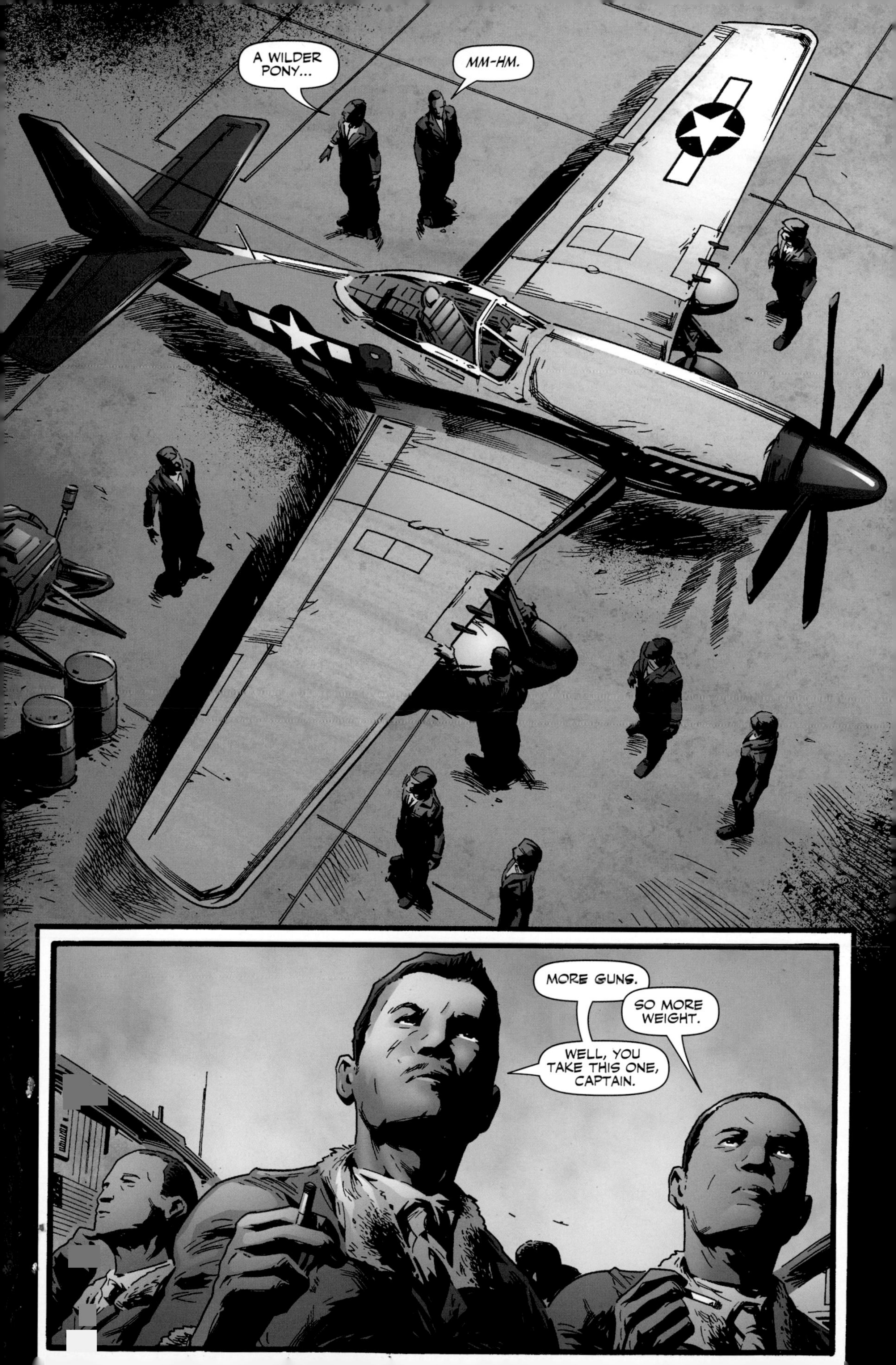
A WILDER PONY...
MM-HM.
MORE GUNS.
SO MORE WEIGHT.
WELL, YOU TAKE THIS ONE, CAPTAIN.

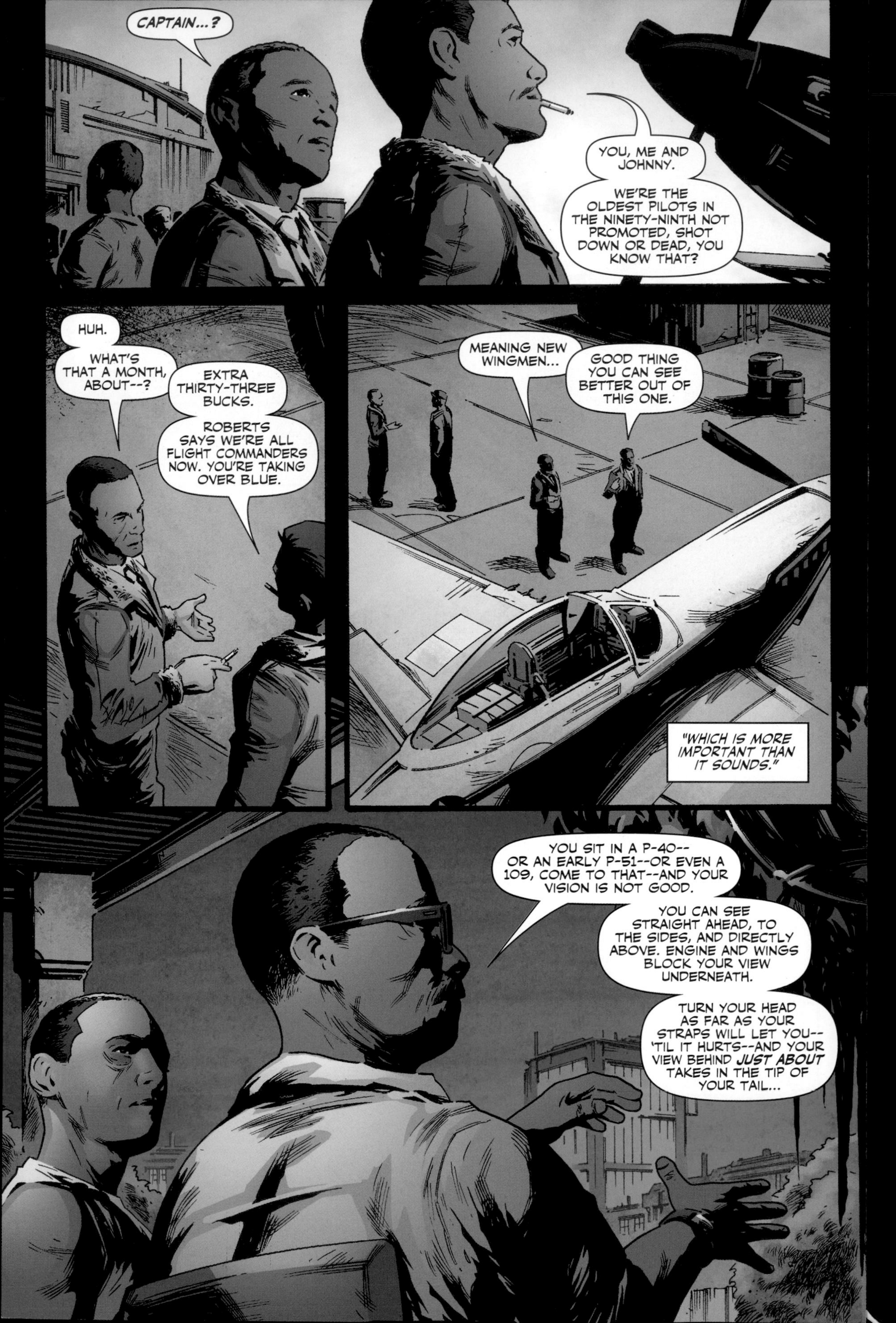
CAPTAIN...?
YOU, ME AND JOHNNY.
WE'RE THE OLDEST PILOTS IN THE NINETY-NINTH NOT PROMOTED, SHOT DOWN OR DEAD, YOU KNOW THAT?
HUH.
WHAT'S THAT A MONTH, ABOUT--?
EXTRA THIRTY-THREE BUCKS.
ROBERTS SAYS WE'RE ALL FLIGHT COMMANDERS NOW. YOU'RE TAKING OVER BLUE.
MEANING NEW WINGMEN...
GOOD THING YOU CAN SEE BETTER OUT OF THIS ONE.
"WHICH IS MORE IMPORTANT THAN IT SOUNDS."
YOU SIT IN A P-40-- OR AN EARLY P-51--OR EVEN A 109, COME TO THAT--AND YOUR VISION IS NOT GOOD.
YOU CAN SEE STRAIGHT AHEAD, TO THE SIDES, AND DIRECTLY ABOVE. ENGINE AND WINGS BLOCK YOUR VIEW UNDERNEATH.
TURN YOUR HEAD AS FAR AS YOUR STRAPS WILL LET YOU-- 'TIL IT HURTS--AND YOUR VIEW BEHIND JUST ABOUT TAKES IN THE TIP OF YOUR TAIL...

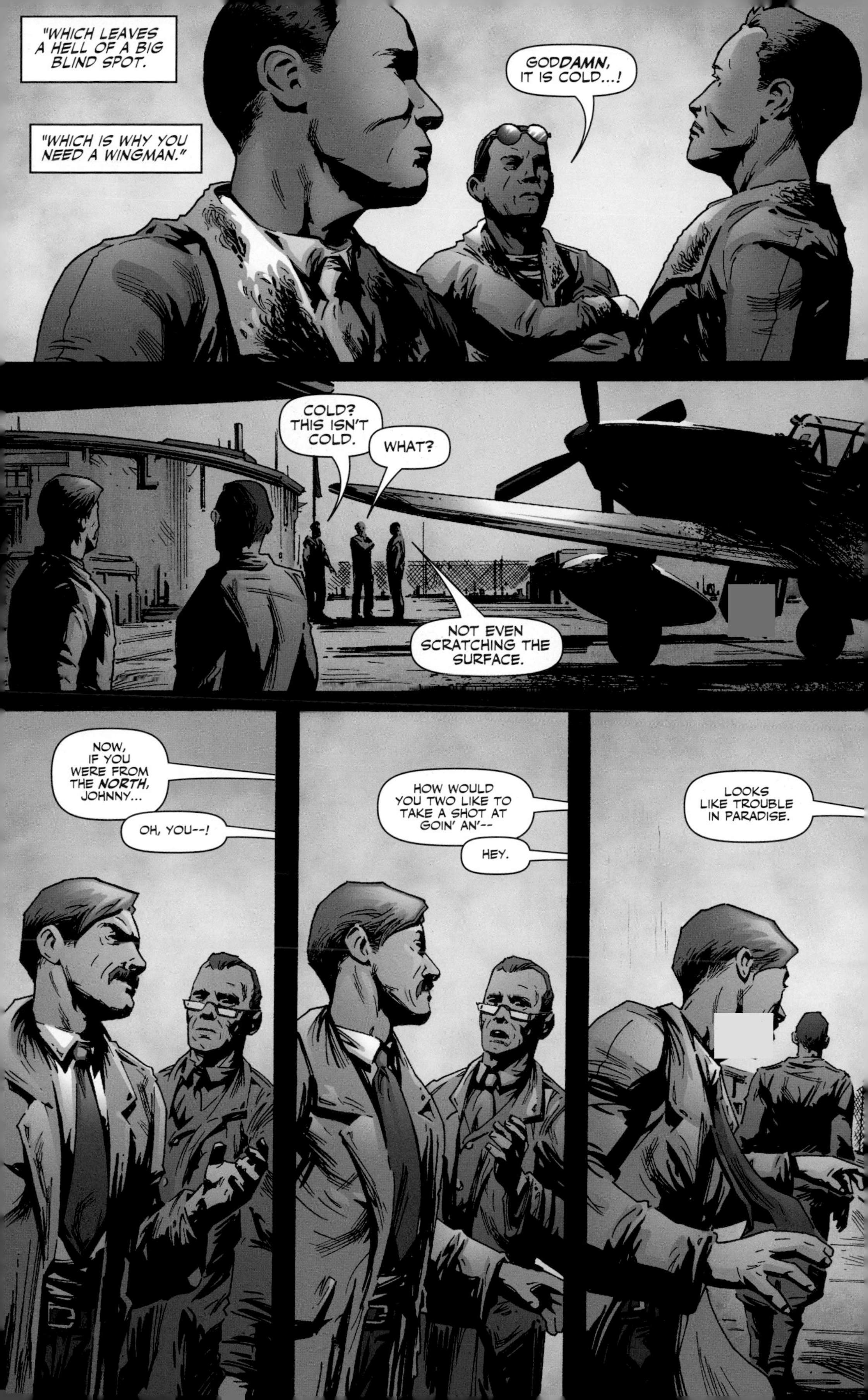
"WHICH LEAVES A HELL OF A BIG BLIND SPOT.
"WHICH IS WHY YOU NEED A WINGMAN."
GODDAMN, IT IS COLD...!
COLD? THIS ISN'T COLD.
WHAT?
NOT EVEN SCRATCHING THE SURFACE.
NOW, IF YOU WERE FROM THE NORTH, JOHNNY...
OH, YOU--!
HOW WOULD YOU TWO LIKE TO TAKE A SHOT AT GOIN' AN'--
HEY.
LOOKS LIKE TROUBLE IN PARADISE.

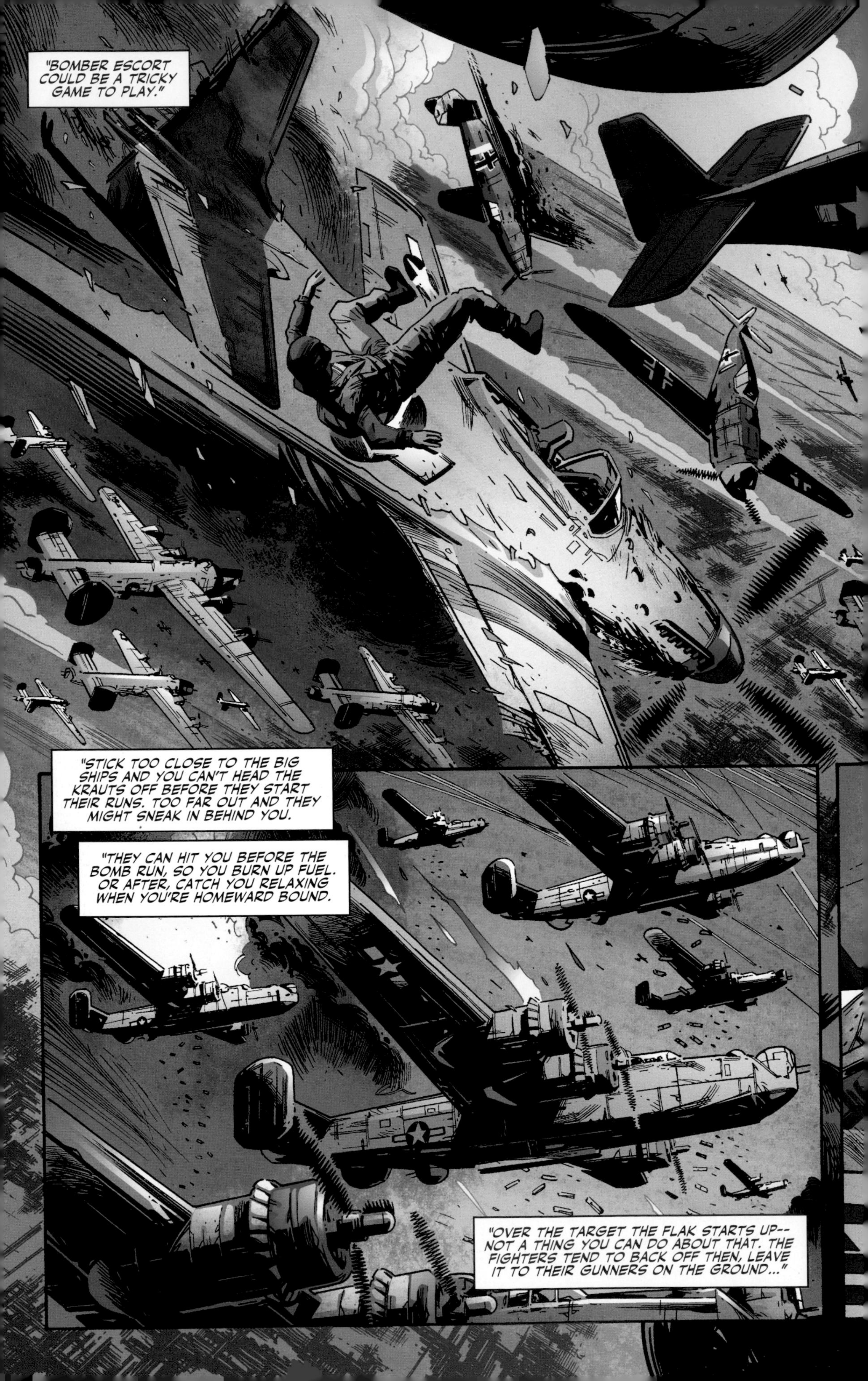
"BOMBER ESCORT COULD BE A TRICKY GAME TO PLAY."
"STICK TOO CLOSE TO THE BIG SHIPS AND YOU CAN'T HEAD THE KRAUTS OFF BEFORE THEY START THEIR RUNS. TOO FAR OUT AND THEY MIGHT SNEAK IN BEHIND YOU.
"THEY CAN HIT YOU BEFORE THE BOMB RUN, SO YOU BURN UP FUEL. OR AFTER, CATCH YOU RELAXING WHEN YOU'RE HOMEWARD BOUND.
"OVER THE TARGET THE FLAK STARTS UP-- NOT A THING YOU CAN DO ABOUT THAT. THE FIGHTERS TEND TO BACK OFF THEN, LEAVE IT TO THEIR GUNNERS ON THE GROUND..."

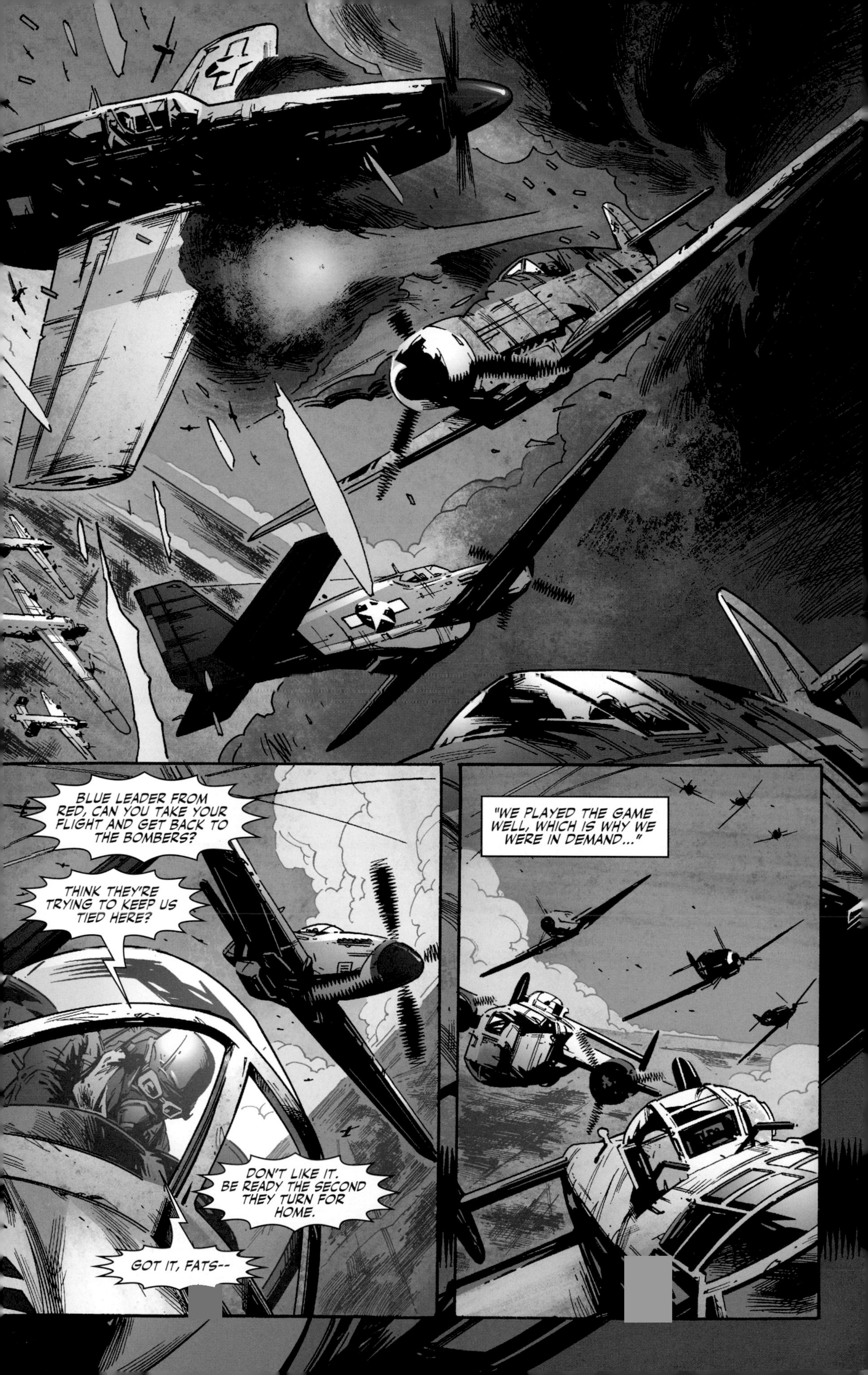
BLUE LEADER FROM RED, CAN YOU TAKE YOUR FLIGHT AND GET BACK TO THE BOMBERS?
THINK THEY'RE TRYING TO KEEP US TIED HERE?
DON'T LIKE IT. BE READY THE SECOND THEY TURN FOR HOME.
GOT IT, FATS--
"WE PLAYED THE GAME WELL, WHICH IS WHY WE WERE IN DEMAND..."

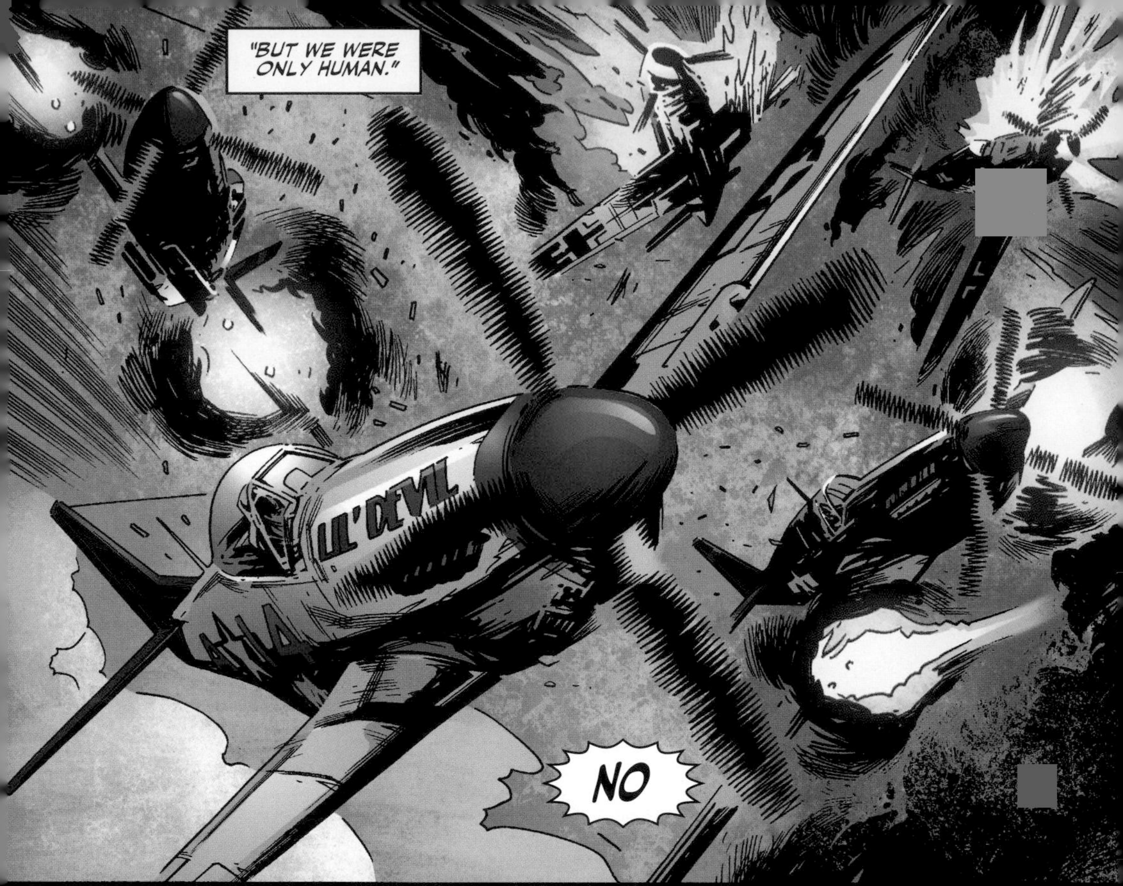
"BUT WE WERE ONLY HUMAN."
LIL' DEVIL
NO

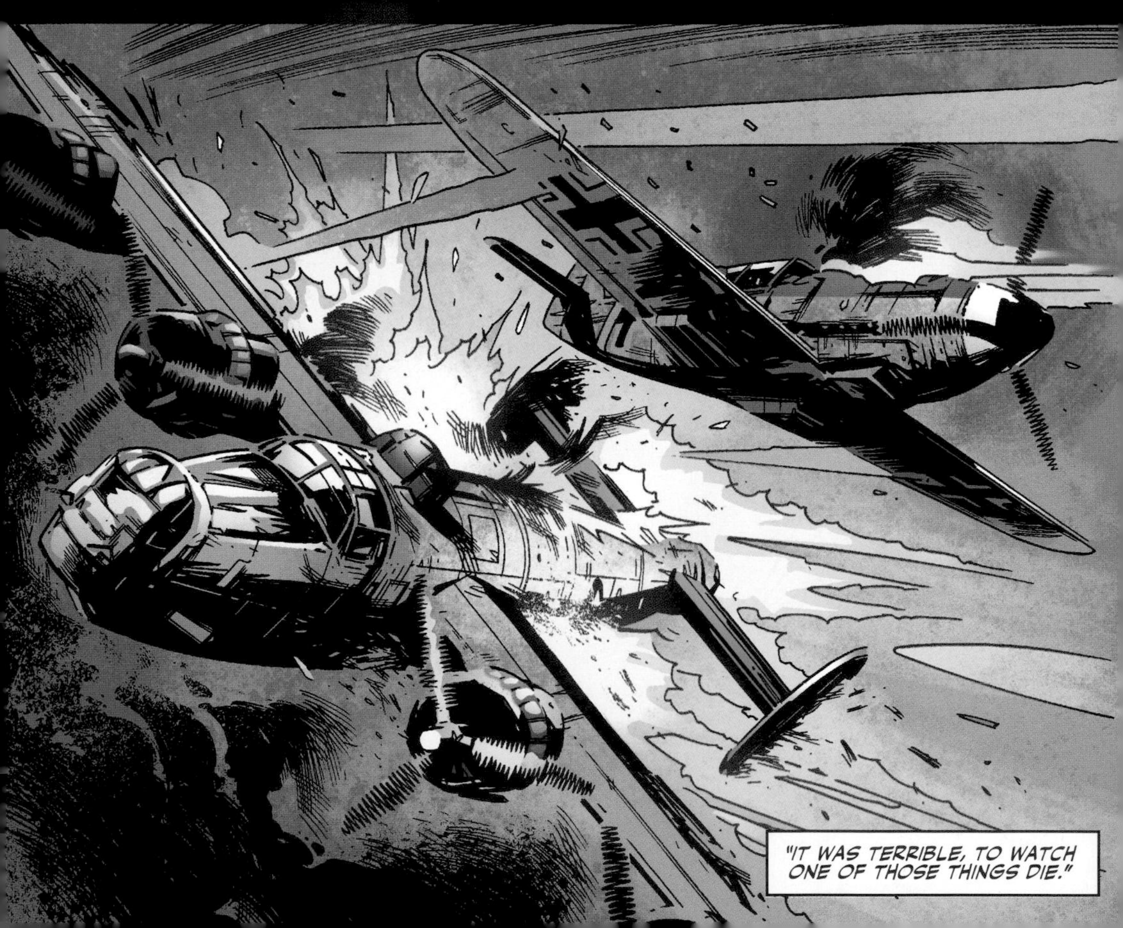
"IT WAS TERRIBLE, TO WATCH ONE OF THOSE THINGS DIE."

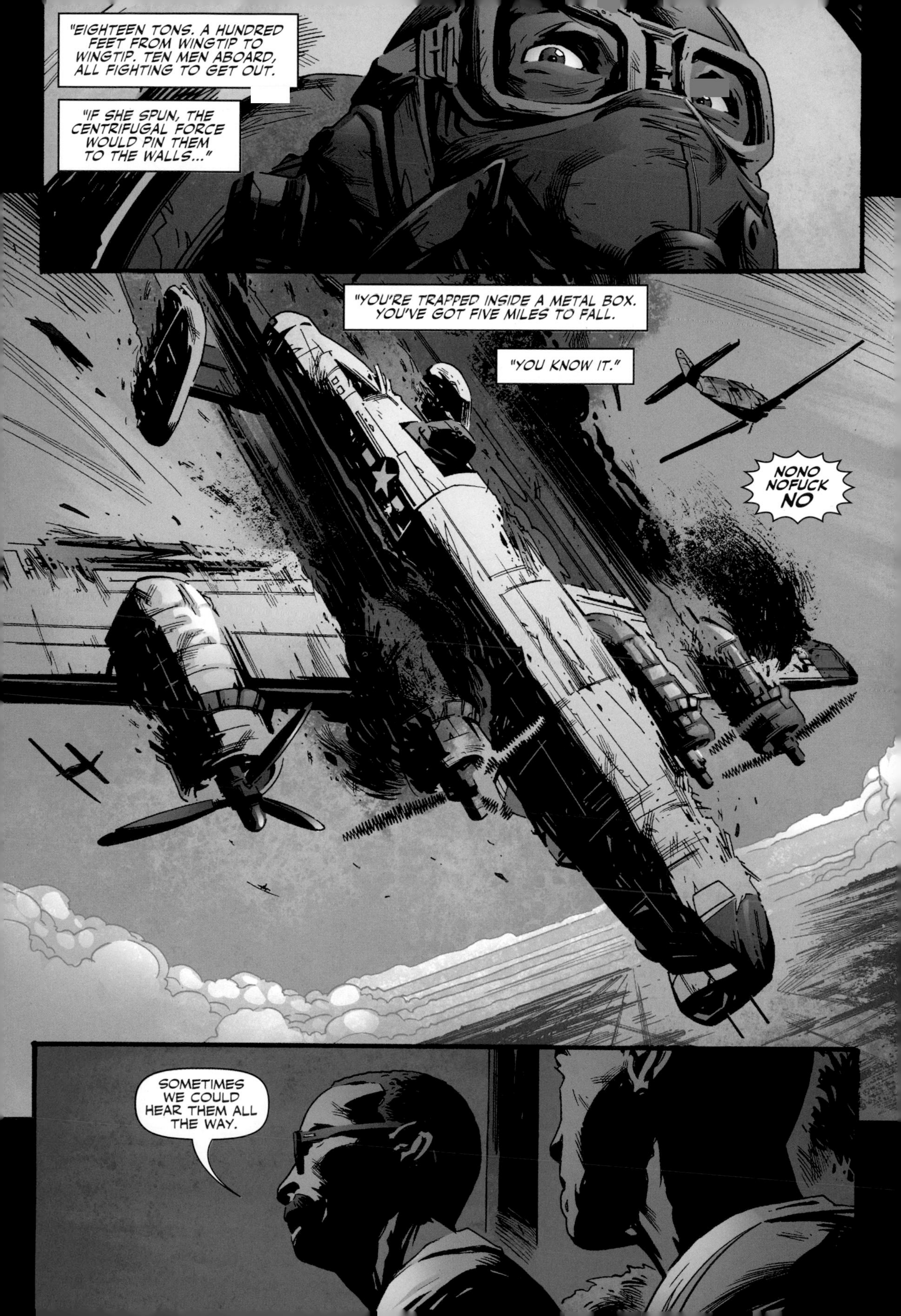
"EIGHTEEN TONS. A HUNDRED FEET FROM WINGTIP TO WINGTIP. TEN MEN ABOARD, ALL FIGHTING TO GET OUT.
"IF SHE SPUN, THE CENTRIFUGAL FORCE WOULD PIN THEM TO THE WALLS..."
"YOU'RE TRAPPED INSIDE A METAL BOX. YOU'VE GOT FIVE MILES TO FALL.
"YOU KNOW IT."
NONO NOFUCK NO
SOMETIMES WE COULD HEAR THEM ALL THE WAY.

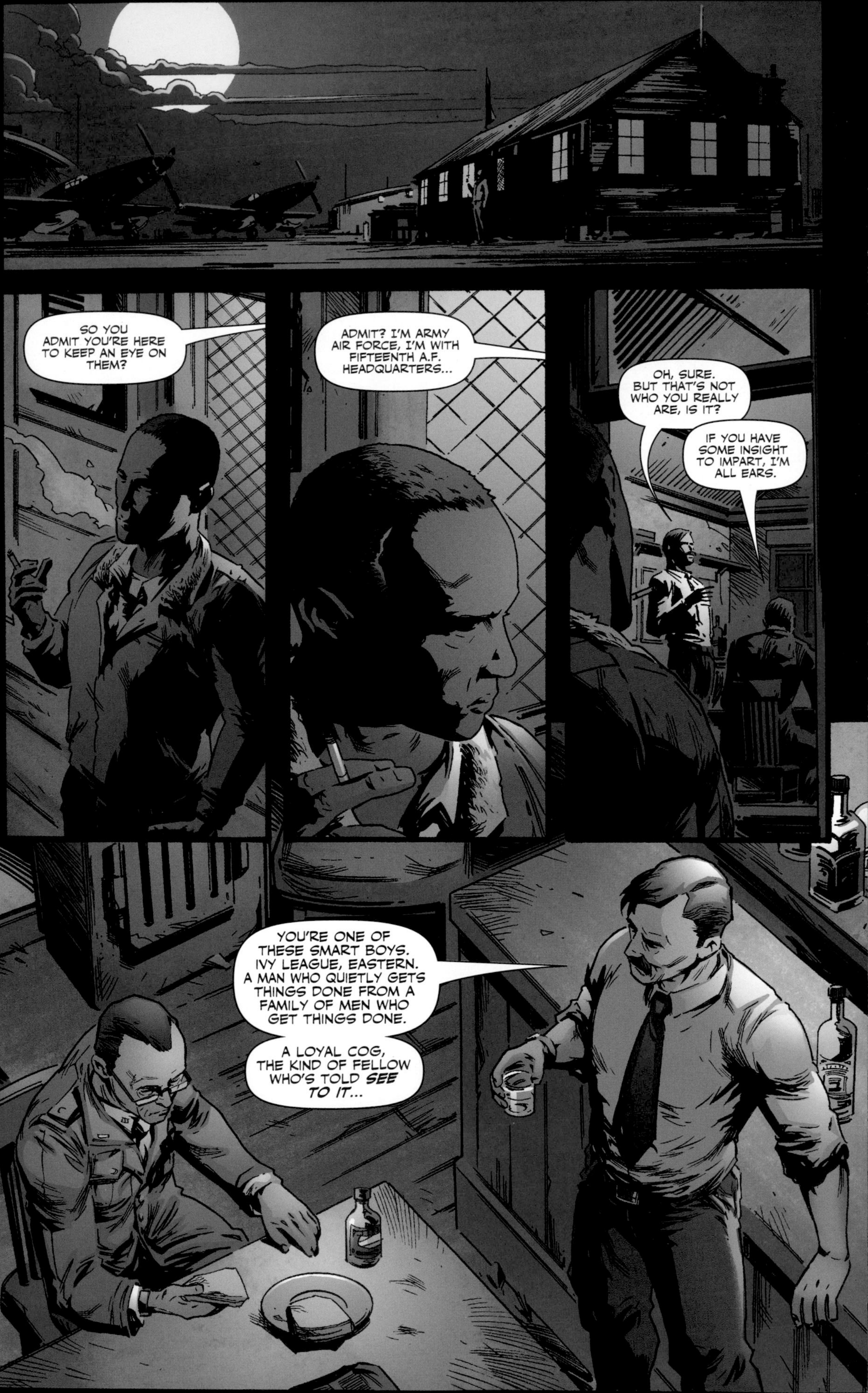
SO YOU ADMIT YOU'RE HERE TO KEEP AN EYE ON THEM?
ADMIT? I'M ARMY AIR FORCE, I'M WITH FIFTEENTH A.F. HEADQUARTERS...
OH, SURE. BUT THAT'S NOT WHO YOU REALLY ARE, IS IT?
IF YOU HAVE SOME INSIGHT TO IMPART, I'M ALL EARS.
YOU'RE ONE OF THESE SMART BOYS. IVY LEAGUE, EASTERN. A MAN WHO QUIETLY GETS THINGS DONE FROM A FAMILY OF MEN WHO GET THINGS DONE.
A LOYAL COG, THE KIND OF FELLOW WHO'S TOLD *SEE TO IT*...

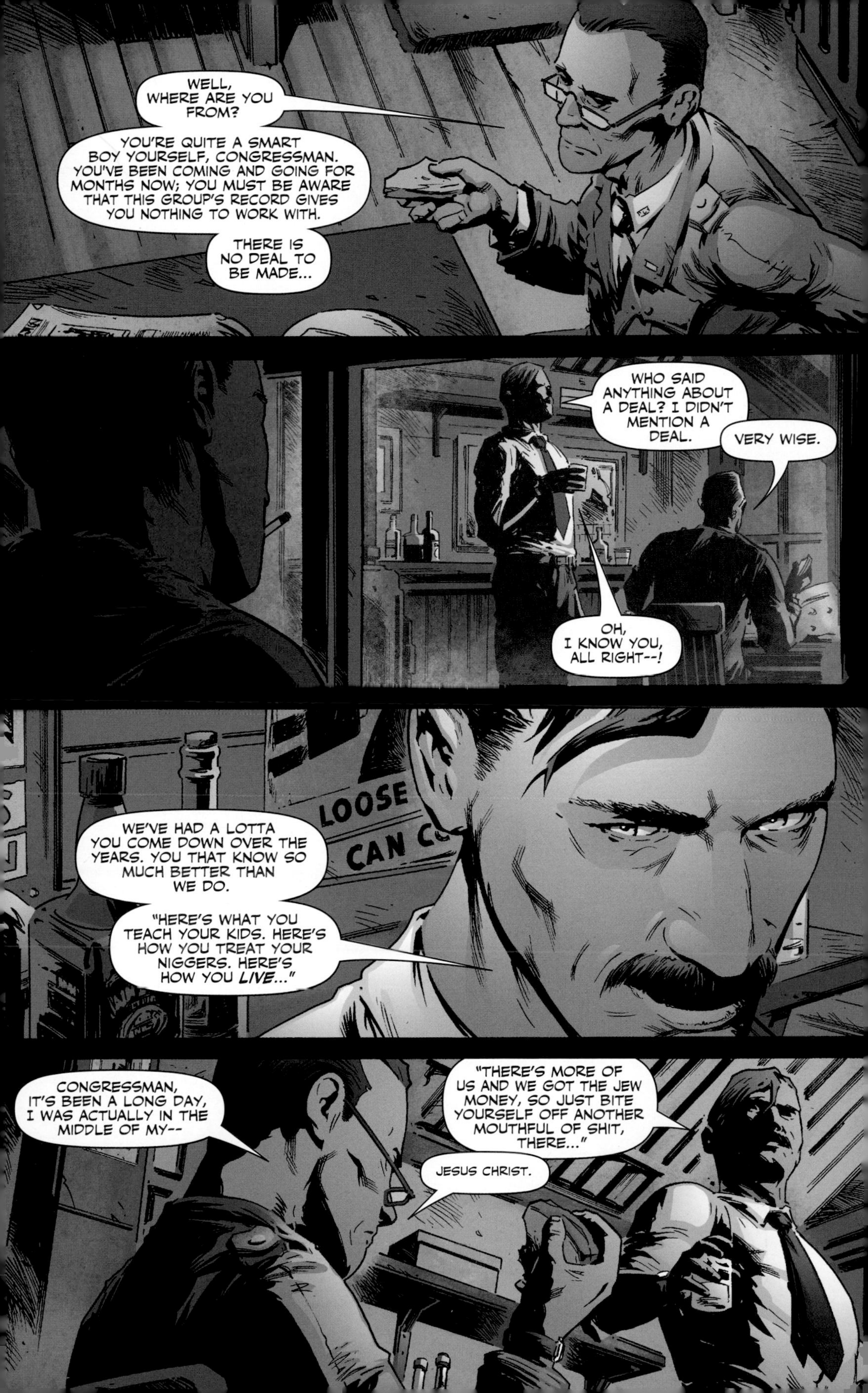
WELL, WHERE ARE YOU FROM?
YOU'RE QUITE A SMART BOY YOURSELF, CONGRESSMAN. YOU'VE BEEN COMING AND GOING FOR MONTHS NOW; YOU MUST BE AWARE THAT THIS GROUP'S RECORD GIVES YOU NOTHING TO WORK WITH.
THERE IS NO DEAL TO BE MADE...
WHO SAID ANYTHING ABOUT A DEAL? I DIDN'T MENTION A DEAL.
VERY WISE.
OH, I KNOW YOU, ALL RIGHT--!
LOOSE
CAN C
WE'VE HAD A LOTTA YOU COME DOWN OVER THE YEARS. YOU THAT KNOW SO MUCH BETTER THAN WE DO.
"HERE'S WHAT YOU TEACH YOUR KIDS. HERE'S HOW YOU TREAT YOUR NIGGERS. HERE'S HOW YOU *LIVE*..."
CONGRESSMAN, IT'S BEEN A LONG DAY, I WAS ACTUALLY IN THE MIDDLE OF MY--
"THERE'S MORE OF US AND WE GOT THE JEW MONEY, SO JUST BITE YOURSELF OFF ANOTHER MOUTHFUL OF SHIT, THERE..."
JESUS CHRIST.

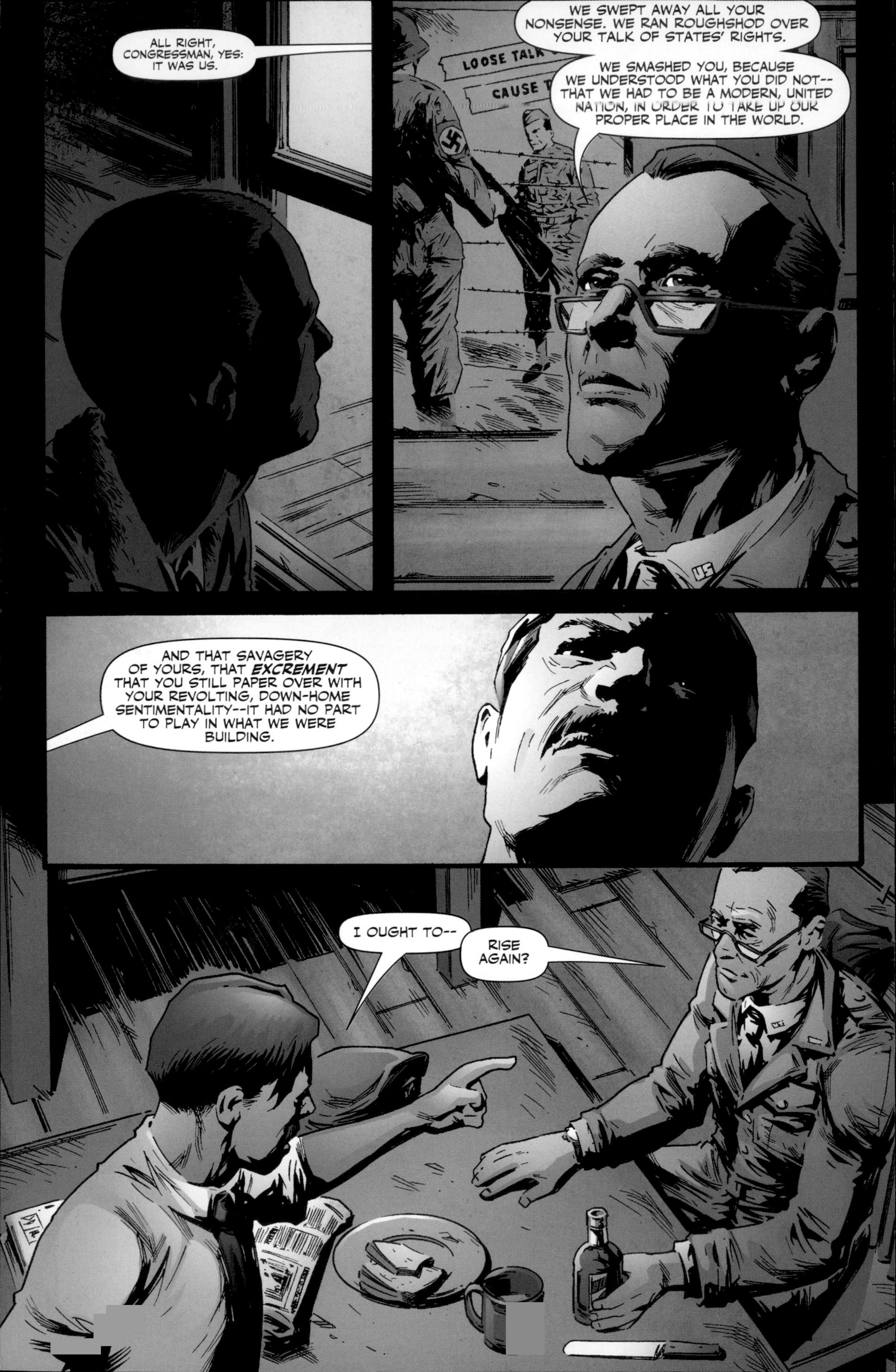
ALL RIGHT, CONGRESSMAN, YES: IT WAS US.
WE SWEPT AWAY ALL YOUR NONSENSE. WE RAN ROUGHSHOD OVER YOUR TALK OF STATES' RIGHTS.
LOOSE TALK
CAUSE
WE SMASHED YOU, BECAUSE WE UNDERSTOOD WHAT YOU DID NOT-- THAT WE HAD TO BE A MODERN, UNITED NATION, IN ORDER TO TAKE UP OUR PROPER PLACE IN THE WORLD.
US
AND THAT SAVAGERY OF YOURS, THAT *EXCREMENT* THAT YOU STILL PAPER OVER WITH YOUR REVOLTING, DOWN-HOME SENTIMENTALITY--IT HAD NO PART TO PLAY IN WHAT WE WERE BUILDING.
I OUGHT TO--
RISE AGAIN?

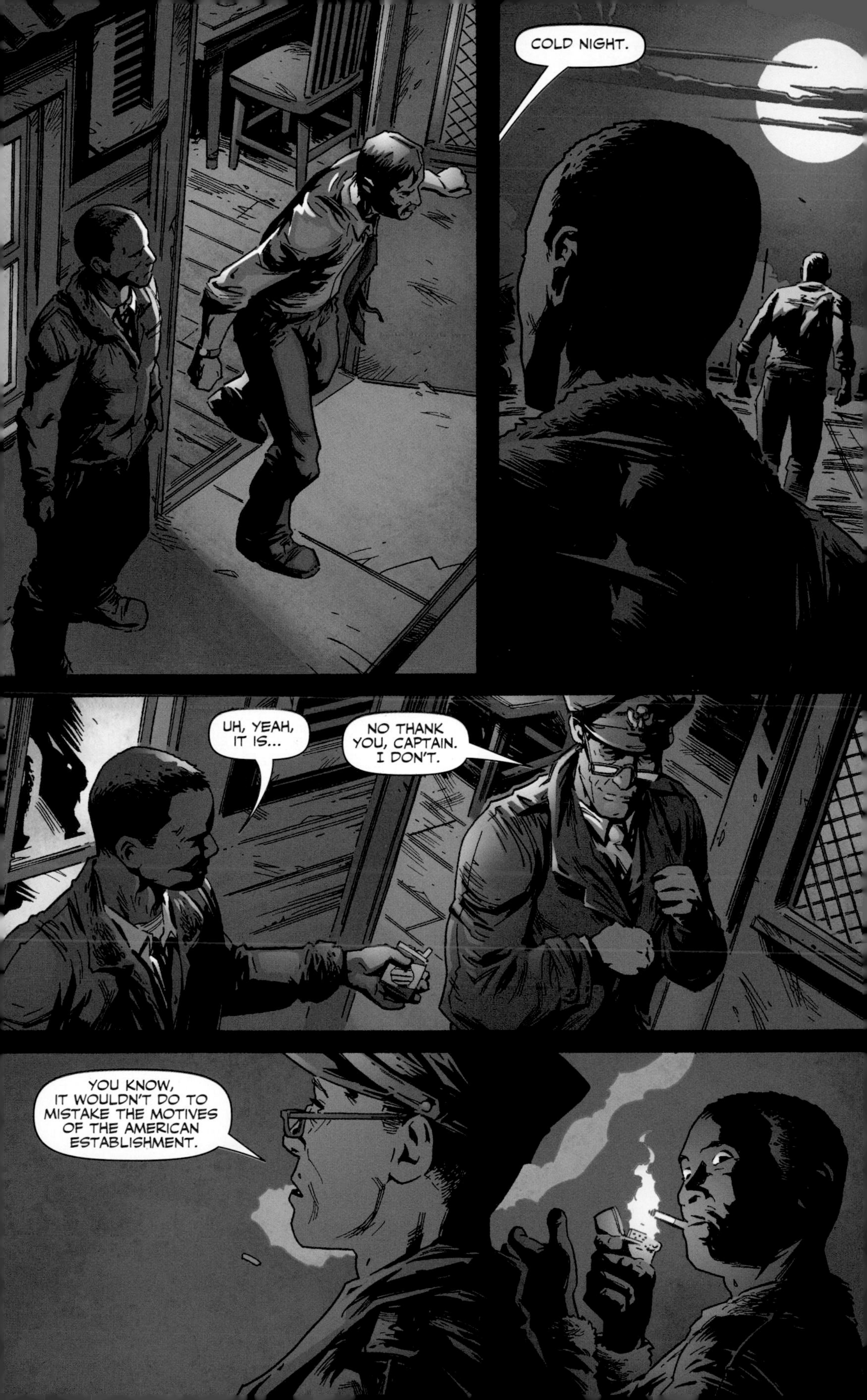
COLD NIGHT.
UH, YEAH, IT IS...
NO THANK YOU, CAPTAIN. I DON'T.
YOU KNOW, IT WOULDN'T DO TO MISTAKE THE MOTIVES OF THE AMERICAN ESTABLISHMENT.

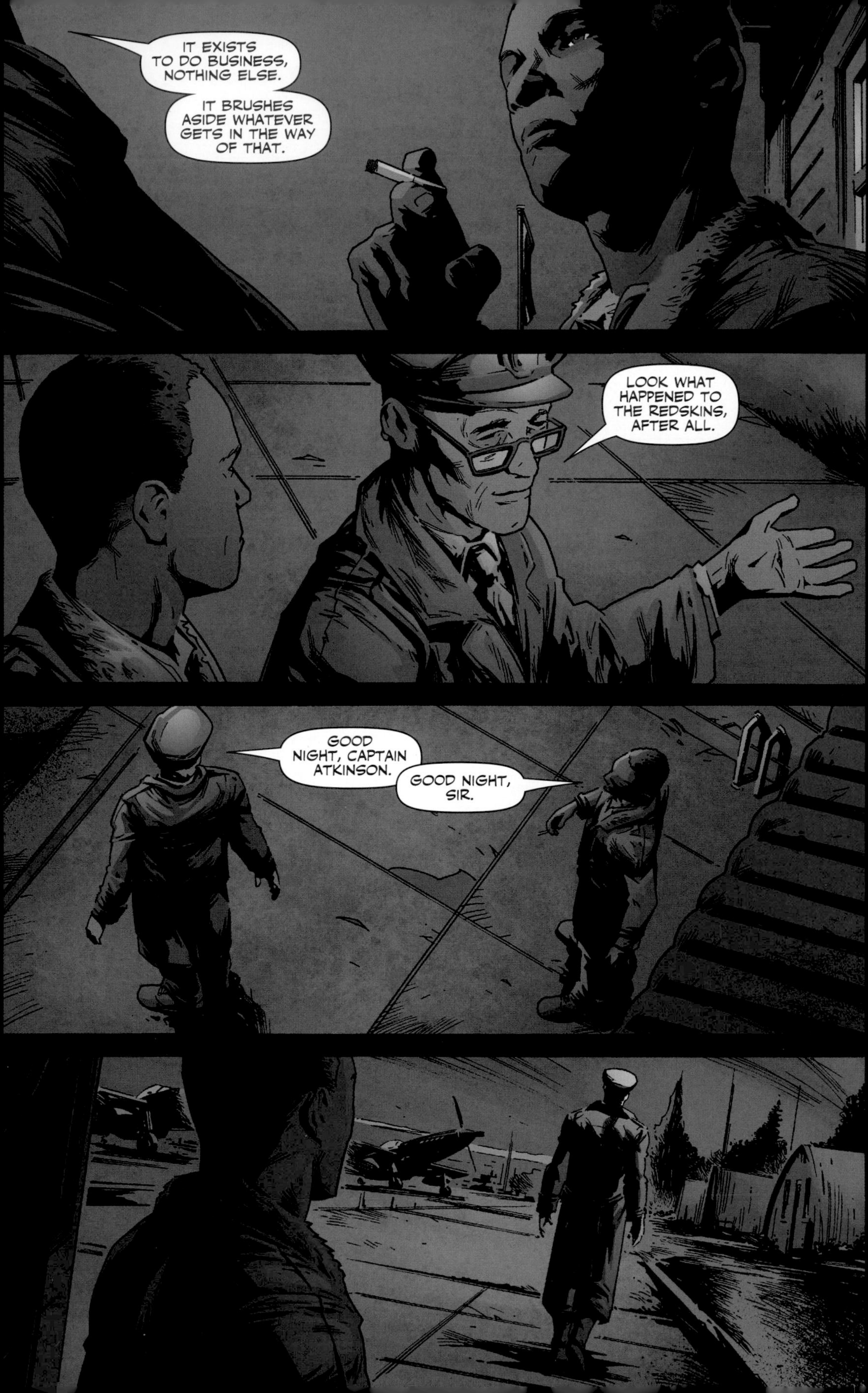
IT EXISTS TO DO BUSINESS, NOTHING ELSE.
IT BRUSHES ASIDE WHATEVER GETS IN THE WAY OF THAT.
LOOK WHAT HAPPENED TO THE REDSKINS, AFTER ALL.
GOOD NIGHT, CAPTAIN ATKINSON.
GOOD NIGHT, SIR.

6: A STONE OF HOPE

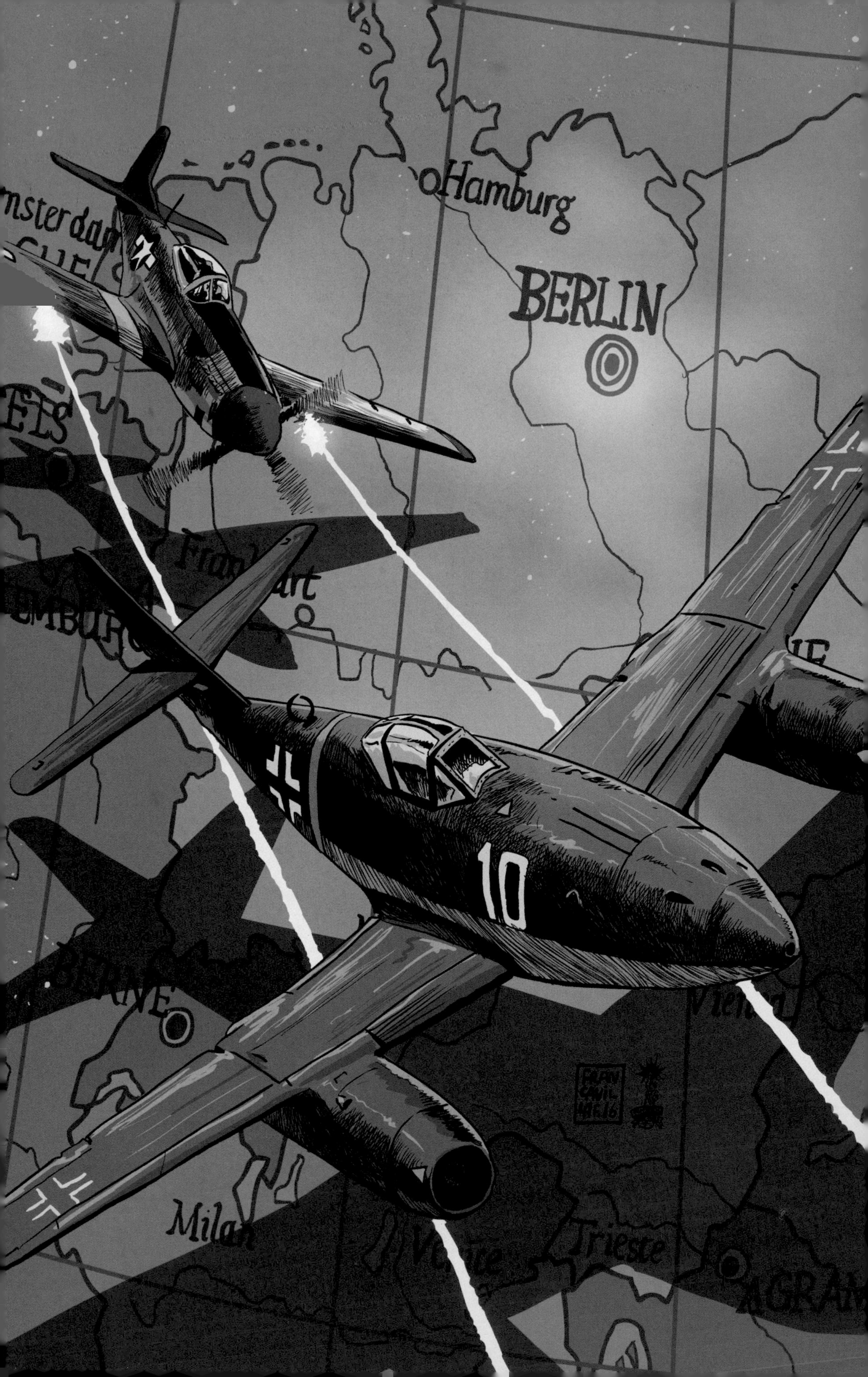
Hamburg
BERLIN
10
Milan
Trieste

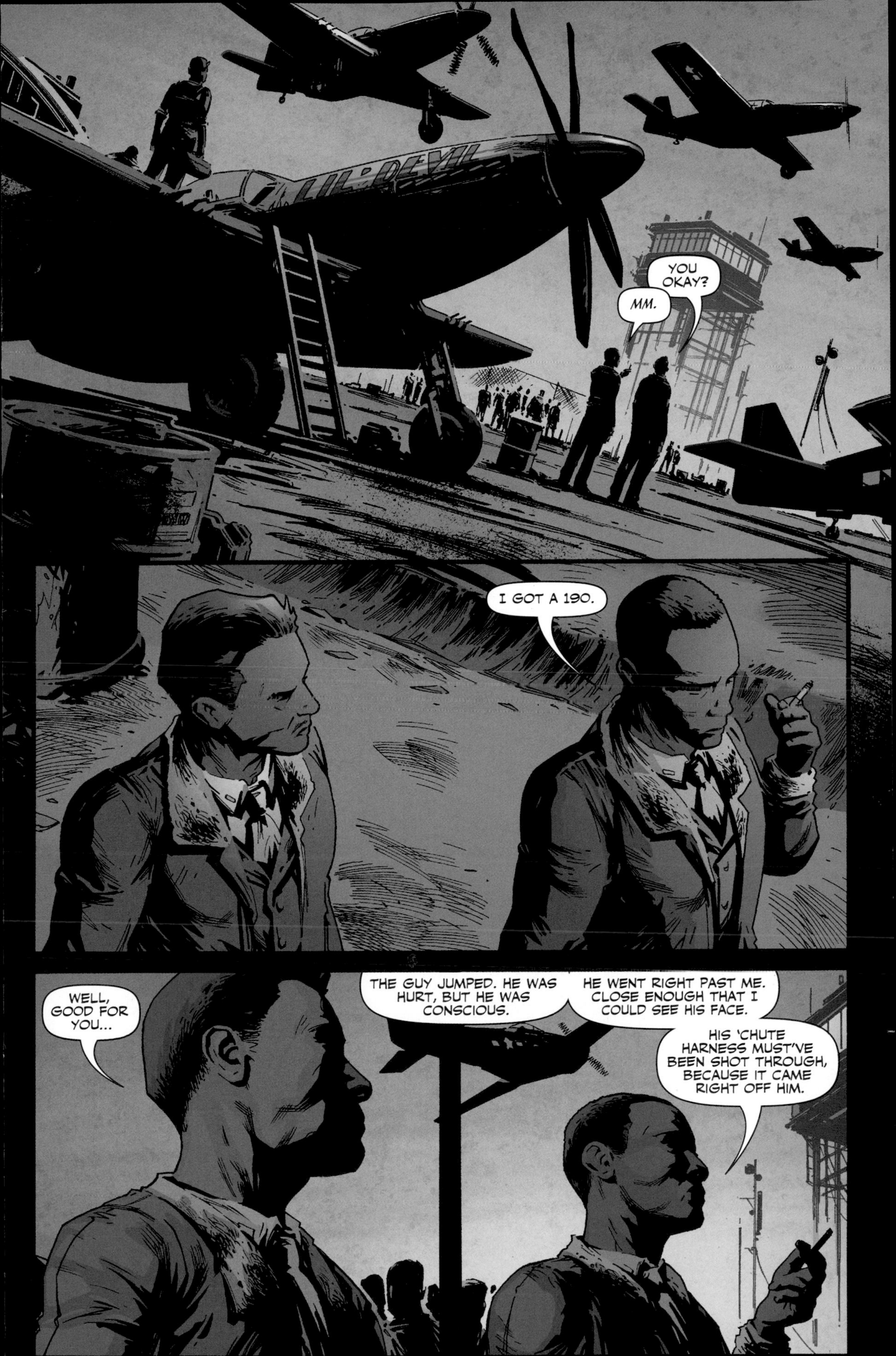
LIL' DEVIL
YOU OKAY?
MM.
I GOT A 190.
WELL, GOOD FOR YOU...
THE GUY JUMPED. HE WAS HURT, BUT HE WAS CONSCIOUS.
HE WENT RIGHT PAST ME. CLOSE ENOUGH THAT I COULD SEE HIS FACE.
HIS 'CHUTE HARNESS MUST'VE BEEN SHOT THROUGH, BECAUSE IT CAME RIGHT OFF HIM.

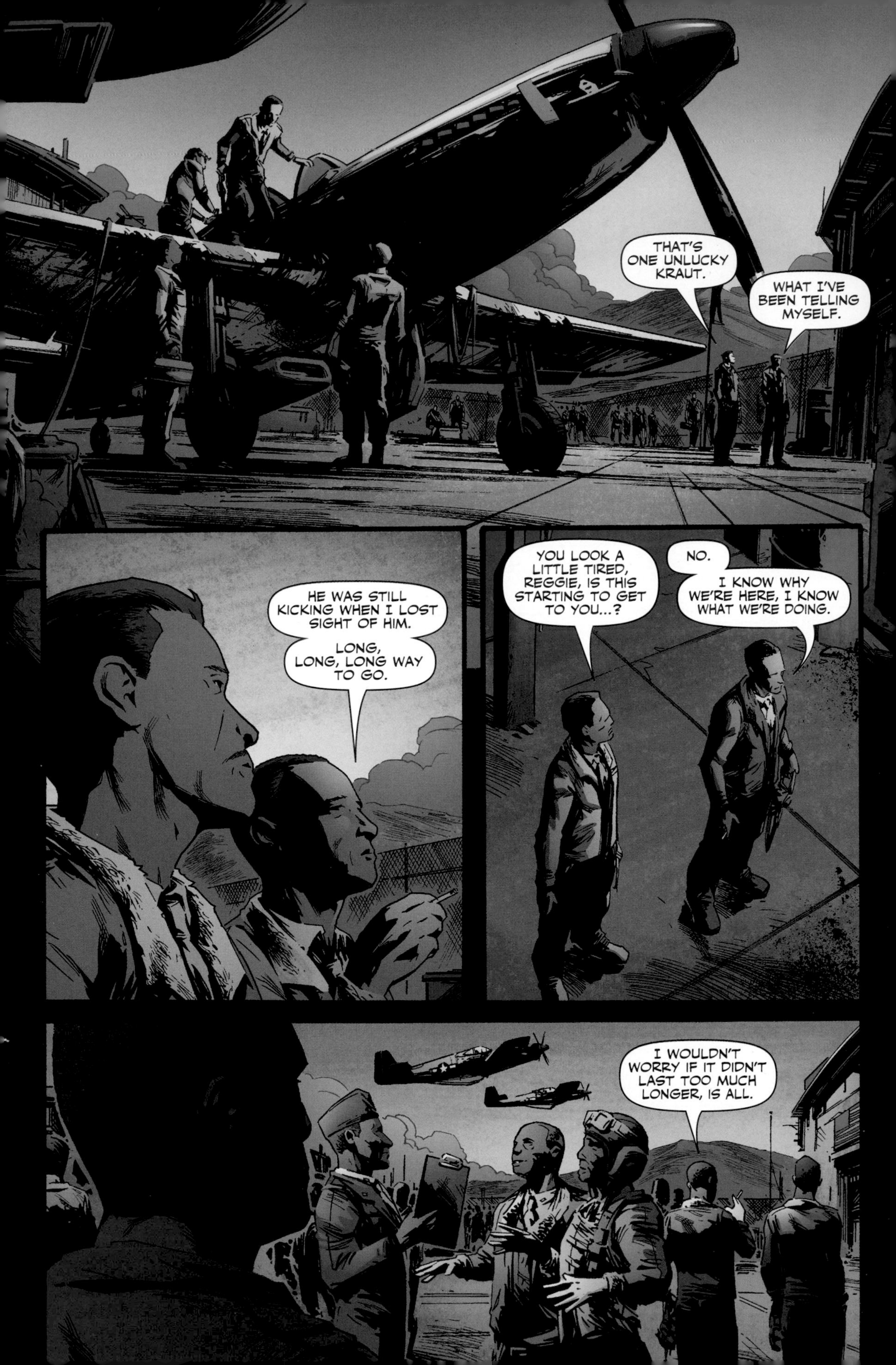
THAT'S ONE UNLUCKY KRAUT.
WHAT I'VE BEEN TELLING MYSELF.
HE WAS STILL KICKING WHEN I LOST SIGHT OF HIM.
LONG, LONG, LONG WAY TO GO.
YOU LOOK A LITTLE TIRED, REGGIE, IS THIS STARTING TO GET TO YOU...?
NO.
I KNOW WHY WE'RE HERE, I KNOW WHAT WE'RE DOING.
I WOULDN'T WORRY IF IT DIDN'T LAST TOO MUCH LONGER, IS ALL.

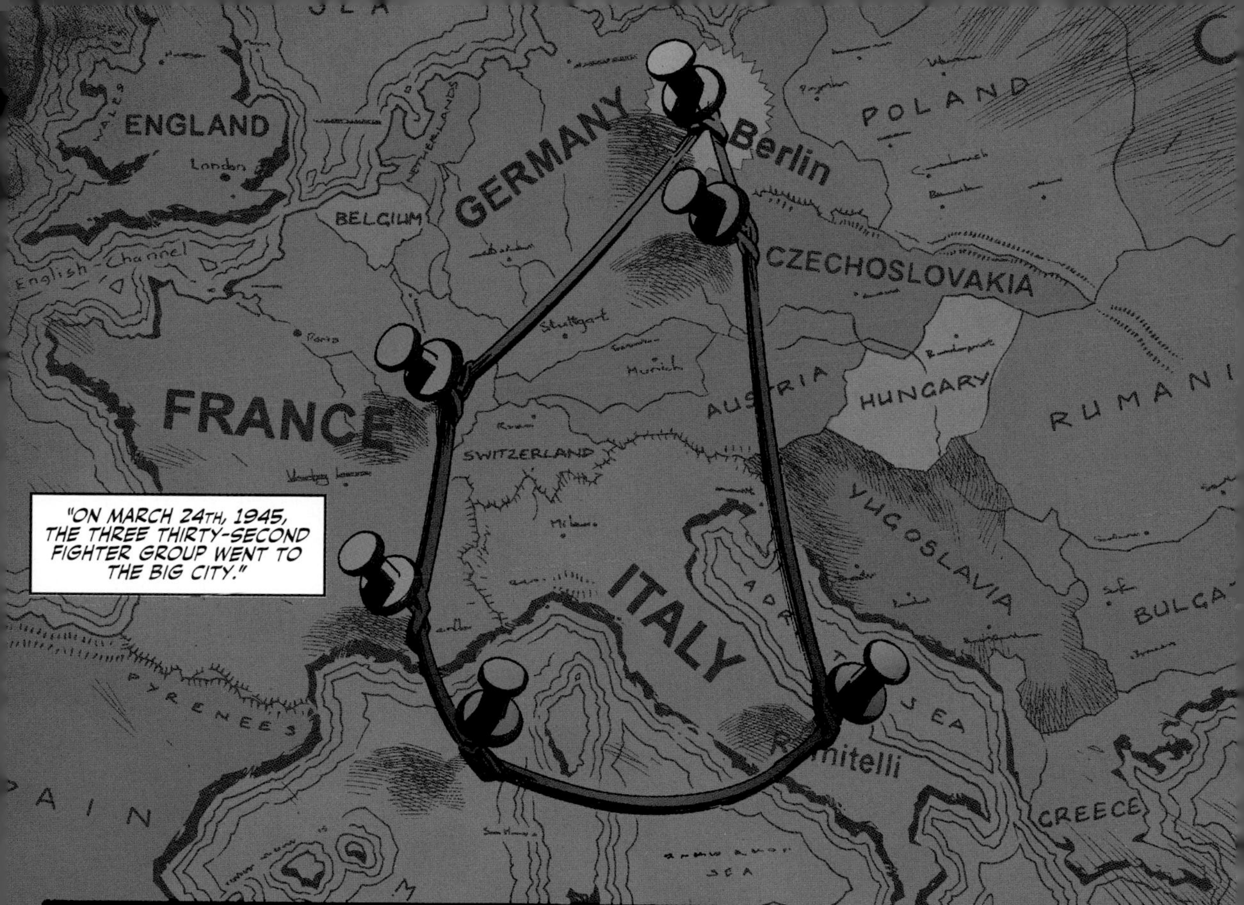
ENGLAND
London
English Channel
BELGIUM
GERMANY
Berlin
POLAND
CZECHOSLOVAKIA
Stuttgart
Munich
FRANCE
AUSTRIA
HUNGARY
RUMANI
SWITZERLAND
YUGOSLAVIA
ITALY
BULGA-
PYRENEES
GREECE
"ON MARCH 24TH, 1945, THE THREE THIRTY-SECOND FIGHTER GROUP WENT TO THE BIG CITY."

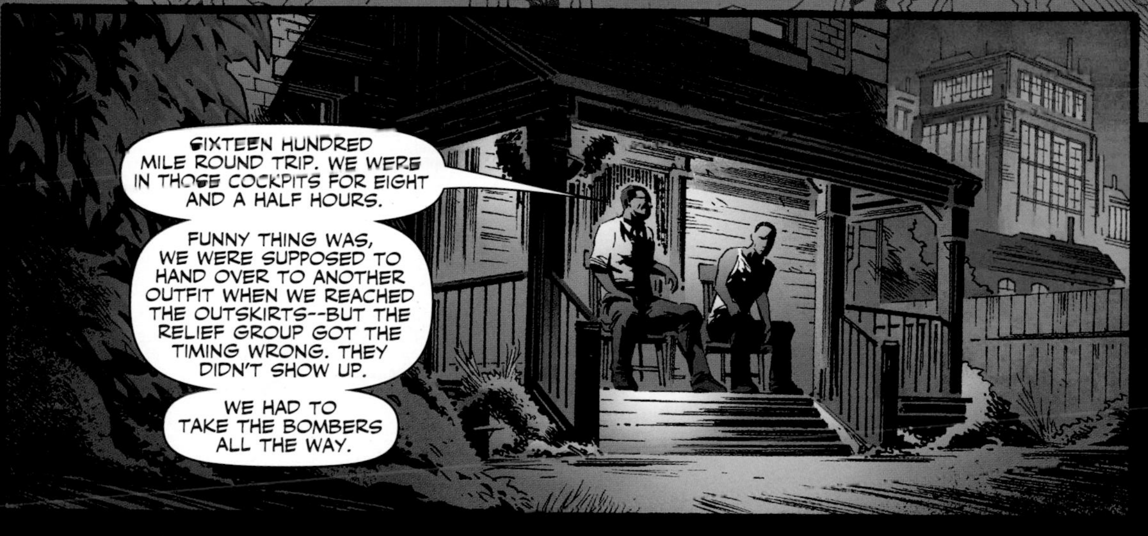
SIXTEEN HUNDRED MILE ROUND TRIP. WE WERE IN THOSE COCKPITS FOR EIGHT AND A HALF HOURS.
FUNNY THING WAS, WE WERE SUPPOSED TO HAND OVER TO ANOTHER OUTFIT WHEN WE REACHED THE OUTSKIRTS--BUT THE RELIEF GROUP GOT THE TIMING WRONG. THEY DIDN'T SHOW UP.
WE HAD TO TAKE THE BOMBERS ALL THE WAY.

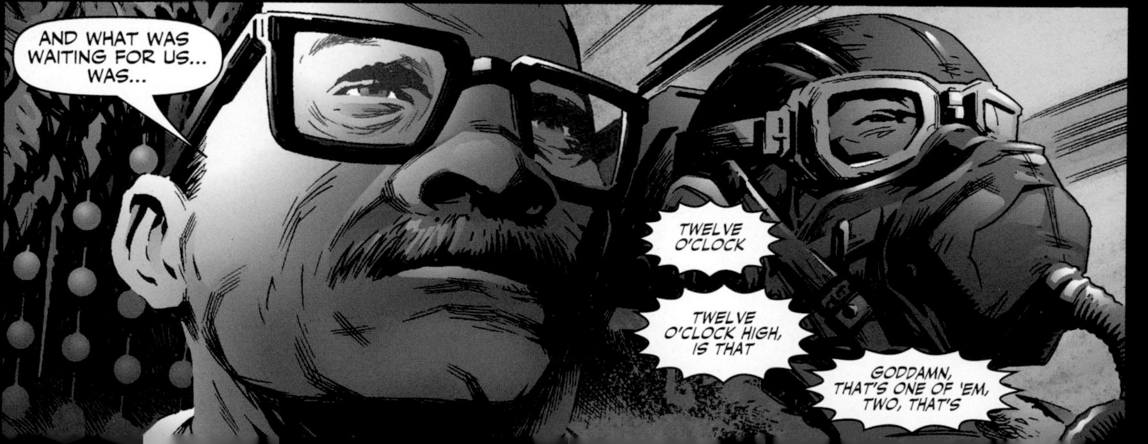
AND WHAT WAS WAITING FOR US... WAS...
TWELVE O'CLOCK
TWELVE O'CLOCK HIGH, IS THAT
GODDAMN, THAT'S ONE OF 'EM, TWO, THAT'S

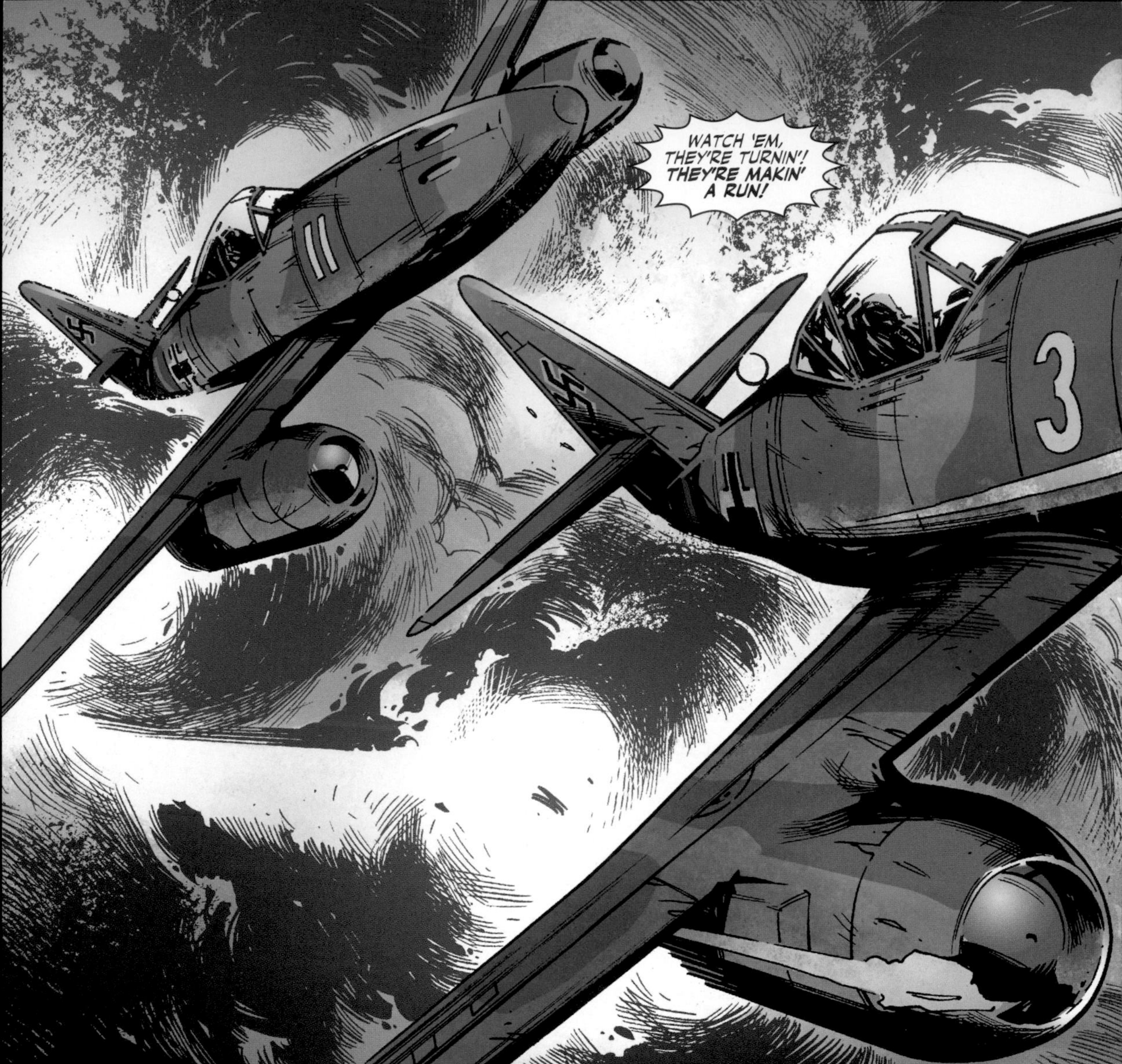
WATCH 'EM, THEY'RE TURNIN'! THEY'RE MAKIN' A RUN!

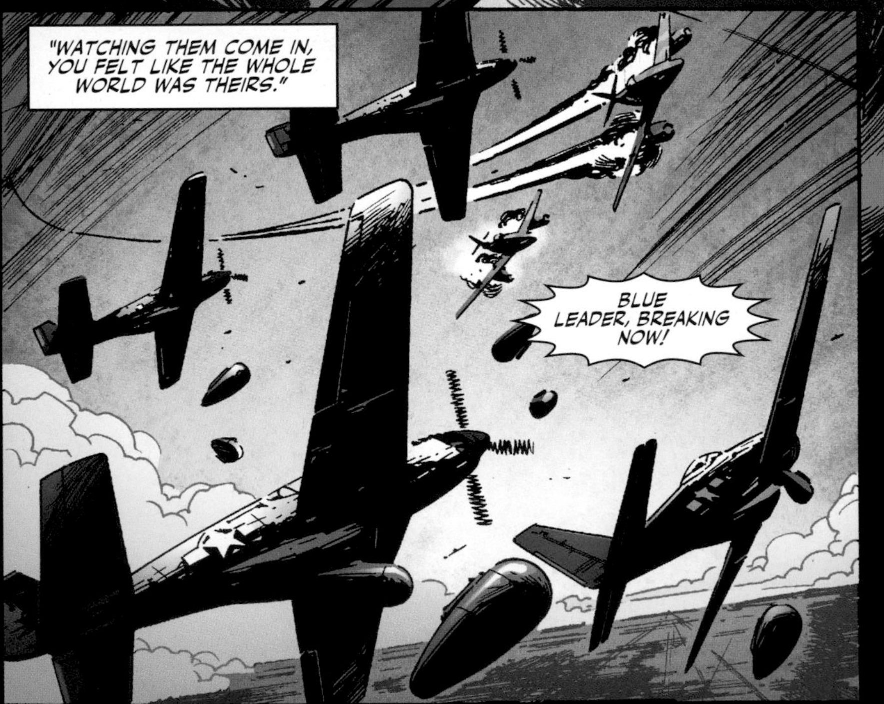
"WATCHING THEM COME IN, YOU FELT LIKE THE WHOLE WORLD WAS THEIRS."
BLUE LEADER, BREAKING NOW!

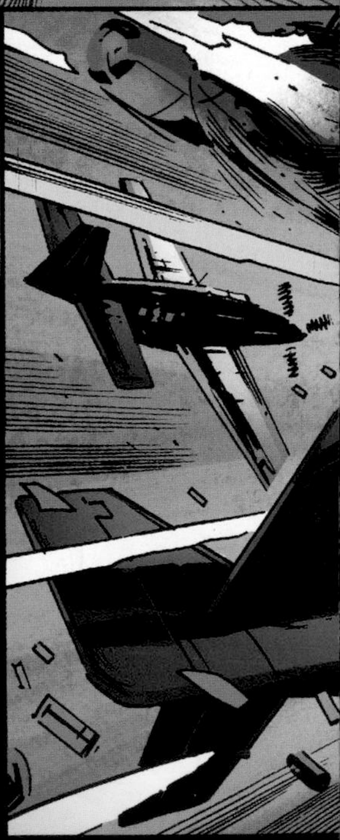

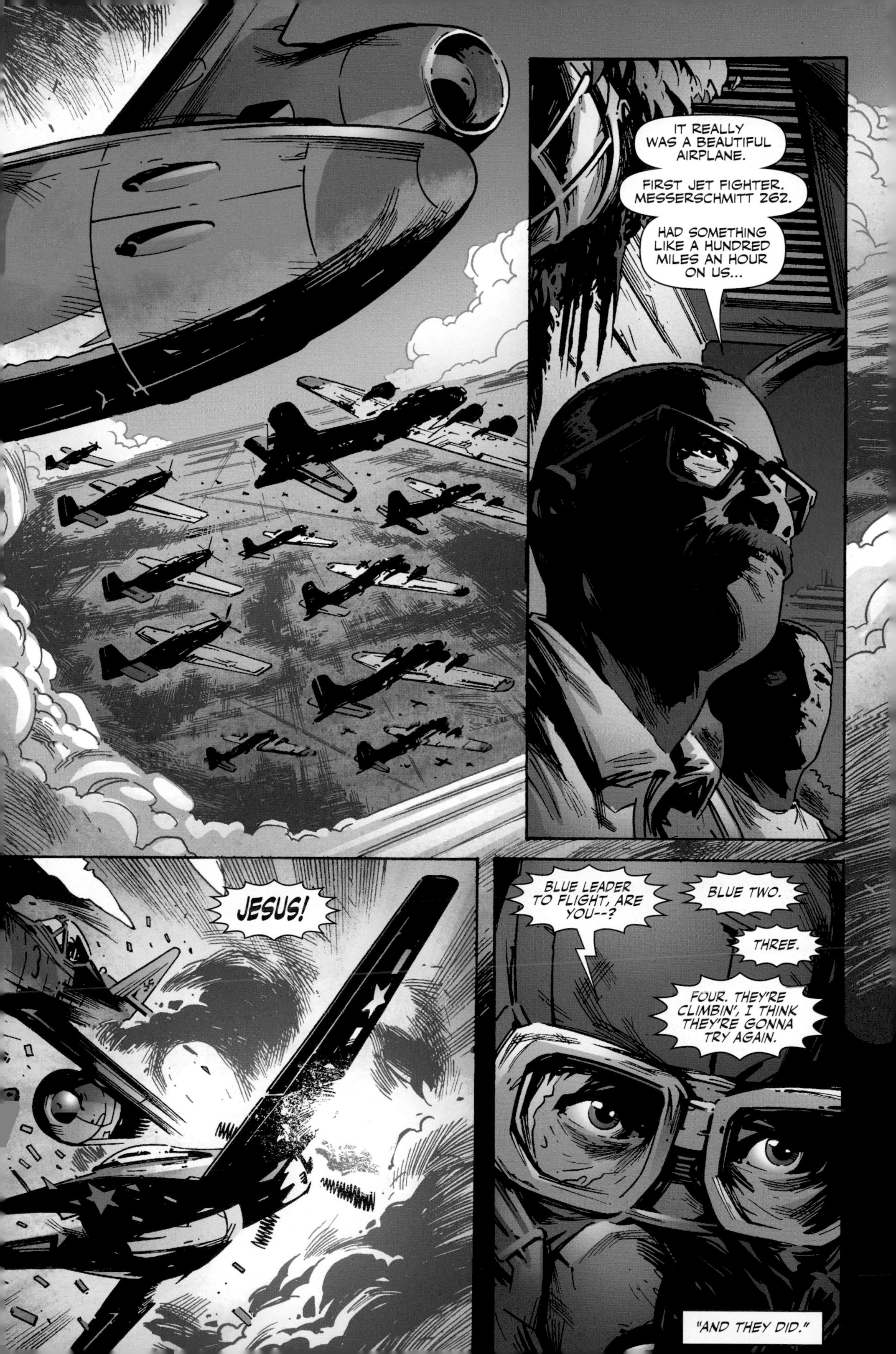
IT REALLY WAS A BEAUTIFUL AIRPLANE.
FIRST JET FIGHTER. MESSERSCHMITT 262.
HAD SOMETHING LIKE A HUNDRED MILES AN HOUR ON US...
JESUS!
BLUE LEADER TO FLIGHT, ARE YOU--?
BLUE TWO.
THREE.
FOUR. THEY'RE CLIMBIN', I THINK THEY'RE GONNA TRY AGAIN.
"AND THEY DID."

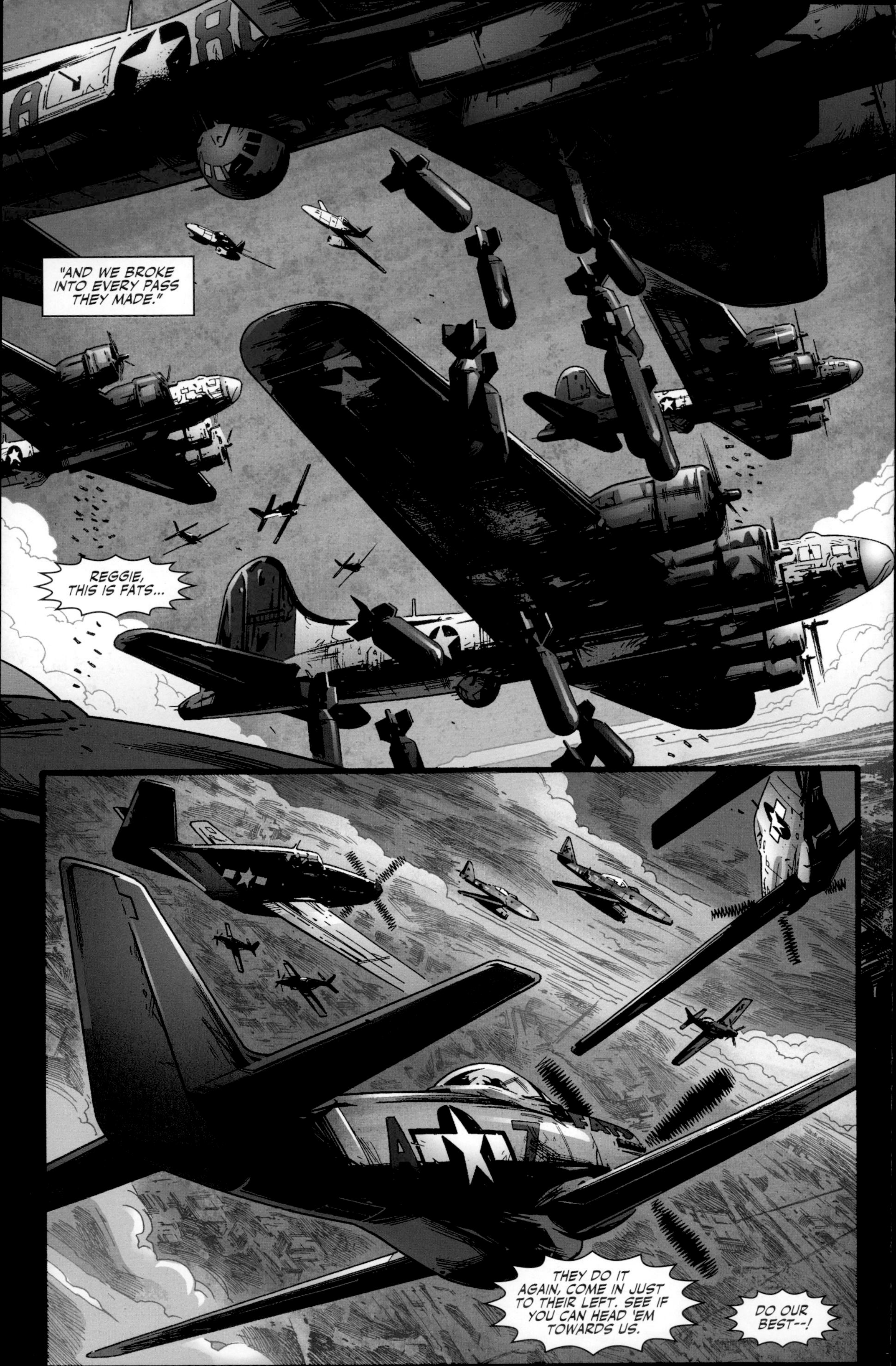
"AND WE BROKE INTO EVERY PASS THEY MADE."
REGGIE, THIS IS FATS...
THEY DO IT AGAIN, COME IN JUST TO THEIR LEFT. SEE IF YOU CAN HEAD 'EM TOWARDS US.
DO OUR BEST--!

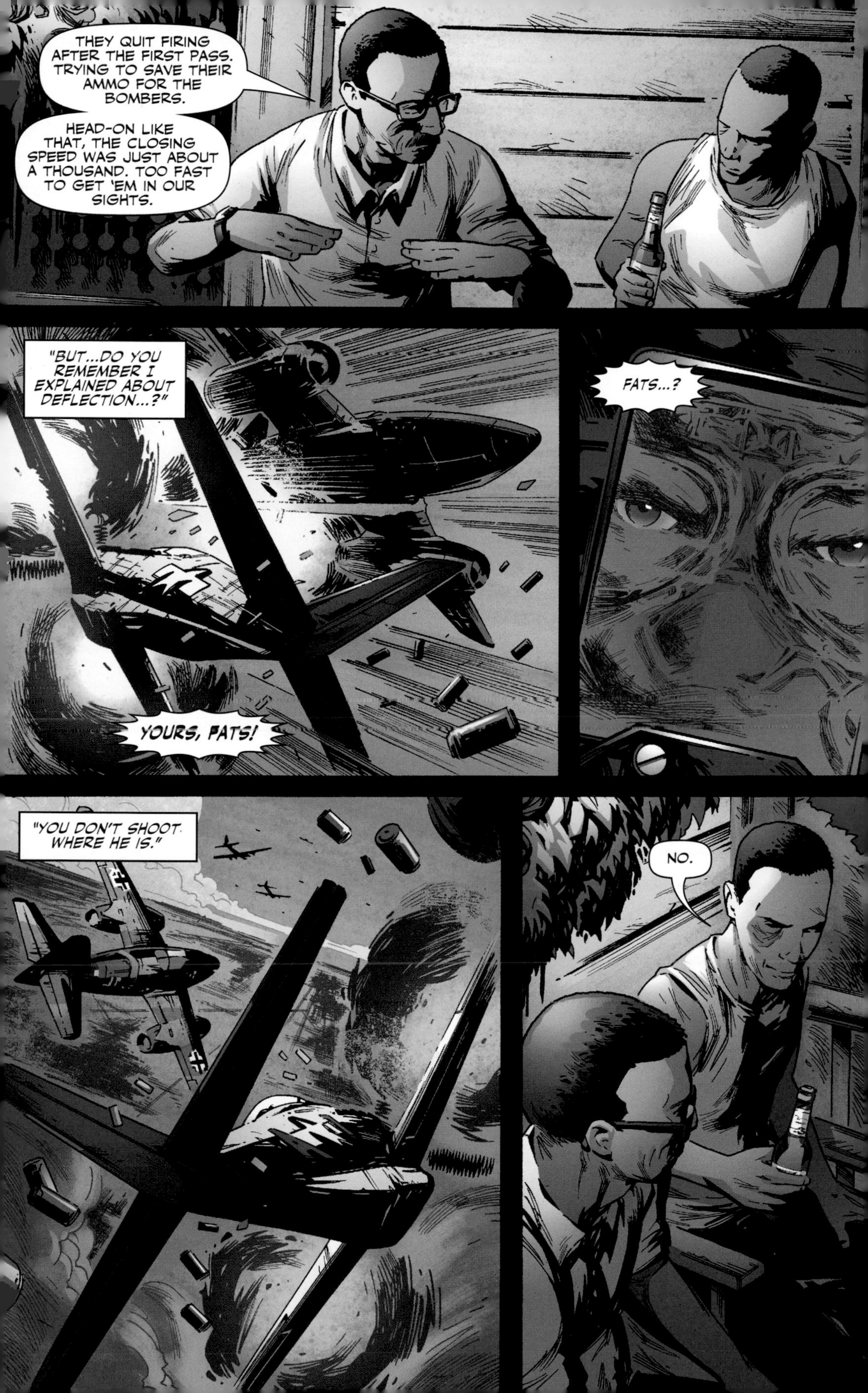
THEY QUIT FIRING AFTER THE FIRST PASS. TRYING TO SAVE THEIR AMMO FOR THE BOMBERS.
HEAD-ON LIKE THAT, THE CLOSING SPEED WAS JUST ABOUT A THOUSAND. TOO FAST TO GET 'EM IN OUR SIGHTS.
"BUT...DO YOU REMEMBER I EXPLAINED ABOUT DEFLECTION...?"
YOURS, FATS!
FATS...?
"YOU DON'T SHOOT WHERE HE IS."
NO.

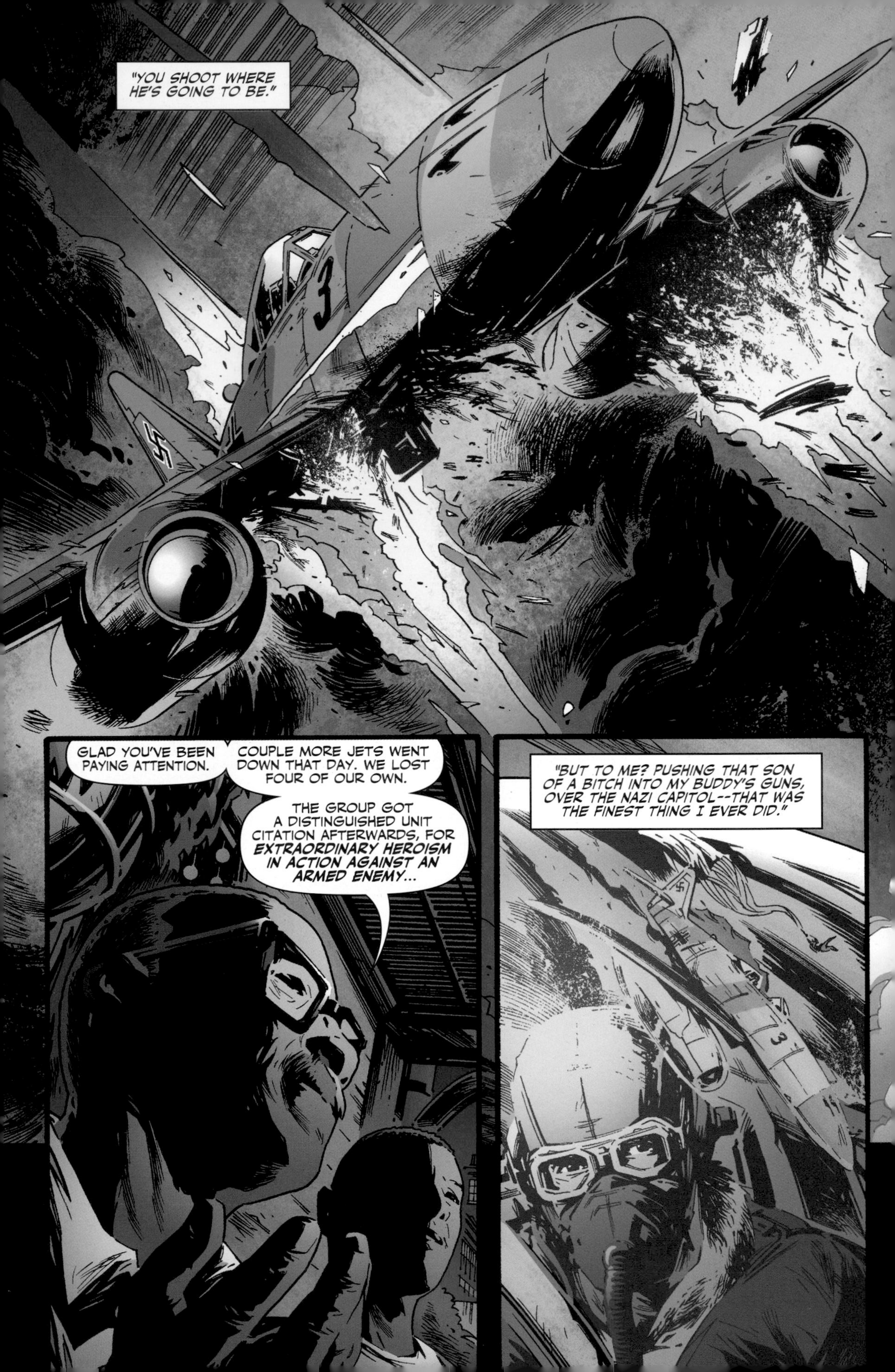
"YOU SHOOT WHERE HE'S GOING TO BE."
GLAD YOU'VE BEEN PAYING ATTENTION.
COUPLE MORE JETS WENT DOWN THAT DAY. WE LOST FOUR OF OUR OWN.
THE GROUP GOT A DISTINGUISHED UNIT CITATION AFTERWARDS, FOR *EXTRAORDINARY HEROISM IN ACTION AGAINST AN ARMED ENEMY*...
"BUT TO ME? PUSHING THAT SON OF A BITCH INTO MY BUDDY'S GUNS, OVER THE NAZI CAPITOL--THAT WAS THE FINEST THING I EVER DID."

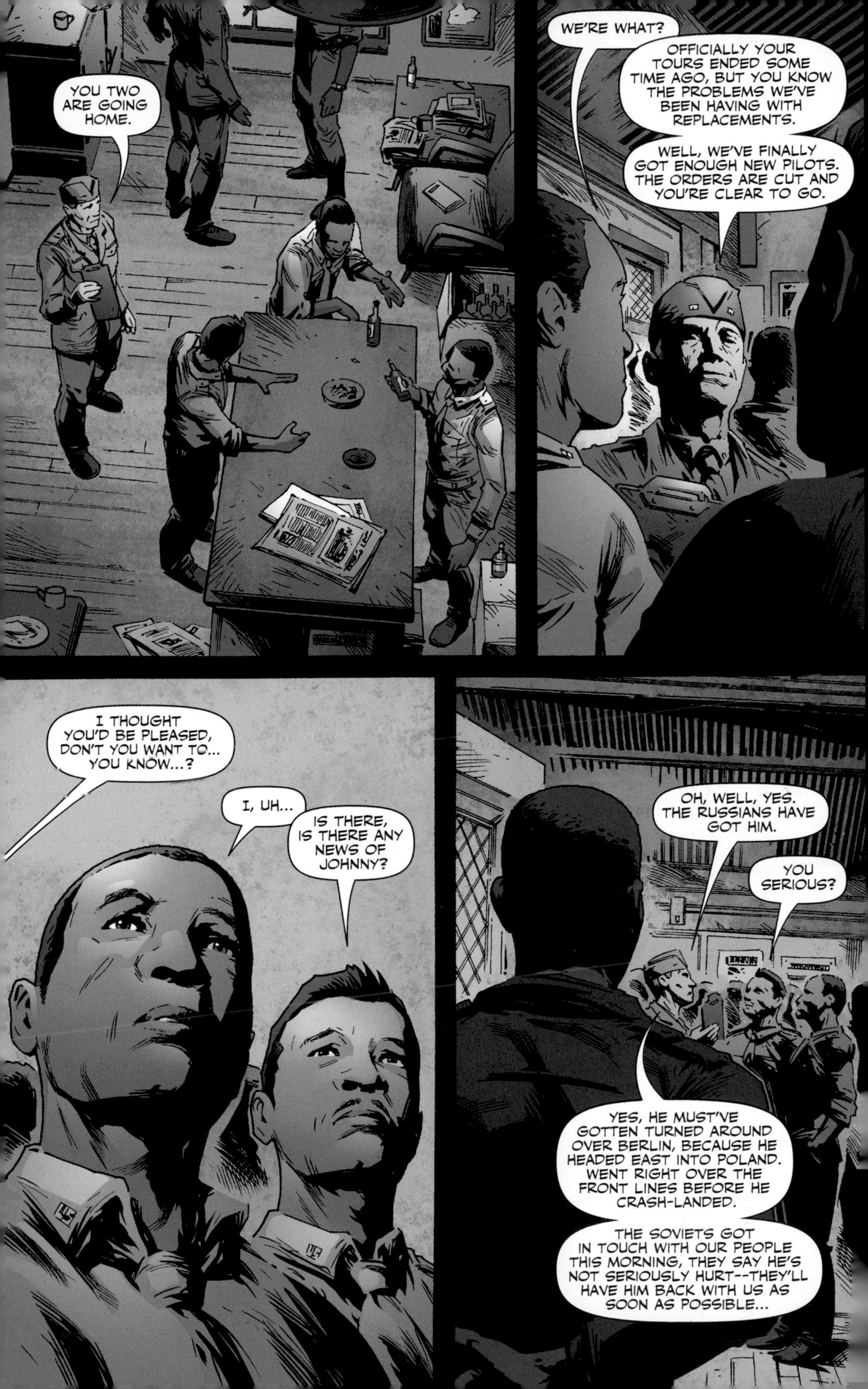
YOU TWO ARE GOING HOME.
WE'RE WHAT?
OFFICIALLY YOUR TOURS ENDED SOME TIME AGO, BUT YOU KNOW THE PROBLEMS WE'VE BEEN HAVING WITH REPLACEMENTS.
WELL, WE'VE FINALLY GOT ENOUGH NEW PILOTS. THE ORDERS ARE CUT AND YOU'RE CLEAR TO GO.
I THOUGHT YOU'D BE PLEASED, DON'T YOU WANT TO... YOU KNOW...?
I, UH...
IS THERE, IS THERE ANY NEWS OF JOHNNY?
OH, WELL, YES. THE RUSSIANS HAVE GOT HIM.
YOU SERIOUS?
YES, HE MUST'VE GOTTEN TURNED AROUND OVER BERLIN, BECAUSE HE HEADED EAST INTO POLAND. WENT RIGHT OVER THE FRONT LINES BEFORE HE CRASH-LANDED.
THE SOVIETS GOT IN TOUCH WITH OUR PEOPLE THIS MORNING, THEY SAY HE'S NOT SERIOUSLY HURT--THEY'LL HAVE HIM BACK WITH US AS SOON AS POSSIBLE...

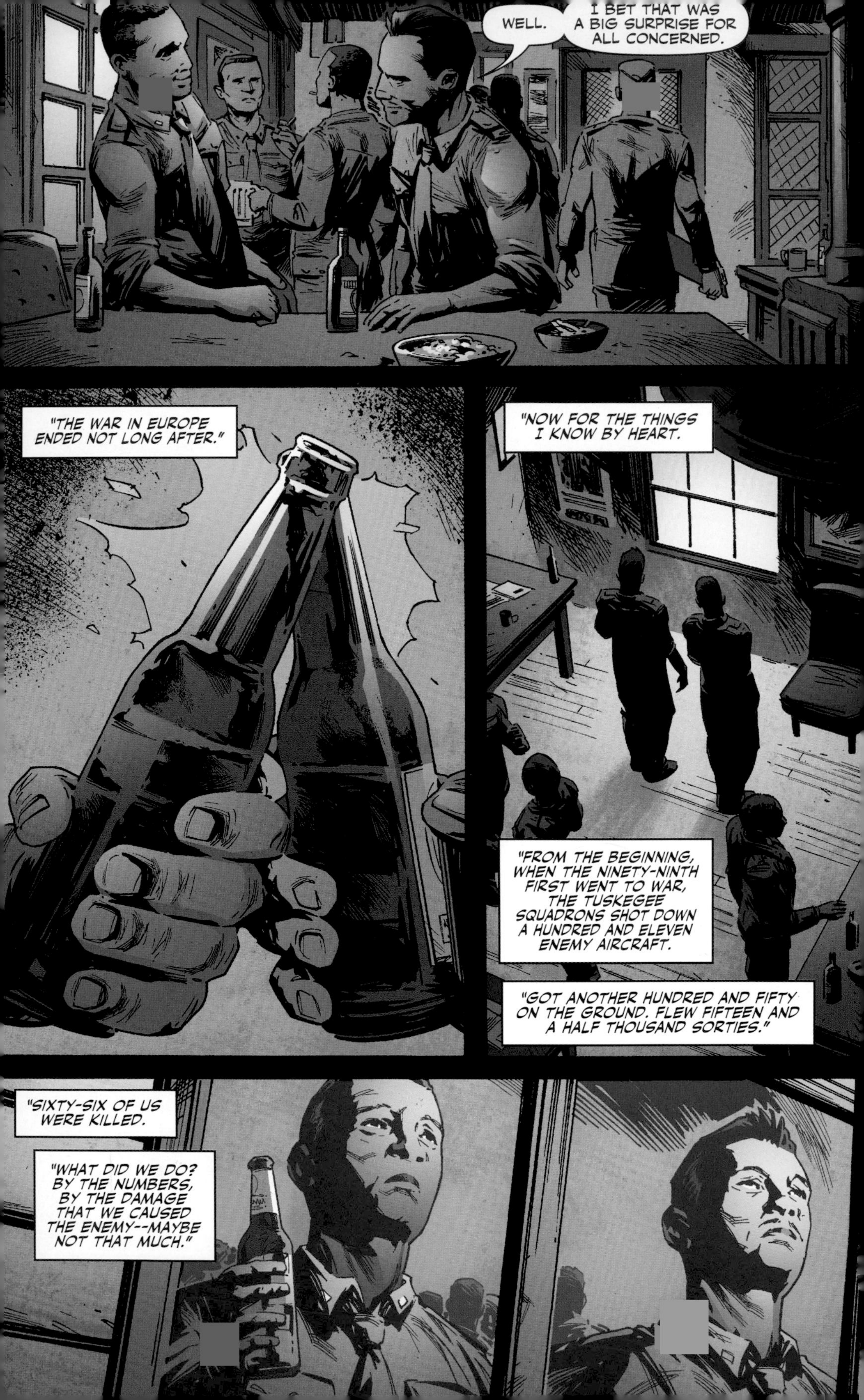
WELL.
I BET THAT WAS A BIG SURPRISE FOR ALL CONCERNED.
"THE WAR IN EUROPE ENDED NOT LONG AFTER."
"NOW FOR THE THINGS I KNOW BY HEART.
"FROM THE BEGINNING, WHEN THE NINETY-NINTH FIRST WENT TO WAR, THE TUSKEGEE SQUADRONS SHOT DOWN A HUNDRED AND ELEVEN ENEMY AIRCRAFT.
"GOT ANOTHER HUNDRED AND FIFTY ON THE GROUND. FLEW FIFTEEN AND A HALF THOUSAND SORTIES."
"SIXTY-SIX OF US WERE KILLED.
"WHAT DID WE DO? BY THE NUMBERS, BY THE DAMAGE THAT WE CAUSED THE ENEMY--MAYBE NOT THAT MUCH."

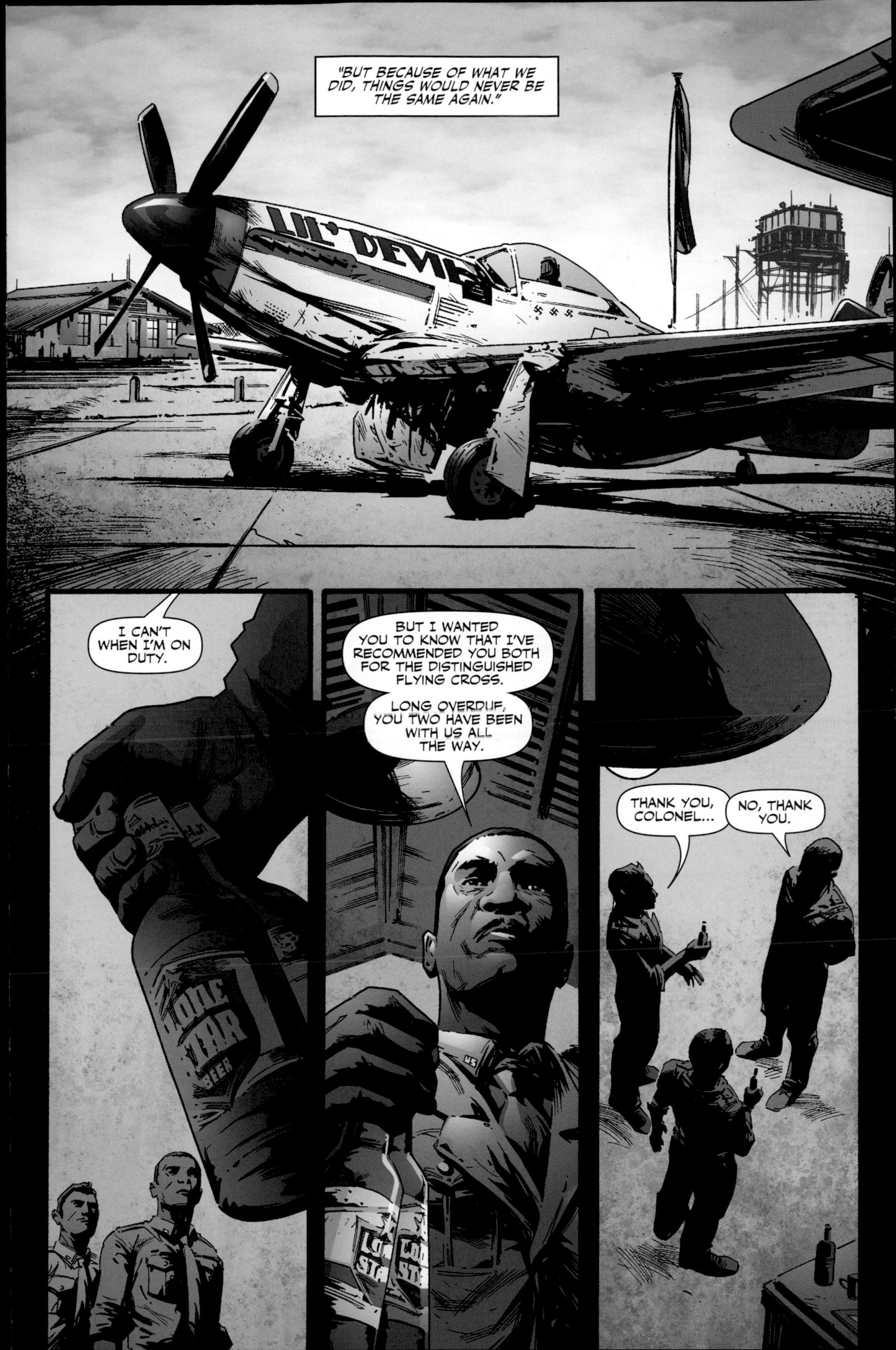
"BUT BECAUSE OF WHAT WE DID, THINGS WOULD NEVER BE THE SAME AGAIN."
LIL' DEVIL
I CAN'T WHEN I'M ON DUTY.
BUT I WANTED YOU TO KNOW THAT I'VE RECOMMENDED YOU BOTH FOR THE DISTINGUISHED FLYING CROSS.
LONG OVERDUE, YOU TWO HAVE BEEN WITH US ALL THE WAY.
THANK YOU, COLONEL...
NO, THANK YOU.

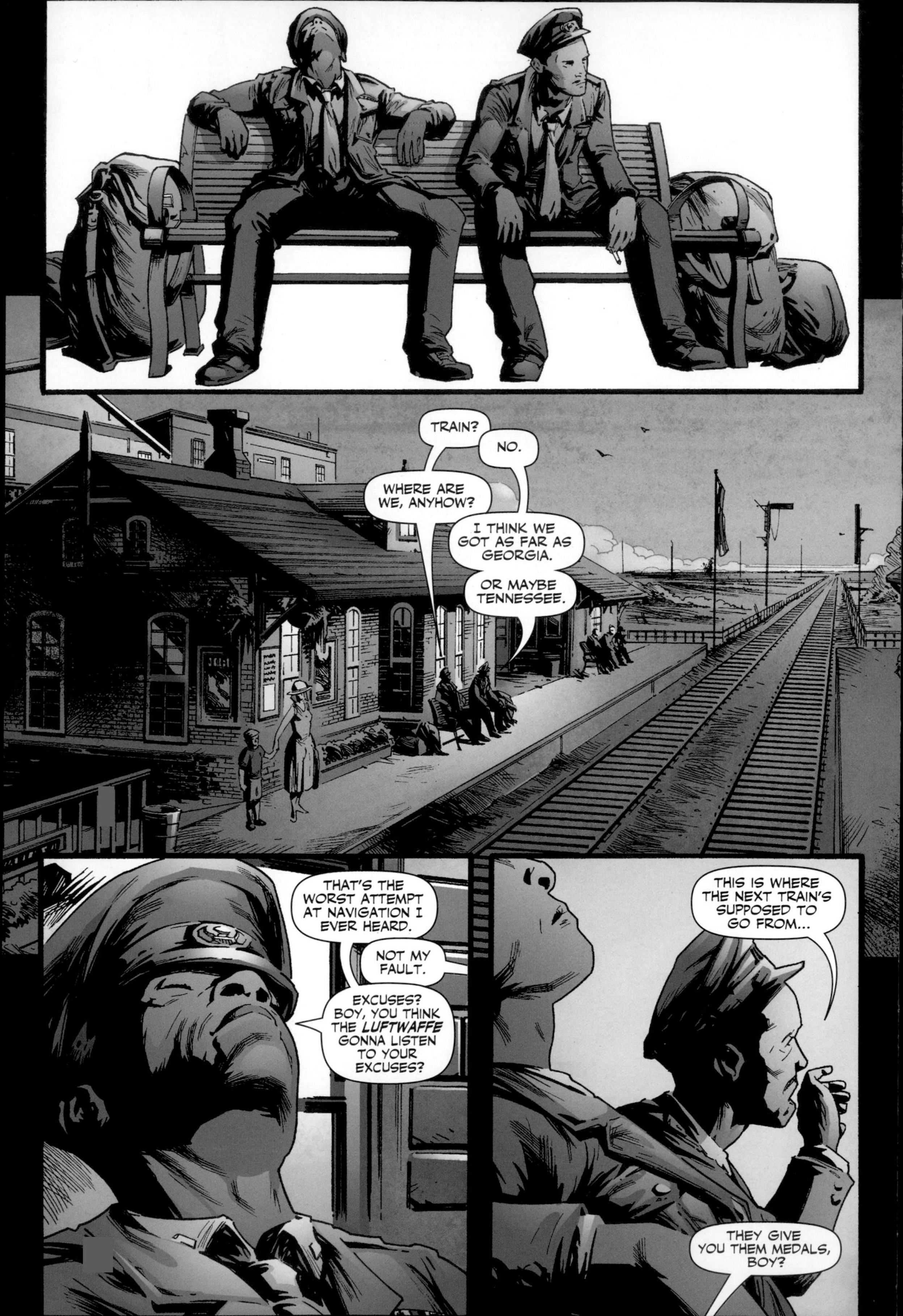
TRAIN?
NO.
WHERE ARE WE, ANYHOW?
I THINK WE GOT AS FAR AS GEORGIA.
OR MAYBE TENNESSEE.
THAT'S THE WORST ATTEMPT AT NAVIGATION I EVER HEARD.
NOT MY FAULT.
EXCUSES? BOY, YOU THINK THE *LUFTWAFFE* GONNA LISTEN TO YOUR EXCUSES?
THIS IS WHERE THE NEXT TRAIN'S SUPPOSED TO GO FROM...
THEY GIVE YOU THEM MEDALS, BOY?

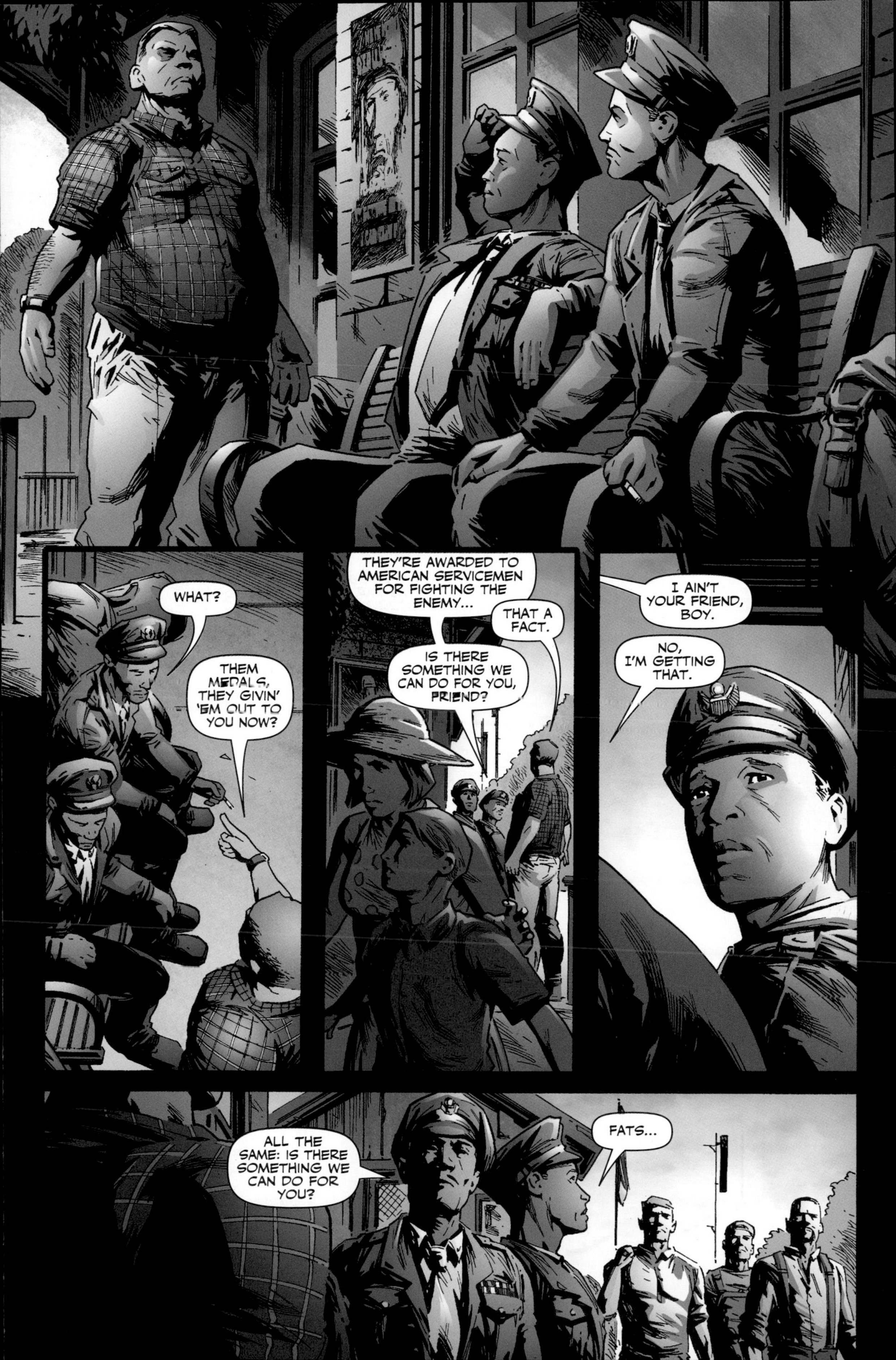
WHAT?
THEM MEDALS, THEY GIVIN' 'EM OUT TO YOU NOW?
THEY'RE AWARDED TO AMERICAN SERVICEMEN FOR FIGHTING THE ENEMY...
THAT A FACT.
IS THERE SOMETHING WE CAN DO FOR YOU, FRIEND?
I AIN'T YOUR FRIEND, BOY.
NO, I'M GETTING THAT.
ALL THE SAME: IS THERE SOMETHING WE CAN DO FOR YOU?
FATS...

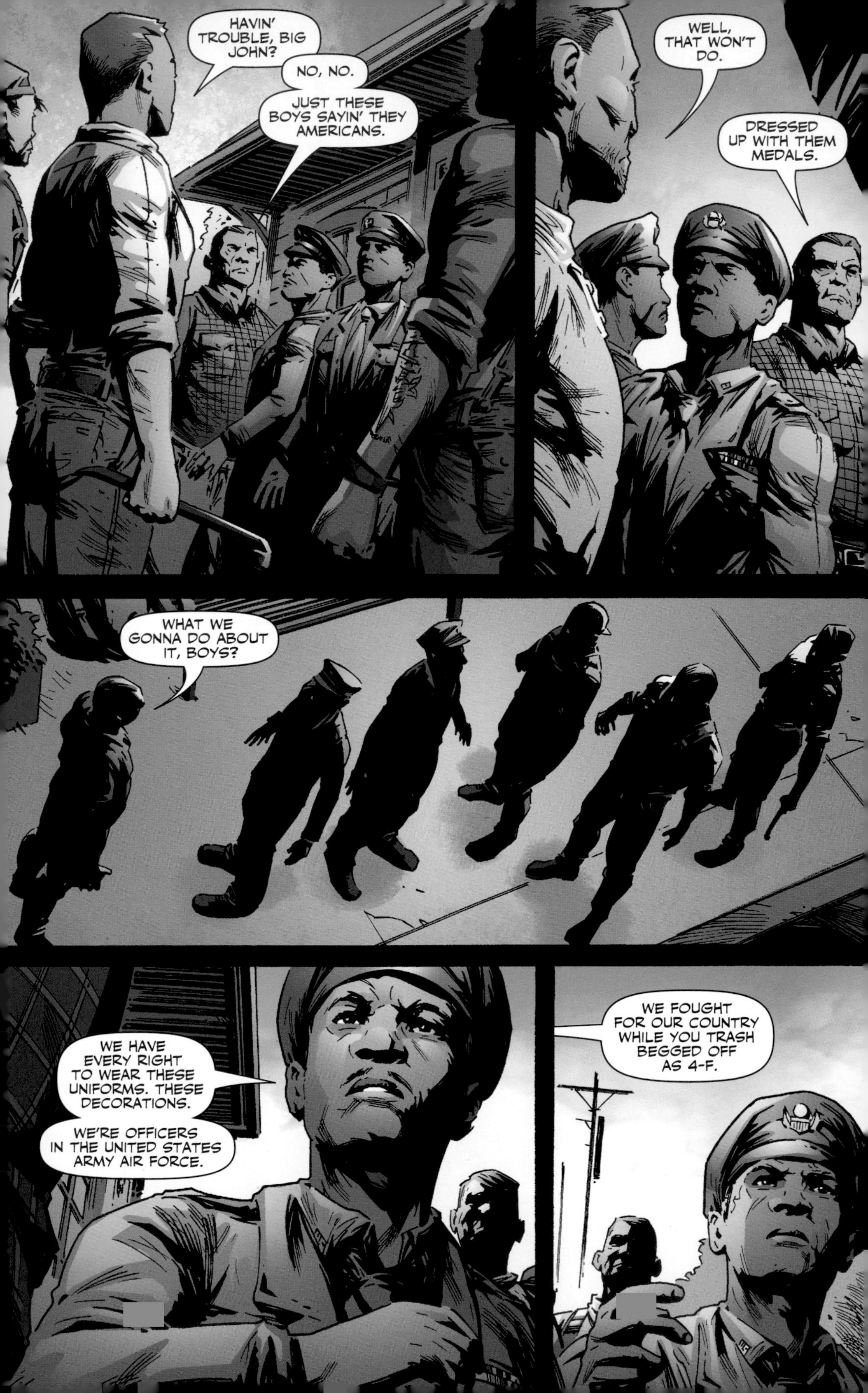
HAVIN' TROUBLE, BIG JOHN?
NO, NO.
JUST THESE BOYS SAYIN' THEY AMERICANS.
WELL, THAT WON'T DO.
DRESSED UP WITH THEM MEDALS.
WHAT WE GONNA DO ABOUT IT, BOYS?
WE HAVE EVERY RIGHT TO WEAR THESE UNIFORMS. THESE DECORATIONS.
WE'RE OFFICERS IN THE UNITED STATES ARMY AIR FORCE.
WE FOUGHT FOR OUR COUNTRY WHILE YOU TRASH BEGGED OFF AS 4-F.

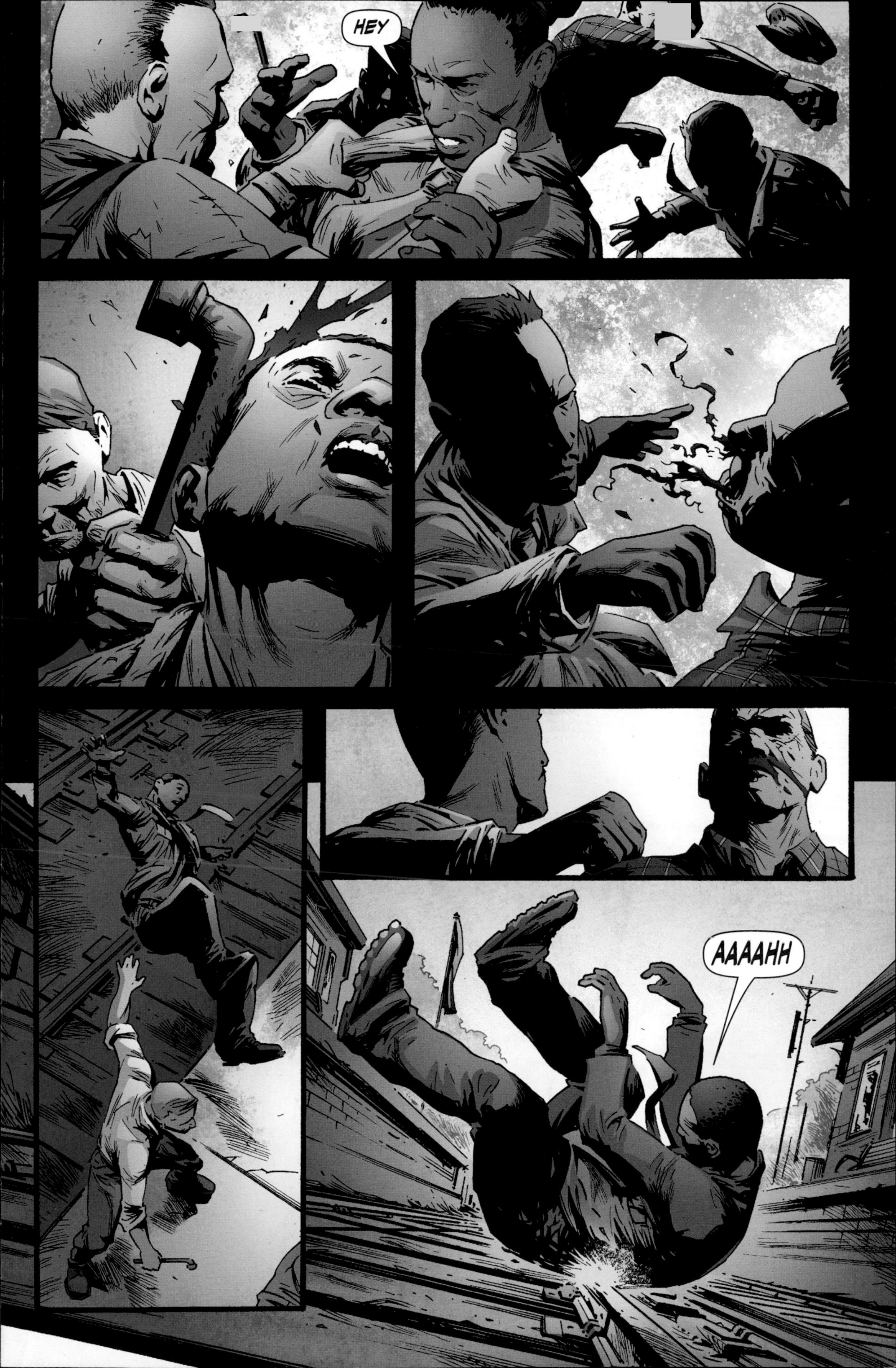
HEY
AAAAHH

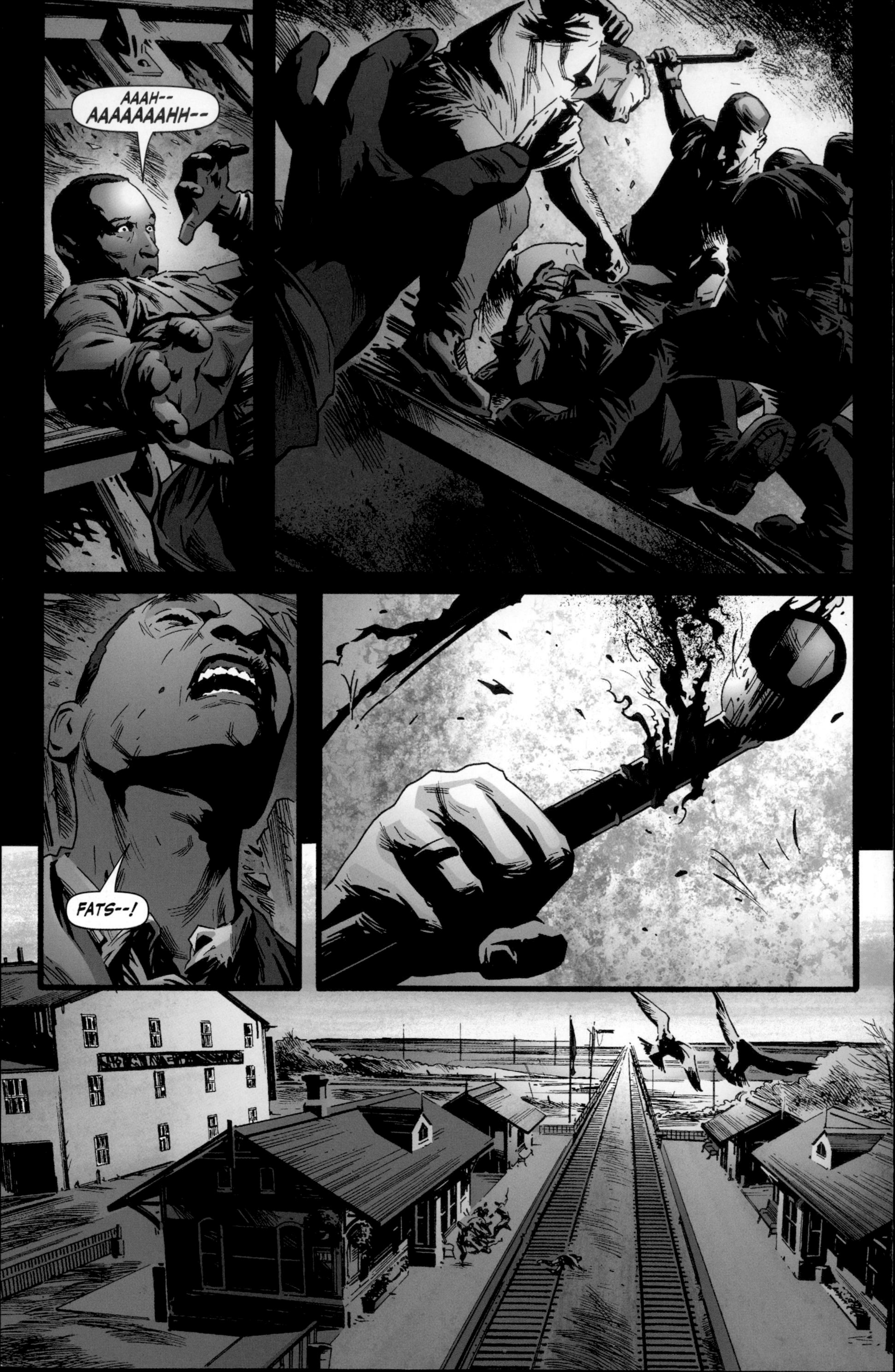
AAAH--
AAAAAAAHH--
FATS--!

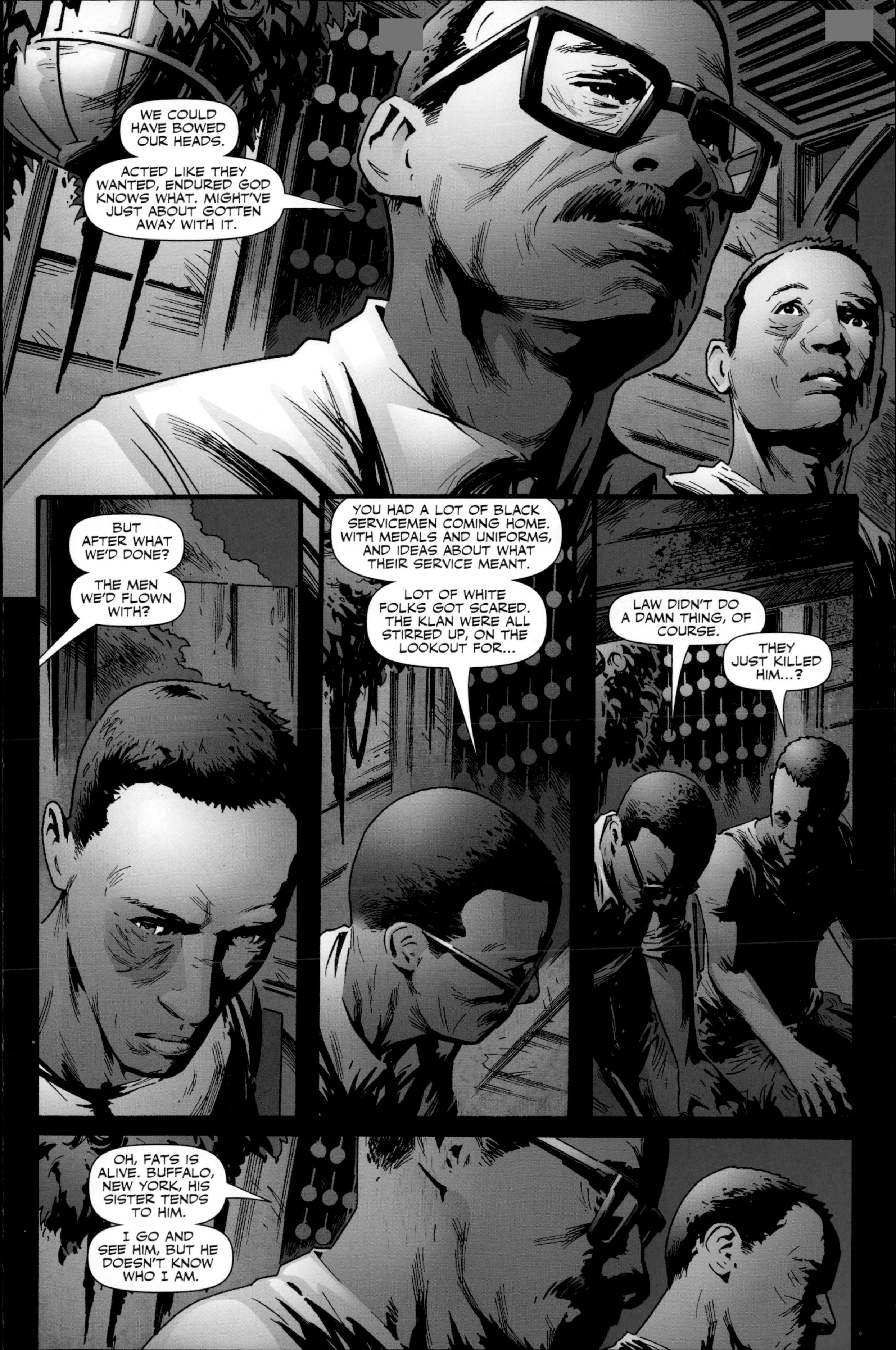

WE COULD HAVE BOWED OUR HEADS.
ACTED LIKE THEY WANTED, ENDURED GOD KNOWS WHAT. MIGHT'VE JUST ABOUT GOTTEN AWAY WITH IT.
BUT AFTER WHAT WE'D DONE?
THE MEN WE'D FLOWN WITH?
YOU HAD A LOT OF BLACK SERVICEMEN COMING HOME. WITH MEDALS AND UNIFORMS, AND IDEAS ABOUT WHAT THEIR SERVICE MEANT.
LOT OF WHITE FOLKS GOT SCARED. THE KLAN WERE ALL STIRRED UP, ON THE LOOKOUT FOR...
LAW DIDN'T DO A DAMN THING, OF COURSE.
THEY JUST KILLED HIM...?
OH, FATS IS ALIVE. BUFFALO, NEW YORK, HIS SISTER TENDS TO HIM.
I GO AND SEE HIM, BUT HE DOESN'T KNOW WHO I AM.

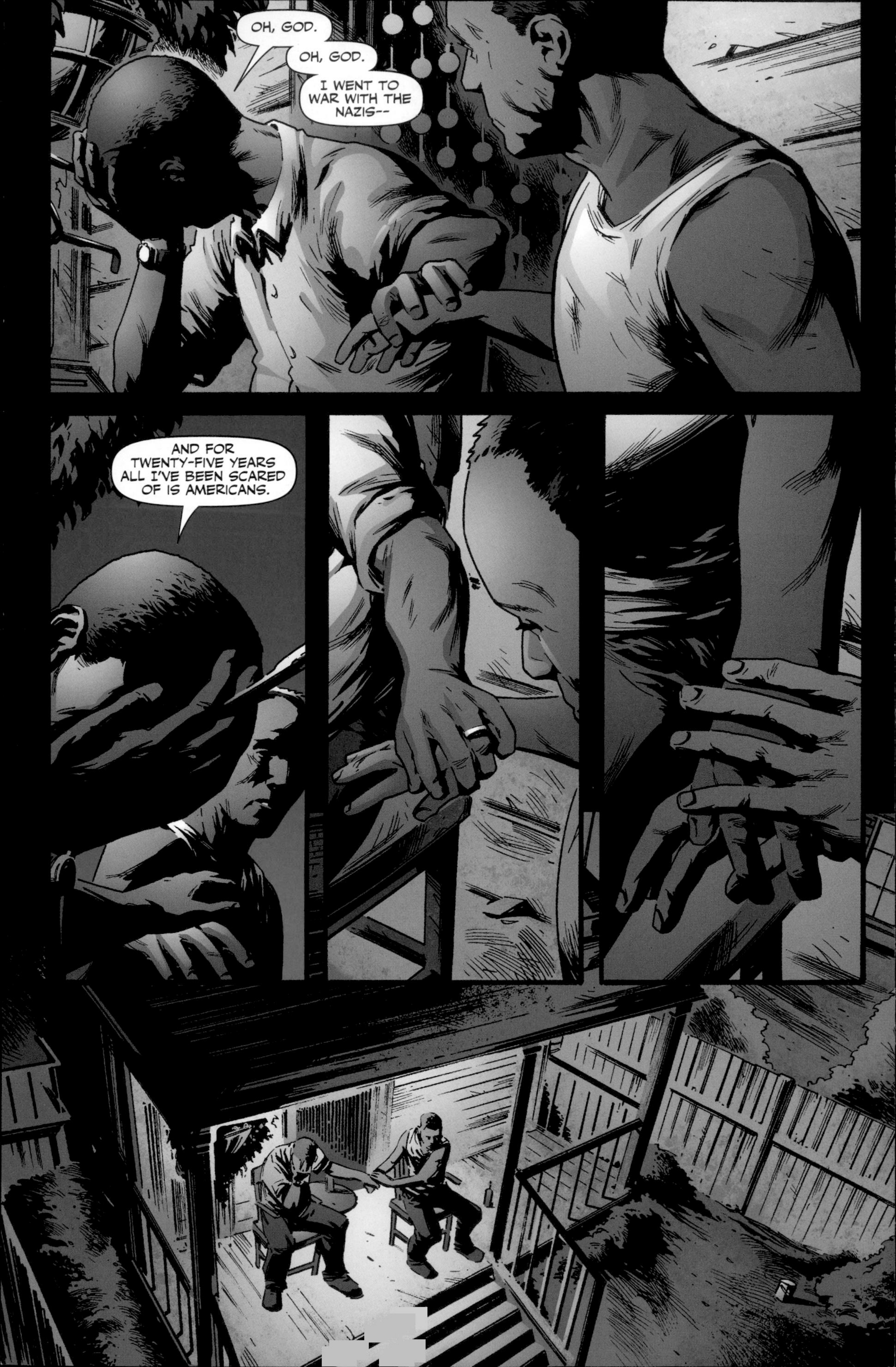
OH, GOD.
OH, GOD.
I WENT TO WAR WITH THE NAZIS--
AND FOR TWENTY-FIVE YEARS ALL I'VE BEEN SCARED OF IS AMERICANS.

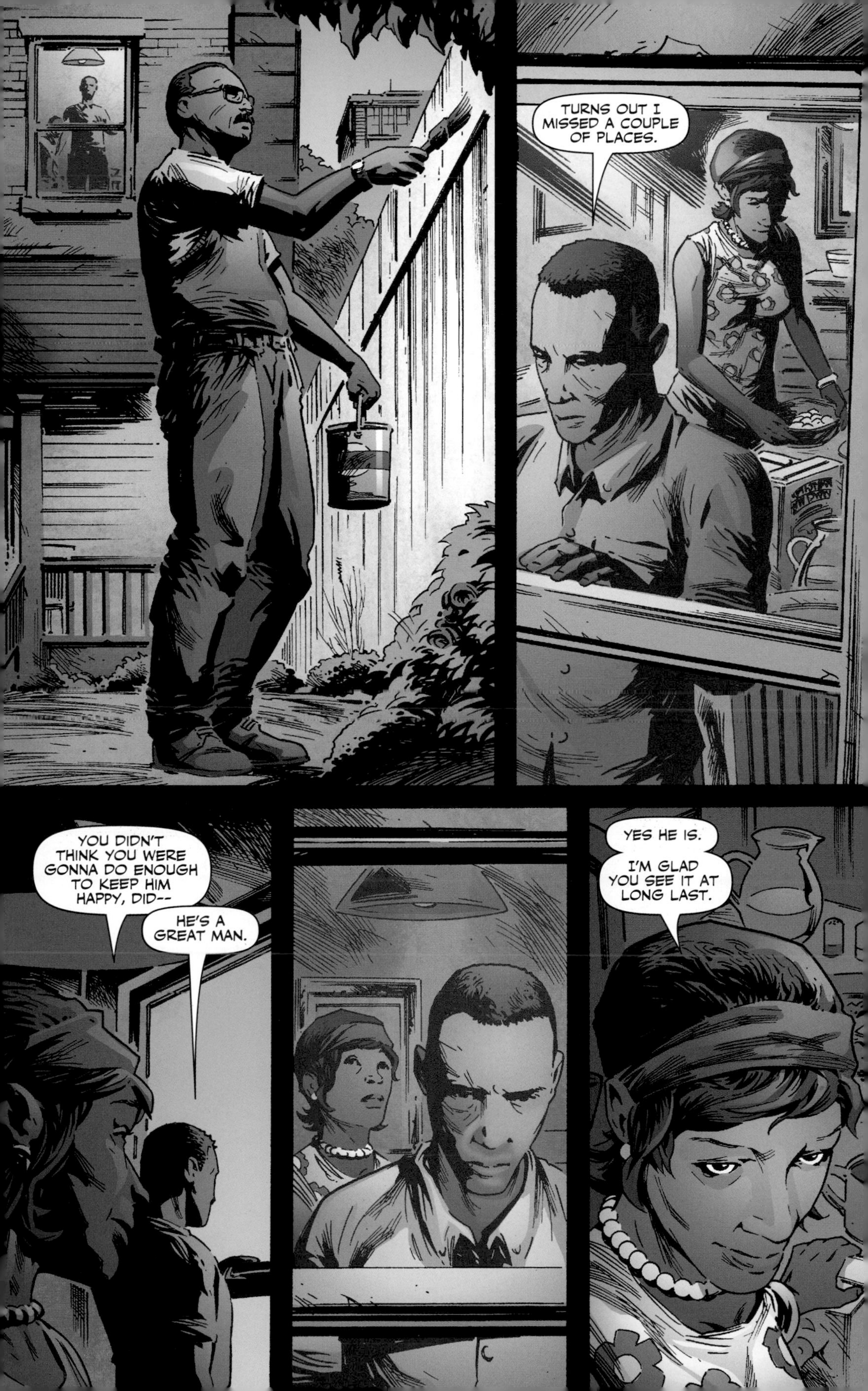

TURNS OUT I MISSED A COUPLE OF PLACES.
YOU DIDN'T THINK YOU WERE GONNA DO ENOUGH TO KEEP HIM HAPPY, DID--
HE'S A GREAT MAN.
YES HE IS.
I'M GLAD YOU SEE IT AT LONG LAST.

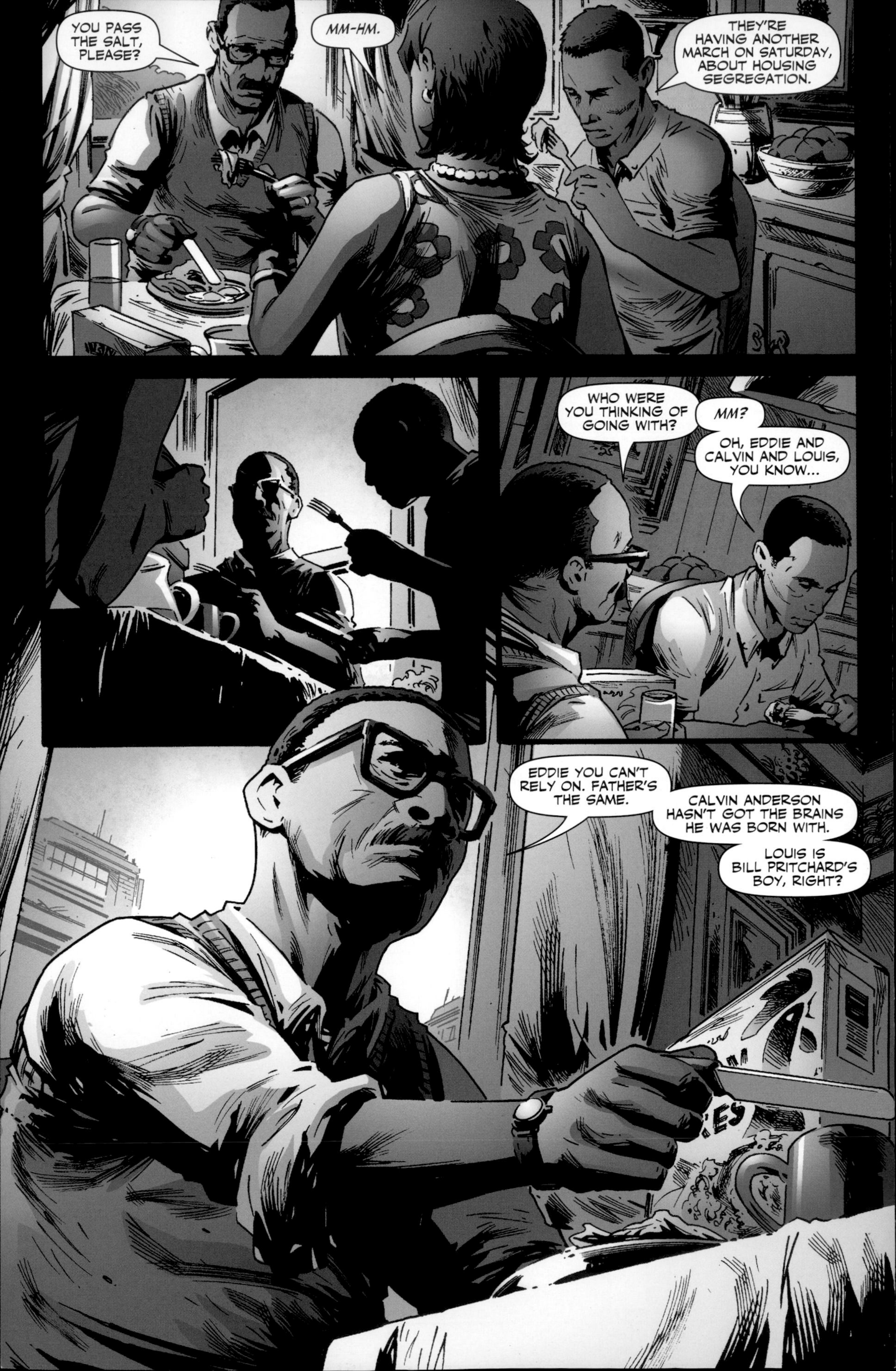
YOU PASS THE SALT, PLEASE?
MM-HM.
THEY'RE HAVING ANOTHER MARCH ON SATURDAY, ABOUT HOUSING SEGREGATION.
WHO WERE YOU THINKING OF GOING WITH?
MM?
OH, EDDIE AND CALVIN AND LOUIS, YOU KNOW...
EDDIE YOU CAN'T RELY ON. FATHER'S THE SAME.
CALVIN ANDERSON HASN'T GOT THE BRAINS HE WAS BORN WITH.
LOUIS IS BILL PRITCHARD'S BOY, RIGHT?

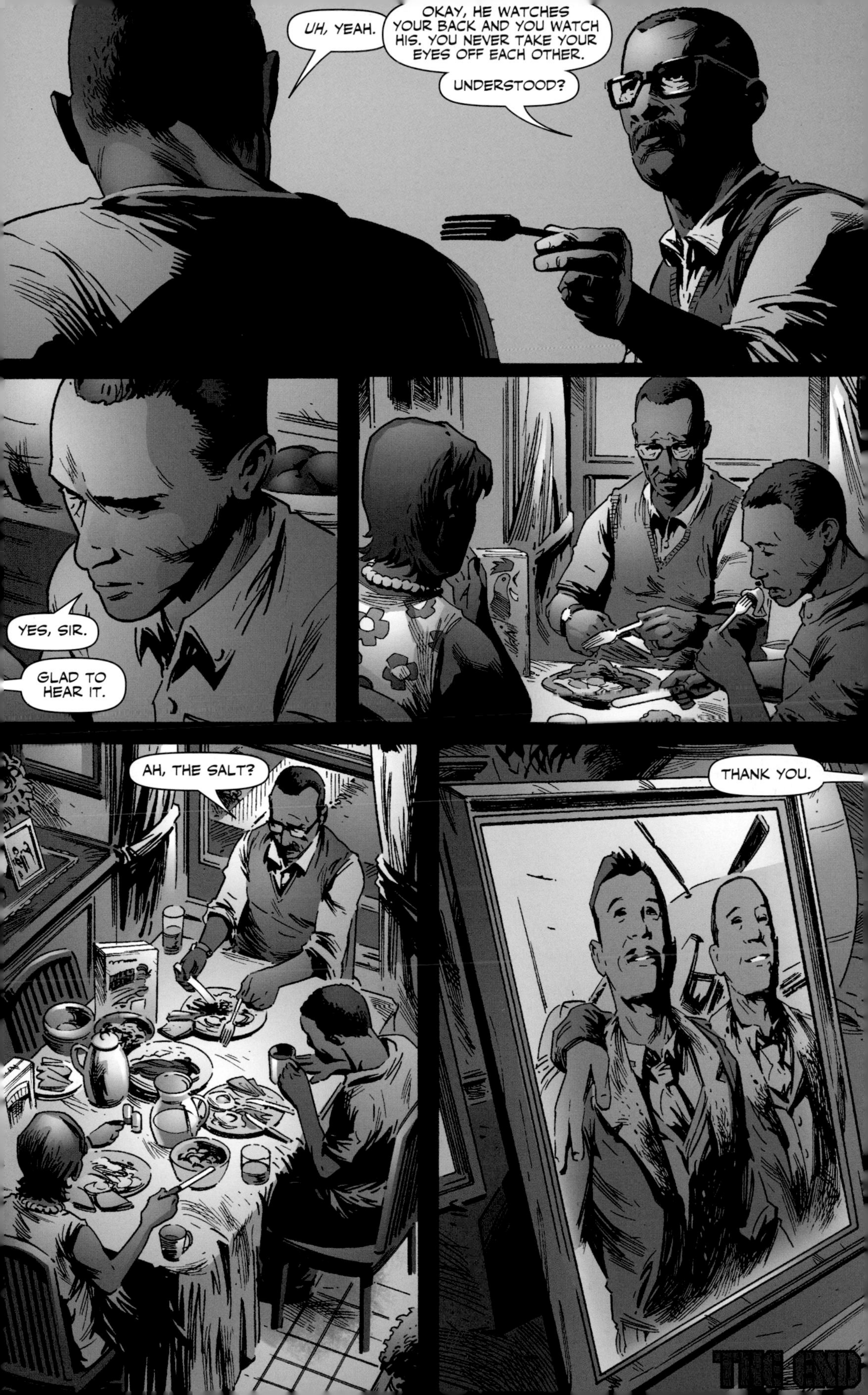
UH, YEAH.
OKAY, HE WATCHES YOUR BACK AND YOU WATCH HIS. YOU NEVER TAKE YOUR EYES OFF EACH OTHER.
UNDERSTOOD?
YES, SIR.
GLAD TO HEAR IT.
AH, THE SALT?
THANK YOU.
THE END

A F T E R W O R D

In the spring of this year, at the kind arrangement of some fellow aviation enthusiasts, I had the honor to meet Doctor Roscoe C. Brown at his home in the Bronx. A little slow on his feet but certainly not frail, hard of hearing but still sharp of mind, he seemed rather less than 94 years old—though his memories of long ago were perhaps that bit more vivid than recent recollections. One in particular stood out: in March of 1945, high above Berlin, he'd blasted a Nazi jet fighter out of the sky.

Which was, apparently, somewhat easier than might be imagined. "I got in his blind spot," he told us, "and I had a computing gunsight so I knew just where to shoot." I found his modesty slightly startling; the Messerschmitt 262 enjoyed a good 100mph speed advantage over his piston-engined Mustang. After the war he met a number of German jet pilots, and quite enjoyed the chance to speak with them. "Being a fighter pilot is like being an athlete—it's interesting to see the quality of the competition."

Having graduated from the Tuskegee school a year earlier, the then Lieutenant (later Captain) Brown joined the 100th Fighter Squadron of the 332nd Fighter Group, United States Army Air Force. He flew 68 combat missions and scored one other aerial kill, earning himself the Distinguished Flying Cross. When the war ended he returned home and gained his doctorate, then entered public life, most notably as president of Bronx Community College. Dr. Brown died on July 2nd, 2016.

Listening to the old aviator speak that morning, my eye was drawn to the many models and pictures of the aircraft he'd flown—mostly featuring his Mustang, *Bunnie*—and then to the view from his apartment window, the green trees of his beloved Bronx stretching to the horizon. I had a sudden sense of a man who served his nation in war but spent the bulk of his life in peacetime, concerned with the needs of his community. *A good life,* I thought to myself, *well-lived.*

* * *

My usual practice when writing military fiction is to get as much of the technical detail right as possible—setting, hardware and so on—and then to invent fictional characters with which to tell the story. Portraying actual historical figures is something I regard as troublesome territory; it's one thing to state that the P-40 was largely inferior to the Messerschmitt 109, because the record shows that to be the case—but including Roscoe Brown, or Lee Archer, or any of the other real-life 332nd FG pilots, and having them express opinions or demonstrate mannerisms that have no basis in fact, would to my mind be more than a little disrespectful. Better to let my own creations speak and act as I deem appropriate, within the correct historical context, and get at the truth of the narrative that way.

In the case of *Dreaming Eagles*, however, this was simply not possible: largely due to the looming figure of Benjamin O. Davis. The man towers like a giant above the Tuskegee saga, with veterans to this day recounting the lessons he taught them and the discipline he instilled in them. For disciplined he was, and indeed had to be. Davis remained undaunted by the thousand slights he suffered in his own life and the endless frustrations strewn in his path by the agents of institutional bigotry; he taught his pilots not to be deflected by such pettiness, not o allow their spirits to be sapped by the apathy or hostility of the establishment. The 332nd commander kept his eyes on the prize; there was never any question of omitting him from the story.

There are several other real-life personas in *Dreaming Eagles*. The unnamed officer who delivers the pep-talk in part two is Major Philip Cochran of the 58th Fighter Squadron, 33rd Fighter Group, who was incidentally the inspiration for "Flip Corkin" in Milton Caniff's famous *Terry and the Pirates*. Men of the 99th FS, attached to the 33rd at the time, remember Cochran's advice on P-40 combat as most helpful. Not so Colonel William "Spike" Momyer, the 33rd's commanding officer, whose adverse report dogged Davis' men much in the manner described. They experienced better treatment from Colonel Earl Bates, 79th FG, with whom they served for a good part of the campaign in Italy.

Apart from the trio of base commanders at Tuskegee, mentioned briefly towards the start of the second episode, the rest of the book's characters are invented: Reggie, Fats, their various comrades and fellow fliers, and others they run across during the course of the narrative. Two of these deserve further explanation, however. The visiting Congressman serves to represent the multitude of establishment critics determined that Davis' "experiment" should fail; some of these came closer to the front line than others. His opposite number, the mystery officer who causes our heroes such puzzlement, was based more on my own speculation than anything else. There is no suggestion that Fifteenth Air Force headquarters ever attached an observer to the 99th or 332nd, but it seems unlikely that various people—up and down the chain of command—weren't keeping a discrete eye on them.

*   *   *

A couple of dozen P-40s are still operational around the world (compared to several hundred Mustangs). Some years ago I had the pleasure of a flight in a P-40N, converted to two-seat configuration but otherwise kept in original condition by its owner. Half an hour aloft in this priceless World War Two classic rendered up a good deal of valuable insight—not least of which was the frighteningly poor visibility from its cockpit. Reggie's observations in part five are based directly on my experience; I would estimate that around three quarters of the pilot's normal field of vision is lost to him. Even in the peaceful skies of Sonoma, California, the thought of so much unknown space—and of the trouble that could develop there—caused a slight shudder down my spine. The need for a wingman was suddenly startlingly clear, brought home to me by means that no written account could convey.

The early Mustangs were no better in this regard, of course; it was the P-51's sheer performance that made it the equal of the deadly Messerschmitt 109 or Focke Wulf 190 (the improved visibility of the later D model was simply the icing on the cake). Yet, as the story makes clear, the P-40 could achieve good results when flown well, so any notion of the 99th Fighter Squadron being given substandard equipment needs closer examination. The majority of American fighter groups were still flying the type until well into 1943, so there is no question of the 99th being singled out in this regard. Which leads me to the subjects of misinformation and myth as they pertain to the story of the Tuskegee Airmen, most obviously in the question of bomber escort.

According to the legend, no American bomber accompanied by aircraft of the 332nd FG was ever lost to enemy fighter attack. According to combat reports filed both by fighter pilots

...nd the bomber crews they escorted, as well as Fifteenth Air Force aircrew loss records, the Tuskegee squadrons may have lost as many as twenty-seven of their charges. Eyewitness accounts of bombers falling to their doom have been found; so have references to such losses even in the medal citations of the men who fought to protect them. Indeed, the initial "never lost a bomber" assertion was actually made on behalf of the 332nd, not by its pilots during the period in which these deadly combats were occurring. Benjamin Davis—a witness as close to impeccable as could be imagined in this context—was asked if he agreed with the claim in a 1990 interview. He replied,

> I do not say that, or if I do say it, it's not an over-enthusiastic statement.
> I question that privately between you and me. But so many people have
> said it that a lot of people have come to believe it.

The peculiar dilemmas facing the escort fighter pilot are detailed in part five, and should be borne in mind when considering what the men of the 332nd were up against. It is interesting to note that the average bomber loss rate per Fifteenth Air Force P-51 group was forty-six, which puts the 332nd well ahead of the curve. Certainly, more and more bomber units began to request the group on escort duties—not because they enjoyed a perfect record, but because they were so much more capable than most. The crews aboard the B-17s and B-24s did not expect the impossible; they knew that as they entered German airspace they were flying into the deadliest skies above the Earth, with some of the greatest fighter pilots the world had ever known intent on their destruction. All they asked was the best chance of survival possible— and what more reassurance could those anxious men have had, watching the little red-tailed Mustangs take up station on their flanks?

In crediting mortal men with feats more appropriate to myth and legend, I believe we do them a disservice. Unlike the bomber crews, we expect too much: we seek to render simple flesh and blood superhuman, and by doing so obscure the truth about their already remarkable service. It is what the Tuskegee Airmen actually achieved that made them special, overcoming monumental bigotry by strength of will and talent. It is what they did with what they had— worn-out aircraft that were replaced all too slowly, a mere trickle of replacements resulting in extended combat tours—that made them heroes. What they might have done equipped with Mustangs from the first, flying with the Eighth Air Force from England into the target-rich skies over the enemy heartland, we will sadly never know.

*   *   *

To the best of my knowledge, no real-life 332nd personnel returned to quite as catastrophic a reception on their native soil as Reggie and Fats suffer in part six. Yet other black servicemen certainly did. Jim Crow had survived the war intact, and throughout the South the Klan and its servants were on the lookout for any who thought their military service made a difference. Some were shot dead, some castrated, some beaten senseless or worse. In South Carolina a black veteran who complained about segregated public transport had his eyes removed with the butt of a billy club. Local law enforcement did little to help the victims or punish the aggressors, and in many cases openly aided the latter.

There seems no end in sight to America's grueling racial saga. Progress is slow and far from steady, with the shadows of the past obscuring too many opportunities for change. Yet in considering the pilots of the 99th, 100th, 301st and 302nd Fighter Squadrons of the 332nd...

Fighter Group, we can say this much with certainty: that Nazi Germany had a vastly more simple answer to the vexing question of race; that those brave men played a small but not insignificant role in the struggle against that regime; and that the Third Reich and its fascist allies are gone from the world.

On May 8th of last year I went to Washington, DC, where a fly-past of vintage combat aircraft had been arranged for the seventieth anniversary of the end of the war in Europe. The fine old warbirds thundered down the National Mall; among their number were two B-17s and a B-24, several Mustangs, even a couple of P-40s. Afterwards I wandered west, towards the melancholy black walls that commemorate America's time in Vietnam, and the lesser-known Korean Veterans' Memorial, the latter sadly as forgotten as its war. But it was the National World War Two Memorial that I'd come to visit, and it was there that I had a surprise in store.

The structure is undoubtedly impressive, divided into Atlantic and Pacific theatres, then again into various battles and campaigns. Among many others Sicily and Italy are featured, so the 332nd's portion of the war is set safely in stone. The names of far-off atolls and islands appear, where so much blood was shed on the long road to Tokyo. I was pleased to see the Murmansk Run get a mention, no doubt to the puzzlement of many, and touched by the red rose lain across the carved words *Battle of the Bulge*. Yet more remarkable by far, drawn up in two long ranks between the fountains and walls of the Memorial, were forty elderly men who'd gathered for the day's commemoration: veterans.

Some stood, some sat. All looked weary, all looked proud. Three quarters of a century before they'd fought America's war across both oceans. These were the men who shivered in ice-walled foxholes, waiting for the grey shapes of Panzers to smash through the trees to their front, or stood to their guns as torpedoes sought their vessels' hulls, or patrolled the lower reaches of the stratosphere in single-engined fighters, far from home. They stormed up beaches, toiled up hills, crossed rivers, crouched behind tin walls atop five miles of void, all while the air around them filled with fire. Cursing and suffering, bearing more than any human being should, they endured against the greatest evil the world has ever known. They kept on going, and when they were done, so were Nazi Germany and Imperial Japan.

On that slow, hazy May afternoon they looked like nothing more than grandfathers, which no doubt most were. Like the other visitors to the Memorial I watched their brief ceremony in silence—after all, what can be said, or even thought, in the presence of such men? Yet the world somehow found its voice. A soldier, a sailor, an airman and a Marine—the latter by far the smartest in his dress blues—stepped forward to salute them. In the rising heat the needle of the Washington Monument shimmered, seeming for a moment less substantial. The old men returned the salute. The gentle spatter from the fountains sounded like applause.

—Garth Ennis
New York City,
August 2016

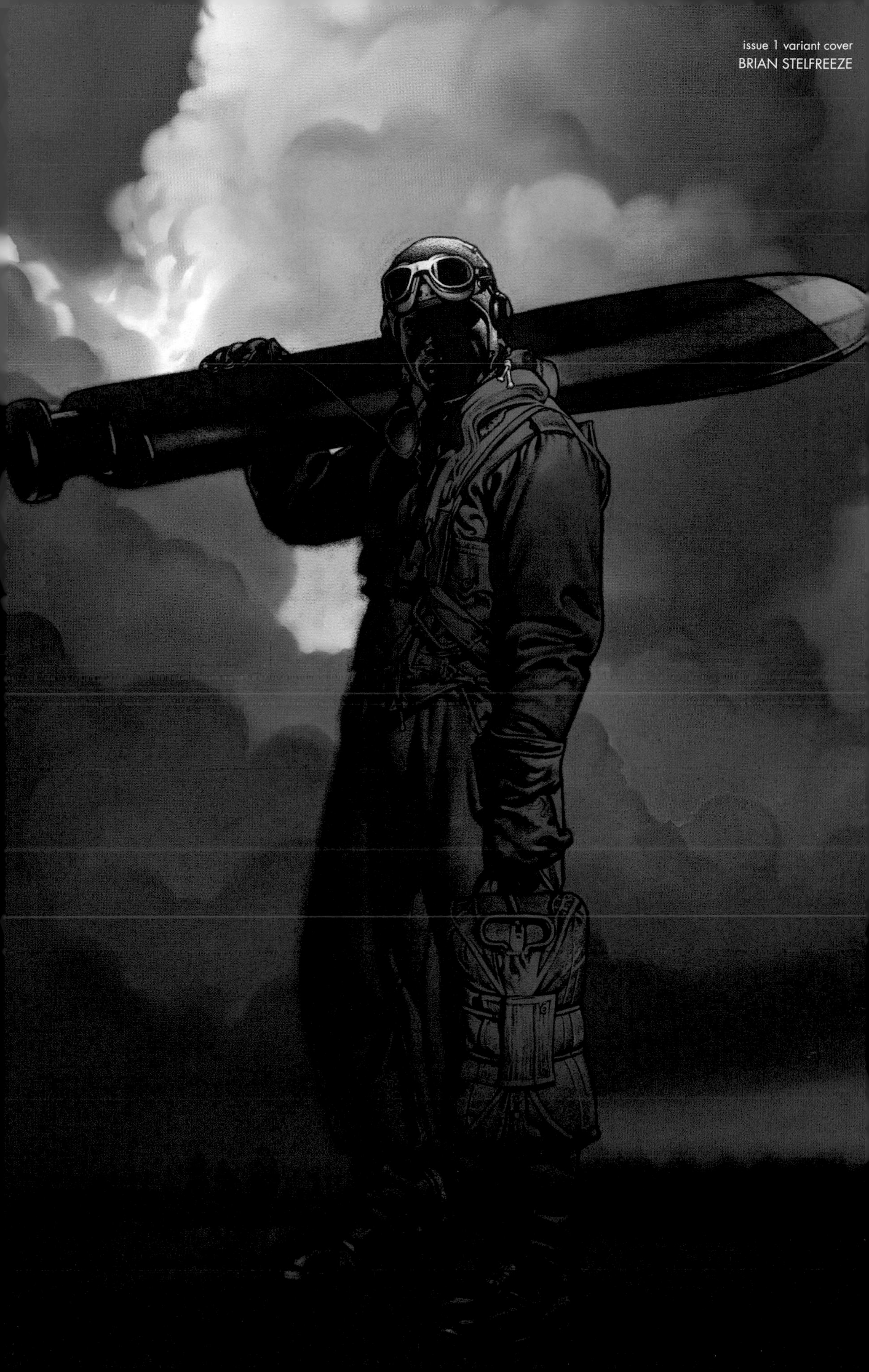

issue 1 variant cover
BRIAN STELFREEZE

issue 1 variant cover
PHIL HESTER

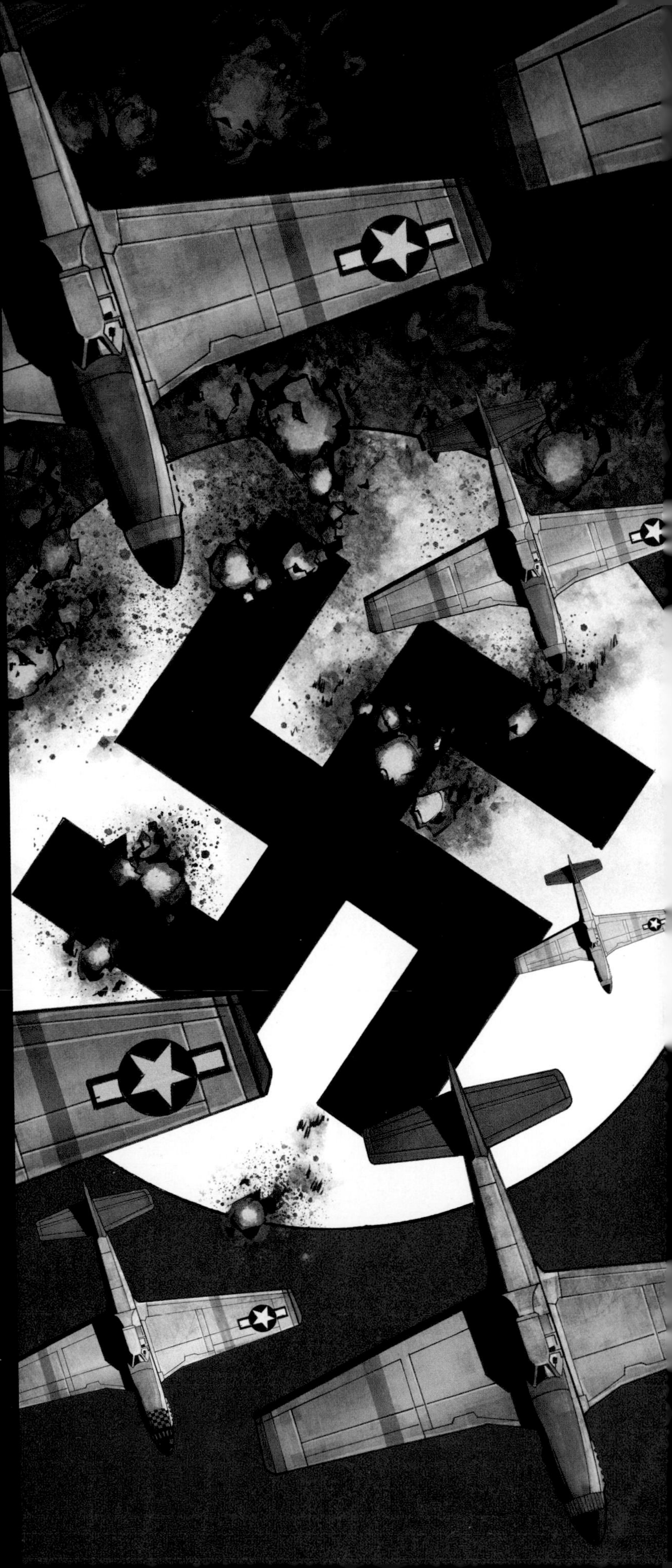

issue 2 variant cover
DECLAN SHALVEY

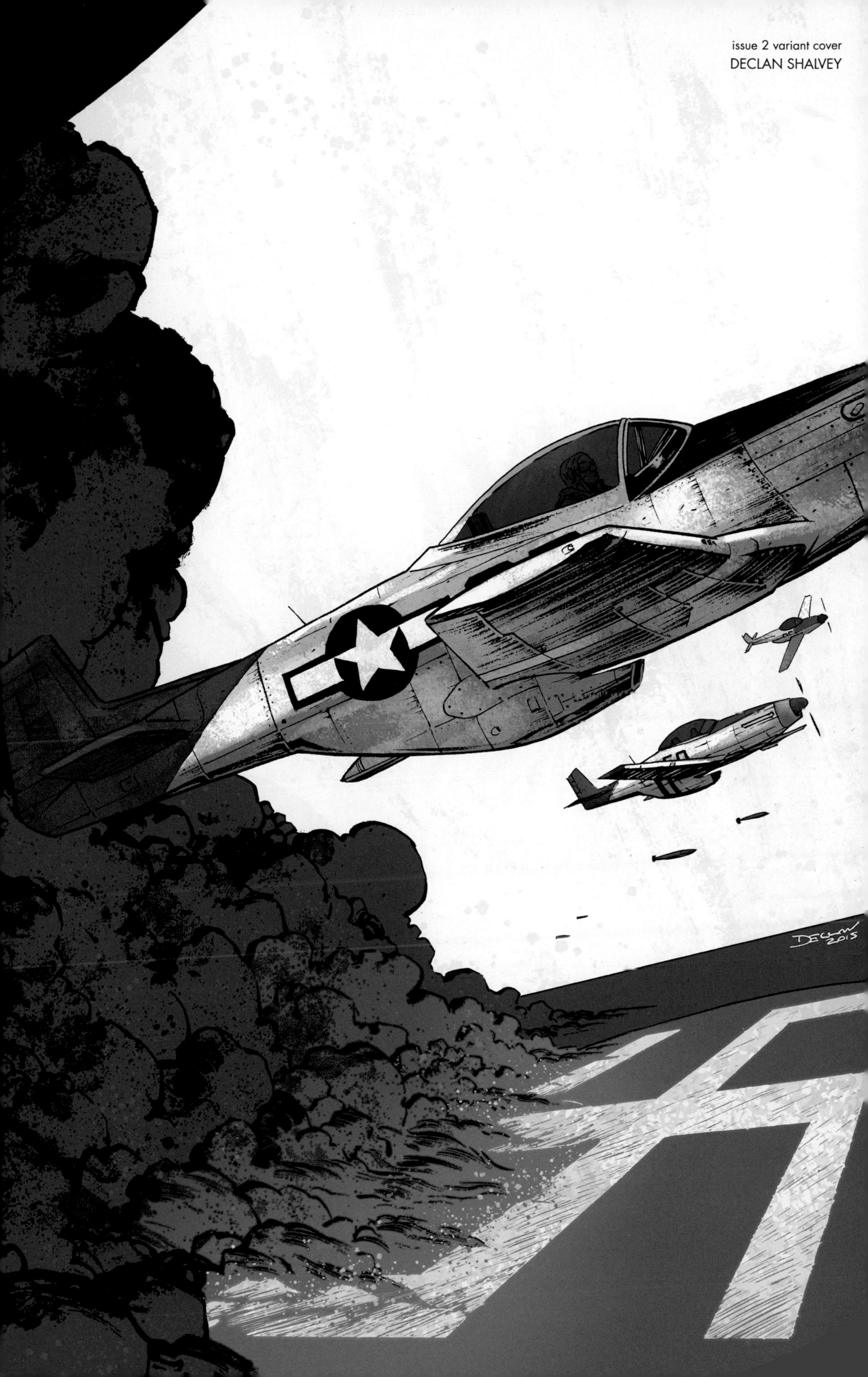
DECLAN 2015

DREAMING EAGLES #1
SCRIPT

by GARTH ENNIS

CLASSIFIED
TOP SECRET DOCUMENTS

DREAMING EAGLES #1

Garth Ennis

Title: 1: WE CANNOT CONSECRATE

PAGE ONE

1.
Beautiful summer evening, sky a deep blue. We're in a black neighborhood in a major city, somewhere in the north like New York or Chicago. Note that this doesn't mean we're in a ghetto, just that most or all the faces we see will be black. Pretty quiet at the moment. Nearest us is a bar, neat and well-kept, THE SILVER PONY. A man stands outside it, gazing up into the sky. Not too close yet.

Caption: 1966

2.
Close up, head and shoulders. This is our hero, Reggie Atkinson, black, late 40s, short but stocky. Short hair and neat moustache. Intelligent air about him, a thinker. He looks upwards with a slight smile on his face, miles away, slightly mesmerized. When we get a better look we'll see he wears black shoes, slacks and a white shirt with the collar loose and sleeves rolled up. Even in informal work mode he seems dapper and smartly turned-out.

3.
His pov: high above the outlines of the buildings on the block we see an airliner climbing hard into the evening sky, gleaming silver, lights winking. Small in shot but recognizable.

Off: MISTER ATKINSON?

4.
Reggie doesn't turn, smile becoming slightly distracted, still gazing up. A tall, slightly stooped bald man emerges from the bar behind him, wearing a barman's apron: Stoney.

Stoney: WE RUNNIN' LOW ON SCHLITZ.

Reggie: SEEMED FAIRLY QUIET TO ME.

Stoney: STILL GONNA HAVE TO CHANGE 'EM OUT.

5.
Reggie turns, still with one eye on the sky above. Stoney is already re-entering the bar.

Reggie: OKAY, I'LL COME GIVE YOU A HAND.

6.
View past Reggie as he pauses, sees a dark figure slipping into the shadows of the alley at the side of the bar.

PAGE TWO

1.
View past whoever-it-is as they dodge in through a door at the side of the bar, down at the rear of the building- hasn't kicked it in, just opened it normally. Reggie has just rounded the corner and seen him, looking down the alleyway that runs down the side of the building, about twenty yards back.

2.
View past Reggie's hand as he gently pushes the door open, using just his fingertips. A young man is bent over a sink within, shirt off, mopping at his face with a cloth. This is a storeroom at the back of the bar, piled high with beer kegs, cases of bottled beer and liquor. Some empty, some sealed. Gloomy, too, the guy at the sink works in the dwindling light from the single high window.

3.
Big. Reggie calmly pulls on a cord and a single naked bulb lights the room- not much better than before, but enough to illuminate the young man at the sink as he stands up and freezes, obviously had no idea anyone else was present. Reggie is almost emotionless, regarding the younger man with what seems like cool detachment. Reggie tends to be quiet and precise in his movements, not a man given to drama.
This guy is his son, Lee, a wiry 17 year old who (we'll soon see) favours his mother more than his father. Already several inches taller than Reggie, very short hair, clean shaven. Simple black suit, with jacket, shirt and tie dumped on a beer keg. Lip badly swollen from a nasty impact, he has bruises down his ribs on one side, and he's developing a serious black eye. The cloth he's been dabbing his mouth with is streaked with blood.

Reggie: YOU WENT TO THE MARCH.

4.
Lee only, turning to look at us, still nervous but resentment coming in too. Injuries plain to see here.

Lee: I WANTED TO HEAR DOCTOR KING SPEAK.

5.
Reggie only, eyes narrowing as he peers at us, noticing something slightly alarming.

Reggie: **DOCTOR.** YOU KNOW HOW I FEEL—

"   "   OH, LORD, DID YOU REALLY THINK YOU WERE GOING TO
             HIDE THAT…?

PAGE THREE

1.
Lee lowers his gaze, fuming a little, unable to look his father in the eye as Reggie comes closer to examine his face. Reggie grimaces with weary disbelief, more practical than annoyed. Head and shoulders on both here.

Lee: IT'S NOTHING.

Reggie: OF COURSE NOT. YOU WERE GOING TO SIT DOWN AT THE
               TABLE IN THE MORNING AND NEITHER OF US WOULD
               HAVE NOTICED A THING.

"   "   THAT MAN STIRS THINGS UP, WE DON'T NEED HIM HERE…

2.
Back a little. Lee bristles slightly, but not enough that he's going to yell at his dad. Reggie turns towards us, quietly wringing the cloth out over the sink, bleak.

Lee: HE TELLS THE TRUTH. HE SPEAKS FOR OUR PEOPLE.

Reggie: IN THE SOUTH, MAYBE. BUT THIS ISN'T THE SOUTH.

Lee: THAT'S—

Reggie: SO YOU WENT TO HEAR HIM SPEAK, BUT SOMEHOW YOU
               ENDED UP FIGHTING WITH WHITE BOYS.

3.
View past Lee as Reggie leans over the inks, turns the tap on. Lee's hand trembles slightly, but we can see his knuckles are skinned from the punches he threw.

Lee: THEY CALLED US NIGGERS…

Reggie: I KNOW WHAT THEY CALLED YOU.

Lee: OH, SO IT DOESN'T JUST HAPPEN IN THE SOUTH?

4.
Close up on Reggie's hands, wringing the blood and water from the cloth.

Up: WE'VE BEEN THROUGH THIS. IF HE WASN'T HERE, THOSE
              FOOLS WOULD MIND THEIR BUSINESS.

"   "   LET ME GET A LOOK AT YOU.

PAGE FOUR

1.
Few minutes later. Lee sits perched on a beer keg with a damp cloth clamped against his eye, Reggie using another to dab gently at his mouth, leaning down to work on him. When we get closer we'll see that Lee has a third cloth tied around his skinned knuckles. Looking across the room at them here, both a little more calm. Lee just seems tired now.

Reggie: DON'T THINK IT'LL NEED STITCHES.

2.
Close in for a headshot on Lee as Reggie's hand dabs the cloth on his mouth. In fact Lee is not tired, he's just dangerously calm, a certain light in his eye as he recalls the fight. Sense of grim satisfaction.

Off: ALL THE SAME, THERE'S NO WAY SHE CAN MISS—

Lee: WORTH IT. JUST TO PUT THAT MOTHERFUCKER ON THE
             GROUND.

" "   HEAR HIM SCREAM.

3.
Reggie only, startled almost to silence. Eyes widening but mouth just a thin line.

Reggie: YOU KNOW IF YOUR MOTHER HEARS YOU USE THAT WORD
             SHE'LL KILL US BOTH?

4.
Pull back. Reggie stares, slightly bewildered. Lee won't look up, resentful, fuming.

Lee: YOU DON'T KNOW WHAT IT'S LIKE. TO HAVE TO TAKE IT.

Reggie: WHAT?

Lee: TO NOT BE ABLE TO DO ANYTHING, AND THEN, THEN GET
             THE CHANCE—

Reggie: YOU THINK I DON'T KNOW WHAT IT'S **LIKE…**?

5.
Lee only, finally looking up at us, snapping. Resentment boiling over in a savage moment

Lee: **IT'S ALL RIGHT FOR YOU, YOU GOT TO FIGHT THEM!**

6.
Reggie only, genuinely surprised now, stunned to silence as he realizes and understands.
Off: YOU GOT TO **KILL NAZIS…!**

PAGE FIVE

1.
Pull back again. Reggie gazes at Lee, troubled, thrown. Wasn't ready for that. Lee glares at the floor, trembling a little. Quietly furious.

2.
Close up on Reggie, still troubled. Picking his words with care.

Reggie: LEE… IT WASN'T EXACTLY A MATTER OF KILLING.

" "   WHICH ISN'T SOMETHING YOU WANT TO MAKE AN AMBITION
             OF, ANYWAY.

3.
Reggie frowns as he tries to explain, an awkward memory for him. Lee stands and pulls his shirt on. We don't see his face, but he isn't looking at Reggie.

Reggie: BUT THE POINT IS, I WASN'T SHOOTING AT MEN. OR IT DIDN'T
             FEEL LIKE I WAS.

" "   I SHOT AT THE AIRCRAFT, I COULDN'T SEE THE MAN WHO
             WAS FLYING IT. I WAS GOING TOO FAST OR I WAS TOO FAR
             AWAY.

4.
Lee only, grim and weary. Just doesn't want to talk anymore. Won't look up as he buttons his shirt.

Off: TO BE HONEST, MOST OF THE TIME IT DIDN'T EVEN OCCUR
             TO ME THAT THERE **WAS** A MAN IN—

Lee: YEAH, OKAY.

5.
Pull back as Reggie watches Lee go, jacket and tie in hand. We don't see either man's face.

6.
Reggie only, gazing offshot as his son leaves, quietly but deeply saddened.

PAGES SIX AND SEVEN

1.
Long shot. Reggie lies in the gloom of his bedroom, next to his wife who lies curled up asleep in bed. We don't get much detail on the room because it's so dark, but Reggie lies on his back and gazes up at the ceiling, pretty obviously not sleeping.

2.
Close up on Reggie. He's awake, eyes open, a certain tension in his expression as he gazes up past us. Quietly but obviously annoyed about something, just can't sleep.

3.
Big. Rear view on a P-51 banked almost to the vertical, pumping bullets at a Focke Wulf 190 just ahead of it- also banked hard over so we get a plan view of it, this is a tight-turning battle. Casings spew from under the P-51's wings and sunlight gleams on its canopy, but the 190 is hit hard, black smoke pouring from the engine, one aileron shot away, black crosses plain to see. Debris from multiple hits flies back past the Mustang, including the 190's canopy which the pilot has just ejected- it whirls back in the slipstream, narrowly missing the American fighter. Clear blue sky beyond.

Jag: -- LEADER, YOU NAIL THAT SON OF A BITCH!

4.
Big. Switch around now as the 190 levels out nearest, pilot just visible struggling in the cockpit. The P-51 stops firing and begins catching up with the German, apparently about to formate on it. High to the rear, couple of hundred yards back, a second Mustang keeps pace without closing in. And in the background, a mass dogfight seems to be taking place around a long stream of four-engined bombers- the aircraft are just shapes against the cloud-streaked blue sky at this range, but there are about a hundred bombers in formation and a couple of dozen little fighters whirling around them. Thin black smoke trails mark the fall of a couple of aircraft, and one of the bombers is trailing smoke too. We're high above the earth, could be anywhere.

Jag: BLUE LEADER, NO DOUBT ABOUT THAT ONE.

" "   YOU FEELING HUNGRY, YOU WANT TO GO LOOK FOR MORE?

5.
Close up on the P-51 pilot in his cockpit, peering out to his left at us- this is actually Reggie 20 years ago, but we can barely see him behind his goggles and oxygen mask. What we can see is that his eyes are narrowing- in confusion rather than anger, he's trying to figure out exactly what he's looking at. Painted neatly on the frame of his cockpit canopy is Lt. R. Atkinson and below that are two swastikas: kill markings.

Jag: BLUE LEADER?

PAGES EIGHT AND NINE

1.
View past Reggie's P-51 as he turns his head to watch the German pilot
struggle out of his doomed machine- we're close enough to see that the man's
in serious trouble, and that blood is whipping back in the slipstream as he
works his way clear of the cockpit.

2.
Close up: the German's been shot through the shoulder and hand on his right
side, having lost all his fingers and a good deal of blood- more soaks his
flying jacket and whips back in the 200mph slipstream. He gasps in dreadful
agony, sick and weak with pain, but determined to keep going. What's clear is
that his parachute harness has also been shot through on the same side as the
wounded shoulder (of which Reggie's .50 calibre bullet has made a dreadful
mess), the severed straps flapping loose in the screaming wind.

3.
Reggie in the cockpit, eyes now snapping open in shock as he makes sense of
what he's looking at.

4.
View past the now-burning 190 as the pilot gets clear and is instantly flung
backwards arse-over-tit, limbs flailing, parachute pack loose but apparently
still attached (note that both German and American pilots wear the kind of
chute pack that they sit on in the cockpit, not the more modern backpack
type). Mustang still visible keeping pace with the German wreck.

5.
Big close up on the flailing German pilot. His parachute starts to open but the
drag of the deploying chute drags the harness off his body- with the strap
shot through on his injured shoulder side, the still intact strap on his other
shoulder is pulled clean off his good arm, leaving the harness secured to him
only by his leg straps. We don't see his face here.

6.
View past the P-51, showing us its belly as it banks hard over, Reggie trying
to keep the German in view. The guy is small in shot, but we can see the chute
isn't opening fully and the harness straps have been dragged down his legs
to his ankles.

7.
Reggie's pov: the flopping, half-deployed parachute detaches completely from
the flailing figure of the German pilot, straps pulled off his ankles, man and
chute flung in different directions by the howling slipstream.

Jag: AH, BLUE LEADER, ARE YOU OKAY?

PAGE TEN

1.
Reggie in the cockpit again, eyes like saucers, utterly riveted as he gazes
out to one side. Can't move.

Jag: BLUE LEADER, THIS IS BLUE TWO—REGGIE, ARE YOU—

2.
Back to Reggie lying away now, unable to sleep. One arm thrown listlessly
behind his head. Grim, bleak, sense of regret. Knows he lied to his son.

3.
Pull back a little as he grimaces with weary annoyance, closes his eyes.

4.
And back further as he rolls over to sleep, facing away from his wife in the
gloomy bedroom.

Bln: HAVE EVERY RIGHT

5.
Black panel, page width.

Bln: OFFICERS IN THE UNITED STATES ARMY AIR FORCE

"   "   FOUGHT FOR OUR COUNTRY

"   "   YOU TRASH BEGGED OFF AS 4-F

PAGE ELEVEN

1.
Big. A grim memory, seen through a dull red haze with a hand held up nearest-
belonging to whoever's pov this is- smeared with blood. Three big men are
holding a fourth man down, got their backs to us so they block our view of
the victim. We see great fat arms and swollen heads, obese torsos. Two pin
the guy, the third holds his head while doing something to his face- again,
we have the vaguest view of this, it's a grainy, indistinct shot with little
sense of location or even time of day. Whoever's watching isn't approaching or
trying to help, the pov is from low down. He's already on the ground.

2.
Reggie snaps awake in bed, drenched in sweat, eyes wide, gasping in horror.
A bad one. He's still on his side with the shape of his wife beside him, but
it's morning now and light is seeping in through the curtains further back.
The room is nicely decorated and neatly kept- not opulent, but tidy.

Reggie: NAAH

3.
Pull back. Reggie sits on the edge of the bed with his feet on the floor,
wearing shorts and a string vest. Gazing into space, breathing heavily,
working to push the dream away.

4.
View past his wife as she slowly raises her head, sees Reggie standing at the
window, having opened the curtains a little to look out. We don't see either
of their faces.

Wife: HONEY?

PAGE TWELVE

1.
Day. Long shot on the bar and Reggie's house behind it- they back onto each other, with a tall wooden fence running around the back yard of the house and a door in it that accesses the much smaller yard at the back of the bar. The latter is piled high with kegs and crates and is open to the street at one side, the former is planted with a neatly kept grass lawn. Note that neither house nor bar are really all that big. A figure can be seen painting the fence at the back of the house, another relaxing in a chair on the back porch.

Painting: THIS THE ONLY BRUSH WE GOT?

Relaxing: NO.

2.
Close in. Lee's doing the painting, stripped to his vest, sweating in the summer heat. His injuries have bruised but not healed, this is only the next morning. He grimaces with weary frustration, the brush is barely an inch across and the fence is taller than he is. Tin of white paint to hand. The person on the porch is a woman, not looking up from what she's reading. Sat in the shade with a pitcher and glass of lemonade on a little table.

Lee: HHHH.

"   "   LIKE I'M A LITTLE KID, OR SOMETHING.

Woman: NOW, WHAT LITTLE KID WOULD ACT AS DUMB AS YOU DID?

Lee: HOW COME HE HAS TO BE LIKE THAT, ANYWAY?

3.
The woman looks up, frowning with mild interest, smiling slightly. This is Lee's mother and Reggie's wife, Alison, an intelligent woman of about 40. Hair gathered up neatly, starting to get a little tubby, flower print dress. Book's some Harlequin romance thing.

Alison: MM?

Off: SO… CALM. SO **EXACT**, EVEN WHEN YOU CAN TELL HE'S MAD.

"   "   IT'S LIKE HE'S THOUGHT EVERY SINGLE THING THROUGH,
              RIGHT DOWN TO THE WAY HE'S GOING TO SAY IT…

4.
Alison shrugs, looks away. Lee turns to face her further back.

Alison: YOU PREFER IT IF HE GOT DRUNK AND GAVE YOU A WHIPPIN'?

Lee: 'LEAST IT WOULD BE A REACTION…!

PAGE THIRTEEN

1.
Alison only, eyes narrowed, slightly exasperated. Like she's thought about this herself and hasn't got an exact answer.

Alison: IT'S THE WAY HE IS. THE WAY HE HAD TO LEARN TO BE AT
              ONE TIME, IT WAS HOW HE FIGURED HE'D GET THROUGH IT ALL.

Off: YEAH, RIGHT, THE WAR. THE BIG FIGHT FOR FREEDOM.

2.
Lee gets more frustrated- stopped painting, gesturing with the brush to make his point.

Lee: SO WHY DOES HE ONLY WANT TO GO SO FAR WITH IT? MOST
              OF OUR PEOPLE ARE IN GHETTOES, THEY WERE STUCK UNDER
              JIM CROW 'TIL DOCTOR KING DID SOMETHING-DOCTOR
              KING THE **STIRRER**, THAT IS.

"   "   AND ME, I'M NOT EVEN FREE TO GO AND LISTEN TO HIM…

3.
Alison pours more lemonade, smiles thoughtfully, bit bleak. Not much humour in it.

Alison: WELL, PEOPLE WHO FIGHT FOR FREEDOM DON'T ALWAYS
              LIKE WHAT GETS DONE WITH IT. WHICH KIND OF DEFEATS
              THE PURPOSE, BUT THERE YOU ARE.

"   "   YOU EVER TRY AND TALK TO HIM ABOUT IT?

4.
Long shot, little figures of Lee and his mother facing each other across the yard.

Lee: CAN'T.

Alison: 'COURSE NOT.

5.
View past Lee as he wearily returns to the fence, gloomy and pissed off. Alison watches from further back, but we don't see her face.

Alison: YOU DONE YET?

Lee: NO…

Alison: WELL THEN.

PAGE FOURTEEN

1.
Inside the bar, long before opening time, Reggie stands behind the bar nearest us with notebook and pen as he takes inventory- one eye on the bottles racked behind the bar. Looks irritated, not turning to Alison as she stands watching from further back. The place is neat and tidy without being particularly high-end: not spit and sawdust but little more than functional in décor. No one else present.

Reggie: WHAT DOES HE KNOW ABOUT **GHETTOES?** I WORKED MY
              ASS OFF SO HE—

Alison: **AHHRRM.**

2.
Alison only, listening carefully, eyes narrowed. Wants to understand and be understood.

Off: WORKED HARD. WORKED VERY HARD.

"   "   SO HE COULD GROW UP IN A REAL HOME WITH FOOD
              ALWAYS ON THE TABLE, SO HE COULD GO TO A GOOD
              SCHOOL…

Alison: WELL, HE DID. AND HE'S LEARNED THINGS WE DIDN'T, AND
              HE HAS DIFFERENT IDEAS TO US.

"   "   HE WANTS THINGS TO BE BETTER, I MEAN THAT'S NOT SO
              HARD TO UNDERSTAND.

3.
Reggie only, little grim as writes in his notebook. Up behind the bar are a couple of small, unobtrusive, framed B&W photos: a pair of Mustangs in flight, half a dozen pilots grouped in front of another one.

Reggie: WHAT HE DOESN'T UNDERSTAND IS WHAT MAKING THINGS
              BETTER COSTS, SOMETIMES.

"   "   I'M NOT TALKING ABOUT THE WAR. I MEAN HERE, BACK
              HERE, THE BATTLE HE'S ALL FIRED-UP TO GET INTO.

4.
View past Alison, watching as Reggie taps the line of bottles with the end of his pen, counting them. We don't see their faces.

Alison: WELL… YOU NEVER TOLD ME EXACTLY WHAT IT WAS
              THAT…

Reggie: YOU'RE MAKING ME LOSE COUNT.

PAGE FIFTEEN

1.
Nearest us Reggie scribbles another note, irritated, not looking up. Alison watches him, hopeful but nervous. Trying to coax him, even plead a little.

Alison: CAN YOU TELL HIM ABOUT IT?

"   "   REGGIE…?

2.
Nearest us Alison slumps a bit, rolling her eyes in weary defeat, turning away from Reggie- who glances up at her, cool.

Alison: NO, BECAUSE MEN DON'T TALK TO EACH OTHER…

Reggie: IT ISN'T AS EASY AS THAT.

"   "   BELIEVE ME.

3.
Pull back for a wide view. Alison warily watches Reggie, who's gone back to his notemaking. Too far back to see either of their faces.

Alison: I'M SORRY.

4.
Alison only, wary but hopeful.

Alison: HE… HE DOESN'T HATE YOU. HE DOESN'T DISRESPECT YOU.

"   "   IT'S JUST THAT HE'S GOING TO LEAVE HOME ONE OF THESE
             DAYS, AND ALL HE'LL HAVE TO LIVE HIS LIFE WITH IS WHAT
             HE'S FIGURED OUT FOR HIMSELF.
5.
Reggie only, not looking up but gently stopping short. This one goes home.

Off: WOULDN'T IT BE GOOD IF HIS FATHER DIDN'T SEEM LIKE
             SUCH A MYSTERY TO HIM?

PAGE SIXTEEN

1.
Night, long shot on the back yard. Lee is still painting the fence, working by the porch light. Doesn't see Reggie emerge from the house, set two bottles on the table. Both small in shot. No Alison.

2.
Close up on Reggie, smiling a gentle little smile, somewhere between fondness and amusement. Enjoying watching his on, without the boy knowing he's there.

3.
View past Lee as he turns, slightly startled, sees the silhouetted figure stood on the porch.

Reggie: ALL THIS WORK COULD GIVE A MAN A POWERFUL THIRST.

4.
Close up on the two bottles of beer, Reggie's hand in shot where he stands beside them.

5.
Lee peers at us, frowning, genuinely taken aback. Huh?

Lee: IS THAT FOR…?

6.
View past Reggie as he slowly sits down, Lee staring at him.

Reggie: THERE'S SODA IN THE REFRIGERATOR. BUT I DON'T SEE ANY
                CHILDREN AROUND HERE.

PAGE SEVENTEEN

1.
Lee is sitting next to Reggie now, with the little table between them, and they each have a bottle of beer (no glasses). Reggie faces front, calm and businesslike. Lee glances at him, slightly startled.

Reggie: I LIED TO YOU BEFORE. OF COURSE IT WAS A MATTER OF
             KILLING AND OF COURSE I KILLED MEN, BECAUSE THAT'S
             WHAT WAR IS.
2.
Lee only, eyes widening slightly as he watches us. Definitely not what he expected.

Off: TO WIN, YOU HAVE TO KILL THOUSANDS.

"   "   IN THAT WAR IT WAS MILLIONS.

3.
Reggie looks a little bleak, shrugging thoughtfully. Lee watches him, quietly riveted.

Reggie: THE AIRCRAFT I SHOT DOWN WERE FIGHTERS. THAT MEANT
             ONE OR SOMETIMES TWO MEN, IF THEY DIDN'T GET OUT IN
             TIME.

"   "   BUT THE BOMBERS MY SQUADRON ESCORTED… THE
             TARGETS **THEY** HIT, THE PEOPLE ON THE GROUND…
4.
Reggie snaps out of it, turns to Lee, quietly serious. Lee is surprised again, but not unpleasantly so.

Reggie: ANYWAY. THE POINT IS I LIED TO YOU, AND I DON'T WANT
             TO DO THAT AGAIN.

"   "   I WANT TO TELL YOU EVERYTHING THAT HAPPENED TO
             ME AND LET YOU MAKE UP YOUR MIND.

PAGES EIGHTEEN AND NINETEEN

1.
Long shot of the two of them sitting on the back porch.

Reggie: IT WAS NINETEEN FORTY-TWO AND THE SECOND WORLD
                 WAR WAS TWO AND HALF YEARS OLD. FOR AMERICA,
                 SIX MONTHS.

"   "   THE GERMANS ROLLED UP ALL OF EUROPE EXCEPT THE
                 BRITISH, WHO HELD ON ALONE FOR A WHOLE YEAR. THEN
                 HITLER DECLARED WAR ON RUSSIA–THEN, WHEN HIS
                 JAPANESE FRIENDS ATTACKED PEARL HARBOR, HE
                 DECLARED WAR ON THE U.S.A., TOO.

2.
Close in. Lee frowns, quietly fascinated as Reggie continues– Reggie will
generally face front unless indicated, and Lee will glance at him from time
to time.

Reggie: IT'S NOW GENERALLY RECKONED THAT'S WHAT FINISHED
                 HIM, BUT IT DIDN'T SEEM THAT WAY AT THE TIME.

"   "   AND WHETHER THAT WAS TRUE OR NOT, WELL, THE WHOLE
                 THING STILL HAD TO BE FOUGHT OUT TO THE END.

3.
Big across the spread. A broad stretch of tarmac on the edge of an airfield,
with the main runway further back and a couple of hangars and other buildings
off in the background. Nearest us a line of monoplane BT-13 trainers are drawn
up on the tarmac, gleaming silver despite the dull grey skies. Windy day,
rather a bleak scene with almost no one around. However, further back and
quite small in shot, a dozen men in civilian clothes are drawn up in two ranks
of six, stood in front of a couple of silver Stearman biplanes. Suitcases on
the ground beside them. A truck drives off having just delivered them. A man
in uniform addresses them, but we're too far away to get much detail.

Caption: "NOW… WHAT WAS INTERESTING ABOUT ADOLF HITLER WAS
                 … HE HAD A LOT TO SAY ON THE SUBJECT OF RACE."

4.
View past the two ranks of men at the guy addressing them, a typically stern
US army senior sergeant– a white man. Here he seems to be lecturing them
matter of factly, grimly laying down the law rather than screaming in typical
drill instructor style. The men wear hats and overcoats, so we don't get a
look at them yet. No faces.

Caption: "RIGHT THROUGH THE THIRTIES HE WAS MAKING SPEECHES
                 ABOUT THE ARYAN SUPERMAN: BLONDE HAIR, BLUE EYES,
                 NORDIC, THE **MASTER RACE** WHO WOULD CONQUER THE
                 WORLD FOR GERMANY.

"   "   COUPLE OF MEN IN PARTICULAR KNOCKED HOLES IN THAT
                 NONSENSE. JOE LOUIS, WHO BEAT THE GERMAN
                 HEAVYWEIGHT MAX SCHMELLING TO BECOME CHAMPION OF
                 THE WORLD, AND JESSE OWENS, WHO WON FOUR GOLD
                 MEDALS AT THE BERLIN OLYMPICS."

5.
Our first proper look at the men lined up: all are black, smart, young and
fit, none older than 25. The nearest is Reggie, early 20s, clean shaven. Like
others he faces front, keeping his face carefully neutral as the drill
sergeant addresses them.

Caption: "LOUIS AND OWENS WERE BOTH AMERICAN.

"   "   "LOUIS AND OWENS WERE BOTH BLACK."

PAGES TWENTY AND TWENTY-ONE

1.
As the men stand at attention– in the sloppy way that untrained civvies do–
three aircraft can be seen approaching from the background in tight formation,
very low. No one turns.

Caption: "WE WANTED TO MAKE A STAND AGAINST HITLER'S RACIAL
                 FOOLISHNESS AND WE WANTED TO SERVE OUR COUNTRY,
                 AND–THE POINT WAS–WE FELT IT WAS **OUR FIGHT.** JUST
                 AS MUCH AS ANYONE ELSE'S.

"   "   "WHICH WAS WHY THE MEN OF CLASS 42-T WERE STANDING
                 ON THE TARMAC AT TUSKEGEE ARMY AIRFIELD THAT
                 JANUARY, BEING TOLD IN NO UNCERTAIN TERMS THAT WE
                 WERE IN THE ARMY NOW."

2.
Reggie now, shrugging as he tells the story. Lee is fascinated.

Reggie: WE WERE AN EXPERIMENT. US AND THE CLASSES BEFORE US,
                 IF WE GRADUATED, WE WERE TO GO ON TO FORM THE FIRST
                 EVER BLACK FIGHTER SQUADRON.

"   "   **ALL** BLACK, BECAUSE UP 'TIL THEN THE U.S. MILITARY WAS
                 PRETTY STRICTLY SEGREGATED. THERE WERE PRECIOUS FEW
                 BLACK OFFICERS AND **NO** BLACK PILOTS–AND THERE WERE
                 GOOD REASONS WHY THAT WAS SO.

3.
Back in '42, Reggie and co. stand nearest us, coolly facing front as the
aircraft cruise low over their heads. They're AT-6 Texans, gleaming silver, in
perfect tight V-formation.

Caption: "WE WERE HOPELESS, WE WERE INFERIOR, WE WERE LAZY.

"   "   "WE WERE THOUSANDS OF YEARS BEHIND THE CAUCASIAN
                 RACE IN THE HIGHER PSYCHIC DEVELOPMENT.

"   "   "WE LEARNED SLOWLY AND FORGOT QUICKLY."

4.
Nice big shot of the Texans cruising directly above us, from the pov of the
guys on the ground.

Caption: "SO SAID A LOT OF PEOPLE IN HIGH PLACES, AND THEY
                 SHOULD KNOW. YOU CAN BET THEY HAD PLENTY OF
                             SCIENTIFIC STUDIES TO BACK THEM UP.

"   "   "ONE GENERAL SAID WE HADN'T THE PROPER REFLEXES TO
                 BE FIRST CLASS FIGHTER PILOTS. ANOTHER, AH, HE
                 RECKONED WE WEREN'T WILLING TO DIE FOR PATRIOTIC
                 REASONS.

"   "   "HENRY STIMSON, SECRETARY OF WAR, SAID **LEADERSHIP
                 IS NOT EMBEDDED IN THE NEGRO RACE**…"

5.
Now. Reggie raises an eye. Lee stares at him, face twisting.

Reggie: BUT HAP ARNOLD, CHIEF OF THE AIR CORPS, HE WAS ON OUR
                 SIDE. HE SAID WE COULD BE USEFUL AS UNSKILLED LABOR.

"   "   WAITERS IN MESSES, WAS ONE OF HIS SUGGESTIONS.

Lee: THAT'S **RIDICULOUS**…!

PAGE TWENTY-TWO

1.
View past the men lined up below as the three aircraft cruise onwards. They're
all still facing the Sergeant as he drones on– except for the two at the
end of the row that he doesn't notice, Reggie and another man, watching the
planes.

Caption: "YES IT IS. EVERY BIT OF IT.

"   "   "BUT YOU KNOW THE REALLY RIDICULOUS THING?"

2.
Closer on Reggie and the other guy, still gazing up and offshot in the
direction of the planes, eyes narrowed, attention caught– and imagination too,
by the look of things. The others just face front, noticing none of this.

Caption: "IT'S THAT SOMEONE WAS GOING TO HAVE TO PROVE THAT
                 WAS THE CASE."

3.
Close in as Reggie and the other guy drop their gazes at the same time and
accidentally make eye contact. Momentarily caught off guard, but pleasantly
so. This guy is taller and skinnier than Reggie but about the same age, a
lanky type with a slim little pencil line moustache: known ironically as Fats.

4.
The two face front again, smiling with a mixture of amusement and quiet
determination. Kindred spirits, looking forward to what's coming, keen to make
their mark.

TO BE CONTINUED

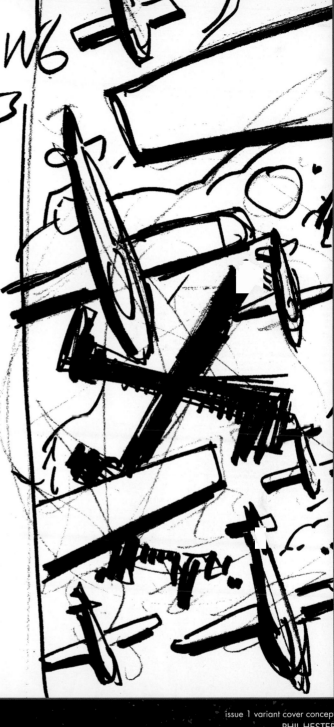

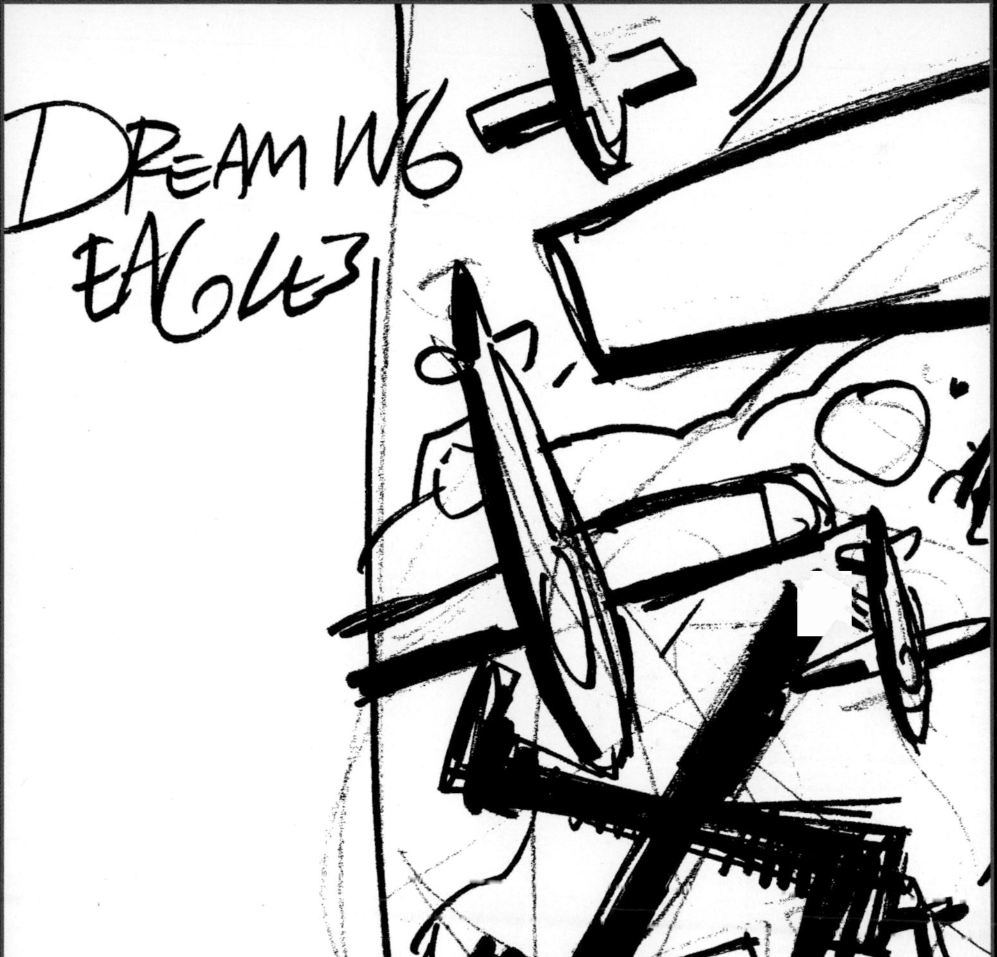
DREAMING EAGLES

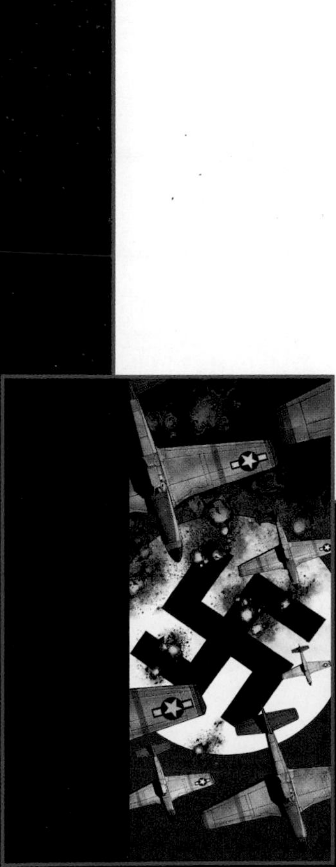

issue 1 variant cover concept
PHIL HESTER

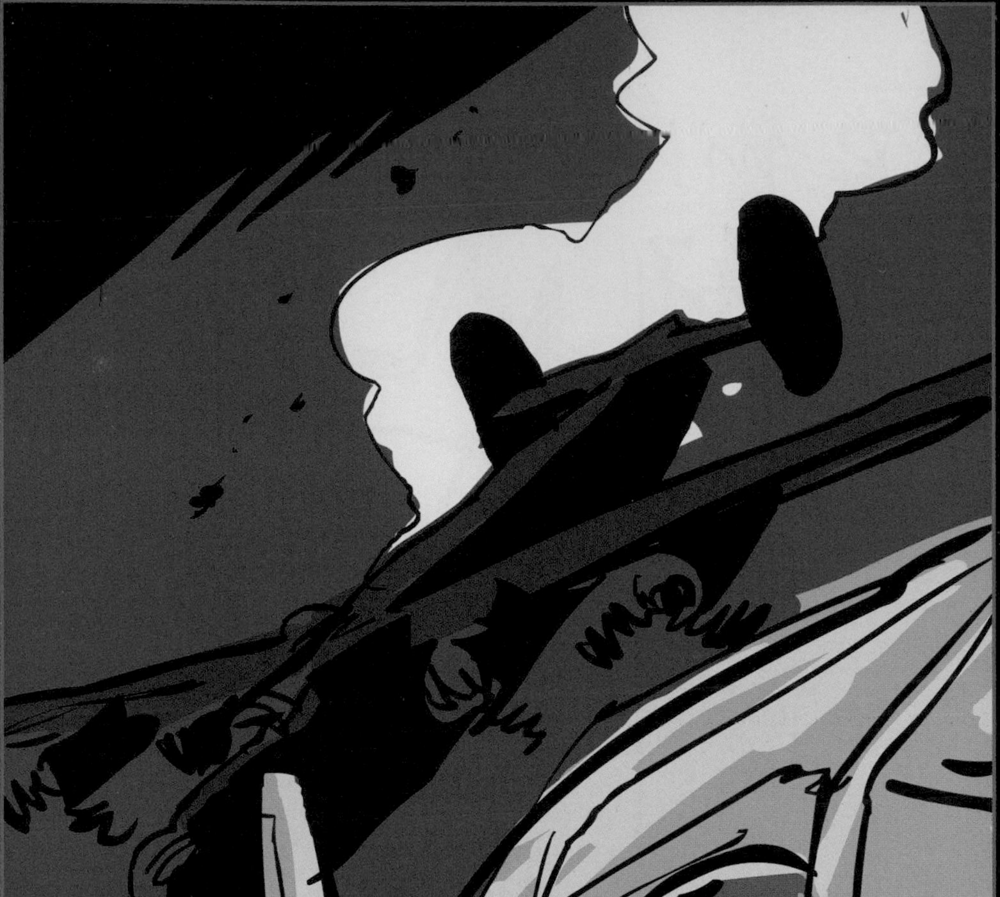

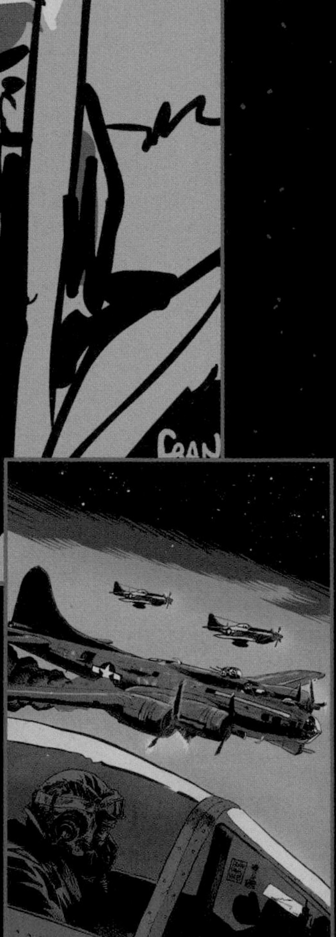

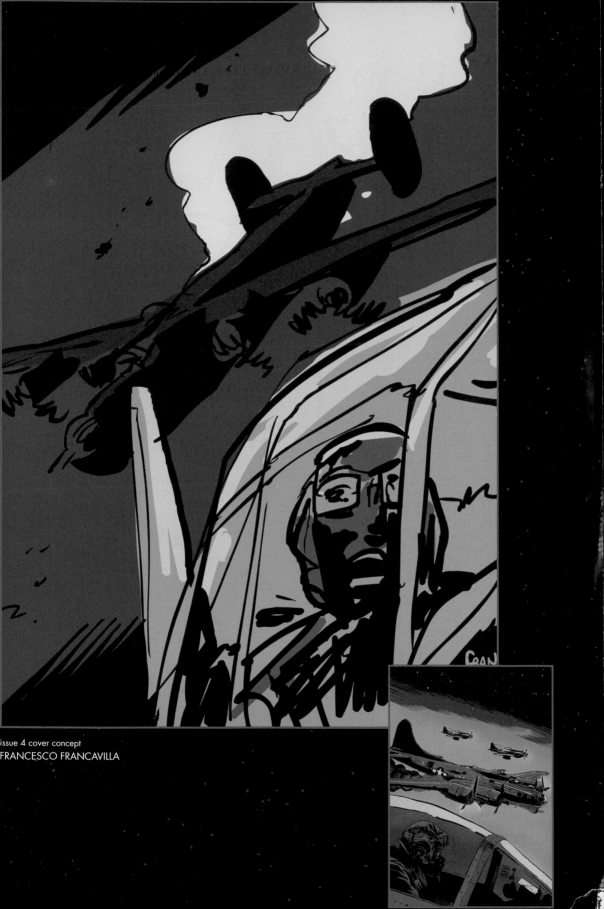

issue 4 cover concept
FRANCESCO FRANCAVILLA

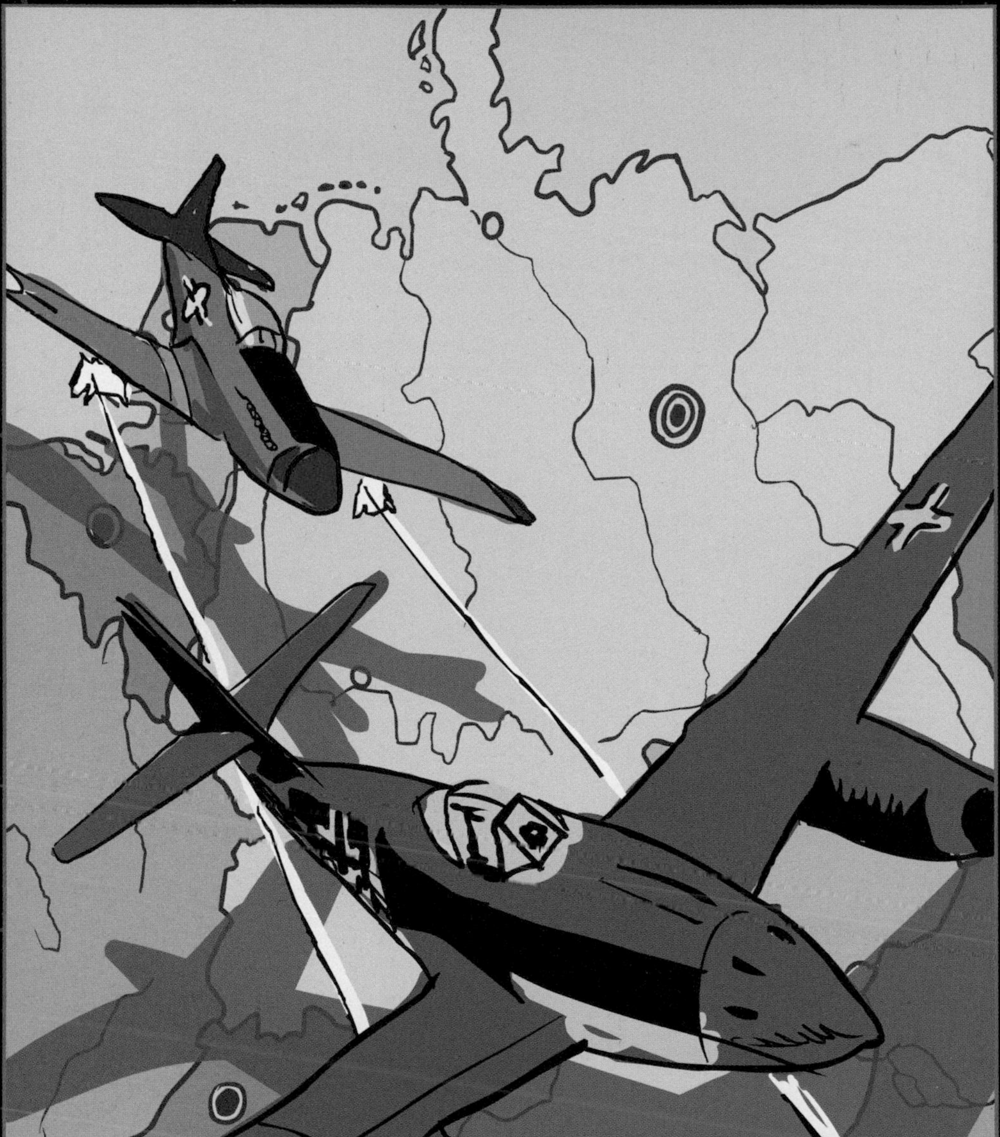
FRAN
CAVIL
LAF.16

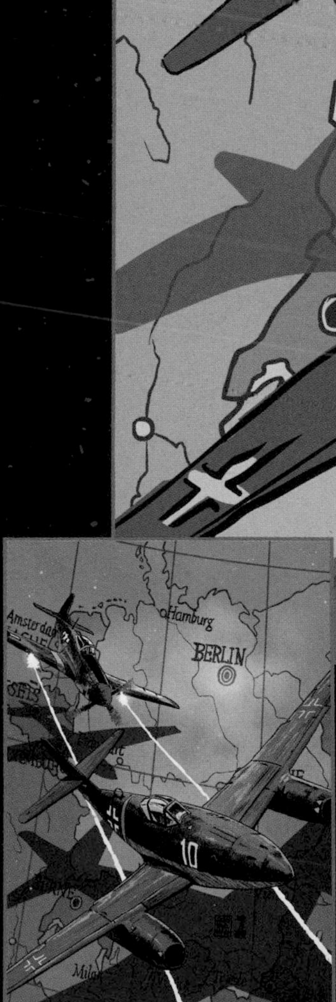
Hamburg
BERLIN
10

issue 6 cover concept
FRANCESCO FRANCAVILLA

GARTH ENNIS writer

Garth Ennis has been writing comics for over twenty-five years. His credits include *Preacher, The Boys* and *Hitman,* along with successful runs on *The Punisher* and *Fury* for Marvel. Among his most acclaimed work are his war comics, notably *War Stories* (published by Avatar Press), *Battlefields* (Dynamite Entertainment) and a recent revival of the classic British series *Johnny Red* for Titan Comics. Originally from Belfast, Northern Ireland, Ennis lives in New York City with his wife, Ruth.

SIMON COLEBY artist

Simon Coleby lives and works on the east coast of England. He began his professional career as a comic book artist in 1987 for Marvel UK. In the intervening years, he has produced work for 2000AD, illustrating stories such as *Judge Dredd, Rogue Trooper, Low Life* and *Jaegir.* Simon has also worked for Marvel and DC Comics, producing art for *Punisher 2099, Batman Eternal, The Authority* and *Royals: Masters of War,* among other titles.

JOHN KALISZ colorist

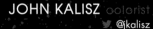
@jkalisz

John Kalisz has been coloring comics for over twenty years, working on just about every major character or book in comics at one point or another...from *Avengers* to *Zatanna* and everything in between.

ROB STEEN letterer

rmd3.tumblr.com

Rob Steen is the illustrator of the *Flanimals* series of children's books written by Ricky Gervais, and the Garth Ennis children's book *Erf.* He is also the colorist of David Hine's graphic novel *Strange Embrace* and letterer of comic books for AfterShock, Marvel, Dynamite, Image,